"...Hi Henry, I just finished reading your latest book in the series. I have loved each and every one of them. Since reading these books I have always dreamed of visiting your Cafe as I think it would just complete my whole experience with the books."

TINA

"...Read all six books ...great read, spellbinding....I guess you are taking a year off or so before number 7? For me left a few questions ....like a Hitchcock book, write your own ending, enjoyed very minute reading, keep up the good work."

JOAN M.

"...I have read all six books and can hardly wait for the seventh one to come out. I have enjoyed very book and am now passing them to my daughters and grand children I am a true believer of God and words encourage us to be even better. God bless you in your good work."

JANET

"...You are one of God's special people! I am reading my bible almost every day because of you, didn't tell you that before! I hope there will be a movie based on your angelic series someday! Keep on writing & painting! Hugs & blessings to you!"

CAROL B.

"...My Mom loved your books! She could not wait for the next one to come out.... This past March 7th she died at age 85....As we were beginning to go through all her possessions in her house, I came upon the five books in the series. I was going to be somewhat housebound following hip replacement surgery in early June, so I thought I would start reading your Angelic series, to see what had kept my Mom's interest. In three weeks I read all five books, and I was so touched by the story and the message. I asked my sister to pickup Book Six for me as I learned it became available at Costco. Now I can hardly wait for Book Seven!! Thank you for writing such a meaningful series.

IRENE G.

"...I am just so amazed at your God given gifts. What an incredible journey you are sharing with so many people! I just finished reading Bk. # 6 and I am so anxious to read the next one coming up. Thank you so much for sharing your talents and expertise. ... I have shared the inspirational reading with family and friends."

MONIQUE S.

"...I love your books and have read them all and read them twice! They are so spiritual and fulfilling!!! Thank God!! And blessings to you Henry!!

CAROLE O.

"...I met you in Winnipeg.... I immediately purchased two books and after reading them I bought all six. They are clean, well written and leave the reader wanting more. I am anxious to get my hands on book seven. Thank you for bringing to others the joy of your work."

DIANE D.

"...I have enjoyed reading your books very much....always looking forward to the next one! The intriguing 'twists and turns' draw the reader into the story, as you skillfully weave wisdom and inspiration throughout with your wonderful descriptive writing style. You have been blessed with an amazing gift..thank you for sharing it !"

BRENDA K.

"...I have enjoyed your books so much, my husband is not a reader but is reading this series. When is book seven going to be for sale?

LORRAINE F.

"...Love this story so much!! Thank you for writing these Mr Ripplinger. Gosh I don't want this series to end"

KENDRA J.

"...From the first page of Book 1 to the last page of Book 5 I have been captivated with the story of Henry and Jenny. There are four of us that are reading this series and I am also happy to tell you that I have the books in print and on my tablet. I'd also like to thank you most sincerely for this beautifully written story."

JANIS Z

"... I'd love to visit your cafe and art gallery!

DEBBIE C.

"...I have read all six of the books and the series and can't wait for number 7. ... I have passed the books on to several friends and kept the series on my e-reader to read over and over again. I have read the entire series 5 times (except book 6 only twice). They are truly enlightening and awe inspiring."

MARY B

"... Each book is a blessing in itself !!"

SYLVIA B.

"…I knew when God lead me to Henry's table that He had a revelation that He needed to share with me through Henry's book series. I am so thankful for the incredible message our Father has shared with us through his faithful servant, Henry. This book has brought much revelation and clarity. Our Lord has been showing me how important His unconditional Love is in our daily lives and these books were confirmation of this message. Thank you so much for sharing heartwarming scripture that enables us to live victorious lives through our Lord and Saviour Jesus Christ."

DEBRA O.

"… Thank you so much for signing all your books for my Mom, Rema . She was beside herself with excitement when I gave them to her. And was a bit jealous that I was able to have a picture taken with you. Thank you again for your kind words.

MICHELLE W.

"… you're books have restored my faith and given me hope! Thank you Henry Ripplinger for sharing your gift of writing the most EPIC love story I personally have ever read."

LORETTA E.

"… I've read the whole series and absolutely love these books!

MAUREEN R.

"…My wife and I have read all 6 and looking fwd to book 7. I have started 5 of our friends on them and one lady's husband has found her reading at 2 in the morning amidst many tears!!!! The story really makes one feel like they are real people that are in our lives. Its hard to stop reading once one has started. I don't know where you get all your ideas from Henry because the story just keeps flowing and never stopping."

JOHN C.

"…My friend introduced me to the Angelic series and right now on book 4; I cannot put them down; I hope Jenny and Henry unite soon; its upsetting and a wonderful read at the same time and inspirational."

MARY G.

"… I am so grateful to you, Henry for inspiring me to know more about the bible, to want to read it, to know more about His love & forgiveness! Thank you! God Bless!"

CAROL B.

"...The best books I have ever read. Love each series 1 to 6
                                                                CAROL S.

"... These are wonderful books! He is a talented author."
                                                                SANDY B

"... Thanks, for the most incredible book of an amazing series. Book 6 I loved it. I gifted my six copies to the sisters of St. Joseph of London Ontario. They are enjoying muchly. God bless and may the sales sky rocked for Christmas. No better gift."
                                                                DIANE M

"...I am so thankful I was blest to be at the Calgary Costco with my daughter and we purchased your series of 6 books I COULD NOT PUT THEM DOWN UNTIL I read every one of them now waiting for book #7"
                                                                JOSEPHINE G.

"...Just would like you to know that your books are the only books in my adult life that I have read and collected the complete series...so true to life, so heartfelt and reminding constantly of the need for God in my life... Thank you for writing!"
                                                                MAUREEN L.

"...I have all six books. Reading book number six. Best books that I have ever read. Looking forward to reading number seven."
                                                                MARCELLA S.

"... Congratulations! ! Such an amazing feat but they are amazing books!"
                                                                SARAH B.

"...Bought the whole set. .Hard to put down after you start reading. One could learn a lot from those books."
                                                                EDWARD Y.

"...I feel very bless by reading, book #6. You have outdone yourself with this one, they keep getting better and better. I think everyone would be blessed by reading this book, not to discount the other 5. This one is amazing. You are such an earth angel to all of us Henry. You have taught us all so much and certainly brought us all closer to our Lord and Saviour, and also our Blessed heavenly Mother. God bless you my friend. I give thanks for your angelic presence in my life. You are definitely a light to all in a darkening world."
                                                                DIANE M.

"...Our family will forever be grateful and thankful for your wonderful stories in the Angelic series and for your precious gift of time shared with our amazing sister-in-law Janice as she prepared to meet with our heavenly father! Words will never be able to express our thanks Henry!"

SELMA F.

"... I absolutely love this series have all six I have a friend who's not a big reader but she absolutely loves them said the best series she ever read and by a Saskatchewan author.

JEAN B.

"...I have read the first five of your books and couldn't put them down. Beautiful books! I look forward to the sixth!"

TERRY S.

"...I love, love, love these books. I met Henry at Costco in cross iron location. He signed my books. At the time, my life was so busy & stressful. Lol. I said to him, for crying out loud, don't you know that I'm busy? Hahaha. His books were my new calm. It was like the Angels were with me. I felt total comfort when I sat down to read them. Now that the new book is out, I intend to sit down & re read the series. .....once again I find myself in need of calm in my life. Thank you for a great read. I look forward to your new book."

PAM R.

"... I have read all six books and I am in anticipation of no. 7. I never cried so much or learned what being a living angel was before. May God bless you and I think he already has."

EILEEN B.

"...One of the "best" series of books you could read. Finish one book couldn't wait to start the next."

RUTH B.

"... Enjoyed meeting you and have read all six of your books since you were in Fredericton. Can't wait for book Seven to be released!!!"

PAULINE M.

"... I enjoyed your books so much...I wish you a long and healthy life... keep on writing, your books are so inspiring. Good luck and God Bless you both!

GEORGINA M.

"…I've had the chance to had a wonderful discussion with Henry when he was in Edmonton. He's an amazing author, artist and even more amazing individual! Have a wonderful and safe trip Henry! Happy Signing!"

DEBBIE M.

"…Great weekend Henry. My books have been shared all over my neighborhood in Ontario. Formerly from Claybank Sk. You are a true inspiration Henry. Thank you for enhancing my life!

ANGELA W.

"… I have gotten your latest book and I can't wait to read it , I have enjoyed all of them so much, thank you , I hope to be able to get to Regina before winter to your art gallery and cafe , thanks again."

SIMONE W.

"… I am reading your 5th book of the angelic letters series. You are truly a disciple of God. I love that you are so humble and yet passionate about your spirituality. God be with you."

LOIS G.

"…Have been waiting to hear this good news… can't wait to read it (BOOK 7)… Hopefully my mom will still be able to read this too… She loves your books so much and was able to read all of them so far with her magnifying glass. So hopefully her vision will still be good enough to read this last one as I know she has been waiting for it too. Thanks Henry!

JUDY M. D.

"… I can hardly wait for 'The House Where Angels Dwell' for Mother's Day!! Your previous 5 books marked me and my life in a noticeable way and I continue to be touched and transformed for the better version of me even only by remembering them. Your work has brought me not only back but also closer to God and our Saviour and His awesome Angels. Bless you, your family and your wonderful work! Thank you."

SANDRA M.

Please write to Henry at: henry@henryripplinger.com or visit www.henryripplinger.com for more information about Henry's work and art. We would love to hear from you

THE HEART
OF AN
ANGEL

THE ANGELIC LETTERS SERIES

Book Seven

———— ✴ ————

THE HEART
OF AN
ANGEL

1992–2007

HENRY K. RIPPLINGER
Best Selling Author of Pewter Angels

Library and Archives Canada Cataloguing in Publication

Ripplinger, Henry, author
    The heart of an angel / Henry K. Ripplinger.
(The angelic letters series ; 7)
Issued in print and electronic formats.
ISBN 978-1-928142-11-9 (hardcover).--ISBN 978-1-928142-12-6 (softcover).--
ISBN 978-1-928142-13-3 (ebook)

    I. Title. II. Series: Ripplinger, Henry. Angelic letters series ; 7.

PS8585.I565H43 2018   C813'.6   C2017-908051-2
                                              C2017-907052-0

TRUE LOVE (from High Society)
Words and Music by COLE PORTER
© 1956 (Renewed) CHAPPELL & CO., INC.
All Rights Reserved
Used by permission of ALFRED PUBLISHING CO., INC.

Author photo: Bruce Vasselin, Designer Photo
Cover concept and design by Henry K. Ripplinger
Cover design and production by Brian Danchuk Design
Page layout by Human Powered Design

PIO-SEELOS BOOKS
Ph: (306) 731-3087, Fax: (306) 731-3852.
E-mail: henry@henryripplinger.com

Printed and bound in Canada by Friesens Printers
May 2018

*This novel is dedicated to the loving
memory of my sister Darlene
…my earthly angel!*

ACKNOWLEDGEMENTS

DEAR JOAN, AS I said when I began to write this series, it requires a lengthy commitment, a withdrawal from the usual routines of daily living, a time to be alone, to reflect, to write. Who would have thought I would still be writing after thirteen years and finally concluding this epic story!? Thank you, Joan, for the gift of this freedom and the sacrifices you have made to allow me to fulfill the dream I had for so many years. Your patience, understanding, friendship and love is deeply treasured.

Thank you, too, Joan and Jen Howie, and Debbie Beedham, Sr Theresia Elder for reading through the manuscript and catching errors in spelling, punctuation and grammar.

To Tracy Jacknife, thank you for proofreading, editing and your helpful suggestions. Very much appreciated!

To Dr. Peter Van Rooyen, thank you for your time, knowledge and assistance in dealing with the medical matters in the story.

Once again, to all of you, my heartfelt thanks for helping to realize this goal and your assistance in making my writing the best it can be.

As always, I thank the Lord for the gift of the Angelic Letters Series! Sometimes the thoughts come, the words flow, and the chapters write themselves so effortlessly, I break out in laughter out of sheer joy for being so blessed with the capacity to write this epic story. From the bottom of my heart, thank you, God the Father, God the Son and God the Holy Spirit and of course, my guardian angel.

PREFACE

I T WAS THE summer of 2005, mid-June when pen and paper met to write this epic story. After 12 years, I am finally in the process of completing my last book in the Angelic Letters Series. Just the other day, I received an email from a young girl who made me aware of this passage of time in a profound way. She started reading the series when she was in grade eight and now in her second year of university has just finished reading book 6 in the series! Other emails, too, have struck a chord indicating the years rapidly ticking by and yet, too quickly for many who were taken to the Lord at different stages in reading the series. Often, I wished I could have written faster and finished sooner but things take time and don't always fit into the plans of our lives.

One thing I have learned over and over in my life and through this series is the importance of daily prayer, meditation and reading the Bible. Coming to God daily and placing Christ at the center of our lives transforms our minds into how we should live and think. It gives us purpose, meaning, and keeps us centered on the truth in a world which can easily lead us astray. Death is something we don't like to think about, yet it can come to any of us in the blink of an eye. How ready are we?

But there are other reasons too, which I have tried to illustrate in the entire series. We have a tremendous effect upon one another by what we say and do; how we live our lives. Jenny and Father Engelmann are two characters in the story who have had a powerful affect upon readers. It's all part of God's Divine Providence how He works through us to minister to each other. Over and over I have seen how insights, lessons or different circumstances in the series have affected the lives of readers in positive ways that I would never have suspected nor anticipated. Once I am made aware of this however, I could see looking back how I was led or prompted to write what I did. Often, I now find myself, on the edge of my chair waiting for the next insight or lesson to come along. I no longer hesitate to get up in the wee hours of the morning and write down certain situations or insights I am given.

It is for these reasons that we need close friendships. I have received countless emails from readers expressing their admiration for Father Engelmann and wishing that they would have such a mentor or person in their lives. They disclose envy for Henry that he is so fortunate to have someone in his life that he can trust and share his deepest thoughts and feelings with. Often such relationships are developed between spouses, but many are through friendships we have established and nurtured over time. Sometimes the Lord gifts us with such a person, but often we have to be willing to seek and develop such close relationships. We need to have a sounding board to get out of ourselves and have new fresh thoughts enter our minds.

I encourage all of you to nurture such friendships and when you find someone, treasure them dearly. It's not really surprising how similar we really are and go through many of the same challenges in life. We are not as unique in our thoughts and feelings as we think. I believe that is why the series has had such appeal and success because readers could so easily see how their own lives entwined with the lives of characters in the story and learned from them.

When I emailed a friend to inform him that I would be writing a seventh book in the Angelic Letters Series, he reminded me of the biblical significance of the number seven. That it represents perfection: something that is complete, full, finished. I would like to think that it was not by chance that I was led to write a total of seven books in the series! When I searched the internet for more information about the number seven as it relates to the Bible, I was amazed to learn that the number seven is used in the Bible more than seven hundred times. It begins in Genesis when God created the world in seven days. In most cases however, it seems that God is communicating the idea of divine completeness, perfection and wholeness by means of the number seven. I was pleased to learn this and confirms to me that this is the exact number of books that I was intended to author in the series.

In any event, what a wonderful thought that the series would be brought to an ending in such a complete way. It comforts me as I struggle to let go of the story. The characters have become family to me as they have for so many readers. We have talked and laughed together, cried together, supped together and prayed together. I feel sad and wish it could go on and on and yet all things must come to an end. Such is our earthly life.

It comforts me also by the many emails you have sent to me sharing how much you have enjoyed the story and how the contents have affected your lives as well. It was wonderful meeting so many of you during my tours and book signing events. I am deeply grateful to all of you too, for investing so much of your time spent in reading the novels. Your love, encouragement and loyal following of the Angelic Letters Series are much appreciated.

The good Lord willing, I would like to continue writing. I think there is still another book or two in me. In any case, thank you again for sharing this incredibly amazing journey with me! Daily, I thank the Lord for this story!

I love you all dearly!
God bless!

Henry K. Ripplinger
March, 2018

"Draw near to God and He will draw near to you."
JAMES 4:18

"If any man be in Christ, he is a new creature; old things are passed away; behold all things are become new."
2 CORINTHIANS 5:17

"Enter by the narrow gate; for the gate is wide and the way is easy, that leads to destruction, and those who enter by it are many. For the gate is narrow and the way is hard, that leads to life, and those who find it are few."
MATTHEW 7:13-14

"You shall love the Lord your God with all your heart, and with all your soul, and with all your strength, and with all your mind; and your neighbor as yourself."
LUKE 10:27

"Let all bitterness, and wrath, and anger, and clamor, and evil speaking, be put away from you, with all malice: And be ye kind one to another, tenderhearted, forgiving one another, even as God for Christ's sake hath forgiven you."
EPHESIANS 4:31, 32.

"I am the light of the world; he who follows me will not walk in darkness, but will have the light of life."
JOHN 8:12

"I count all things to be loss in view of the surpassing value of knowing Christ Jesus my Lord, for whom I have suffered the loss of all things and count them but rubbish in order that I may gain Christ"

PHILIPPIANS 3:8

"A new command I give you: Love one another. As I have loved you, so you must love one another. By this everyone will know that you are My disciples, if you love one another."

JOHN 13: 34-35

"Learn of Me, for I am meek and lowly of heart."

MATTHEW 11:29

"Whosoever will be chief among you, let him be your servant, even as the Son of man came to serve."

MATTHEW 20:27

Everyone then who hears these words of mine and does them will be like a wise man who built his house upon the rock; and the rain fell, and the floods came, and the winds blew and beat upon that house, but did not fall, because it had been founded on the rock."

MATTHEW: 24-25

PROLOGUE

A THOUGHTFUL MAN ONCE said that he is saddened to see so many of God's children lay on their deathbed regretting that they did not become all they could have become. In their dying breaths, as their life flashes before them, they finally see the countless moments, hours, days and years wasted in worry, harboring unforgiveness and anger and resentment and pursuing worldly goals which have offered nothing and no lasting value. So few of those moments were well lived. So few of those moments being really happy, thankful, or spent serving others and making a difference in the world. They see their legacy left behind is shallow and empty; one which will soon be forgotten. Instead of leaving an endowment exuding streams of living water flowing through the lives they have touched, their legacy is more like a cistern filled with cracks and holes dried up like a desert, parched and bare.

Sure, the message of another way to live their earthly life passed them by. All of us at one time or another has heard the plea to come to Him but we refused to listen. We are too proud; we don't need God, we don't have time for Him. I am too busy, I don't believe in that stuff and I really don't see anything in it for me.

And what have we achieved by our choices and independence? Have we been happy, joyful people? Have we become better on our own? Have we brought light to the darkness? Have we made a difference leaving the world better because we have lived?

Choices, choices, choices. It's all about the millions upon millions of choices we have made struggling to find happiness, security and inner peace when it could have come down to one choice: to accept Jesus Christ as our Lord and Savior; to place Him at the center of our lives, pick up our cross daily and follow Him.

That's it.

Once we have made that choice, we come into God's family and claim our inheritance. We are a child of God and His spirit comes into our minds, hearts, and very soul to give us the joy, peace and freedom which God promises to those who love Him.

As we lay dying, death so near that we can count the number of breaths remaining in our existence, it's now too late to relive those choices. The gift of life we once had, to become all we were capable of becoming, is over. We see the dead ends we chased and the emptiness it offered. Worldly values and pursuits have no lasting value. We have failed to see that they are all illusions while just a breath away we could have followed the way, the truth and life which Jesus wanted so desperately to give to us. We failed to see the incredible gift of love He offered us. His love so deep that He gave His life for us; so that we may have life, not only on earth, but eternally with Him and the Father.

But there is a lesson here. Even a life, that is moments away from departing can make an act of repentance. God's love is never ending, never changing, ever there. Look at one of the thieves who was also hanging on a cross beside Jesus on Calvary. Moments away from his death he asks Jesus to remember him. His last-minute faith and belief in Jesus restored him into God's family and eternity. "Today you will be with Me in heaven," is how Jesus responded. Imagine Jesus responding with such love, mercy and forgiveness to a sinner; a thief while just moments away from his own death too!

This was the thief's purpose in life: it all came down to this one moment; to show us that we too, until our dying last breath can still ask for mercy and forgiveness. We can offer our lives to others to be used as an example of a life that has squandered all too many opportunities to live for Jesus by the choices we made. Perhaps, like the thief at Calvary, our example of repentance will motivate others to make better choices.

But what if we don't wait until the end to see the folly of our ways? What if we chose to make it our goal to follow Him and strive to be holy? It is a road less travelled but the results are much different at the end of the journey.

I know of such a man.

While others chose wealth, possessions, power and the praise and honor of men, he chose a simple life to honor and be obedient unto the Father. Yes, an ordinary life has become an extraordinary life; a saintly life.

Let me share with you what I have learned about holiness. It is not the proud who shall inherit the earth. It is not the strong, the powerful, the wealthy, but the meek, the lowly, the humble; those who forget about themselves and live to serve and love their Lord and others.

Come, let us go out back and sit on the two old crates where the school of life takes place. I will take you on a journey that will impact your life profoundly. It's a love story all right, but the real love story is not about two people. That was only the lure to draw you into the real love story. No, it is the pure love of a man who died for you and me. Yes, let me tell you about a man who chose to become all that he could be. Here is the legacy of one who was least among men yet led a life we shall never forget.

There were no regrets as this man sacrificed his life. There was joy and heavenly choirs of angels who lifted him up to the Father. Yes, my dear brothers and sisters in Christ, it is true as we shall see, there is no greater love than this, than to lay down one's life for a friend.

CHAPTER ONE

HENRY CALLED FATHER Engelmann at the care home. He didn't recognize the person answering the phone but she knew of him. She informed Henry that Father had left for the hospital to see Mrs. Pederson.

When Father came into the dimly lit room, Henry was seated at Jenny's bedside holding her hand. Father rushed to their side. Henry had to take a second look; he wasn't used to seeing Father in his black suit and white collar rather than his brown Franciscan habit. The concerned priest placed his hand on Henry's shoulder and asked, "How is she doing, Henry?"

Tears were sitting at the edge of his eyelids and began to spill over. He wiped the rolling tear off his cheek and said, "Jenny had a seizure and somehow they stopped it by inducing a coma. Hopefully, she will awaken in a day or so."

Henry shook his head. "It's like reliving the same nightmare when Julean was in the hospital with meningitis. I don't know if I could cope if Jenny died too."

"What do the doctors recommend?"

"That's the thing, Father. The doctor is adamant about terminating the pregnancy. He maintains that it is the safest and best option at this point and would quickly restore Jenny's blood pressure to normal and end the condition she is suffering from."

Henry paused and then said, "I am inclined to agree with him, Father. I don't want Jenny to die. He said to me this

5

morning that time is running out and a decision has to be made. If Jenny doesn't wake up, the doctor wants me to decide… to go ahead with the abortion or not."

Father shook his head, "Oh, mein lieber Gott. Such a decision, Henry. What would Jenny want?"

"We both know Jenny's heart, Father, but should we just let her die without doing anything?"

Father nodded and kept shaking his head.

"If we don't terminate the pregnancy, both Jenny and the baby are at risk of dying. If we do, we can save Jenny…" Henry's words trailed off.

"Can they possibly deliver the child without aborting it?" Father wanted to know.

"Yeah, we discussed that. The doctor thinks the baby is too underdeveloped and won't be able to breathe. And to bring on the labor will be too stressful. It might kill Jenny."

"Yet, it might deliver the baby."

"Yes, that is a possibility, I suppose. I'm not sure even the doctor can predict that. Jenny is extremely ill and becoming more so. If Jenny doesn't wake up soon, I'll have to make a decision."

"I brought communion for you and Jenny." Father reached into his jacket pocket and pulled out a small gold Pyx. He unscrewed the lid and took out one of the consecrated hosts. He turned to Henry and said, "The Body of Christ."

Henry replied, "Amen" and made the sign of the cross. He bowed his head and said a private prayer. Father stepped in between Henry and Jenny so he could put one hand on Henry's head and the other on Jenny's forehead and prayed, "Oh, heavenly Father, creator of life, if it is Your divine will, restore Jenny's health and that of the child within her womb. In the same way Your Son on this day lay in the darkness, let Jenny, Henry and their daughter, Hannah resurrect with the Lord into new life. Through the power of Your Holy Spirit give Henry the wisdom to know Your will in this situation and the trust, strength and courage to carry it out. Fill their hearts with peace, praise and thanksgiving for all of Your blessings. We ask this in Jesus' name, Amen."

HENRY WENT HOME shortly after six, had a light dinner and was on the phone continuously for over two hours. He called Lauren and Alison to give them an update on Jenny's condition. He told the girls that he was struggling with the decision whether or not to terminate the pregnancy. Matti and Chloe were also surprised to learn that Jenny's condition was worsening. In all cases he asked for their prayer support.

He did however, ask Chloe about the decision he was faced with and asked for her opinion. All she said was that she had seen many cases where the mother's life was at risk yet, when the mother went ahead with the pregnancy it all turned out and both baby and mother quickly recovered. In the end, the decision was his and that she and Robbie would pray for him and his loved ones.

Early, Easter Sunday morning, Henry, along with Justin, travelled into the city. Henry hoped he would see his dear wife awake, but she was still in a coma. The similarities between Jenny's situation and that of Julean's were eerie to Henry. So many memories flooded his mind. Just as Henry and his son sat down on either side of Jenny's bed, a nurse came in and took Jenny's blood pressure. It had come down a tad but was still way too high; it was at 195/95. Henry asked if Jenny had woken up at all.

"No, she hasn't."

"Is there a danger that she might not?" Henry was anxious to know and needed reassurance.

"She was given a very strong tranquilizer yesterday. The drug has a half-life of a day or so. She may not wake up until tomorrow."

"Was Doctor Webster around yet?"

"No, he doesn't usually come around on Sunday unless there is an emergency."

For most of the morning, it was just Henry and Justin in the room other than nurses coming in periodically to check Jenny's vitals. Henry was surprised to see Justin just sitting quietly for all that time. Occasionally, Henry noticed his son wipe away a tear or two. He wasn't much good at hiding it.

In many ways Justin was like him; his son wore his emotions on his shirt sleeve.

Henry knew Father wouldn't be in until after lunch as he celebrated two Masses that day at the care home. He knew there would be too many people coming for Easter Sunday.

At one point in the afternoon, the room was filled. Jeremy and his son Joshua, Camilla, Father, Carlos and Maria and several of Jenny's friends were there. For almost an hour, a prayer vigil was held for Jenny and Hannah. There were tears, hugs, and well wishes floating around. Even the attending nurses left with tears in their eyes.

Around four thirty everyone had left except Henry. Justin went home with Jeremy and Father caught a ride back to the Care Home with Carlos and Maria. Henry was glad to learn from Carlos that Thomas and Neela were coming to Regina for a visit. In the few days he had spent in Ottawa before James' passing and again just that past summer, Henry had observed Thomas to be a godly man, who in many respects possessed a wisdom similar to that of Father Engelmann. He looked forward to the support of Thomas and his wife.

Despite all the prayers and discussion that day about what to do in Jenny's critical situation, Henry was still struggling with the decision of whether or not to abort the baby. If Jenny didn't come out of her coma by tomorrow morning, he had to make up his mind what to do. Every passing minute was having its toll on Jenny and the baby.

Just as he was praying deeply to God to know His will in the matter, Doctor Carter walked into the room. He could see the tears of worry and sorrow in his son-in-law's eyes. He had read in Jenny's charts that she had a seizure and was put in an induced comatose state. He was concerned over the woman who had taken his daughter's place in Henry's life but just as worried about Henry's state of mind and wellbeing too. He got one of the chairs, pushed it beside Henry, and sat down.

"When Vera was pregnant with Julean, I was just as worried as you, Hank. Sometimes life throws us a curve that's too much for us to handle. I know you're a man of God, so I don't need to tell you to go to Him. I was on my knees more than once when Vera was struggling with the same condition. High blood pressure can be the cause of many serious complications."

Henry nodded. "I am struggling with the decision to abort the child, Jack. Jenny is getting worse by the minute. She wanted to hold off as long as possible so the baby grows and develop more but we have run out of time. Doctor Webster feels the best option at this point is to terminate the pregnancy. He feels the risks to do a C-section or induce labor is too risky."

"And what do you and Jenny think?" Doctor Carter wanted to know.

"Jenny is absolutely against aborting the child. She would never agree to do that. I am the same but I don't want to lose Jenny. I thought my world would end when Julean died and here again is almost the exact replay of what happened. What good is it to try and save the baby if Jenny dies? And we are not sure that the baby will even live and how healthy it still is. It could already be suffering from many complications."

Jack nodded. "I understand your reasoning, Henry. It is sound logic and Doctor Webster's assessment of the situation is correct. Jenny is dying. The latest lab tests confirm the prognosis for both the mother and child. I am older than you and considerably older than Doctor Webster and Vera tells me each year to hang up my stethoscope but I love what I am doing. I can't begin to tell you after all these years how in awe I am over the human body and all its workings and how it strives to heal itself.

"God outdid Himself when He created man.

"Marvelous Hank, truly marvelous. I have lived long enough to see miracles before my eyes; impossible cases more serious than this, miraculously pulled through. And yes, I have seen unfortunate deaths and much sorrow as well. This is the life we live, Hank. At the end of the day we have to be obedient to God's laws and will and trust Him to turn it into good. If we place our faith in Him, He will turn it into good, perhaps not now, but at some time He will use our faith and suffering and sorrow for His purposes but we must give it to Him."

Henry nodded and listened to the wise doctor; it was so similar to what Jenny said the other day on the way in to the hospital.

Doctor Carter continued by posing a question, "What is God's will in this matter, Hank? Would He want us to abort the child or try to save both the mother and child?"

For the first time, a surge of confidence swept through him. "The latter Jack, that's what God would want."

"Well then, what are our options?"

Henry thought for just a moment; those options had been floating in and out of his mind all day. "Well, we could do a C-section but the tests show Jenny's blood count is too low and she might bleed to death. The other is to induce labor. The problem with that is if it's a long labor with her high blood pressure, the stress might kill her." Henry was beginning to feel like one of the medical team, weighing the options; as if he knew as much as the doctor next to him.

"But then again, Hank, the labor might be short and it's a small baby, the cervix wouldn't need to dilate that much. And what did I just say how God creating the body that always works towards healing itself and to follow His laws?"

Henry nodded and for the first time in days felt his indecision and hopelessness beginning to lift…a surge of certainty flooded his being.

He had made up his mind!

He wanted to get up and hug the old doctor. "Yes, Jack, that's what we will do. I know Jenny would be in full agreement. I know if she hadn't woken up and I decided to abort the baby, Jenny would forgive me but she would never forget the child that was killed within her womb. She would be as good as dead for the rest of her life."

Henry was amazed not only with the doctor's assessment of the human body but also how God, through His divine providence, works through people to minister to one another. Had he gone home, he would have missed the doctor. Why would he be making rounds at four thirty on Easter Sunday and not be home with his wife? Surely, at his age he wouldn't have that many patients to see.

Yes, God answers prayers!

Henry gave his father–in-law a warm hug and told him to extend it to Vera. He couldn't thank Doctor Carter enough for coming in.

"So, tell me Jack, how many patients were you seeing today?"

Jack looked at Henry and replied, "Only one."

"That is my good fortune that you also stopped by to check on Jenny. "Who was your patient on this floor?" Henry wanted to know.

Jack smiled and softly said, "It was you."

CHAPTER TWO

H ENRY DECIDED TO spend the night at the hospital. The nurses were able to get maintenance to bring in a small cot. He wanted to be there when Jenny woke up.

Around five thirty, Jenny came out of her deep sleep and was surprised to see Henry sleeping on a bed next to her. She didn't want to wake him but a nurse came in and was happy to see Jenny had come back to the land of living. "Oh, Mrs. Pederson, you're awake! The doctors will be so pleased!"

Henry woke and he too, was more relieved than words could say to see his dear sweet wife's blue eyes! He approached Jenny and bent down to kiss her tenderly. Oh, Honey, I was so worried…"

The attending nurse interrupted Henry and asked him to go to the waiting room while they gave Jenny a sponge bath and ordered breakfast. At the nurse's station, Henry learned that Jenny's condition was still critical and her blood pressure not responding to the medication. They were waiting for Doctor Webster to come in and decide how to proceed. Henry knew something had to be done.

When Henry returned to Jenny's room, he told her of Doctor Carter's visit and advice. Just as he finished, Doctor Webster rushed into the room. He was both surprised and glad Henry was there so early. He already knew that Jenny had come out of her deep sleep and had great news for her, or so he thought.

"Good morning, Jenny, Mr. Pederson..." He paused for a moment and walked closer to Jenny's bedside. "The signs, symptoms, lab results, blood pressure and multi-organ involvement are not good. The seriousness of your condition cannot be over stated. The chances of your infant surviving are slim and even if she does, serious complications may already have developed. Your pregnancy, in my opinion, constitutes an obstetrical emergency."

Both Henry and Jenny's eyes were filled with tears as the doctor spoke. Jenny was about to respond when Doctor Webster went on. "Fortunately, Jenny, there was a weekend conference in which Doctor Smith from Chicago spoke on new procedures in abortion. He is highly skilled and has performed hundreds, if not thousands of abortions. I told him of your case and he has agreed to stay over and terminate your pregnancy. You would be in excellent hands, Jenny. Terminating your pregnancy is the best and safest option at this point. It would quickly drop your blood pressure and restore your organ function. It would put an end to all of the complications you are presently enduring. Your blood pressure wou—"

"No, Doctor Webster, I'm afraid you do not understand," Jenny said with compassion. "I know you have my best interests at heart but I could never harm Hannah in any way. We are in this together and she has just as much right to life as I do."

Jenny brushed away tears sliding down her cheek and continued, "I do not want a doctor who has terminated the lives of thousands of infants or acquired all of the skill and techniques on how to abort infants. To me, such a doctor does not respect the sanctity of human life. I would sooner have a doctor who has never done a single abortion. I would choose a doctor who still believes in the original Hippocratic Oath not to destroy a woman's child. I would choose a doctor who respects the life of the mother and child equally. A doctor who sees that neither the life of one is better than the other or one has the right to live over the other. I want a doctor who sees the value of the mother as equal to the life of the child still inside her womb.

They are one and the same human life, Doctor Webster. We either live together or die together.

Once again, Jenny paused and gazed directly into her doctor's eyes, "For this reason, I am requesting that Doctor Carter be my primary care giver from here on in. If you wish to assist him and learn from him that is your choice."

Doctor Webster was flabbergasted by Jenny's comments.

"Mrs. Pederson, I don't want to undermine any of my colleagues but Doctor Carter is not familiar with all of the new procedures and drugs. His knowledge is not as up to date as younger doctors. You are in a very dangerous point in your pregnancy—"

"Doctor Webster, I am fully aware of my condition thanks to all the tests which you have done but my decision is final. I want a doctor who shares my views of human life. I don't mean to offend you, but you don't understand. I do not want a doctor to choose to save one human life over another. I want a doctor who obeys God and does not try to play God. I want a doctor who is concerned about saving both lives."

As soon as Doctor Webster left the room, Henry went to the nurse's station and asked if Doctor Carter was available in the hospital. Henry was informed that the doctor only came up occasionally and didn't have that many patients there anymore. They gave Henry his office number and permission to call him.

"Dr. Carter's office, how may I help you?"

"Hello, this is Henry Pederson, I'm Doctor Carter's son-in-law—"

"Yes, I know who you are, how may I assist you?"

"Is the doctor in? This is an emergency."

"He is seeing a patient... just one moment and I will see if he can take your call."

After a few minutes, Doctor Carter came to the phone.

"Hello, Hank, what can I do for you?"

"Jack, I spoke with Jenny this morning and she would like you to deliver her baby. We have informed Doctor Webster of our decision and he may or may not assist you. And in fact, if you don't want him to, the choice is yours."

"But Hank, Doctor Webster is a highly skilled doctor with much more training and up to date on all the drugs and procedures. I am of the old school. And I haven't delivered a baby in years."

"It doesn't matter, Jack. We want you and we hope you will accept the job." Henry wasn't sure how else to put it.

There was a momentary pause... "Okay, if Doctor Webster knows of your decision, I will call him and discuss this with him. I'm sure things will work out fine. Okay, Hank, I'll do it."

"So, when later this week will you be able to induce labor?"

"Hank, there is no further time for any delay. I will be at the hospital within the hour and begin making arrangements. Hopefully as early as two o'clock this afternoon, we will induce labor. We need to get the job done straight-away!"

Chapter Three

T RUE TO HIS word, Doctor Carter had the delivery room scheduled for two o'clock and Jenny was wheeled into the room. There was some discussion between Doctor Carter and Doctor Webster whether to administer medication to induce the contractions or to rub a gel on Jenny's cervix to soften and open it. They decided on both and Doctor Carter also went ahead to break the amniotic sac.

Henry sat in the waiting room area with Father Engelmann who had come up earlier. Father anointed Jenny with oil and also gave her Holy Communion. Henry tried to pray with Father but he couldn't concentrate on anything. The doctor did give him the option to be present in the delivery room but he opted out of that. He recalled delivering Justin in the back seat of their station wagon; it was an amazing miracle. He did something which he never thought he could. But with Jenny's illness, if something happened and emergency procedures were needed, he would only be in the way.

Within an hour, a nurse came out and told Henry that Jenny was in labor; her contractions had started. Henry burst with emotion at the news. He stood and walked to the window and gazed outside, "Oh, please dear God, let Jenny and the baby be okay." Father came up behind Henry and put his hand on his shoulder startling him. He reached back with his hand and placed it on top of Father's. The two men just stood there for the longest time and then went to their respective chairs and sat down. The brown beads of the rosary slid silently through Father's fingers.

The minutes seemed like hours as Father and Henry had both stood up again and had begun pacing the floor. If it hadn't been for Father's age and elderly appearance it would have been difficult to tell who the expectant father was.

Another hour passed by and Henry was beside himself. A nurse was coming down the hall. He didn't know if it was the same one as before; he knew she was from the delivery room by how she was dressed and wore a mask. When she came, she lowered her mask and said, "The doctors wanted you to know that your wife's cervix has begun to dilate and the delivery should be soon."

"How is Jenny doing!?" Both Henry and Father Engelmann were anxious to know.

"She is doing as well as can be expected under the circumstances." The nurse turned and walked away down the hall. They watched as she disappeared around a corner.

Just under an hour later, Doctor Carter came rushing down the hallway. "Hank the baby girl is born but you better come, Jenny is exhausted and very weak, I'm not sure if she will make it. Come!"

Both men rushed down the hall and into the delivery room. He momentarily saw the baby in a nurse's arms. But straight ahead on the table was Jenny with her eyes closed.

Was she alive or dead?

He slipped slightly on the wet floor. A nurse was beside Jenny holding her wrist. Henry couldn't tell from the nurse's face the condition of his wife.

Jenny lay flat on the table all wired up with an IV tube going into her arm. An oxygen mask covered her nose and mouth. Henry wanted to know if she was still alive but was afraid to ask or go over. He stepped slowly forward, shaking his head from side to side bracing himself for the worst.

He was startled by the baby as she began to cry and scream. The sound was deafening. He came to Jenny's side and looked for signs of breathing. He recalled the time when he rushed into the hospital when she was dying of cancer. He looked for a sign then, too. His heart skipped a beat when the sheet covering Jenny showed signs of life.

He began to openly cry.

He was emotionally spent. The nurse holding Jenny's wrist offered Jenny's hand to Henry and stepped aside. He took her hand and gently squeezed it. "Oh, please Jenny, stay, please stay, don't go away like before." He brought her hand up to his lips and kissed her hand. It was limp, lacked life, and yet, felt warm and soft…He looked at the sheet again for signs of life.

For that brief moment, he had shut out the screaming but it was back. He heard one nurse say, 'she has good lungs'. The words were hopeful. He turned to the sound and noticed the baby already had a tube going to its nostrils. Hannah, like her mother, was being given oxygen. The baby was being placed inside a mobile incubator.

He turned back to Jenny. Doctor Carter came up on the other side of the bed and took Jenny's hand. He studied the monitors for vital signs. "She is weak, Hank." He nodded. "Pray, she makes it."

"Once again, Father Engelmann startled Henry. He came up behind the distraught father and placed his hand on his shoulder. Father could no longer wait in the waiting room, he had to see Jenny too. Both men just stared at their beloved Jenny. The nurses and doctors were busy cleaning up. Out of the corner of his eye, Henry saw a nurse wheeling out the baby inside the glass womb. He knew that would be Hannah's home for a long while.

"How is the baby?" Henry asked the nurse as she wheeled by with the newborn.

The nurse's mouth was covered with a white mask, however, she smiled with her eyes to offer Henry some hope.

He wanted to ask more; when would Jenny come home? How soon would she recover? He wanted to spread that glimmer of hope to his dear, sweet wife. "Oh, Jenny, please stay with me, with us. I love you so much." He wanted to kiss his dear Jenny and look into her sparkling blue eyes.

Finally, Doctor Carter spoke. "We have to clean Jenny and will have her in ICU within fifteen minutes. I will come and get you as soon as she is ready. Just pray Hank, Father Engelmann. She needs prayers. She is in God's hands now."

Within thirty minutes, Doctor Carter came to the waiting room as he said he would and took them to the intensive care unit. On the way, the three men looked in on how the baby was doing. It was hard to tell with so many tubes and wires attached to the infant.

"She looks remarkably well to me, Hank," observed Doctor Carter. "Lungs seem to be good but we need to do more tests; in the end, time will tell. The baby is small and the skin tone shows signs of being malnourished but that was to be expected as the blood flow to the placenta was so constricted due to Jenny's high blood pressure. But like I said, the body desires to heal and live, that's how God wired it. In the days ahead, you will see God's handy work being accomplished.

"I must say, Hank your wife is rare person. When we started the labor process she told us all in the operating room that if complications should arise and it came down to a decision whose life to save, it must be Hannah's. She looked me and Doctor Webster in the eye and insisted that we abide by her wishes."

"Oh, Jenny," was all that Henry could say.

The men walked along in silence and then another thought popped into
Henry's mind. "What about food? How can Jenny nurse the baby in her condition?"

"Apparently that has been looked after. Your wife and daughter have already discussed that. Camilla, I believe is your daughter-in-law. She will be feeding your daughter. Fortunately, she has given birth just in time to nurse her son and be a wet nurse to your daughter."

Father and Henry were flabbergasted. They were speechless and didn't know what to say. However, Father Engelmann always had the appropriate comment, "Ach mein leiber gutt. You have thought of everything."

Chapter Four

WHEN THE THREE men entered the room, Jenny was still unconscious and had wires and tubes coming out of her everywhere. Doctor Carter looked at the monitors and said, "She is still very weak but I do think there is a slight improvement. Her blood pressure is still high but it has dropped slightly."

Jenny heard the doctor speaking and her eyes fluttered and then opened. Henry rushed to her side. The sight of her clear blue eyes gave him hope. "Oh Jenny, you did it. Hannah is born..." Henry could no longer speak; he was so choked up emotionally.

"How... is she?" Jenny asked faintly.

Doctor Carter came up to Jenny and took her hand. "You did a fine job, Jenny. The baby girl is doing well. She is in an incubator as she came into the world a bit early; she couldn't wait to see her mommy and daddy." Doctor Carter smiled and Jen forced a smile and closed her eyes. She was drifting off, overtaken by exhaustion.

Doctor Carter stepped back and whispered, "It's best she rests."

Father Engelmann came to where Doctor Carter had just stood. He placed his hand over hers and said a prayer. Doctor Carter pushed up a chair for both Henry and Father.

"I don't know how to thank you Jack for delivering the baby and your support." Henry shook his head and gazed appreciatively into his father-in-law's eyes and said again, "I can't thank you enough."

Jenny opened her eyes and said, "Yes, Doctor Carter, God has gifted you as a doctor and a comforter. His Holy Spirit is with you. Thank you, too."

Doctor Carter nodded. "Doctor Webster's assistance was a vast help but, in the end, all thanks go to Him. We all know that but thanks just the same. My ego still needs a little boost every now and then and I'm sure Doctor Webster's does too."

The two men smiled at one another and Father Engelmann nodded his head clearly understanding the meaning of the doctor's insightful words.

Doctor Carter shook Henry's hand once more, patted Father's shoulder and then quietly left. A few minutes later, Doctor Webster came into the room. He lightly stepped over to Henry and mouthed his congratulations to the new father. Henry thanked him for helping to deliver the baby. Doctor Webster nodded slightly and then reached across the bed and shook Father's hand.

The doctor studied the monitor for a moment and then turned to Henry. "I will check in on her later. The readings look hopeful."

THE ROOM WAS quiet and dim. Jenny periodically opened her eyes and each time she did, Henry squeezed her hand letting her know he was there. At four thirty there was a staff shift change as a different nurse started to come into the room, check on Jenny, and change the IV bag. At six o'clock, Father Engelmann said he was going to go see Hannah in the Neonatal Intensive Care Unit and go back to the care home. Henry was to call at any time if he was needed. He patted Jenny's hand and once again said a private prayer.

Father came over to Henry who stood by the time he came there and the two men hugged one another.

"Thanks for staying with me and being here for Jenny."

Father nodded. "Perhaps, go to the cafeteria and have some supper. Jenny will be fine, Henry. I will be back in the morning.

I will call Jeremy and the girls and let them know, Hannah is born."

Henry liked the way that sounded, "*Hannah is born.*" Henry thanked Father and shook his hand before he left. He returned to his chair and watched Jenny and held her hand and prayed. Each time her eyes fluttered or made a twitching movement, he was filled with hope.

About fifteen minutes after Father left, Camilla wheeled herself into the room. She came by Henry's side and they embraced one another. "Congratulations, Dad. How is Mom doing?"

Henry shrugged his shoulders, "So far so good. Have you seen Hannah?"

Camilla nodded, "She's adorable, Dad. I could eat her up."

"Doctor Carter said you fed her."

"I pumped some milk for them. Premature babies need more than just breast milk, so they will tube feed Hannah a little at a time along with other supplements for a while. Both Doctor Carter and Webster were in the Neonatal Unit when I was there, planning a feeding schedule. I think they have Hannah scheduled to eat eight to ten times a day. They will watch closely that Hannah doesn't become dehydrated. Mom's milk should be coming in soon and she will probably start pumping to get her milk up."

"Oh, Camilla..." said Jenny, weakly.

Camilla wheeled herself to Jenny s side and kissed her forehead. "Oh Mom, it's so good to see you awake. How are you feeling?"

Jenny raised her hands and let them fall almost as dead weight. She was very weak.

"You need to rest Mom, don't talk, Dad and I are here. I saw Hannah. They took some of my milk for her and will give her a tiny bit. She is adorable, Mom."

Jenny smiled and again closed her eyes. When the nurse came in, Camilla asked if Jenny could be given some oxygen. The nurse went out to the nurses' station and returned and hooked up a mask to Jenny.

"Do you want to come to the Neonatal Unit, Dad? I can show you your little angel."

Henry smiled and said, "I did very briefly earlier but I really want to see her with Jenny at my side. I would like to very much but I will wait."

"I better get back before they send a search party for me. Jeremy is coming up later. Perhaps it's best not to have too many visitors for the rest of the day. Mom looks very tired."

"Yeah, I'm going to see if they can roll a cot in here for me. I want to stay until Jenny gets up."

Camilla gave Henry a hug. "Mom, will be fine, Dad. I see a lot of girls after they have delivered their baby and they too, are exhausted. In Mom's case there was a lot of stress accompanying her delivery as well as medical issues. She did very well."

Camilla looked up at the monitor in the same way, Doctor Webster did earlier. She noted the blood pressure was still high but decided not to say anything. She smiled and left.

Around ten, Jenny was wide awake. She slipped the mask off and was so happy to see Henry still sitting on the chair.

"What time is it, Henry?"

"It's just after ten."

"Aren't you going home?"

"No. They brought up a cot for me. I thought I would stay here until you're strong enough to visit Hannah. Are you hungry?"

"Yes, I am, but I would love to see Hannah. Is it too late to go there?"

Just then a nurse walked in. "Oh, it's good to see you are awake, Mrs. Pederson."

"She said she was hungry, is it possible for her to get something at this hour?"

"Oh, I think I can manage that. In fact, that is a good sign."

"And we were also wondering if we are permitted to visit the care unit at this hour. Jenny and I would love to see our little girl."

"Yes, if Mrs. Pederson feels well enough to be wheeled there, I can arrange for someone to accompany you. The nurses work around the clock and so to them it doesn't matter what time of day patients or families come in."

Both Henry and Jenny's eyes brightened. As soon as the young nurse left, Henry went over to Jenny, took hold of her shoulders, and kissed her tenderly, "I love you so much, Mom." Unbidden tears surfaced in both their eyes. "I think we are going to get through this okay, sweetheart."

Jenny smiled and nodded. "I am dying to see her. She would be so tiny. I hope I can look without wanting to hold her."

Henry nodded and smiled. For the first time that day he began to relax. Silently, they looked at one another. Every now and then, Henry thought of something to tell Jenny.

"Father was with her until six o'clock and then he went back to the care home. He will be back in the morning. And, oh, both Doctor Carter and Doctor Webster were in to check on you."

"Yes, I remember Doctor Carter but not Doctor Webster."

"You were asleep at the time. I'm so happy Doctor Carter got involved; he gave me such a sense of confidence in all of this. He's a wonderful man."

Henry thought about his early relationship with Jack when he first started to date Julean how stressful and strained their relationship was. Henry shook his head and smiled at how God's divine Providence is always at work.

"Why are you smiling, Honey?"

Henry didn't want to get into his not so good years with Doctor Carter. He was glad the nurse came back with a sandwich and fruit tray under a plastic lid and diverted the attention to the food.

"Oh, that looks good," said Henry. He cranked Jenny's bed more into an upright position so she could sit up and then he rolled the hospital table over the bed with the food in front of her. She drank the water and asked Henry to pour some more. She took the lid off and began to eat the sandwich. She didn't quite eat half, then said she was full. Henry ate the other half.

Jenny looked better and a little stronger. "I have to go to the bathroom."

"Better call the nurse, in case you need some help."

Henry got up and pulled the cord alerting the nursing station. Immediately, the same young nurse as before walked in.

Henry spoke for Jenny. "She has to go to the washroom; she might need some help."

Henry left the room. A few minutes later the nurse came and told Henry it was okay for him to return and that she was going to get a wheelchair and assist them to the NICU.

Jenny's heart was racing as they approached the entrance. Henry was given a gown and mask to wear. The room was filled with about ten incubators. The nurse left Henry and Jenny momentarily while she approached one of the nurses on duty. They both went over to an incubator on the far side of the room. They discussed something for a few minutes and then the nurse returned to their side. "Your baby is sleeping. Don't be alarmed by all the wires and tubes. We are trying to assimilate the womb as much as possible and also monitor how your baby is doing."

Jenny barely heard the nurse's words as she was wheeled over to the other side of the room. Jenny and Henry's gaze held steadfast on the incubator the nurses had looked at.

From the seated position, Jenny could see the baby through the side of the clear, acrylic chamber. As soon as Henry saw Jenny attempting to stand he and the other nurse supported her.

"Oh, Hannah," was all Jenny could utter as tears filled her eyes. Hannah was so tiny and thin. Her skin was so transparent that the red blood vessels were visible. The poor little thing hardly had any fat under her skin. Her face was smooth and delicate and very sparse, light colored hair grew from the top of her small head. It was impossible to tell which parent she looked more like.

Jenny brought her hands up to her mouth, so overwhelmed to see her little girl all hooked up: to an oxygen supply, intravenous lines which went to the baby's arms for food and medicine, monitors attached to her tiny chest to check heart rate and breathing. Jenny shook her head and longed to pick Hannah up and hold her. She knew she was still too weak to do so and didn't know if the baby could be touched or held.

The nurse intuitively guessed what Jenny was thinking, "You can reach in and touch her or hold her hand if you want."

Jenny slowly brought her hand to one of the openings that appeared sealed by a rubber shield and slid her hand into the incubator. Her heart skipped a beat as her finger brushed Hannah's body and then her hand. Hannah made a closing motion around Jenny's little finger.

Henry was speechless as he watched on.

An attending nurse came over. "Her breathing is surprisingly strong. The few extra days before delivery must have developed her lungs more. She still requires assistance. Her heart rate is also very good. We are feeding your daughter with Camilla's milk until you start producing."

"When can I hold her?" Jenny wanted to know.

"It may be a few days or even a week or two. Your little girl's blood pressure and heart rate are still stabilizing and we want to make certain oxygen is reaching Hannah's cells and vital organs. So, we move small preemies as little as possible for the first day or so to avoid big changes in her circulation. But each preemie is different. We'll take one day at a time."

The nurse paused and then went on. "However, even though you might feel helpless seeing so many barriers, wires and tubes between you and your baby, Hannah needs you more than ever. With clean warm hands you can reach inside and touch your baby. We will show you how to comfort hold Hannah and soon give her 'Kangaroo care' as well. We encourage you to come as often as you can to talk to her. Soon, whenever the tubes are removed and you feel comfortable to do so, you can help with the bathing and care and also hold your little girl."

"Oh, she is so beautiful," Jenny kept saying, over and over.

Jenny began to wobble and had to sit back down in the chair. She leaned forward and kept her gaze on Hannah. After about ten minutes, the nurse said, "We better go back to your room. You need rest, Mrs. Pederson. We will notify you when you can come back in the morning if you feel strong enough."

They returned to Jenny's room and as soon as they were alone, both Henry and Jenny began to cry. They were so thankful that everything was turning out for the good. Jenny quickly dozed off while Henry was holding her hand. The nurse came in and directed him to the cot and he too fell into a deep sleep.

When Henry awoke in the morning, he was alarmed to see Jenny's bed was empty. Just as he made his way to the door, a different nurse came in. "Oh, hi Mr. Pederson, I just came in to check on you. Your wife went to NICU and we were instructed to take you there when you awoke. If you want, you can freshen up in the washroom before we go."

"Yes, just give me a few minutes."

When they arrived at the care unit, Henry saw Jenny holding Hannah through the clear plastic incubator. He was helped with the gown and mask and then taken into the room. Jenny was so focused on Hannah, she didn't notice Henry standing at the doorway, however the attending nurse next to her did. She alerted Jenny that Henry was there. Jenny turned immediately in her husband's direction. Her tear-filled eyes glowed with an inner joy as the father of her dear little Hannah approached them.

Henry came to Jenny's side and kissed her on the forehead. He looked at Hannah. She looked so tiny and fragile. Jenny had her one hand gently wrapped around Hannah's feet and her other hand touching Hannah's head. His heart went out to both mother and child.

Henry didn't notice at first that Camilla was there as well partially hidden by the attending nurse. Her eyes were filled with tears as well. When she saw Henry she just nodded and slowly shook her head from one side to the other out of the sheer wonder of it all. Jenny removed her hand from the incubator and took hold of Henry's hand and guided it into the opening of the plastic chamber. As soon as his finger touched the infant, an electric pulse seemed to flow through him at the feel of the new life he and Jenny had brought into the world. Henry shook his head at their tiny creation. Jenny gently patted Henry's hand inside the incubator. Henry instinctively knew the message his dear wife was conveying to him by the gesture. Hannah, was her gift to him.

Her dream had come true.

CHAPTER FIVE

CARRYING THE BABY in her womb for an extra week or so, accompanied by steroid injections, did help to mature the infant's lungs more quickly. Both Doctor Carter and Doctor Webster were amazed by the ease with which Hannah breathed and prepared for life outside the womb. However, it did come at a cost. Jenny did suffer some organ damage, but the extent of it was not yet known.

The good news, as Doctor Webster claimed was that the preeclampsia would quickly go away as soon as the baby was delivered. Within three days, Jenny's health improved significantly. Her blood pressure which was over 200/100 had gone down to 140/90. The protein in her urine was all but gone. Jenny was also happy to note that along with the lowering of her blood pressure, the diuretics were able to work more effectively in removing most of the fluid built in her ankles. Much to Henry's and everyone else's relief, Jenny was looking more like her usual self.

On the fourth day after Jenny delivered Hannah, Camilla was scheduled to be discharged. She was ready to go home and her services as a wet mother were no longer required. Jenny's milk had come in and she was pumping her breasts regularly. Although Hannah did not attempt to nurse yet, Jenny always held the baby close to her bare breasts giving the infant as much love and attention as possible. Henry especially enjoyed listening to Jenny talk and sing to Hannah. Jenny also said the guardian angel prayer over and over to her darling little girl.

When Jeremy came to the hospital to pick up Camilla and the baby, Henry, Jenny, Justin and Father Engelmann were waiting for them in the NICU. Jenny and Henry had decided to baptize Hannah just in case any complications arose. So far, Hannah was checking out beyond their expectations. It was a simple ceremony. Jenny removed Hannah from the incubator and gave the infant to Camilla. She and Jeremy were designated the god parents. Jenny had decided that several months ago. She and Camilla had several discussions that if anything happened to her that Camilla and Jeremy would have to help Henry raise the child.

Several nurses in the unit stopped what they were doing to observe the simple ceremony. While in Camilla's arms, Jeremy touched the infant as Father Engelmann baptized Hannah in the name of the Father and of the Son and of the Holy Spirit. Hannah was startled when Father poured a small quantity of warm water on her head. Father also anointed the baby with oil and prayed for speedy growth and health. This was followed by the distribution of Holy Communion. Both Henry and Jenny felt relieved that their little girl was now a member of the Christian community.

JENNY WOULD HAVE dearly missed the daily visits by Camilla when she was in the hospital if it hadn't been for the many other visitors. Now that her health was better, her friends felt more comfortable in coming to see her. She was dearly missed at the group meetings and many of the ladies were still giving Jenny positive feedback from the talk Father Engelmann gave at their social event last year in November.

Although she knew Thomas and Neela were coming for a visit to Regina, Jenny was still surprised to see them walk into her room, accompanied by Carlos.

"Oh, Thomas and Neela, it's so good to see you!" exclaimed Jenny.

Her dear friends rushed to her side and took turns giving Jenny a hug.

"You are looking fine, Miss Jenny. It is a pleasure to see you as well."

"It's very nice to visit with you," replied Neela.

Carlos simply remained quietly at the doorway and smiled. Jenny didn't know whose teeth were whiter or smile kindlier between the two men. She loved both dearly and over the years they had been such comforting and supportive friends.

Thomas gave Jenny a package he was holding. It had the shape of a bouquet of flowers hidden inside. "We know how much you love these but I can see your room is already filled with nature's beauty."

"Oh Thomas, you have such a way with words. They always paint a picture." It was true; Jenny's room looked like a garden in full bloom. Every flower possible in all the florist shops in Regina seemed to be on display. Jenny opened the wrap and two dozen white daisies with a yellow center were exposed. Jenny immediately smelled them and said, "Thank you so much, Neela, Thomas. They are my favorites. I love daisies."

"We also got you several things for the baby; a blanket, full length pajamas and a rattle. We will leave them with Carlos to give to you when you are released from the hospital."

"Oh, that is so kind of you and Thomas. Thank you so much." Once again, Jenny brought up her arms and extended them towards her dear guests from Ontario. First, Neela and then Thomas came to Jenny to receive a warm hug of appreciation and thanks.

"How is the baby doing?" inquired Neela.

Jenny laid the flowers on her lap and said, "Surprisingly well for being born almost eight weeks early."

"I can hardly wait to see her. Is she nursing yet?"

"She shows signs of wanting to when I rest her on my chest. I think she will be in a few more days. The doctors and nurses are so pleased with her progress."

Then looking at Thomas, Jenny continued, "So, you won't be able to see the flowers or what the yard looks like at this time of the year."

"No, but I do recall how beautiful it all looked when you and Henry married. Carlos also sent me photos of some of the changes that you and he decided upon. I assure you, Miss Jenny, there is nothing I could add. You both did such a fine job."

"Did you see the shrine of the blessed Mother, Mary?" Jenny wanted to know.

"No, what shrine are you referring to?"

"It's in the back yard, but, I guess with winter still here it would be covered over," Jenny replied, looking to Carlos for confirmation.

"Yes, Senorita Jenny, it is as you say but I will show Thomas and Neela where it is and Maria has taken some photos of it as well."

Just then, Henry arrived. After a warm greeting, they all went to the NICU to see Hannah. One the nurses had just changed the baby. Together, Jenny and an attending nurse wheeled the incubator over to the viewing window. Jenny took Hannah out of the incubator and held her so her guests could have a good look at the newborn infant.

Jenny could see the joy in their faces, especially Thomas'. He knew of the difficulties which developed after she gave birth to J.J.. She was so restricted in nursing and raising the child in a normal family setting. Thomas could see the happiness glowing in Jenny's eyes. Her love for Hannah was pouring out of her entire being.

Henry couldn't be happier or prouder as he looked on at Jenny holding their daughter. Her fine yellow, wheat colored hair, almost white, lay flat on the baby's head. It was still difficult to see who she resembled more at this stage as the features had not yet filled out. Henry hoped she would be the spitting image of his dear wife.

As Henry gazed on, all the days of worry and concern seemed to be melting away and were being replaced by a future filled with hope. He silently thanked God for the gift of life and family and friends. He was thankful how it all seemed to work out in God's divine providence. How Doctor Carter came into the room that Sunday when he was so troubled over the decision of whether to abort the child or not. *He now could see that such a decision would be unthinkable.*

After the viewing, they all returned to Jenny's room and chatted some more. Jenny was happy to learn that J.J. and his family were coming to Regina at the end of April to visit and see the new baby. Jenny was doubly overjoyed that Matti would also be coming. What a joy it was for Jenny to see her family and extended family on the estate grow so close together. Silently, she thanked God for all His blessings and mentally placed a flower in the Angel of Thanksgiving basket.

CHAPTER SIX

W ITH EACH PASSING day, Jenny and the baby bonded more and more as mother and child. Henry loved to watch tiny Hannah tucked inside Jenny's gown, lying on her breast in what the staff called the 'kangaroo' position. Although the infant wasn't able to nurse directly, Hannah was tube fed while resting 'skin to skin' with Jenny. Henry could see how this time was so precious for both mother and child.

It was the perfect picture of pure bliss. If he had his easel and paints there, he would set to painting at once!

The baby's lungs had developed much sooner than the doctors expected and she seemed to be breathing fine on her own. They were also pleased to note the baby was growing in size and weight. After the third day, Hannah was just under three pounds. It was so true what Doctor Carter had said, "God created the body that always works towards healing itself and to follow His laws."

Doctor Webster was very pleased that he hadn't aborted the child. The day after the delivery, he commended Jenny on her wise choice to go with Doctor Carter and that he had learned a thing or two from the wise, elderly, prairie doctor. "There are some things which you don't learn in school." He further told Jenny that he took her words to heart and thanked her for reminding him of the main reason why he chose to become a doctor: to save lives. Doctor Webster came to realize more and more the value and beauty of life and he made an internal decision to always look for ways to save the child and mother when complications arise.

One thing which was quite noticeable by the nursing staff and Doctor Webster was the aura that surrounded Jenny when she was with her baby. Doctor Webster had to admit there was something very special about his patient. Her radiance seemed to go beyond anything he had seen in his practice before.

Each day, Jenny's room was filled with more colorful flowers. Just as Thomas felt on the day of his visit, as well as friends and family who came to see her, it was as though they were visiting Jenny in a spectacular garden. As beautiful as the flowers were however, they could not outshine the glow of happiness on Jenny's face. No matter who entered Jenny's room, they were immediately attracted to this aura of light.

Jenny often communicated with her guardian angel as well as her baby. Her infant was named after her own protector. The child within her arms was her earthly angel. Jenny was thankful for both. But there was still another reason for the name; both her guardian and baby had the same name as Hannah, her biblical heroine in the 1st Book of Samuel, the woman she emulated. It would forever remind Jenny of how the Lord answered her tearful cry for help to conceive the child. Jenny had not forgotten the promise she had made to God. If He blessed her with a child, she would, like Hannah in the Bible, dedicate the child back to God from birth.

One morning, at the end of the first week when Henry came in, Jenny reminded her husband of the covenant she had made.

"Honey, do you recall when I told you of the story about Hannah in Samuel 1, she had made a vow to God that if she were blessed with a child, she would give it back to God?"

"Yes, after the child was fully weaned, Hannah gave the child to the priest at the shrine where she prayed, but Jenny, times are different today. One does not give up their child to some religious order."

Jenny smiled. "I understand that, however, I did promise to dedicate the child to the Lord. So, if Hannah feels inclined to enter a religious vocation, we won't interfere. If she is meant to go in that direction, I'm certain God will incline her so."

Henry nodded, "It would be wonderful if Hannah became a nun or dedicated her life to God in some way. I have no problem with that, Jen. I was very happy to see Alison enroll at the Bible College."

"That's wonderful, thank you, Henry."

Henry smiled. "I recall in the story, the name, Hannah, means 'favored one'. Perhaps, God has something special in mind for our little girl."

A silence fell over the room as they held hands and gazed lovingly into each other's eyes. "Oh Henry, I am so happy we had this child together. I have yearned and dreamed and prayed for this so long. I love you so much."

Henry nodded. "I love you all the more, sweetheart. Every day I love Hannah more as well. I can hardly wait for the two of you to come home.

"Just saying three little words, 'I love you' doesn't seem like enough, Jen. Or saying those words doesn't seem to express or capture all I feel or want to say to you."

Jenny gazed lovingly at her dear husband and said, "It's a way to capture so many things that would take a life-time to show and convey. It's your presence, friendship, patience, kindness, consideration, the little things you do, the way you talk and walk, your expressions and the sacrifices you make. These are just a few of the things encapsulated in the words, 'I love you', and yet, when we think of God as love there simply are no words to describe it and we never will."

"That's how I feel towards you, Jenny; there are no words to convey how I feel for you. If something would have happened, I don't know if I could have gone on."

Jenny remained silent. She loved to hear Henry's words and yet it concerned her. So, she said, "When we got married, I loved when we put Jesus at the center of our lives and marriage. He is the glue that keeps us together and is our teacher and guide. I remember Father Engelmann saying how the two commandments which Jesus gave us, capture the heart of the Gospel. The first was to love God with all of our strength, mind and heart and that the second was to love others as ourselves. Father stressed the order; that we are to love God first and foremost. I am so glad that Father Engelmann made me aware of that because if something should happen to you, I would easily get stuck and perhaps no longer able to carry on as you just said. If I felt that I was totally dependent upon you for the love I feel, you would have control of my very life and your departure would be devastating. Father Engelmann made me realize however, it is through God, through Jesus, that I love you, Henry, with all my heart, all my strength and very being. That love I feel for you comes from God, who is love. It is you which stirs my being to enter into the source of His divine love. *But it all comes from Him.*"

Henry remained silent, trying to take in what Jenny said, it was true that in many relationships, a spouse feels the other is the source of their happiness and it keeps them stuck in the death of their partner at times for years and at times, one never gets over it. *Would he be such a person?* He loved Jenny more than life itself. It was the same with Julean and how deeply he loved her. She may be gone at a physical level and yet, he still sensed her spirit and love. *Would it be the same in Jenny's case?*

It was as if Jenny were reading his thoughts. "We are never really alone, are we, Henry? When we have God, I love you freely, Henry. If you should leave, I will deeply mourn and grieve but it will be God's love that will sustain me and help me to carry on. Thankfully, it all comes from Him, otherwise what would we do? When I see you and yearn for your touch or caress, it's that love within me that comes from God which I feel in my heart for you. God is first and foremost in our lives and the wellspring of all love." Jenny paused and gazed tenderly at Henry and then added, "As I said, if it came from you, I would be crushed when you're gone. I would be enslaved to you, locked into a relationship that has no escape. True love is free just like God's love; He loves us no matter what. True love is divine, a precious gift from God that gives us untold happiness in this life and also the source of untold comfort in life's trials and challenges."

Henry didn't know what to say. Just the way his dear wife expressed those words, it seemed as if she wanted to prepare him for that day of departure which all of us have to eventually face.

Jenny broke into Henry's thoughts. "Doctor Webster said that I will be discharged next Monday. That will be two weeks since Hannah was born. We will need to make daily visits to the hospital for several weeks."

"That's fine, honey. Soon, the both of you will be home."

They both gazed down at the little angel asleep on Jenny's chest and almost in unison they said the Guardian Angel Prayer which Jenny continued to say countless times to Hannah:

"Angel of God, my guardian dear,
To whom His love commits me here,
Ever this day be at my side, Jenny's, Hannah's and
*   Henry's...*
to light and guard, to rule and guide.
Forever and ever. Amen."

CHAPTER SEVEN

O N MONDAY, APRIL 26, 1993, exactly two weeks after Hannah was born, Jenny was discharged. Everyone was elated but especially Justin. Both Henry and Jenny were surprised at his expression of concern for his step-mother. He helped with the supper dishes and generally wanted to be around her more. It was as if he finally realized the gem he had and wanted to polish it in any way which he could.

J.J. had to put their coming to Regina on hold until the middle of May due to a business commitment. Henry was relieved as he thought it might put too much stress on Jenny just being released from the hospital and still not fully recovered. Since the baby would be in the hospital for at least another month, they also decided to rent a condo near the hospital to eliminate the daily driving to and from the hospital. Jenny was already feeling fatigued from the rigorous routine. She stayed at Camilla's home but thought it was too much for her daughter as she also had a new baby and was a busy mother as well. She did pump extra milk for Hannah just in case she couldn't make it in.

As the first week at home came to a close, Jenny found that sitting in a more upright position when sleeping allowed her breathe easier. She also noticed that her ankles were swelling again. She was to see Doctor Webster the following Tuesday. On Saturday, she decided to stay home as Henry went into the city to finalize the lease of a condo near the hospital. She also pumped some extra milk for Hannah for Henry to drop off at the NICU.

On Sunday morning, they both were awoken by the sun streaming in through the open blinds. Jenny loved the warmth of the sun and didn't mind that it woke her up at times when she would have liked more rest. Henry would have preferred to have the blinds closed but he also readily accepted it as it gave him joy to see the happiness the sun gave Jenny. Besides, the light allowed him to see Jenny's beautiful sparkling blue eyes upon awakening.

At first, Henry wasn't sure where the soft noise was coming from and then he realized, Jenny was wheezing slightly. She had propped herself up on two pillows like the day before as it seemed to help her breathing.

"Are you okay, Honey?" Henry asked, not sure if she was awake as her eyes were still closed.

"Yes, just a little tired."

"Perhaps, you should stay home today?"

"Oh, no, I have to see Hannah and nurse her."

"How is your breathing? You seem to be short of breath?"

"I think it's because I'm still tired and not fully recovered. Maybe, I will stay at the condo and rest for the day after I nurse Hannah and leave some milk for her. I hope I can walk, I feel a pain in my right leg."

Henry got up and made his way over to the other side of the bed. He slowly pulled down the covers and looked at Jenny's right leg. The calf looked a little red and swollen. He felt the calf and asked, "Does it hurt when I touch it?"

"No, it's just a minor pain. Perhaps I slept in an awkward position. If you want, you can get dressed and start breakfast, I'll be down in a few minutes."

Henry was reluctant to leave. He wasn't sure if he should take Jenny to the hospital or call the doctor. She did have an appointment Tuesday but was that waiting too long? What if she needed attention sooner? What of the swelling and shortness of breath?

As if reading Henry's thoughts, Jenny said, "Oh, I'll be fine, Henry. I can't wait to see Hannah. Wild horses can't keep me away today. I could hardly sleep last night just thinking of her and holding her close to my heart."

Fortunately, Justin was up and preparing breakfast. He had the ingredients out to make pancakes. He hoped Jenny would make some as they were his favorites. Henry was telling Justin that Jenny seemed overly tired when they heard a loud thump in the foyer. Henry rushed out and saw Jenny lying at the foot of the stairs. She was on her side. He immediately went over and rolled her on her back. She had hit her head on the tile floor. There was a large red bruise that threatened to bleed. He took hold of her shoulders and gently shook her. "Jenny, Jenny, are you okay?"

Jenny remained unconscious. She was breathing heavily.

"We have to get her to the hospital right away!" cried Henry. "Call 911, Justin! Quickly!"

Justin dialed the number and told the operator who was calling and their land description. He then brought the receiver to Henry to answer questions he was asked and didn't know the answer to. Luckily, the cord was long enough for Henry to hear the operator. "My wife is unconscious, she is having difficulty breathing. She is very stressed out from having a baby a couple of weeks ago."

"Is she conscious, yet?"

"No. She hit her head when she fell at the bottom of the stairs, so I'm not sure if the fall made her unconscious or she just passed out."

"Do you know how to do CPR?"

"Yes, but how long will it take the ambulance to get out here? I could put her into the back of the SUV and start to head to Regina and meet up with the paramedics at exit B...it's the one near the turnoff to Condy. That would save ten minutes."

Jenny began to stir and opened her eyes and saw Henry's frantic face looking down at her. "What happened, Henry? Where am I?"

"She just woke up, operator. How are you feeling Jenny?"

Jenny was gasping, "It's hard to breath, Honey. Please help me up."

"She's having difficulty breathing, should I prop her up? She used two pillows last night when sleeping and it seemed to help."

"Yes, do that now. Get several pillows. We want you to stay at the farm and keep contact with me. The ambulance is on their way. We know your land location. They can drive faster than you and will be there in no time."

Justin heard the operator and ran to the guest room on the main level and quickly returned with three pillows. They placed them behind Jenny's back. Justin knelt down and acted as a backrest and supported her head.

"Is she still conscious?"

"Yes."

"Do you have Aspirin in the house?"

"Yes."

Henry could see Justin had a good hold on Jenny and quickly got up and ran into the bathroom. He brought out a bottle of Aspirin. He knelt down and said, "Oh geez, I forgot the water."

"That's okay. Just give her two and ask her to chew on them."

Henry did as he was instructed.

"How is your wife doing, Mr. Pederson? Is she breathing easier?"

Jenny nodded, "Tell her it helps when I'm in this position."

"Did you hear what she said? She can breathe better in this position."

"That's good. You are doing fine. The paramedics will be there soon. Is your wife wearing any tight clothing?"

Jenny had on a white blouse that was buttoned all the way up to her neck. Henry loosened the first three buttons without being told to. She was wearing black slacks. Henry looked at Jenny and asked, "Is the belt too tight around your waist?"

"Perhaps, loosen it a bit. It seems okay though."

"Okay, I loosened her clothing. What else can I do?"

"If you have a blanket nearby, cover her, so she is warm."

Henry was upset with himself for not thinking of that. Justin had an expression on his face that echoed Henry's sentiments.

"Okay, I have her covered."

"You are doing fine. Just stay calm and let your wife know that help is on the way. Was that your son who called?"

"Yeah, that was Justin."

"Tell him he gave clear instructions to your acreage. How old is he?"

Henry had to think for a moment. Justin looked at his father and whispered, "Fifteen."

"He's fifteen."

"I have a daughter who is a year older. How is your wife doing?"

Jenny nodded and whispered, "I love you, Henry, with all my heart." She reached up for Justin and said, "I love you too, Justin."

Just as Henry was about to respond to Jenny he was interrupted by the operator. "Is that your wife speaking?"

"Yes, that was Jenny."

"What a beautiful name. I have an aunt whose name is Jennifer. We call her Jenny too."

Just then, Henry became aware of a siren.

"I think the ambulance is here!"

"I was just going to ask if there is a red barn on your property?"

"Yes, it's at the top, soon after you enter the lane into the acreage. There is a row of evergreen trees behind the barn. Tell the ambulance to keep following the lane down into the valley around the hill. It leads to a two-storey cedar log house."

The siren was getting louder. Both Henry and Justin felt a sigh of relief.

"Keep holding her Justin, I'll get the door."

Henry rushed to the door and opened it. The paramedics were already at the back of the ambulance taking out a gurney. Henry waved to them.

"She's just inside."

Henry held the door as the two paramedics rushed in. One was a male and the other a female.

"Mr. Pederson, I'm Shirley. This is George."

Henry nodded but didn't take time to shake hands. He quickly stepped aside as Shirley brushed by him carrying a case. George wheeled in an oxygen tank. They both knelt down and began to assess the situation. Shirley took out a gauge to measure Jenny's blood pressure while George positioned the stethoscope to his ears and the other end to Jenny's chest. "Her lungs have water," he said as Shirley gave Jenny a thermometer to measure her temperature. She also took Jenny's left hand from underneath the blanket and wrapped the blood pressure cuff around her arm. She also listened to Jenny's pulse with her stethoscope at the same time. "Its low," she said, keeping the numbers to herself. Henry assumed it was not to upset them.

"We need to start her on oxygen right away."

George had already unraveled a long cord attached to a clear oxygen mask and placed it over Jenny's nose and mouth. He instructed her to breathe deeply.

"What is the problem, George?" Henry asked with deep concern.

"It could be her heart—"

"You mean she is having a heart attack!?" Henry wanted to know.

George just tightened his lips and shrugged his shoulders. He quickly got up and went to the door and brought in the gurney and positioned it as close to Jenny as possible and lowered it. Justin moved out of the way as George took his place, while the female paramedic took hold of Jenny's feet. On the count of three, they transferred Jenny to the gurney and raised it. Just as they were going out the door Henry said, "She also complained of a pain in her right leg this morning. It looked red and swollen."

They immediately stopped and pulled up Jenny's slacks. Shirley felt around the swollen calf and then looked at her partner. "It could be an embolism." She pulled the pant down again and covered Jenny with a blanket.

Henry followed them to the back of the ambulance. They raised the gurney as far as it could go and pushed the stretcher inside. Both of them went inside. Shirley set up an IV while George prepared to insert a needle into Jenny's arm. Her veins were so fine. Henry recalled the difficulty they had at the hospital. Fortunately, the first try was successful and they quickly started to give Jenny some medication. Henry assumed it was to remove the water. He wondered why that was happening. Surely, Jenny couldn't be having a heart attack. *Could she?*

He was surprised how calm and collected he still was. He was happy Jenny was conscious. He stepped up and stood at the door and gazed at Jenny. He reached to the top of his shirt and unbuttoned his first two buttons and took out the pewter angel. He read the inscription, "*Watch over my beloved.*" Tears came to his eyes. Jenny took her free arm and reached for her pewter angel as well. It danced in the light. Henry thought she was whispering something too but couldn't tell as the mask covered both her nose and mouth. She did bring the tips of her fingers from her free hand to the mask and threw Henry a kiss.

The paramedics were all set up and George came to the back door. "You will have to leave now. You can follow us. We will have your wife to the hospital shortly and she will be placed in the ICU."

Henry side stepped George and saw Jenny's sparkling blue eyes. "I love you honey. My heart goes with you."

Henry threw her a kiss and then asked if he could quickly give her a kiss. Shirley nodded. Henry quickly squeezed around her to Jenny's side. "Oh Jenny, you are in my prayers. I love you so much." He lifted the mask and kissed her tenderly.

"I love you all the more," said Jenny.

Their tears mingled as Henry withdrew and backed out of the ambulance. He kept his gaze on his dear wife for as long as he could, burning the image of her deeply in his mind.

George closed the doors and rushed to the driver's seat. Henry stepped out of the way as the ambulance quickly sped down the road. Just as they disappeared around the bend to ascend to the top of the flat prairie, Henry was startled by the wailing sound of the siren. He never did like that sound. He hated it even more so now. He stood motionless as the sound diminished into a dead country silence. He turned and there was his son. Justin's eyes were filled with tears and fright. Henry went to him and they embraced.

Chapter Eight

H<small>ENRY AND</small> J<small>USTIN</small> quickly got ready to follow behind the ambulance and then Henry thought to call Father Engelmann. Father was planning to come back to the Poustinia right after saying Mass at the care home. He called his room but there was no answer. *Perhaps he is with one of the residents.* He called the main reception area and instructed them to let Father know Jenny was ill again and to come to the ICU at the Grey Nuns Hospital as soon as he was able to.

When Henry and his son arrived at the hospital, it was shortly after ten. He wondered if he should call Doctor Carter and let him know. Unbelievably, just as they were entering the emergency area, Doctor Carter was approaching the front doors, too.

"I was about to call you Jack. Jenny was just admitted. The ambulance came out to the farm to get her."

"Yes, I know. They called to let me know since I am one of her caregivers."

"That's wonderful. It makes me feel better that you will be there." Justin held the door for the two men and they all rushed in.

"She will be in ICU after they carry out some tests, Hank. If you and Justin want to go to the waiting room up there, I will let you know what is going on as soon as I know. Oh, yes, check with admittance first to see if anything needs to be filled out."

JENNY WAS WHEELED into one of the emergency rooms and was immediately attended to by one of the doctors on duty.

He lifted her mask and asked, "How are you feeling, Mrs. Pederson?" the doctor asked.

"My head is sore where I fell but...I am...having trouble breathing..."

The doctor replaced the oxygen mask and then proceeded to take her blood pressure. He then listened to her chest and examined her hands, legs and feet and then immediately ordered a diuretic to be administered through the IV. He also ordered chest x-rays.

Just as Jenny was wheeled to the lab, Doctor Carter came in. He rushed to Jenny's side and smiled. He patted her arm, reassuringly. As they walked towards the elevator, the resident doctor informed Doctor Carter of Jenny's status. Jenny overheard part of their conversation but didn't understand the terminology. The one word was "cardiomyopathy" and assumed it had something to do with her heart. The rest of their discussions centered on her respiratory condition. She wondered how on earth she got fluid in her lungs.

Dr. Carter came back to Jenny's side and said, "We are going to take a chest x-ray and get you to the ICU as soon as possible. I will see you up there. Hank and Justin are there already waiting for you."

Jenny nodded and lost sight of Henry's father-in-law, as the elevator doors closed.

HENRY FELT QUEASY as he and his son rode the elevator up to the fourth floor. It was a little over three years since he was in another elevator on the east ward rushing up to see Jenny in the palliative care unit. He recalled vividly, thoughts of never seeing his dear, sweet, first love still alive. Those same thoughts and feelings inched their way up from the bottom of his stomach to the top of his head. He was deeply concerned over Jenny's well-being. Although she didn't look to be in eminent danger when she left with the ambulance that morning, there was just a pervasive feeling of fear swarming around inside of him that wouldn't go away. He sensed his sensitive son had similar feelings. Every now and then he noticed Justin swiping at a tear or two rolling down his cheeks.

The elevator came to a jarring halt and both men stepped out into the large foyer that led in four directions. They followed the sign that read:

Cardiac Intensive Care Ward Unit
All Visitors must check in at Nurse's Station.

Henry told Justin to sit in an area that looked like a waiting room, then continued on to the nurses' station.

A nurse didn't look up right away when Henry stood in front of the high counter. He was too impatient to wait on her and asked, "Is Jenny Pederson in this ward?"

The nurse looked up. Her face quickly shed a look of annoyance as soon as she saw Henry's concern written clearly on his face.

"No, we are expecting her any time now from X-ray. If you wish to wait in the waiting area, I will let you know as soon as you are able to visit with her."

"Is Doctor Webster here, today?"

"No, but he was informed that your wife was admitted."

Henry walked slowly back to the waiting area almost bumping into several nurses who were going in and out of rooms in the hallway. He was in a daze. How could this be happening? Jenny was finally at home. Hannah was doing so well and then, suddenly, out of the blue, life throws him another curve. But not just him, Jenny, too, who had over the past years of her life been confronted by so many trials and challenges.

Life, just isn't fair.

WHEN FATHER ENGELMANN heard that Jenny was admitted into the ICU he immediately recalled his second mission which he was assigned during his stint on the other side. When Jenny's pregnancy developed such serious complications, Father thought his second mission had to do with her grave condition. That notion was dismissed however, in lieu of Jenny's successful delivery of the baby and her seemingly quick recovery. When Henry called that morning and left the message that Jenny was admitted into the ICU at the Grey Nun's Hospital, something triggered deep within Father Engelmann which told him this had something to do with the vision he had seen on the other side.

His first instinct was to pray.

He would ask the residents for their support, too, just like he did when Jenny was dying of cancer in the hospital.

The chapel was packed with both residents and nearby neighbors. Before he began the Mass, he informed the gathering of Jenny and Henry's situation. He related more of the story than he needed to but he wanted to revive the memory of several of the residents who were there at the time when they had that incredible prayer session for Jenny's healing. He was hoping that the few remaining residents would be able to muster up that surge of faith like a mustard seed to heal Jenny once again of whatever she was admitted for that morning. Father just knew that the power of prayer was needed.

His dear friend, Edith, had gone to see the Lord a year ago. Johnny was making records somewhere in Toronto, Father had last heard. Margaret passed on just six months ago and two days later, Shirley followed. However, there were still a few faces before him that he recalled being at the last faith filled prayer session. He appealed to those when asking for their prayers and hoped they might instill fervor in the surrounding neighbors visiting the care home.

Father began the prayer but the intensity was not the same. There just weren't enough prayer warriors in the room to lift the ceiling like they had done in the past. However, all prayer is heard by God and along with the offering of the Mass for Jenny, all would be heard by the Lord to do what He willed.

DOCTOR CARTER FOUND Henry and Justin seated in the waiting room. Henry immediately stood and let out a long sigh of relief.

"How is she Jack!?"

"The lab had to re-take some of the chest x-rays. She will be brought up here shortly."

"Is Mom going to be okay, Grandpa?" Justin interjected.

Doctor Carter tilted his head and displayed a serious face. "It's her heart. In her heart's main chamber, the left ventricle, her heart muscle has become enlarged, Hank. This has weakened its ability to pump blood through her body. She has acute pulmonary edema which means that fluid is accumulating in the lungs. She is also in right ventricular failure as evidence by the swelling in the ankles, feet and legs. The x-rays will confirm our diagnosis."

"Is this the reason she is having trouble breathing?"

Doctor Carter nodded. "Yes, with less blood flow carrying oxygen throughout the body and the build up of fluid in the spaces between the tissues of the lungs, makes it more and more difficult for the lungs to expand. She is not getting enough oxygen."

"How could this come on so suddenly? She was doing so well." Henry lamented.

"I suspect it has to do with the preeclampsia, Hank. Jenny had uncontrolled high blood pressure for several weeks which placed tremendous stress on her heart and caused it to become inflamed. Other complications may have developed in the kidneys and liver. We are waiting for the lab results and then we will know more."

"If only Jenny hadn't waited so long to deliver the baby." Henry said absently.

Doctor Carter nodded. He understood Henry's reasoning and offered an answer, "She was informed by Doctor Webster that complications could develop which could endanger her life as well as the fetus. She intuitively felt however, that if the fetus was healthy and that its chances for survival would be better if she kept the baby longer so the lungs would develop more. She was adamant to do this and, in the end, she was correct. The baby's lungs were remarkably strong at birth and free of abnormalities but it was at a great cost to her health.

In defence of Jenny's decision, cardiomyopathy can occur in any pregnancy."

"Even women who don't have preeclampsia?" Henry quickly asked.

Doctor Carter, nodded, "Yes."

There was a momentary silence and then Doctor Carter added, "I am going to see where things are at and will keep you and Justin informed, Hank."

"Are you able to deal with heart problems, Jack?" Henry wanted to know.

"I have basic knowledge but there is a cardiologist on staff who will be looking after Jenny in that regard. She will be hooked up to a heart monitor as soon as she comes into the ICU. She will be in good care, Hank."

Henry and Justin watched the elderly doctor walk down the hall towards the nurses' station. Henry pulled out Julean's rosary and motioned to his son to sit down. They sat together near the window. The sun was just working its way around the corner of the south-west wing of the hospital and its rays struck both Henry and Justin's face. They squinted and looked up. It felt warm and soothing. Henry wished the sun could touch Jenny. The sun was her friend and on so many occasions lifted her spirits during life's trials.

Henry ran the crystal beads through his hand and squeezed the silver cross of the rosary with the tips of his fingers and made the sign of the cross. Justin did the same and the two men began to pray for Jenny.

CHAPTER NINE

A FTER HENRY AND his son finished saying the rosary for the Blessed Mother Mary to intercede to Jesus, they became more restless by the minute. They could no longer relax in the waiting area. Henry suddenly realized he needed to make some phone calls. First, he let Camilla know what was happening to her mother. He explained as best he could to his daughter-in-law what Doctor Carter had told him. She took the news hard and immediately began to cry. She was hoping and praying that no complications from the pregnancy would develop as so many girls in her care were not so fortunate. She was so hopeful and relieved when Jenny was discharged that she would beat the odds. Jeremy was called into work because two staff didn't show up due to a sudden illness and said that she would come up as soon as he got home.

Henry thought of calling his two daughters but decided to wait until later that evening. He did however decide to call J.J.. He was Jenny's son and needed to know that his mother was very ill.

How serious, Henry couldn't say.

He also called Carlos and Maria to pray. Thomas and Neela had returned to Ottawa several days ago. Carlos said he would call them however and ask for their prayer support. Carlos also said that he would call their parish priest to ask for intercessory prayers and that a Mass be offered up for Jenny.

When Henry came back to the waiting area, Justin was standing by the window looking out into the courtyard. He saw his son's reflection in the window but it wasn't clear enough to read the distress on his face. Regardless, Henry knew his son was hurting. He came up to him and put his hand on his shoulder to alert him that he was there. Henry then moved still closer and put his arm around his son. They both gazed out the window and watched people come and go in the courtyard below.

Henry recalled looking out a similar window at the General Hospital when Julean was critically ill. Those memories flooded back to him now. He remembered the day she died and how he was walking down the hallway when a nurse shouted. He instinctively knew it had to do with Julean. How quickly he ran to Julean's room to see the medical staff trying to revive his dear wife who just had another seizure. Henry hoped and prayed that he would not hear a similar cry from a nurse and have to deal with another departure of a loved one.

Henry wished Doctor Carter would come out and tell him what was going on. Almost two hours had passed and the tension was building. Justin was beginning to tremble and shifted his weight from one leg to another. He couldn't stand still. He began to pace in front of the window. Henry asked his son if they should say another rosary. Justin shook his head negatively at first and then when he saw his dad pull out his mother's crystal beads again, he nodded affirmatively.

As the two men stood there in front of the window praying, Henry began to see an image of Julean. He stopped midway saying, "The Our Father." It reminded Henry of the time when he was at the farm after he had discovered Jenny's diary. He heard the words now as he did then which spurred him into action to rush to the Santa Maria care Home. "Quickly, hold my hand," was a thought which began to form in Henry's mind. He wondered if Jenny was beckoning him.

Justin must be seeing a vision of his mother as well as he went to the window and began to rub the glass. Just as he turned to ask his dad something, they were both startled by someone calling Henry's name.

"Hank, come, come quickly! Your wife insists on seeing you."

Henry turned and looked down the hallway and saw Doctor Carter rushing towards him. "Hank, Jenny's blood pressure is falling and not responding to medication. She is calling for you to come quickly. She wants to hold your hand. Come, Hank, come."

Without hesitation, Henry rushed to the elderly doctor who had already turned his direction back to the intensive care room when he saw his son-in-law coming. The words, 'quickly, hold my hand,' resonated in Henry's mind; Jenny was waiting for him to hold her hand. Julean tried to alert him.

Doctor Carter pushed the door open to Jenny's room and stepped aside for his son-in-law. Henry rushed into the intensive care unit, panic blitzing through his body. He expected to feel the same terror and see a similar horrific scene as the day Julean died, but the atmosphere was filled with a peace he had never felt before.

The scene before him was divine...

It was as if an aura of light emanated from Jenny. Her glow gave light to the two nurses who stood on either side of her at the head of the bed like angelic sentinels. Jenny lay still and was in a sitting position. Her breathing was assisted with an oxygen mask over her mouth and nose. Through the maze of wires and tubes coming out of Jenny, Henry could see the sparkle in his dear wife's eyes. The nurse on the left side bent over Jenny and lifted Hannah off Jenny's chest, partially exposing her breast.

What was going on? How could a baby be nursing amidst such a critical situation? Henry was flabbergasted. Yet, the important thing was that Jenny was alive. It was almost a re-run of the same scene when Jenny delivered Hannah three weeks ago.

Henry heard the monitor just above her bed displaying the heart beat and rhythm. He didn't look, as his eyes were fixed on his dear, sweet, Jenny. When she saw him, her eyes brightened and she raised her left hand and removed the mask.

"Oh, Henry, quickly, hold my hand."

She raised her right hand but it immediately fell back. The nurse at her side helped raise it up again by gently grasping her wrist. When Henry was half way to Jenny, she looked up, her eyes opening wide. Her gaze was intensely staring at something that no-one else was seeing.

Henry took hold of his beloved's hand but Jenny's stare remained fixed on some vision. Her next word revealed instantly to Henry what it was that she was witnessing.

"Hannah! Hannah, it's so good to see you again. Yes, I am coming."

Jenny's gaze lowered slowly towards Henry and as soft as a feather, she whispered, *"I love you...cherish the gift I leave with you, our little angel..."* her words trailed off... as her cerulean blue eyes closed forever on earth.

Henry felt her spirit rise out of her body through his hand which was holding Jenny's. Intuitively, his eyes seemed to follow something up to the ceiling and then... it all came crashing down.

"Jenny, come back! Don't go!" cried Henry. Then, with a deep sorrowful groan, he cried again, "Noooo! No, God? Why God, why? Why have you taken my life away?"

Henry's loud shout frightened the baby and she began to cry. Doctor

Carter rushed to Henry's side and put his hand on Henry's shoulder and patted it.

Justin, who was standing at the doorway, could no longer just watch what was going on. He rushed into the room and went to the other side of the bed and began to weep uncontrollably. "Oh, Mom, please don't go. Please come back to us."

His sobs were so grieving, it compelled a nurse to come over and put her arm around the young boy and tried to comfort him.

Henry brought Jenny's hand up to his lips and kissed it. It felt warm and soft. It was as if he was holding Jenny's hand for the first time like that morning they crossed Victoria Avenue in front of Mr. Engelmann's Grocery store. He searched for that electrifying thrill that surged through him then but it was no more. The world stood still for them at that special moment but now was all seeping away and it pained Henry so deeply. He had to somehow cushion the shock, lest he completely fall apart.

He raised his head and gazed at his loved one. She looked peacefully asleep. Perhaps, that's what was happening. They had given her a sedative. She couldn't be dead. He tried to fool himself, but not for long, until he bent over and kissed his dear sweet wife. Her lips were still warm but from a great distance. She had gone, too far…

Her life was gone.

The nurse, holding Hannah, placed the infant into the incubator and began to wheel it back to the NICU. The baby was still crying loudly but Henry no longer heard her wailing as the infant's cry was drowned out by the screams rising from his heart and soul. The nurses and doctors except for Doctor Carter began to leave and let Henry and his son stay awhile with their loved one. Doctor Carter didn't know what else to do but to be available. He just stood there in the background, regretting that he wasn't able to save the life of the woman who had replaced his dearly missed daughter as Henry's second wife. Jenny should have died while delivering the baby. Her blood pressure was so high that he still found it hard to believe that Jenny was able to withstand the stress of her labor. Yet, her heart held out long enough to deliver the baby and have some time with her new-born.

The weary doctor shook his head and marveled at the strength and determination of Jenny; how she refused to be sedated so that her body could calm down and begin to restore itself. Rather, she was adamant to see and nurse her baby. She knew how critical her condition was and there was no way she wanted to die in some deep sleep or induced coma. He never thought that he would agree to bring a premature baby into an ICU to a critically ill mother. *But she was immoveable.* He shook his head and compared the two women in his son-in-law's life. He had to acknowledge that Jenny was just as strong in spirit as Julean. Perhaps, it was the nudge of Julean which made him agree to Jenny's wishes.

So many thoughts flooded Henry as he hovered over his dear wife. Waves of sorrow and loss swept through him as he stared steadfastly at her pretty face. The thought that he would never see her again sent a sharp, clutching pain to Henry's innards and he moaned.

Why did they need to have the baby at this stage of their lives? Why did she have to risk her life?

He was angry with himself for blaming Hannah but he had to strike out and find some relief. How would he possibly be able to go on? His life would never be the same again. Despair and hopelessness began to mingle with his grief. So many emotions were violently colliding with one another like a hurricane, smashing everything in its path. Words of sorrow, regret, sympathy, compassion, joy, and happiness came towards him in meaningless waves. No one, no one could ever understand what was raging in the depths of his being.

And just as he was breaking apart and ready to collapse, he felt a soft touch on his shoulder as if his guardian angel had come to his rescue. For a brief moment, he thought it was his mother. In a flash, he re-lived that time when Jenny left for Ottawa, driving off in the taxi with her parents, to the airport. His world had collapsed then as it did now. It was the touch of his mother that pulled him out of the abyss of utter despair but he knew who it was now. He didn't need to turn to see his dear, lifelong friend, teacher, comforter …

But what could he do now?

Father Engelmann patted Henry's shoulder but he could no longer console his hurting son as he too, was overtaken with sorrow. He needed comfort and support just as much, perhaps even more. The holy man couldn't hold back the dam that was building in his heart. He loved Jenny dearly as his own daughter. She had a light within her that he loved. She was so much like his dear Anna. Both women, were such dear, accepting, God fearing souls who were beacons to all those around them.

Because Father's heart was grief-stricken, he felt to the core of his being the utter pain that his dear adopted son was going through. The death of Jenny would be Henry's complete un-doing. In a flash, Father was beginning to see the vision of what he had seen when he was on the other side. He was beginning to catch up to the future which he was allowed to see back then. It finally had come into the reality of this very moment. He knew in the days ahead what his mission was; to help his son grieve and mourn and deliver him from the depths of a deep, deep sorrow.

It was to save his son, his very soul.

A nurse came in and saw the three men weeping over Jenny. She thought she could help them break free from the clutch of such sorrow. She came to the side of the bed where Justin stood and gently took hold of the sheet and moved it upwards to cover Jenny's face. Immediate anger flared into Henry's eyes and he thrust his hand towards the nurse's wrist instantly stopping all motion. The nurse winced and quickly pulled her hands away. She tugged twice to free it from Henry's grip. No words needed to be spoken; the nurse understood and walked away. At the doorway, she stopped and looked back. Despite what just happened, her heart went out to them.

It was difficult for her to tell which man loved Jenny more.

CHAPTER TEN

"**D**AD, DAD, ARE you alright!?" Justin yelled, as he stood over his father, lying in the bed.

Henry tried to sit up but the water bed wasn't firm enough to support him and he fell over on his side. Perspiration was pouring off his forehead and his clothes were soaked with sweat. He stared at his son with both a disorientated and horrified look in his eyes. He had just re-lived Jenny's dying moments in the ICU. If only he got there sooner, he might have been able to save her. His love pulled her back once and he thought for certain, he could have done it again. Since their marriage, their love for one another grew stronger by the day. It was like steel…inseparable!

And yet, death pulled her away from him.

Henry could see the concerned look in his son's eyes and tried to alleviate his worry. "I'm, I'm okay, Son. Just a bad dream…how did I get here…what time is it?"

"It's two thirty, Monday afternoon. You have been sleeping for over a day. Jeremy and I brought you home. Grandpa Carter gave you some medicine to help you sleep…" Justin's words trailed off.

"I must have been very tired. I don't recall coming home and…" Henry looked down… "I still have my clothes on."

"Yeah, we tried to take off your clothes but you just flopped on the bed and Jeremy said to just leave you."

Henry couldn't recall any of it. He was in such a state of shock and despondency, his mind shut down lest he lose it. He could tell he had been sedated. His head was groggy and heavy; he could hardly support it.

"Look, Justin, I'll change and take a shower and be down in about half an hour, okay?"

Justin studied his father; he looked a mess. He had never seen his dad look so lost and in such disarray. "Can I get you something, Dad? Need a drink of water?"

"It's fine, Son. I am thirsty but I'll get up right away and have a drink in the washroom. I'll be down shortly."

Justin turned and walked away. He stopped at the door, looked back at his dad, and then disappeared down the hallway.

Henry turned over in his water bed and lay on his back. He hoped it was all a dream but he couldn't escape the nightmare of Jenny's passing. It was vivid in every detail. She definitely saw her guardian angel in those last moments. He wondered if she saw Gabriel, his protector as well. Why is it only in death we can see our messengers and protectors? Once Jenny crossed that threshold, Henry knew it would be next to impossible to revive her. Yet, if he only had held her hand sooner, spoke to her, distracted her from the vision she was seeing, perhaps, perhaps...if, if, if...at the end it doesn't matter. She was gone. He was helpless to do anything then and the same now.

He looked at the empty bed. Feelings of melancholy immediately overtook him. With each thought, the wave of despair began to return. Thoughts of how he would ever survive without his Jenny at his side kept hitting him like waves against the rocks. He wondered why he hadn't yet collapsed or turned to stone...

The drugs had worn off and the full blunt of pain and sorrow was returning like a cyclone. He tried to ward off the rising anxiety with questioning thoughts...trying desperately to find some justification for what happened but he could not grasp onto anything. He began to cry into the silence and aloneness of the room, the bed seemed so cold and empty. The sun dancing off Jenny's features in the early morning as the sun found its way into the room would never come again. Her luminous skin shimmering in the light was what he loved to watch as she lay sleeping there beside him. The thought of not seeing his sweetheart there in the bed overwhelmed him with dread.

Memories would not be good enough.

Memories would not be strong enough. Memories were just that, *memories.* They could never replace the warmth of her touch and beauty of her face or sparkle in her eyes. Memories would turn on him and remind him minute by minute of what once was! He didn't want memories now...he wanted to turn off the memories...

Please, Lord, bring me peace

"Why did you have to have the child, Jenny? Our life was so happy without her. Our days so filled with love and life..." Henry paused and looked up as if God were in the room and he continued, "Why did You have to take her? Why is there so much pain and suffering and death?"

Henry knew the answers but asked them anyway. They were the same when Julean died. He knew the world was imperfect. He gives us free will to choose and when things don't turn out, we blame Him. Father Engelmann explained that all the time. Henry's thoughts began to go in circles and he asked once more, "Oh, Jenny, why did you have to have this child?"

Henry tossed from side to side in the water bed like a ship in a storm. He was losing control, fast. A complete spectrum of emotions: anger, dread, hopelessness, despair...surged through him over and over like they did at the hospital. Once again, he cried out, "What will I do without you, Jen? How can I go on?"

Fear gripped him with every thought. Despair clutched him without any hope for the future. Depression overwhelmed him and began to make its home in him. Life was going out like a dying burning ember. It struggled to stay alive but there was nothing to sustain it. The oxygen was gone.

Henry gasped for air.

He lay there choking and began to realize that the storm was not only within but also without. The wind just outside his window sighed and howled about the house and just then it struck with such force that the entire home seemed to tremble. He could hear the groan of the high fir trees as they waved back and forth driven by the wind. It seemed as if nature itself was releasing its fury over Jenny's death as well.

Suddenly, a flash of lightening lit up the room, followed by the roar of thunder echoing in his innards. He desperately tried to hang on but was sinking back into the abyss of darkness…

"Oh Jenny, I need you so…" he cried.

There was a knock at the door and Justin opened it.

"Dad, are you all right? I heard you shouting again." Justin looked

frightened. Tears surfaced in the young boy's eyes.

Henry pushed himself up, his hands pressing aside the water hidden in the mattress until they hit the bottom of the wooden frame.

What was happening to him?

The sight of his son snapped him back to a wobbly reality.

"Oh Justin, I'm sorry. I don't want you to worry… I just miss Jenny."

Justin began to weep. "I do too, Dad." He quickly went to his dad's side and sat on the frame surrounding the rubber mattress. Trying to be older than he was, he placed his hand on Henry's shoulder. "How can I help you, Dad?"

His son's tear-filled eyes and deep concern touched Henry's heart. It pulled him out of the clutches of despair. He knew he had to get up immediately and get on with the day otherwise he would be sunk. He recalled that same feeling the day after Jenny left for Ottawa when he was lying in bed after he awoke that morning. Thoughts similar to those, he was dwelling on now, flooded into his mind like the advancing storm outside. Even at his young age, he knew if he didn't quickly apply the advice Mr. Engelmann had given him the day before, he would drown. "It's all about choices, Henry. You can accept what happened or dwell on your loss. You can feel sorry for yourself or think about helping your son…*what do you want to do*? Look on the positive or the negative? Yes, we live by choices but the positives don't offer enough. Nothing can possibly replace Jenny. But—"

"Dad, what's wrong?"

Fear, returning to Justin's eyes, snapped Henry back once again into the reality of the moment.

"I'm so sorry, Son. I promise, I'll get up right away."

Justin stood up as Henry pushed himself out of the bed. He looked down at his wrinkled clothes. It looked as if he was wearing a crumpled paper bag. Henry shook his head.

"Look Justin, I want to wash and change...I'll be down in a bit."

WHEN HENRY CAME into the kitchen, Justin was on the phone with his brother.

"Yeah, he's here now, do you want to speak to him?"

"Here, Dad, its Jeremy, he wants to speak to you."

"Hello, Jeremy."

"How are you doing, Dad?"

"Okay, I just got up..." Henry's words trailed off. He didn't know what else to say.

Jeremy hesitated as well, then gently said, "Camilla and I made funeral arrangements. I hope you don't mind. I'll go over it with you tonight. Camilla and I thought we would drive out to see you...would that work for you?"

Henry was silent for a moment. He didn't want to bury Jenny. He wanted to enclose her in glass and preserve her forever. It was a foolish thought yet, the thought to put her into the ground was so final...so, so very, very final...

"Are you okay, Dad?" Jeremy asked with a concerned tone in his voice.

'Yeah, it's just that...well, I hate funerals..." Henry stopped and couldn't speak. The thought of standing at the open grave with Jenny in a coffin was too much for him to bear at that moment. He wasn't ready...*would he ever be ready?*

"Look, Dad. Camilla and I will be out in an hour. We are going to pick up something to eat on the way...Is there something special you would like...Chinese, KFC, pizza?"

Food was the last thing on Henry's mind. "Whatever you want, Jeremy, is fine with me. Justin likes pizza."

Henry slowly hung up the phone. He didn't hear what else his son had asked. He thought it had something to do with ordering flowers. Henry was certain it would come up again when they got there.

Justin was staring at his dad when he turned. Henry forced a smile and went over to his son. He wrapped his arm around Justin's shoulder.

"Let's go out and sit in the sun for a while."

They made their way onto the deck. It reminded Henry of the day Anna died at the store and he and Mr. Engelmann went out back to sit on the old grey crates. Henry had never forgotten Mr. Engelmann's words. He told Henry about his life and marriage with Anna. Henry could have done the same with Justin, but Justin pretty much knew everything there was to tell. They simply sat on the deck in silence and looked down into the valley. He wondered if Father was in the prayer house. Justin seemed to have read his thoughts.

"Grandpa is at the care home. He wants to make preparations for Mom's funeral..." his words trailed off.

After a bit, Justin moved his chair closer to his dad. He sat down again but this time put his hand over Henry's, resting on the arm chair. They didn't look at one another, just straight ahead. Justin had his father's heart. He knew words were not needed to show how much he cared. Henry recalled how he had done the same for Mr. Engelmann when he was in mourning over his wife's loss.

The air cooled quickly as the sun made its way to the west. It was still early spring and the men should be inside. But despite the crispness in the air, Henry and his son made no move to go into the warmth of the house. Perhaps the cold froze their feelings or diverted their attention from the grief and devastation of what had happened.

The shadows began to lengthen across the valley floor and still they sat there. The growing darkness of the day seemed to compliment the darkness within the two men. It would be hard to tell just when Henry or Justin would have made a move to go inside had it not been for Jeremy sliding open the patio door.

"Oh, there you are. We were looking throughout the house for you. It's too cold for you to be out here."

Jeremy walked over and nudged Justin to come in. He went to Henry and did the same.

Henry had a bite of a pizza but couldn't eat any more. Justin mimicked his dad and just sat there as Jeremy and Camilla went over the funeral plans.

His son and daughter-in-law had thought of everything and more. Henry couldn't think of anything to add to the funeral arrangements his children had made. Camilla tried to be strong for Henry and Justin but every now and then, she broke down and wept over the loss of her mother. Jeremy tried his best to console his dear wife, younger brother and father at the same time. At times, however, the atmosphere was so heavy with sorrow no-one spoke; the silence was penetrated with unpredictable, soft moans and bursts of weeping.

Henry was comforted to hear that Father Engelmann would be officiating at the funeral, along with Father Knuka. Henry wondered what his teacher would say about Jenny.

In a way, Father would be describing himself; he and Jenny were so much alike.

Just before they left, Camilla had to ask Henry something which she regretted to do but had to. "Dad, the funeral home director asked me to bring in clothes which we want Mom to wear. Would you like me to help you pick something out, now? I could come out in the morning and pick them up if you need some time."

Henry stared at his daughter-in-law from across the dining room table. His elbows rested on the table and his hands were clutched together under his chin. As soon as Camilla had spoken those words, the knuckles in his hands turned as white as the candle that was flickering off to the side of the table. His mom had picked out Julean's clothes. He had always regretted not sharing in that task. The dress Mary had chosen was very nice but he liked the black dress she had worn that day on their anniversary when he met her at the Hotel Saskatchewan for lunch. She never looked more beautiful and stunning. Black may not have been the best choice and perhaps that is why his mom had selected a soft blue dress.

But this time it would be different.

He nodded and then said, "It won't take me long, Camilla. There is one dress that I need to see Jenny wearing. Henry got up and went upstairs to their bedroom. He was gone not more than five minutes and came down holding a yellow dress draped across his arm and his fingers interlocked on the matching pair of yellow pumps. His other hand held a bottle. He handed the items to Camilla and said,

"Tell them to use makeup sparingly."

Camilla nodded and looked down at the bottle he had handed her. It contained Jenny's favorite perfume; lilac.

Jeremy and Camilla made their way to the door without a further word. At the front entryway they hugged Henry and Justin. Tears were in their eyes. The house seemed so empty and barren without the life and sparkle of Jenny there. Camilla wiped a tear rolling down her eyes and said hesitatingly, "I've been to the hospital to feed Hannah."

Henry nodded, he had assumed that she would have done so but didn't want to ask. *There was too much a part of him that wanted the mother more than the child.*

CHAPTER ELEVEN

BOTH ALISON AND Lauren had arrived that morning. Jenny's death was so sudden, no-one was prepared. If it had been a weekend, Lauren might not have been able to get a flight home. Although the girls felt sorrow over Jenny's death it wasn't to the same depth that Justin and Jeremy felt. The girls had been away from home long enough to lessen the spell of love and beauty and light that Jenny exuded to all who came in contact with her. The loss to the boys and Camilla and her children was immediate. To them and Henry, *it was as if the sun had suddenly stopped shining.*

Henry waited with his family in the main parlor just outside the viewing room at Speers Funeral Home. Several of Jenny's friends were there saying their goodbyes. As Henry stood there, he couldn't help but count the number of times he had been at this parlor for the viewing of other family he so dearly loved in his life. His son, Benjamin was the first to make a fissure in his heart. He never even had the chance to hold his first born whose life lasted for less than a day. How sorrowful and painful that time was for him and Julean and yet, somehow, they survived the tragedy and went on to have four more children.

The death of his father found him here next. It was unexpected, although his dad did have a brief illness which helped to prepare them for his passing. Still, one just doesn't expect death to be lurking around the corner. Most times it just seems that life will go on forever until it comes from out of nowhere. That's how it was with Julean. Who would have thought that returning home after a weekend in Minot, celebrating their anniversary, a nightmare would begin in which his dearly beloved wife would be taken away? The crevice in his heart widened and deepened over that departure. For days, months and years on end, he struggled to climb out of the depths of sorrow and loss over his dear wife.

For a brief moment, Henry questioned why he didn't feel the depth of pain over his father's death than he did at Julean's passing. Somehow, it was different when a parent dies as opposed to someone you're so intimate with; one that you live with and love day in and day out. In a way, when one leaves home to begin their own life with another, it sort of begins the journey of growing apart from parents. Time and separation, makes one realize that it is now your turn to begin carrying on the legacy of family and heritage. One expects that eventually, those that gave you life will have to go; it's all part of the never-ending cycle of life and death. Yet, we are never ready, especially when it comes so soon and early in life.

Fortunately, Henry's mom was there when Julean passed on to give him comfort and encouragement to go on. She was a pillar of strength much like Father Engelmann. They were close and when she departed it was difficult to deal with. Henry recalled the evening he viewed her in this same parlor but it was the next day at the cemetery site when he opened the coffin and had his own private farewell that he would never forget. Perhaps his catharsis and expression of his deep love for her gave him some closure and aided in accepting her passing.

The fracture in his heart grew with each loved one's passing but now with the death of Jenny, he could feel his heart break completely into two. How could he possibly accept the passing of his first love, the girl who was the first to steal his heart? A flame was lit the very moment they laid eyes upon one another and it never went out nor ever will. It burned still now, so deeply that his entire being was scorched by the pain of loss. He shuffled from one leg to the other, no longer able to wait until the others viewing Jenny left. He yearned so much to reach out and touch her hand.

Oh, why did she have to go? His mind screamed. Who would have possibly conceived that after she was so miraculously healed and came back that she would leave so soon again? The happiness they shared was so immense and in the blink of an eye it all turned into sorrow.

Henry nodded to the visitors as they came out of the viewing room. He felt some relief that he would soon see Jenny, yet it was quickly covered over by a deep emptiness. Jenny's beautiful face would all too soon be out of view forever.

There wasn't a sound when Henry and his family stood at the entryway into the viewing room. Lauren had her arm wrapped around one of Henry's arms while Alison held the hand of his other arm. This would be the last time he would see Jenny. The thought choked him; it was so unthinkable. The room was dim except for a light shining down on the open coffin. The inside of the lid was padded with puffs of white satin yet in places it had the sheen of gold. It was as if the sun lay below reflecting yellow rays of light. Henry didn't know if the tinted light was from Jenny's dress or from Jenny herself.

Colorful flowers of all kinds surrounded the coffin except for the viewing area. Henry hesitated at the door. He wanted to remember his dear Jenny alive and not...dead. And yet the desire to see her, to touch her...to kiss her forced him to make the first step.

Slowly, they made their way forward.

Steadily, they were drawn towards the light shining directly on Jenny's face. Justin followed close behind. They couldn't see all of her face just yet from the doorway. But with each slow step, Jenny's radiance was exposed more and more. Henry shook his head from side to side as he stopped at the edge of the coffin and gazed down at his sleeping beauty.

She looked beautifully asleep and at peace.

Many nights, Henry would wake up and gaze down at her asleep much like she was now. He had to force himself to turn off the night light. If only this was all a dream and she would open her sparkling blue eyes like she did and say those wonderful words, "Morning darling, I love you so much." *Henry wanted to hear them now.*

"Please, Jenny, just say it one more time." He whispered under his breath.

She shone like the sun as she lay there in her yellow dress nestled in the soft clouds of white satin. It would take his breath away when she wore that dress with matching yellow pumps. She looked heavenly, more beautiful than all the flowers combined in the world. He didn't know how else to say or describe it. Not even death could take away the luminosity of her fair skin as it shimmered in the soft light.

It was such a beautiful sight of a sleeping beauty before him and yet death reminded him of the nightmarish dream he had the day he met Jenny while waiting to take her to Balfour to register for high school. Death was after Jenny as she lay asleep like the Sleeping Beauty in a meadow of wildflowers. It was Father Engelmann who had diverted death then but not even his holy friend could intervene or bring back his dear sweet Jenny now.

She lay still, so very, very still.

The faint scent of lilac drifted up from her body and Henry fell apart. He began to weep. It was her favorite perfume and his as well. It conjured up so many memories of Jenny chasing butterflies amongst the lilac shrubs. Henry could easily follow her even if he were blindfolded just by the trail of the scent she left behind. She was an earthly angel, as if taking wings as she flitted about like the monarchs she so dearly loved. If only she was just in a cocoon now like the little creatures enter into a deathlike sleep and then…burst forth from its tomb with new life!

He wished it so deeply in his imagination, he momentarily looked up to see if she had taken flight!

The girls tightened their grip on their father in an effort to console him but it was in vain. Henry slowly loosened his hand and arm from their tender hold. He wanted to touch his dearly beloved. He bent over and kissed Jenny just as he had Anna, Julean and then his mother. They were all beautiful, dear women in his life and yet there was something special about Jenny. Perhaps, it was because she was his first love and all the storms of life they had gone through. They had defeated all the odds of ever coming back to one another, even death. It was their guardian angels who had fulfilled their promise and brought them back together.

Could they again?

He reached towards the neckline of Jenny's dress. He stuck his finger inside and quickly caught a silver chain. He gently pulled on it and soon the pewter angel seemed to fly into sight. The light reflected so strongly off the shiny metal, it momentarily blinded Henry. She had vowed to always wear it forever. He did too since the day he discovered it in his mother's treasure chest. The one around his neck seemed to burn in sympathy.

As much as he wanted to remove the angel as a keepsake, he couldn't. It was the matching one around his neck that was important. It was from Jenny, unbelievably the same he had sent her for Christmas in 1956; both identical with the exact same inscription. He shook his head in awe of the miracle which had transpired!

Henry wasn't even aware that Camilla and Jeremy had come in until their son, Joshua wriggled his way in front of Henry. At first, the young boy placed his hands on the edge of the coffin and looked at his grandmother. Then he reached out his hand and grasped Jenny's wrist. He tried to shake it but it was too stiff to move. With tears in his eyes, he looked to Henry and asked, "Why did Grandma have to die, Grandpa?" Henry just shook his head and barely shrugged his shoulders. It reminded him of that day Julean died and Justin came into the room and shook Julean's hand, trying to wake her up from the deep sleep she had fallen into, too.

Henry turned towards Justin, he had forgotten that his son was there and hurting. His boy was quietly crying. Henry slightly stepped away from Alison and put his arm around Justin and drew him in. Henry wondered what thoughts were going through his son's mind as he watched Joshua do what he had done so very long ago.

Suddenly there was a commotion just outside the viewing room in the parlor. Instantly, they knew who was there by the sound of her distinctive voice. It was Matilda asking in which room be layin' her dear mistress?

A moment later, she entered the room leading the J.J. entourage behind her. They all turned to greet Matti, J.J. and his family as well as Thomas and Neela, who were just there visiting not more than two weeks or so ago. Henry would never have thought that he would see the gardener and his wife so soon again.

After they greeted and hugged one another, Henry and his family stepped back so that the new arrivals could see Jenny and say their goodbyes.

Matilda was the first to rush over and audibly express her deep love for Jenny. Henry was surprised over how many of Matti's thoughts reflected his own.

"Oh, Jen, why the good Lord be takin' you from us. You be such a light in this dark world. You show us how to be and how to love. We needs people like you to show us the way. You be such a good friend, closer than my sister and even my own momma. You take me like your sister…oh, Jen, I loves you so. I miss you every day on the estate, seein' you chase the butterflies like an angel be takin' off any minute."

Matti stopped to wipe her tears and blow her nose and then she went on, "There be no–one like you, more lovin', kinder and forgivin'. Always countin' your blessings and thankin' the Lord for everyt'ing including your trials. How can that be? You have the heart of an angel; there be no way around it. You be feelin' so deeply for others all the time. The whole world could be against you and still you be calm in the midst of it all. Oh, dear Jesus, she be trustin' Your Daddy so much to turn everyt'ing into good. Why, she be obeyin' Your Word as if You be right beside her all the time. Why couldn't You leave her here for a spell longer?"

After a while, Neela came up to her and put her arms around Matti. The comfort quieted Matti and the two women softly wept.

One by one, they approached the coffin and said their good-byes. Thomas was quiet, so quiet. His tears glistened in the light as they silently slid down his brown sun baked cheeks. He turned to Henry and asked if he could kiss Miss Jenny.

Henry nodded.

Thomas kissed Jenny's forehead and whispered something that no-one could make out.

J.J. couldn't hold back the tears and surprisingly, was much like Matti. Over and over, he kept asking his mother to forgive him. He knew she had never held her love or any spirit of unforgiveness against him and yet, he wanted to punish himself somehow, for his foolishness. All the time he wasted rebelling against her when he could have received her love and the joy of knowing her heart. Nora stepped forward much like Neela did for Matti and tried to comfort her husband.

Surprisingly, Camilla, too, came to her stepbrother's aid and patted his hand which was resting on Jenny's.

"It is so good to know you, J.J. and that we had the same mother. I am so thankful to God for bringing her back to me and the few years we had together."

Camilla went on to say how it was such a great miracle how they all found each other and became such close friends. She was also going to add that so many of the girls under her care at the school miss out on so much by holding grudges against their parents or parents not accepting the beauty she sees in the girls. However, she held back as it reflected what J.J. was already deeply regretting that he had done. Camilla simply added,

"Life can be so needlessly complicated at times."

No-one realized what time it was getting to be when the funeral director came in and told Henry that the viewing room would be closing at ten thirty but if they needed more time, he would wait until they all had said their goodbyes.

Henry checked his watch. It was ten minutes past ten. He was hoping everyone would go so he could have some time alone with Jenny but no-one made a move to leave. Perhaps, they all had the same thought in their mind. Henry wished they had postponed the funeral another day as there were still people coming late that night and early in the morning from out of town. Alison had told him Chloe and Robbie with his fiancé were flying in at six thirty in the morning.

Alison made the first move to make some closure to the evening.

She took her rosary out of her purse hanging over her shoulder and softly whispered, "Would it be okay with everyone if I led us in prayer?"

Matti was quick to respond, "Yes, my dear child, we all be needin' the healin' and strength of God to carry this burden. Say what be on your heart, child."

No one else responded audibly, however, there were several nods and it was enough for her to begin. She thought it might help to invite the great Healer and Comforter in times of sorrow.

"Dear Father, we know Mom is up there with you. Heaven must have gotten brighter, as earth seems to have lost a great light. Mom lived for You and was such an example to all of us what You had Your Son, Jesus teach us. Jesus, too, grieved when His dear friends departed. Help us with Your grace and strength to accept Mom's passing and go on with life as Jesus did too, in times of strife. Help, especially Dad, who is in such sorrow and pain. Please comfort him. We offer up this prayer for Mom. It's our bouquet to her for the joy and happiness she gave to all of us. She was such a beacon of light…" Allison reached out her hand to the person next to her. The gesture was immediately repeated until the group circled Jenny's coffin on the viewing side; "Our Father," Alison began, "who art in heaven, hallowed be thy name, thy king…"

At the end of her prayers, Alison said, "The funeral room will be closing soon. If anyone wants to say final goodbyes to Mom please do so now."

Thomas was the first to make a move. He whispered a private prayer to his beloved mistress, made the sign of the cross, touched his lips with the tips of his fingers and reached out to touch Jenny's forehead. He turned and made his way to the door. He was followed by Neela and slowly all the rest said their farewell and made it out into the main foyer.

All that was left were Matilda and Henry. They refused to go. Each wanted to be last. They stood there and waited for the other to make a move. Matti understood and made her way to Jenny and gazed tenderly down at her sweet mistress. Matti was at a loss for words and began to weep uncontrollably. It drew Henry out of himself and he went over to comfort Jenny's dear, faithful friend.

Slowly, Matti regained her composure and whispered, "You be my soul mate, Jen. You will be forever in the heart...you be an angel always at my side, hear? I feel your presence now. I loves you. Someday we be seein' each other again. That's for sure."

Matti touched Jenny's hand, patted it and stood erect. She turned to Henry and said, "You be her one and only man. All the days I know Miss Jenny, I see in those clear blue eyes a hidden treasure in her heart. The day I saw you come to the estate, I know straight away that you be her secret treasure. She loved you deeply, Henry. I know you be knowin' that but I just have to say it. I know you be hurtin' for a long time. You, me and everybody who knows her, never be gettin' over our sweet Jenny...no sir, none of us ever will."

Chapter Twelve

WHEN MATTI LEFT, Henry moved over slightly, almost to the same spot that Matti had just occupied. He gazed at Jenny's glowing face and let his eyes follow her arms down to where her hands gently intertwined. He recalled doing that, that same evening when he viewed Julean's hands in her coffin. She was holding her rosary between her fingers. Julean had a special relationship with the Blessed Mother and said the rosary often.

Henry recalled the struggle he had deciding whether or not to take the rosary. It was the last thing his dear wife was holding in her hands before she died. It was what she loved so much and he wanted to feel that love and her touch through the rosary. He thought it would be difficult to remove the rosary as it was threaded in and out of her fingers.

Would he even be able to remove it?

But when he touched her hand there was no stiffness or coldness. Her hand was warm and soft and so tender and pliable, as if she were alive. Her fingers opened so easily, it was as if she were handing it to him. It was her last gift to him, her gift of love and faith. From that day forward, he always carried it with him and took it to bed with him at night.

It was still in his pocket.

After he and Jenny got married, he was going to remove it and stop the practice of saying it at night when they went to bed. Jenny seemed to accept it and didn't mind and yet, Henry thought it best to stop the practice, thinking that Jenny was just being kind, with her accepting way of others. So, one day, he removed the rosary and placed it in the top drawer to send Jenny the message that she was his wife now and that he had moved on.

Jenny, however, was quick to notice what Henry had done and placed it under his pillow. Henry recalled her words, "She is a part of us Henry, she shared me with you for all the years we were apart and I want to do the same."

Henry was always amazed how the two ladies seemed to be so close and understanding of one another and yet, had never met!

Henry gazed at Jenny's hands and how bare they looked. James' huge diamond ring and his narrow gold band were partially hidden by the fingers of the right hand. They added a gleam but…Henry wondered if he should place Julean's rosary in her hand…his two loves. He recalled Father Engelmann's words, *that to give away to another, something we cherish, is a sign of deep friendship and love.*

In the same way Julean gave her rosary to Henry as her last gift of love to him, Henry in turn wanted to give the rosary now to Jenny. He took the rosary from his pocket and rested it just above Jenny's hands. He gently began to separate her hands. He knew they would separate just as easily as Julean's did. *His instincts were correct.* Jenny's fingers separated just the same as when Julean gave the rosary to him in this very same room the evening of her wake.

Jenny's hands felt warm and soft and pliable as he tenderly entwined the crystal beads around her fingers. Tears fell on the rosary as he worked, adding even more sparkle to the beads. "Let each bead be like a flower, Jenny. Flowers were your rosary and way to get near the Blessed Mother and to God."

Henry walked to the foot of the coffin and looked amongst the flowers in the vases and picked one. It was a white daisy with a yellow center, the one that looked like the sun.

He went back and slid the stem underneath her hands. It now looked complete. He bent over and kissed Jenny again and began to weep. He couldn't walk away. Tears of sadness flowed from Henry's eyes. His children heard him and came back into the viewing room and huddled around him, to console him. His chest heaved as sorrowful, groaning sounds came forth. The image before him blurred. He wiped the tears away so he could see Jenny one last time. He wanted to burn the image of her lying asleep. The thought of the coffin closing permanently was too overwhelming.

"Come, Dad, we have to go. The funeral director is waiting at the door. Everyone's gone," Alison said softly.

But Jenny's gone, Henry screamed in his mind. I want her back…please come back.

Alison tugged at Henry again.

At the doorway, Henry turned and pulled his arm away from his daughter and went back to the coffin. He stared at Jenny for the longest time and then bent over and kissed her for the last time. It was so warm and tender…

"Oh, Jenny, I love you so much."

In the silence of the room, Henry could hear his dear, sweet, first love whisper back…

"I love you all the more."

CHAPTER THIRTEEN

ENRY STOOD IN the large foyer of St. Mary's Church with his family as they waited for the usher to lead them to their pew at the front of the church. He barely had any sleep last night. If he hadn't taken a half of a sleeping pill Doctor Carter had prescribed, he wouldn't have slept at all. He missed Jenny being beside him in their bed and the thought of the funeral and burial filled him with unbearable dread and finality.

He glanced down the long aisle of the church and saw that it was almost full. The majority of people didn't know Jenny but came to pay their respects to Henry. He had already received many phone calls and cards from well-wishers. He did see some of the ladies who were in Jenny's counseling groups. Seated off to the right of the aisle were Matti, Thomas, Carlos and their wives. Henry assumed that is where he and his family would be seated as well.

Henry tried to get his mind off his deep sorrow and focus his thoughts on J.J. who was talking with Camilla. He showed such remorse and regret at the viewing last evening. Over the years of his upbringing, he had been hard on Jenny and difficult to deal with. Henry was so relieved along with Jenny when he made his turn around just before his father's death. Although it was late and long in coming, at least he did it. Henry could only imagine how devastated the young man would be now if he hadn't reconciled with his mother.

The counselor in Henry couldn't help but think of all the families he had counseled and the struggles parents have with their children at times. Death puts an abrupt stop to it all and suddenly there is a void; it's all too late to heal differences now. What is left in all too many cases is regret, guilt, sorrow and the eventual realization that it's due to just foolish stubbornness and pride.

The funeral director nudged Henry and asked him to get in line; he was ready to escort the family to their pew. Henry took a deep breath; he tried to show a tough exterior but inside the pain was unbearable. He thought of Anna's funeral and how Father Engelmann loved his dear wife beyond words and yet he survived; but could he possibly survive, too?

The choir began singing "Peace is Flowing Like a River." He found it soothing as the procession began down the long aisle. Jeremy and his family led the way followed by J.J.'s family and finally Henry and his children.

Earlier, when he had peeked into the church, he hadn't noticed the coffin up front at the foot of the altar. About half way down the aisle, he now understood why. All he saw were flowers. Lots of flowers; in fact, there was a huge mound of colorful flowers.

He looked to the left and right to see where the coffin was but it wasn't there. Perhaps, it was behind the flowers. As he came closer, however, it was evident the coffin wasn't behind the mound either and then… it dawned on him, where it was. He saw part of a wheel sticking out of the floor which the flowers didn't cover. It's the wheels of the frame holding up the coffin. The coffin was hidden beneath the mound of flowers!

Unbelievable!

The flowers were so well arranged and hanging over the sides of coffin that they draped right to the floor like a blanket. Whoever the florist or florists were who created this, they had done a magnificent job! Henry couldn't go into the pew. He was spellbound by this incredible image of flowers!

It immediately conjured up an image of his dear wife lying asleep in the garden as radiant and beautiful as ever. Every conceivable wildflower was interwoven with another into one immense bouquet. Henry had never seen so many different species of wildflowers. Daisies, daffodils, red poppies, baby blue eyes, lilies...*where did they all come from?*

Surely, there couldn't possibly be any florist in the city of Regina that would carry this many and so many different kinds. Henry doubted all the florists in the entire province wouldn't have had this many. They must have come from all over the world! He thought Jenny had grown every possible wildflower in her backyard that there was but he was wrong. *God's creation and creativity was endless!*

Henry could only imagine Jenny's sparkling eyes filled with so much gladness, joy and excitement looking down to see what had been arranged for her. It was perfect! It captured perfectly, Jenny and her love of flowers. Her thoughts were constantly on God's creation. They were her source of spiritual energy and love and peace.

She was like the wildflowers that she so loved.

Surely, everyone around could smell the spiritual fragrance given off by this mountain of flowers. The aroma was intoxicating. Where the scent of one flower could send Jenny into ecstasy, it took this huge display of God's creation to make him completely understand why flowers had such an incredible effect on his sweet wife. He breathed deeply. *He breathed in Jenny.* He could smell her now. The purple and white lilacs at either end of the mound made the aroma of the display complete!

Yes, any moment now, she would spring up from the bouquet full of life and spontaneity! He could see Jenny alive and racing merrily through the meadows chasing butterflies.

Jenny wasn't dead!

Henry's eyes grew wide; it was so real! He raised his hand in anticipation of hers and he softly whispered those magical words,

"Quickly hold my hand"

He felt a warm, soft hand entwine in his. "Come, Dad, come, let's sit down in the pew."

Henry looked at his concerned daughter-in-law, tears erupting from deep within her heart. Henry was momentarily disorientated. Suddenly, he realized he was the only one standing there. He was so intrigued with the beautiful bouquet, he hadn't followed his family into the pew. He simply turned and allowed Camilla to lead him like a lost lamb.

HIDING THE COFFIN beneath all the live flowers helped Henry cope with the funeral. As he sat there, he visualized his dear sweet wife swinging in the gazebo in front of the wildflower patch. In the next instance, she was running through the valley at the farm or offering daisies to the Angel of Thanksgiving for all the blessings she was given. One uplifting scene after the other swept across the screen of his mind. Rather than seeing a dreaded coffin which symbolized the finality of death, he was able to feign life...*anything to keep Jenny alive with him.*

Henry was so transfixed by the flowers and the vision his creative imagination kept conjuring, he wasn't even aware that after he had sat down, Justin had gotten up in the pew where he was seated and passed Jeremy, Camilla and himself and sat down next to him. Justin had slipped his hand into his while his other hand was still wrapped lovingly in Camilla's. Henry was suddenly made aware of their presence and love when he felt them both squeeze his hands as Father Engelmann began to say the eulogy.

Chapter Fourteen

FATHER LOOKED LIKE Moses as he stood there in his white robe surveying the congregation in his usual style. His white beard and flowing long hair exuded the image of a sage ready to impart the wisdom he had garnered during his long journey through life. Henry knew his mentor would say words that would catch the essence of Jenny's life. He hoped too, that Father would say words which could possibly justify the good Lord's early calling of his dear wife. Henry needed more than memories to hang on to.

"We are here to celebrate the life of Jenny Pederson, who has now returned home to the Father. Heaven just got a little brighter."

Father gazed at the flower coffin and continued, "How fitting it is to see so many flowers blooming in all their radiance before us. In all the years of my life as a priest, I have never seen such a spectacular display of God's creation. It's all so full of life and beauty, just like Jennifer. She may be gone in her human form but spiritually, she is here with us, very much alive in her new glorified state.

"Over the past few years, I have often heard of others speak of Jenny as having the heart of an angel. I often wondered what it was about Jenny that caused people to perceive her in this way. After all, an angel exhibits heavenly traits that are not so easy to come by for people on earth. You see, angels constantly see the face of God. They see Love and thus exude love for the one they are assigned to guide, protect and love throughout their life journey. Angels never abandon us; they always accept us unconditionally, pray to God on our behalf, prompt us to reach out to others in need, to do good, to be kind, patient...the list is endless.

"Jenny may not have seen the face of God directly as our heavenly protectors do but she did so through all of God's creation. Whether it was nature, flowers, people, the sun, moon and stars...whatever it was, it was not only seen through the mind but the heart as well. Because of this, Jenny saw all things human in a divine way; through the eyes of God. When life is viewed in this manner, all thoughts in the human mind are filtered through love because God is love. It is no longer about me, my self-centeredness or ego but about God and others.

"And this is how it was with Jenny and that is why Jenny had the heart of an angel."

Suddenly, Matti, in the pew behind them, whispered, "Amen, that be Miss Jenny, that's for sure!"

Henry had to agree with Matti and tuned back in to Father as did the rest of the people within earshot.

"It gave me and others such joy to be in her presence because she had such a buoyant spirit and happy heart and cheerful face. She was like a butterfly; uplifting, spontaneous and free! Did Jesus not say that we must become like little children to enter the gates of heaven? That was Jenny! Her attitude in life was like a child; she lived in the moment, quick to forgive and forget, trusting and obedient to Jesus. She loved to run through the meadow filled with flowers, dance in the rain, sway on the swing in her gazebo and bask in the sun. She had no time to worry, dwell on the wrongs of others, or be controlled by life's trials and tribulations.

"This is why, Jenny was an earthly angel!"

"That preacher man sure be knowin' Jenny's heart!"

"Jenny knew joy and peace and contentment because she chose to live moment to moment with a grateful heart. God loves a heart that sings praise and thanksgiving for all things. Jenny's life was not easy and yet she picked up her cross daily and followed her Master who was her teacher, guide and example. She gave praise for all that came her way. Even when she treaded in the valley of darkness, when God was silent, her faith was unshakeable. Daily, Jenny made it a practice to put flowers into the basket of a marble statue of an angel holding a basket which adorned her garden in thanks for all things, whether they were trials or blessings. She trusted in her Lord to turn all things into good. How many of us can let go and let God!? Jenny did and as a result knew perfect joy.

"And that is why, she had the heart of an angel."

"Amen! Halleluiah!"

"Jenny understood both the pain and the mystery of suffering. Just over three years ago, Jenny lay dying in Palliative Care at the Grey Nun's Hospital. Her body was completely ravaged by the painful attack of cancer. Before she died and the good Lord brought her back to life completely healed, she had a vision. Through her pain and suffering, she could see the joy and good that the Father brought out of the pain, suffering, anguish and death which Jesus endured for our salvation. Through that vision, Jenny found meaning in suffering. One cannot love without suffering. She understood the redeeming power of suffering and joined with our Lord to bring peace and salvation to the world. The more we can understand the great necessity to lay down our life to Jesus as He did for the Father, we too could develop wings as she did. We too, could be perceived as an earthly angel. If we come before the Lord as a broken sinner and ask to be filled with the Holy Spirit and be lifted up and then we too, could be seen as having the heart of an angel as Jenny was.

"I can only imagine how high in the heavens Jenny's spirit was flying towards the waiting arms of our heavenly Father.

"Jenny received great solace and strength from nature but what was it that brought her so close to Jesus and the Father? Part of the difficulty that many of us have is that we don't place our Lord first in our lives. We have too many idols, too many masters that distract us from obtaining the peace and inner joy which Jenny enjoyed. Jenny gave her 'all' to Jesus and when we give our 'all,' our ego vanishes as does our self-centeredness and we become the perfect vessel for God's Holy Spirit. This is a tremendous blessing available to all of us, yet very few receive because we refuse to give our 'all' to the Lord.

"As long as we hold on to our sin, our pride and ego, or place earthly treasures first in our lives, we will be forever separated from God.

"Over and over we witnessed how Jenny died to herself and gave her 'all' to Jesus in service of others. She emptied herself and thus she was filled with the power, strength and grace of the Holy Spirit. It was He who helped Jenny to fill her heart with the indwelling presence and love of Jesus and by Him to reveal the Father in our lives. Because Jenny gave her 'all,' she experienced the 'all' of God the Father, God the Son and God the Holy Spirit. Jenny exuded the fruits and gifts of the Spirit to all whom she encountered: love, joy, peace, patience, kindness, generosity, faithfulness, gentleness and self-control. She freely witnesses the outward expression of an inner life energized by the Holy Spirit!

"And that is why, my dear children, Jenny was seen as having the heart of an angel."

"Thank you, sweet Jesus, for the gift of Jenny! We be lovin' her so!"

"One of Jenny's heartfelt prayers was to bear a child for Henry. Like Hannah, who was barren in the first book of Samuel, Jenny, too, cried out to the Lord to bless her with a child. Miraculously, despite her age, her prayer was answered. As the pregnancy developed, so too did a rare condition that made her blood pressure very high. The medication wasn't able to correct the condition and Jenny was advised to abort the child which would immediately restore her health."

"Jenny do no such 'ting!" Matti blurted out and was immediately confirmed by what Father Engelmann said next.

"Jenny refused; she did not see the child within her womb as having any less right to life than herself. She even chose that the life of the infant be saved over hers. At the risk of her health and very life, Jenny made the decision to carry the child as long as possible to give the infant a better chance to survive by developing longer in the womb. When it was becoming increasingly dangerous to the child, she relented and agreed to give birth the natural way. The stress of labor could very well have claimed her life, yet, the child was born and Jenny survived. However, the organ damage, the high blood pressure and stress of the birth eventually took its toll and claimed her life.

"Jenny's loving heart gave out.

"She knew life is a miracle, a gift from God who would not will for any of his children to be destroyed in a mother's womb. Just as Jesus gave his life for humanity, Jenny laid down her life for her child. She gave her 'all'…

"And that is why our angelic Jenny, has the heart of Jesus."

"Oh, Jenny we be missin' you so!"

"Jenny lived with eternity in mind. She was a beacon of light for all to admire and see and want to emulate. While so many seek the riches and comforts of the world, Jenny saw her main purpose to love the Lord our God and others. She was constantly giving, accepting, healing and loving. What did Jesus say in Matthew 16:19-21? "Do not store up for yourselves treasures on earth…but store up for yourselves treasures in heaven…for where your heart is; there your heart will be also." We can see how quickly the Lord can call us but she was always ready and prepared for eternity. Her candle was lit and easy to see in the darkness. In 1 Corinthians 2:9, we read, "No eye has seen, no ear has heard, and no mind has imagined what God has prepared for those who love him."

Father paused and shook his head, "No, no-one can even begin to imagine the treasures she will now have in heaven!? And it's all because of the endless acts of love she did on earth. This is where Jenny's heart was…

"And that is why she is lifted up and rewarded because she had the heart of an angel. She was a saint!"

"Yes, dear Jesus, she be in your lovin' arms. You and Your daddy be fightin' to hold her next! That for sure!"

Matti's spontaneous comment brought a smile to Henry's face. Camilla let out a soft chuckle.

"Oh, meine lieben Kinder, let Jenny be an example to all of us, how to love, and grow in holiness and ever nearer to the heart of God."

"Amen, hallelujah!" interjected Matti.

"Jenny was so filled with the Holy Spirit and the indwelling of Jesus that she shone with light. At times, Jenny glowed with such radiance, others have said, she could be mistaken for the sun. I can only imagine how high in the heavens Jenny's new wings have lifted her up to the Lord."

This time, Matti began to clap but quickly stopped herself. She just kept shaking her head in agreement with Father's words.

"When such a saintly person is called home, it leaves emptiness in our heart. How can we go on without Jenny who brought so much light into our lives? She was a beacon to all of us as to how life should be lived. She made us see beyond our daily lives and lifted us to higher and more inspired levels which we never knew existed.

"Oh, how can we go on without her?"

"To stay stuck here would be to miss the point of Jenny's existence and example to all of us. Jenny would be the first to say that it was not her that brought joy to others but rather Jesus working through her. It was His light, not hers that stirred within us a desire to have what she had. And that is precisely how God works in our lives. It is something which we can all have if we are willing to come to the cross and give our 'all.' We can all be like a glowing Jenny and that is her wish and desire for all of us. We, too, can become a light brighter than the sun, more beautiful than the flowers of nature but we must choose to do so. Daily, Jenny would retreat in prayerful thanksgiving and in turn be filled with the light of Jesus.

"Are you willing to do the same?

"To exude the light, we must be filled with the light, the truth and way. There is only one person who can give you that and more and that is Jesus Christ. The more we can empty ourselves, the more the Holy Spirit can come into our hearts and re-create us to become more and more like Jesus.

"That was the secret to Jenny's life and happiness. *She was filled with truth and grace of Jesus.*"

"Amen, and again I say, amen!" said Matti a bit louder than she should have.

Father paused and directed his gaze to the incredible display of flowers and concluded, "When I look at all of the flowers covering the coffin, I don't just see the beauty of God's magnificent creation but for the gift of life. Only humans can see and understand the miracle of life and its potential of what it can become if we give our *'all'* to Him. Jenny did and what a beautiful light she lit in all of our hearts. Let us be thankful. Let us see the flowers not just as her love of nature but our appreciation and love for Jenny for being the child of God that she was. Let the flowers be our celebration to Jenny who was a faithful servant to God. This is our gift to Jenny, our lasting bouquet to her.

"May she always be covered with this beauteous blanket of our love."

As Father returned to his chair there wasn't a sound in the large church. After several minutes of silence and contemplation of all that was spoken and inspired other thoughts in the mind and heart of each of those present, Margaret Tearhorst came to the foot of the altar and sang a song with her angelic voice which Henry hadn't heard before; I Believe In The Sun*...

It captured Jenny's spirit; her loving trust and faith.

I believe in the sun,
Even when it isn't shining;
I believe in love,
Even when there's no one there,
And I believe in God,
I believe in God,
Even when He is silent.

I believe in miracles,
I believe in light,
I believe there can always be a way.
I believe that nothing is impossible...

* Father Carey Landry

Chapter Fifteen

It was the internment which Henry dreaded. The final curtain to Jenny's life on earth had come down marking the end of her earthly journey. Could he make it through the last act? He was surprised that he was holding up as well as he was. He was grateful that the coffin was covered with flowers to help ward off this moment.

The shiny black limousine had just entered the gates to the cemetery. The sunroof was opened, letting the warm spring air enter the spacious interior. It felt good; like a healing balm to Henry. The sun flickered on and off his face as the trees lining the road alternated light and shadow across the slowly moving vehicle. Neither the girls nor Justin spoke to their father or each other the entire time since they had left the church.

Henry appreciated the silence.

They waited in the limo until the pallbearers carried the coffin to the grave site. It was like watching a garden of flowers moving in and out of the tombstones. Henry learned after Mass that it was J.J. and Thomas who had come up with the idea of covering the coffin in such a creative way. And he was right as he thought earlier; Thomas had to make dozens of calls all over North America to come up with that spectacular assortment of flowers. It must have been a feat in itself to get them all to the florist in Regina on time and then to make this immense bouquet. Truly, it was such a lovely tribute to

Jenny. Henry really liked the way Father Engelmann saw it as a blanket of love.

Jenny would like that.

Once the casket was in place, the family and close friends got out of the limos and made their way to the grave site. Father was already standing at the head of coffin and waited until everyone was gathered around before saying the final prayers. Henry heard Father's words but shut them out, he didn't want to hear any words of farewell, he just desperately wanted to see Jenny again. He wasn't ready to admit that she was really gone.

Henry tried to see how a small portion of the flowers could be removed so he could open the casket and gaze at his sleeping beauty once more. Maybe a final kiss would bring her back. He knew it was a silly thought but it had been known to happen. But then, he had said his good bye last night and the image of the beautiful flowers radiating with color and fragrance in the end would be best way to leave it.

The breeze flowing through the trees was warm and soothing to the skin. Every now and then, the sound of birds chirping in the trees overhead could be heard between Father's prayers. "Dust thou art and to dust thou shalt return," were words that echoed in Henry's ears but he quickly exchanged them for thoughts of hope. He didn't want to see Jenny that way but rather full of life; greeting all the people there, smelling the different flowers and reveling in the glorious spring day!

Soon the internment would be over and they would head back to the hall and for the last time that day, he would have to put on a brave front. Henry wanted it to be over. He was glad to see J.J. and his family and Matti and Thomas but was also relieved that they would be leaving later that afternoon to head back to Ottawa. He ached to be alone so he could mourn and let go.

Suddenly, there was coolness in the air and the sky dimmed as if a storm was forming and about to shower the earth. Henry was usually good at smelling moisture in the air and detecting an oncoming rainfall but there was none. The air was dry and warm and gentle. Henry turned sharply to a sudden cry by Carlos who was so taken by what he saw.

"Santa Maria!" he shouted, "the monarchs have come early for Señorita Jenny's funeral!"

Father stopped the concluding prayer and everyone followed Carlos's hands which were raised to the sky. Thousands of monarchs swarmed in the heavens above the mourners instantly lifting their spirits! They looked like tiny angels flitting about trying to cheer everyone up. The sight seemed to capture Father Engelmann's eulogy about Jenny's angelic heart of gaiety, spontaneity and free spirit!

As they stood there observing this heavenly sight, Henry overheard Carlos telling Thomas and Neela that this had happened one other time when he looked after Jenny's parents' estate. Jenny was so forlorn and concerned at the time over her friend, Tammy who was deciding whether to abort the child she was carrying. But the monarchs came back a month early then too, just to cheer up Jenny and lift her spirits. Carlos was sure of it then and knew in his heart they had come to bid their farewell to Jenny, too!

Henry had to agree!

By now, hundreds of monarchs were nestling in amongst the flowers. Many, too, were resting on people's heads, shoulders and outstretched hands. *Amazing,* Henry thought as he looked on at the spectacular sight. It seemed as if the heavens were joining in on this celebration and unseen angels were all about!

He felt Jenny's presence.

Henry wondered if the coffin was going to be lowered with the flowers intact or whether they would lift the blanket off and cover the mound of dirt after the burial. In either case, Henry knew it would take a long time for the flowers to wither and die, if ever. Henry could easily imagine if the flowers were buried and if the grave was dug up a hundred years from now, they would be as fresh as the day they bloomed. Jenny's love would sustain them.

Love lasts eternal.

After Father concluded the prayers, he began to walk around and shake hands with many parishioners he hadn't seen in awhile. It was quite a sight to see Matti and Father greet one another. It was as if Matti had met the Pope!

"Oh, Father Engelmann, your words about Jen be touchin' my heart for the rest of my days. Everyt'ing you say is the gospel truth! I just don't know what I do without her. We be such good friends…Oh, Father, please pray for me so my heart don't be breakin'." Matti began to cry and hugged Father.

Henry wanted to visit the grave sight of where Julean was buried but never did make it over there. Many people were going straight home and not returning to the hall and so Henry was kept busy just saying good bye. Chloe and her dad had a flight to catch to Chicago. Robbie was guest speaker at a conference there that same evening and so they had a brief chat with Henry before bidding their farewell and best wishes to him. It was what Chloe said to Henry that lifted his spirits.

"Henry," said Chloe. "Auntie Jenny told me a beautiful story when my mom died. We were walking in the estate amongst all the monarch butterflies and I was so sad. I was only eight at the time and had difficulty understanding the death and what happened to my mother. Auntie Jen helped me see dying in an entirely different way. She compared Mom's death to that of a caterpillar dying in a cocoon. In many ways, it's like us dying, being placed in a coffin. We mourn for the insect and feel sad and yet it has only gone through an amazing transformation as we do too when we die. Instead of looking down at the dead caterpillar in the cocoon, look up and see the new life it has become! See the beautiful butterfly fluttering about so radiantly happy overhead. From that moment on, I saw Mom or anyone who dies, being transformed too, into a new heavenly spirit, which continues on into the next life. Like Father Engelmann said about Jenny's passing, there is another angel in heaven."

With tears in his eyes, Henry said, "That's beautiful, Chloe."

Chloe smiled as she gazed up at all the butterflies flitting all about and went on, "I sometimes think God not only made butterflies for the beauty and joy they give us but also to remind us of this beautiful new life that awaits us all. I can just see my mom, Tammy, greeting Auntie Jenny. They were the best of friends. I can just see them flitting about in the meadows of heaven like two angels!"

Henry thanked Chloe for the beautiful, uplifting sharing. They hugged one another and then she and Robbie were off.

Henry couldn't recall much that went on at the hall. He never was one for having a social after a loved one died. He couldn't eat anything and had no appetite to do so. The many distractions of the day, however, did have the beneficial effect of distracting him enough from falling into a state of deep sorrow like the day Jenny died. He was surprised how well he was holding up. He thought that perhaps he was going to make it.

But Henry would soon find out that he was dead wrong.

FATHER ENGELMANN AND Henry sat on the deck in front of the Poustinia. The sun was just setting and twilight was rapidly spreading across the valley. Both men liked this time of day as much as the sunrise. The air was crisp and cool but not enough to penetrate through the extra jacket Henry was wearing nor Father's hooded Franciscan habit. Furthermore, Coco was lying directly at the base of Father's chair covering his sandals. Father always maintained if his feet were warm so was the rest of him. Besides, after an exhausting, trying day, the serene atmosphere pervading the valley helped to relax and fill them with peace.

They were just discussing the day and how nice it was to see everyone. Relatives and friends had come not only from Saskatchewan but all over Canada.

Gradually, the conversation came back to the funeral Mass.

"The tribute you said to Jenny was beautiful, Father. I have to agree with what Matti said, the words you expressed were so true and I'll never forget them, as well. Sometimes, I wish you would write what you say down as I would like to read and study them. In so many ways what you said of Jenny today, I also see in you. You were so much alike in spirit."

Father simply nodded and raised one hand and waved his fore finger side to side gesturing, 'no' to the compliment."

"The song Margaret sang after your eulogy was so beautiful, Father. It was the first time I ever heard, *I Believe In The Sun*."

"Yes, I came across it in one of the church hymn books. It's written by a very gifted priest, Father Carey Landry. It captures Jenny's spirit and her trust in God."

Henry nodded, "And the way Margaret sings it touches one's very soul."

"Yes, the church has been blessed to have someone in the parish who is so gifted."

Henry nodded once again. "She could have gone on to be a recording star for certain, yet she chose to raise a family and be there for the community. The second song she sang after communion that Nana Mouskouri made famous, *The White Rose of Athens* also touched my heart. I can't get the words out of my mind:

"Till the white rose blooms again,
You must leave me, leave me lonely,
So goodbye my love till then,
Till the white rose blooms again."

Henry's words trailed off…"

This time Father nodded, "Yes, the words are very appropriate. Someday, Henry, we will all be together again."

"Nana sings that song incredibly well; yet, Margaret's angelic voice just seems to touch the core of my being."

A silence fell between the two men. A tear, sliding down Henry's cheek, glistened in the moonlight.

As he went to swipe it away, Henry suddenly sat up and pointed his finger towards the pond, "Look, Father!"

Coco instantly lifted her head to Henry's sudden cry.

The moon had not only exposed Henry's tear-filled eyes but also the V-shaped wave formed by a beaver cutting quietly through the still water. The sun had now completely set and the reflection of the trees in the pond were almost black; a perfect backdrop for the moon to detect anything in the water.

Henry sat back and once again no words were spoken but the sounds of nature became more prevalent. The chattering of the stream flowing through the dam, the cooing of an owl, crickets and every now and then the splash of a beaver tail against the water frightened by some movement near the shore; perhaps a deer or coyote.

"How did you ever cope when Anna died, Father?"

The question startled his teacher. It quickly brought back that time which was still embedded in his heart. He, too, loved Anna, just like Henry loved Jenny. He understood the pain of separation only too well. Many times, the nights were still too long without his loved one at his side.

"Yes, Henry, it was a very difficult time. It is important to mourn and grieve for our loved one but is even more important that we don't get stuck there. It was you who helped draw me back into daily living."

Henry was shocked by Father's words.

"Do you recall how my absence in the store concerned you and how you came upstairs and sat with me for several days? You listened to me as I grieved over Anna and reminisced about our past. It was just your caring and loving presence which made me realize that life goes on and that there are others who need me.

"You helped me live again."

Henry was touched by Father's words. He never fully understood the power of caring.

"I know how deeply you love Jenny. The days ahead will be challenging. I am here for you, Henry, but you will need the comfort of our heavenly Father. Quickly, go to Him and ask for His grace and strength to move on."

Henry wanted to say more, express the rising anger growing within him and all the what ifs and if onlys they had done, but he knew Father was tired and so was he.

"I best head up to the house, Father. I want to visit with Alison a bit more. She is going back to the Bible College in the morning and Justin may need me."

"Yes, yes, your children need you, Henry. I understand, Lauren stayed in the city?"

"Yeah, she is spending the night at Jeremy's place. Lauren's flight back to Ottawa leaves at 6:15 in the morning. She thought it would be easier to get to the airport from there. Did Alison tell you about her and Carson, the young man she met at the College? They're thinking about getting married after they graduate in another two years. She seems very fond of him."

"She mentioned that to me as well at the hall. Alison is a fine, intelligent young woman. I trust the choice she will make. She has good judgment."

Henry nodded, "Yes, she has a good heart and good head on her shoulders. Well, Father, thanks again for all your help today. The eulogy touched my heart. We are all so fortunate to have you as a friend and priest to be able to so personally tend to marriages, baptisms, anniversaries, deaths and all sorts of occasions. Your blessings are a God send. Thank you, Father."

Henry and Father hugged. Coco nudged her nose between the two men. Both men bent down and patted their shared friend.

"Are you going up to see Hannah tomorrow?" Father wanted to know.

Henry hadn't thought much of the baby that day or since Jenny died. He tightened his lips and just shrugged his shoulders.

As Henry made his way to the truck, he gazed heavenward. He noted as the darkness grew, more and more stars had blossomed in the infinite meadow of the sky. With no light other than the moon, the heavens were ablaze with millions of twinkling diamonds. Somewhere up there, too, was Jenny and yet he was certain he felt her presence. Just before he climbed into his truck to head back to the farm, words began to form in his mind,

"Quickly, hold my hand."

Chapter Sixteen

HENRY FOUND HIMSELF asleep in his chair by the fireplace in the sunroom. The reading lamp beside him was on and the book he had been looking at had fallen to the floor. Half of the cover lay resting against his foot. It must be past eight in the morning, he thought, as the sun had advanced almost to the end of the sunroom. From years of waking up early and sitting in the sunroom to watch the sun come up and travel south, he had come to know just about to the minute what time it was by the feel of the light in the room and where it was concentrated.

He had slept there all night. There, just across from him, lying on the couch, was his daughter, Alison. She, too, must have fallen asleep and spent the night there as well. They had been up late talking about all sorts of things including the new man in her life. Henry wondered if his interest in native art and artifacts he collected for years and displayed in his home was a premonition of what was to happen in his family. He wondered what it would be like to have a Métis in the family with a different cultural background. He learned more about Carson and his family last evening.

Alison wanted to get an early start to head back to Alberta so he'd better get her up and get breakfast started. Justin must've still been sleeping. Henry couldn't believe that his thoughts had actually drifted away from Jenny. Last evening, he couldn't think of anything but his dear wife. So much so, that he avoided going up to the bedroom. The thought of her not being there with him and looking into her sparkling, blue eyes, would be just too devastating.

"Morning, Dad, how long were you there?"

"I actually was here all night; I just woke up, too. It must be going on to eight thirty. What time do you want to head back?"

"Right after breakfast. There's a speaker coming to the College tonight from Cochrane that is supposed to be really Spirit filled. He is having a three-day retreat and I don't want to miss the opening night."

Alison made her way over to her father and asked, "Are you going to be okay, Dad? Do you want me to stay for a few more days?"

"No, I'll be fine. I prefer to be alone at this time."

"Hannah looks so beautiful, Dad. When Lauren and I saw her after the funeral, we both thought she had some of your features, especially the nose but she sure looks like Mom."

Alison began to tear up. "Oh, Dad, Jenny left you a part of her...*she will always be near to you.*"

Henry was already in tears and couldn't speak. He just nodded.

Alison gave Henry a hug and then went to the washroom while Henry made his way to the kitchen window and gazed through the opening into the sun room and valley beyond. Out of habit, he reached out his arm to wrap it around Jenny as he usually did when they stood there every morning and said prayers. What would his day be like without Jenny? He was beginning to feel the emptiness already. When Alison left and Justin was gone to school for the day, he would be by himself.

Fear began to grip him.

The phone rang soon after Justin and Alison left. It was a blessing as the silence and aloneness was quickly drawing him into an unknown emptiness.

"Hello."

"Hi, Dad, how are you doing?" Camilla wanted to know.

"Alison left about fifteen minutes ago and Justin's off to school. It feels a bit lonely right now."

"Yes, after being surrounded by so many people the past few days, getting back into the routine of things will be a bit difficult especially with…" Camilla's words trailed off as she didn't want to mention Jenny being gone and add to the sorrow he already was feeling. She thought it best to just get to the reason why she was calling.

"I am going up to the hospital to feed the baby in a half hour. You haven't seen Hannah in a few days; would you like to meet me there around eleven? We can go out for lunch after…" Camilla's words trailed off again.

Surprisingly, Henry had not given much thought to the baby; he was so consumed by the death of his dear wife that the child she bore him was forgotten.

How could he forget?

Jenny lived every day in the hope to give him a child and he considered it as nothing, not even worthy of his thoughts! It was the same when Father Engelmann asked him about Hannah last evening, too.

What is wrong with me?

It was as if he had shut out the most precious gift one could ever give him. Jenny had given her life for this gift and he had forgotten…!? He should have been with his daughter day and night after Jenny died and…here he has to be reminded of his little girl.

"Dad…, Dad, are you still there?"

"Yeah…, to be honest, Camilla, I've been so pre-occupied over Jenny's passing, I haven't been able to think of much else other than do what has to be done and with all of the people here…"

"I understand, Dad. I'm still in a state of shock myself and I miss Mom terribly. If you're not ready to go up to the hospital, that's okay. We can go up another time or when you're ready."

He didn't know if he would ever be ready. He desperately wanted Jenny and not the baby.

How could he be thinking so selfishly!?

"No, that's good of you to call, honey. I'll meet you there at eleven."

"Okay, see you then, Dad. Bye."

CAMILLA WAS IN the lobby waiting for Henry. She wanted to both escort and support him to the NICU. Henry stopped in his tracks as soon as he saw his daughter-in-law. For a moment there, he thought it was Jenny!

"My, God," Henry whispered, from a distance. "They look so much alike." Camilla had cut her hair short and wore it just like Jenny so it would be less work to keep. Camilla was wearing a spring floral dress which buttoned up at the front. Jenny had one that was similar and would have been wearing it any day now as well. Henry shook his head to make sure he wasn't seeing things.

"Dad…, Dad, I'm over here," said, Camilla as she hurried towards her father-in-law. She gave Henry a hug and a kiss on the cheek. He resisted from holding onto her longer.

It felt like Jenny.

"Come, hold my hand and I'll take you to see Hannah!"

Without thought, he quickly slid his hand inside hers. *My God, what am I doing?* At the elevator, he pulled his hand away from hers to press the button even though his other hand was free and nearer.

It just was all too much like Jenny!

As soon as the doors to the elevator opened, Camilla once again took hold of Henry's hand, "Come on, Dad."

As they rode up the elevator, Camilla was talking about the wonderful progress Hannah was making but Henry didn't hear a word. It just felt awkward holding Camilla's hand. Her gesture to hold his hand to comfort and support him was right but thinking that it was like holding Jenny's hand on his part was wrong.

Dead wrong.

She was his daughter-in-law, his son's wife!

He slowly pulled his has hand away and moved slightly to the side. As soon as the doors opened, he was the first to move out to avoid being led by the hand.

Henry knew the way to the room; he had been there a hundred times with Jenny. His heart was always filled with joy and could hardly wait to see Hannah but that was then. Jenny should be at his side, not Camilla!

He slowed as they approached the doorway. His thoughts oscillated between Camilla and Hannah. They were both Jenny's daughters. Except for the one he fathered, they both should be a comfort to him. They were both a direct link to his dear wife, a part of her own flesh and blood. They were both alive and so a part of Jenny would always be with him. And yet, they both reminded him of Jenny too much. He ached to see her now and hold her and tell her how much he loved her and missed her.

Henry hesitated at the door to the room that held infants which were premature and having special needs. Camilla walked past him and then turned. She studied Henry for a moment and said, "Come, Dad."

Once more, she reached out to him to take her hand and lead him in but Henry refused, pretending he didn't see her hand and instead walked in. He recalled the room. Almost every incubator was full over a week ago when Jenny was here. Half were now empty. The babies were at home in the loving arms of their mothers as they should be. Soon, his little girl would be out too, ready to live in the real world but no longer in the loving arms of the one who gave her life.

Camilla stopped at one of the incubators and stooped over. She looked at Henry and waved for him to come. He walked slowly ahead and gradually the infant came into view. Camilla began tapping gently at the clear cover and softly said, "Hi, Hannah, Mommy's here."

The words shocked Henry. What was going on? Camilla wasn't her mother, she was her wet nurse…

Yet, still, she was a mother. *How else would you like it be, Henry?* he asked himself. He just didn't like the sound of it. Jenny was Hannah's mother and yet, he should be so grateful that Camilla was here to take over. It was almost as if this was all planned!

Henry knew Jenny and Camilla had talked about this possible eventuality. Jenny made Camilla promise that she would raise the child if anything happened to her.

Who would have dreamed that such a scenario would happen?

Finally, Henry broke the silence, "How is she doing?"

"Incredibly well. She is almost four pounds and so alert. The doctors have done so many tests and so far, everything is normal. Her lungs and heart are very strong. She is breathing on her own without the aid of oxygen and she nurses so well, better than Jacob."

Henry nodded, "That's good to hear. Jenny would be ecstatic." *He felt so torn.*

Camilla grabbed Henry's arm and nudged him to come closer. Hannah was sleeping. Her hair was golden like Jenny's but very fine. The redness from her face was gone and the wrinkles had smoothed out. Her skin was thicker and denser, not translucent like before. He could tell Hannah had put on weight and seemed a bit taller. He wished she would turn so he could see more of her face. Without the wrinkles, she looked different, more like him. He wished it be more like Jenny.

Henry gazed at the tiny infant, so delicate and fragile; her tiny chest rising and falling with each breath. She was fully alive and… and Jenny should be, too! He wanted to accept the child; to love the child and yet… surely, he couldn't blame the child for the death of the mother. Henry's love for Jenny did not extend to the child, while Jenny's love for Hannah was for both the child and Henry. It was her last gift to him and Henry found it hard to accept!

Guilt and shame swept through Henry as he stood there almost immobilized. He tried to ward off the negative thoughts but they just kept coming.

If only she hadn't given birth to Hannah, Jenny would still be here. Even though Jenny looked so young, she was on in age. The doctor cautioned her about the possibility of complications. She was prone to high blood pressure but she felt invincible. She was certain this was one of the main reasons for her return; to give birth to this child.

She was so adamant to have the child; regardless of her own life. And…and it came down to that. In a low audible voice, Henry muttered, "Oh, Jenny…why didn't you listen to my pleading and the doctor's caution…"

Camilla stood erect and gazed at her troubled father-in-law. She now knew the thoughts that were troubling him. Tears welled up in Henry's eyes and he began to weep over his emptiness; his inability to give love to his beautiful daughter.

"Do you want to hold her, Dad?" Camilla softly whispered.

Henry shook his head and just continued to stare at the infant. It seemed as if he was uncaring and mute and unloving yet, a battle was going on inside his head. It wasn't Hannah's fault, he kept saying over and over. He wanted so much to love his daughter. She was Jenny's and his daughter; a life that they both had brought into the world through the gift of creation. Jenny may be buried but she left a part of her behind in this infant.

How could he be so blind and uncaring?

To reject the child was to reject Jenny. Hannah was the link that Jenny left behind who would give love and joy in her absence. Jenny would always be there through her daughter; their daughter. The thoughts seemed so wholesome and comforting, yet Henry was not ready to let go and accept.

He wanted Jenny more.

All he could do was reach his hand inside the clear acrylic case and touch his daughter. The moment his finger felt Hannah's body, an electrifying warmth surged through him.

Softly, ever so gently he stroked the smooth skin of the newborn…

He felt his Jenny.

CHAPTER SEVENTEEN

THE DAY AFTER Jenny's passing, Camilla began nursing Hannah. She would go up in the morning and then again later in the afternoon. Each time she would pump extra milk for the baby to feed during the times she wasn't there. On days when Jeremy was off, Camilla tried to go up in the evening as well. She wanted to bond with the baby and give it as much motherly love as she could possibly do.

Camilla also wanted the father of the child to bond as well. Hannah and Jenny knitted a close relationship when Jenny was in the hospital but Henry still didn't really develop the feeling of true fatherhood. In most cases, the child was at home and the dynamics of having a new member in the home quickly takes hold with the father and the rest of the family. This hadn't happened yet in Henry's case since the baby was born premature and with the death of Jenny, the bonding with the father was further impeded.

She was so happy when Henry agreed to come to the hospital to visit with Hannah. Perhaps seeing the new baby would help her father-in-law to alleviate some of the sorrow and grief he was feeling and divert his attention on the living instead of on Jenny's passing. As soon as Henry entered the foyer of the hospital though, Camilla felt intuitively he was struggling with accepting his child. Despair covered his face. She had seen that look on Henry's face before, especially when Jenny was suffering with the complications of her pregnancy.

Camilla should have anticipated and expected that. After all, the mother was gone and he would feel lost. How would he possibly raise a child? He knew that his daughter-law-was going to help but still, the dynamics of it all would seem very complicated to him.

Henry's insightful daughter-in-law was correct in her analysis of the situation so far. Henry was concerned over the raising of his child and how this all was going to take place but what Camilla didn't expect was the remote possibility that Henry would blame the child for the loss of his dear wife and reject it. She would never have anticipated such a circumstance until her highly trained empathetic abilities as a counselor began to read his body language that day at the hospital. When he stood in front of the incubator and gazed at his beautiful daughter, there wasn't any emotion or look expressed that exhibited any kind of joy or happiness which a father normally feels.

There was nothing.

That was the first obvious clue but the words her dear father-in-law expressed as he gazed upon his little girl revealed that a serious concern had developed. The words, "Oh, Jenny...why didn't you listen to my pleading and the doctor's caution..." reverberated in her mind now.

Camilla was going to ask Henry to stay and watch his daughter nursing and to hold her but thought it better to wait. She could see it would be too painful for him to see someone else, other than his dear loving wife, feeding the baby.

Rather than concern her husband about all this, Camilla thought she'd wait a while and hope things would just naturally work out and in time heal itself.

But she was wrong.

One day, when Jeremy came home from work and the kids were playing in the family room, Camilla expressed her disquiet to Jeremy.

"Two weeks have gone by and your father still hasn't been back to the hospital to see Hannah. I'm worried about him, Jeremy. He missed church again last Sunday and when I call, he doesn't answer the phone."

"Yeah, I talked to Justin about it yesterday. He said Dad just sits out on the deck or front yard all day. Sometimes he reads but most of the time he just stares into space. Justin tried to get him to throw the football around or play catch, but he refuses which is unusual for Dad."

"I think your dad is suffering from postpartum depression as well as grief, Jeremy and he should see someone."

"Isn't that some condition women get after delivering a baby?"

"It can affect men, too. I've dealt with at least two cases and probably there have been more that didn't come to my attention. A lot of times, men don't like to talk about their mood swings or emotions. But men can become just as depressed when a baby is born as women. In your father's case, it's different. It's not so much concern about the care of the baby, financial issues and so on. It has more to do with not wanting the child and blaming the child for the death of the mother."

"Geez, Camilla, I don't think Dad would think that."

"Well, he did make a comment the day he came to see Hannah with me that expressed those sentiments. I didn't want to concern you with that but it seems to me he may need professional help. I'm not sure if Father Engelmann will be able to help Dad in that regard."

"I don't know, honey. If anyone can help Dad, it would be Father Engelmann."

Jeremy paused for a moment and then said, "I'm glad you brought this up. It's been so busy at the café, I haven't given it much thought. You're right, he hasn't been into the gallery since Jenny was hospitalized almost two months ago. Customers keep asking about him. Yeah, I'll have one of the assistant managers cover for me and drive out to the acreage tomorrow."

Just then, Joshua came out of the family room, "Hi, Dad."

"Hi Josh. Where's Noah?"

"He's watching a cartoon. I've seen it before so I think I'll go to my room and read till supper time."

"Well, come over and give me a hug. Maybe after dinner we can toss the football around."

"Yeah, that would be great, Dad!"

"He's sure growing up fast," observed Jeremy as his son left the room.

"Takes after his dad; you're well over six feet and very handsome I might add."

Jeremy nodded and winked at his lovely wife. "Well, you sure have your hands full, Camilla. It's a good thing you're on maternity leave. Running back and forth to the hospital everyday must be tiring you out. How were the two-babies behaving today?"

"They're fine; so easy to look after. Neither seems to fuss at all. Both fall asleep right after feeding. I either lay the one back into the incubator at the hospital and the other in the crib when we get home and they both continue to sleep on."

"That's great, honey."

"The attending nurse at the hospital says Hannah is such a good baby and making excellent progress. The doctors are considering taking her out of the incubator next week and placing her in a regular crib."

"Does that mean, she will be allowed to come home soon?"

"Yes, I'm sure another week or two at the longest and little Hannah will be here."

Jeremy came over and wrapped his arms around Camilla, "It's so wonderful of you honey to take care of Hannah."

"Oh, I love doing it. She is just like my own little baby. At the start I was concerned that I wouldn't be able to produce enough milk for both Jacob and Hannah but very quickly, nature took over. I am producing more than enough and to be honest, I feel so blessed to be able to do this. I wish the circumstances were different and Mom was just temporarily ill."

"It's almost as if this had all been arranged. How you became pregnant and delivered Jacob a month before and were able to immediately take over the care and nursing of Mom's baby the same as she would have done." Tears welled up in Camilla's eyes. "Yes, in a way, it's all so wonderful; as if I had given birth to twins. And yet, it's so sad that Mom didn't live and raise her little girl. I know how terribly grief-stricken, dad must be feeling.

"He loved her so much."

"Yeah, they shared a long tumultuous relationship and a very victorious and miraculous one at that, too, I might add."

"Those are quite the adjectives you used but I must admit, very accurate. I'll never forget the day they re-united with each other at the hospital when Mom was just moments away from dying of cancer. The way he came into the room in a daze and so in love. Never would I have dreamed that Mom would come out of her coma and kiss Henry.

"Wow! What a sight that was."

"And that was the same day you met your biological mother for the first time. It was so overwhelming for you, too."

"Yes, but the real dilemma was that I thought that your dad was also the man who fathered me! It's a good thing Matti and Chloe were there to straighten it all out."

Jeremy chuckled over it all and shook his head. "It would make a good soap opera, that's for sure!"

"I see you are still hanging on to Matti's phrase when she was here for the funeral. She sure is a great lady and yes, 'that's for sure'. Mom and Matti loved each other so much. She was Mom's closest friend when she lived on the estate."

"Yeah, I guess the entire staff were Jenny's closest friends. I have to admit, Thomas, Matti, Carlos and who was the butler again?'

"Charles."

"Yeah, that's right, Charles, they're all great and J.J. seems like a great guy, too. It's hard to believe his relationship with Jenny was so strained."

Camilla just nodded. "Well I'm glad they resolved their differences in time."

Just then, Jacob began to cry. Camilla got up. "I may have to nurse him, honey. He has been sleeping a long time. Dinner may be late."

"No problem, I can get things going if you like. You know how you love my Alfredo pasta and I see some fresh shrimp in the fridge. I'll sauté them in garlic and throw them on top."

"That sounds wonderful, honey." Camilla came over and wrapped her arms around her husband and they tenderly kissed. "I love you so much, Camilla."

"I love you, too, darling."

Camilla walked down the hallway thinking how terribly Henry must be missing those words from his dear Jenny.

CHAPTER EIGHTEEN

FATHER HAD PURPOSELY left Henry to himself for the past two weeks. He needed time to grieve and mourn over his dearly departed wife. This was the first time, too, Father needed to have time to grieve himself. He loved Jenny dearly and missed her uplifting heart and cheerful face. She was like a ray of sunshine in his life.

Immediately after saying Mass at the prayer house, Father slowly made his trek all the way up to the farm house. It was exhausting for the old man but every now and then he would stop and look back at the beautiful valley. He never got tired of looking at the Poustinia and how it reflected in the mirror like surface of the still pond. Summer was officially here and the valley was ablaze with fresh green leaves and dotted with colorful wildflowers. He had even spotted some monarchs flitting about in the air. Jenny would be in seventh heaven if she were here, ecstatic trying to take it all in.

At the top of the hill was a large boulder at the bend of the road just before the house came into view. It overlooked the valley and offered a spectacular view from north to south. Often, he would see Jenny sitting on the boulder and he would join her when he came to visit Henry. He could imagine Jenny sitting there now, her golden hair shining in the sun. The mirage didn't last long as he made his way over to the huge stone and sat down to rest a bit before visiting Henry. Coco immediately lay at his feet and was quick to close her eyes feeling the touch of her master at her side.

Father began to pray for his dear adopted son.

He was interrupted by the school bus coming down the lane. The children inside saw him and waved as the bus passed by heading towards the house. Justin was ready at the front entrance and hurried to the open door of the bus. When the vehicle drove past Father again, Justin waved with a surprised look on his face, to see Father sitting on the large boulder. The dust swirled, hiding the vehicle as it made its way to the top of the valley and disappeared down the dirt road.

Father prayed for another ten minutes or so and then feeling rested, he and Coco made their way to the house. Rather than go to the front door, Father decided to go on the deck which ran all along the side of the house where the sun room was, overlooking the valley. As soon as he turned the corner of the family room and stepped on the deck, he saw Henry sitting on the far end of the deck gazing out on the valley before him. Most times, Jenny was there next to him. It wasn't the same without her there, the mood already felt heavy and mournful, even from a distance. Father walked slowly trying to adjust to the pain he felt in the air.

Henry was unaware of Father's presence until Father was right next to him and said, "Good morning, Henry."

He was so deep in thought; he was startled by the friendly greeting. The sun rising in the eastern sky shone brightly onto Henry's face and he squinted as he looked up at his dear friend.

He placed his hand over his eyes to shield the bright rays and said, "Oh, hello, Father. How did you get up here? Did someone drive you?"

"No, Coco and I walked up the hill. I had forgotten how long and high the road was. I may be getting too old for this," Father added in jest.

Henry didn't take notice of Father's lighthearted remark. Instead, he seemed a little annoyed that his solitude was interrupted. Coco tried to lick his hand but he pulled it away.

Father got a chair and pushed it beside Henry and sat down. Usually, Henry didn't hesitate to welcome Father and get a chair for him or offer his. Henry was not his usual self and this immediately signaled to Father that his dear friend was still hurting deeply. He looked tired as if sleep had eluded him for days. His eyes were sunken and lackluster. Father's heart went out to his grief-stricken son.

He reached over and patted Henry's hand, "How are you doing, Henry?"

Henry stared straight ahead, tears surfacing in his eyes. He couldn't speak and so he just shrugged his shoulders and tilted his head as if to say, "I don't know."

"I miss her, too. It will take some time to heal the heart."

"Oh, Father, my heart will never heal. I miss her too much."

Henry hung his head down and began to weep. Father moved his chair closer and put his arm around his shoulder. Father began to weep as well. He hurt for his son and missed Jenny so much, too. In this instance, Father seemed to have lost his ability to really help his son from an objective point of view and yet, perhaps he was reflecting Henry's sorrow and helping him to carry the load.

A good half hour elapsed and neither man had said a word. They had stopped weeping but their sorrow continued inside their hearts. Perhaps, Father thought, a discussion about life and death might help to remind Henry about the fragility of this life and that there comes a time when we all must face separation.

Father spoke softly, "Sooner or later in life, my son, we all pass from this life into the next. We hang on to this life; what we know from day to day and the problem is that we lack faith in the hereafter. We fail to live with eternity in mind, yet, it is the door we must all pass through. This is life the way our Lord created it. Just as Jenny had to die, so will you and me, too. Your father went years before your mother and yet, Mary adjusted and accepted it."

"But Jenny and I have only had three short years together, hardly enough time."

"Yes, but many couples don't have that. Look how many men went off to war barely knowing their spouse or seeing the child their pregnant wife carried. Regardless of the time we have, inevitably, we will have to face death again either sooner or later. It was the same with my Anna. I still miss her, but life had to go on. We have to accept and let go, eventually.

"It was the same with Julean. She was taken at such a young age and what about your first son, Benjamin, not even a day old. This is life, Henry. This is the lot we have been given and we have to accept it. You can question and fight it for days but nothing will change."

Father removed his arm from Henry's shoulder and pushed his chair back so that he could face Henry and continued, "God is not here to take trials away from us but that is when he is closest to us. He wants to comfort us and help us to move on. What else can He do, Henry in a world where death is a part of life? I can feel Him near to you. Don't turn your back on Him. He is here so close; I can feel the warmth of His breath.

"Come, let us pray."

Henry shook his head, "I can't, Father. I'm sorry, I'm just not ready to let go or to turn to God or, or…" and then almost in a whisper he added, "If I ever will."

Father nodded. He understood Henry's deep sorrow. He could remember only too well when Anna died, he didn't want to work or do anything but recall and relive one memory after the other they had shared. However, he sensed something deeper going on inside Henry, an anger and rebellion towards his Lord. In such a state, one can easily be maneuvered by evil forces to expand those thoughts and feelings and slip further into despair. Father realized Henry had only been grieving for two weeks and everyone has their own time to heal emotionally and mentally but his son needed to see hope. He needed to see the first and most important step to break free of a broken self is to turn to the Creator. He and He alone can give us the comfort and love to heal a broken heart; but we must give Him the pieces. If Henry didn't want to pray then he needed to be aware of this crucial first step. Father took a deep breath and then risked going on, trying desperately to reach his hurting son.

"Perhaps then, Henry, listen to God in the silence of your soul. He is whispering in the depth of your heart, words of sweetness and peace and hope. Place your trust in Him and believe with all your heart. I know the death of Jenny has broken the ties of your deepest love and affection. But if you turn from Him and rebel, you will only increase your difficulties. You open the door to bitterness and the evil one which will only expand your pain and suffering."

Father gazed at Henry to see if he was taking in and considering his words.

He decided to continue, "Henry, to the degree that you allow your sorrow to go on, it must be overshadowed with a greater trust and love in the Lord to deliver you. Please try to accept and live as Jenny would want you to do. God will give you the strength to do so. What does He promise, Henry, 'Come unto me all ye that are burdened and heavy laden and I will give you rest. My yoke is light and easy.'"

Father's face dripped with compassion and concern. He reached out and grasped Henry's hands and pleaded, "Trust me, my son, and rays of hope will scatter the darkness from your soul. A calm peace and serenity will put your anguish and despair to flight like a flock of birds jolted by the healing hands of the Almighty. He will console you, comfort you, and deliver you. He will give you a new life to go on. He has great plans for you just like He did for me. Who would have thought when Anna died, that at my age, I would become a shepherd but it happened! All things are possible with God. God is a God of possibilities. He can turn all darkness into light! Come; let us see what the Lord has in mind for you!"

Father's words were so uplifting and promising. Henry marveled at his mentor's ability to start a flame amidst a rainstorm in one's heart. Henry could vividly see the picture of hope and the path to freedom that Father had so skillfully painted with his comments but he wasn't ready to let go. Henry pulled his hands away from Father and placed them to either side of his head as if to shut his teacher out and cried, "Father. I don't want my thoughts of Jenny to be dissipated by life. I don't want to forget her tender touch or the sparkle in her eyes. I don't want to lose any memory or picture of her in my mind's eye. I don't want anything to interfere or lessen my thoughts of love or sorrow or anguish or...She was my life..."

Just then Jeremy came out of the sunroom patio doors and saw how distressed his father was. "Geez, Dad, what's going on? How are you doing?"

Henry was startled once again by another intruder. "Jeremy!" Henry shook his head in disbelief, "What brings you out here?"

"We are concerned about you. Justin called and says you are not sleeping well or eating. I can see he is right. My good Lord, Dad, you don't look so good."

"I'm okay, my wife passed away and I'm grieving. I just want to be left alone. I'm okay, don't worry about me."

Jeremy came closer to his father; he had never seen him in this state before. He was always so confident and in control and he looked just the opposite. Maybe Camilla was right. Perhaps, he was in some kind of postpartum depression.

"Maybe Dad, you should see someone."

Henry turned sharply and said, "For God's sake, Son, I'm okay. If Camilla died wouldn't you be mourning for her? How long would you grieve? Wouldn't it be for as long as it takes!? Look, I'm okay and just want to be left alone. Is there a problem with that?"

Jeremy was at a loss for words. He went over and pulled up a chair and sat down. He looked at Father and then at his dad and shook his head.

A silence fell between the men. Neither of them wanting to speak, lest they upset Henry or get into an argument.

Finally, Jeremy spoke, "Okay, Dad, maybe you're right but please take a shower and have something to eat. I don't want to go with you looking so run down. Please, Dad, we love and care for you. We don't want you to get sick. Please, let us help you."

Henry nodded, "I understand your concern, Son. Okay, I'll take a shower and if you want to make some breakfast for

Father, that would be great. I'm not really hungry but maybe I'll have a coffee or cup of tea."

Jeremy nodded and got up. "Okay, let's do it." He waited for his dad to get up.

Henry could see Jeremy wasn't going to move until he did. Finally, Henry got up and made his way upstairs. When he came down, it was evident he had showered but didn't have a change of clothes. Father would find out the reason later that evening. Henry avoided going into the bedroom he and Jenny had shared.

Jeremy made some toast and bacon and eggs and coffee. They sat at the island counter in the kitchen. Father said grace and then the men began to eat. Henry nibbled away at his food to satisfy his son more than his hunger. Not much was said at the table and finally they made a move to go back outside to the deck.

"Hannah will be coming out of the hospital next week. She is making excellent progress, Dad. It would be great if you could come up and see her."

Henry shrugged his shoulders, "Yeah, I might do that in the next day or so."

"The doctors moved her out of the incubator and into a regular crib. She is really doing well. It's so good not to see her with all those tubes and wires going to her."

Henry nodded, "That's good to hear."

"The doctors are amazed how well developed her lungs are. Camilla laughs about it; when Hannah is hungry, she sure lets everyone know about it."

Henry nodded.

"I can go up with you to the hospital," Father offered, trying to encourage Henry to follow his son's excellent suggestion.

Henry shrugged his shoulders. "Yeah, we'll see how things are tomorrow."

Jeremy and Father could sense Henry's resistance and didn't know how far to push him. They could sense he was uncomfortable and wanted them to leave.

"I see the kitchen needs some attention. I'll go in and clean up a bit."

"No, that's fine, Jeremy, I'll do it. You probably have lots to do at home."

Jeremy got up and said, "It's okay, Dad, I have the day off and want to help out."

Jeremy went back inside. Dishes had been piling up and Justin hadn't really done anything either. Henry and Father could hear dishes clanging and water running.

Father was startled when Henry said, "I'm ashamed to say this, Father, but I don't want to see Hannah—"

Jeremy suddenly opened the patio door and stopped Henry from sharing something to do with Hannah to Father.

"Would either of you like some more coffee? Jeremy asked.

"No, I'm good," said Henry. Father just shook his head.

When Jeremy went inside, Father waited for Henry to say what he started but Henry remained silent.

Jeremy cleaned up the kitchen, straightened the family room and then decided to head back to the city. He invited Father and Henry for Sunday dinner and both agreed. Henry wasn't really enthusiastic about going but agreed to it more to appease his son and get him to leave.

After Jeremy left, Henry was growing more and more uncomfortable with Father sitting there. He wanted to be alone.

"Would you like me to drive you back to the prayer house, Father?"

Father didn't want to leave Henry alone, so he said, "If it's okay with you, I would like to stay and visit with Justin when he gets home. Perhaps, I will go into the guest room and have a nap."

Before Henry could say no or put any more pressure on him by his presence, Father rose and excused himself. Later, when Father got up from his nap, Henry was gone, nowhere in sight.

Henry had gone for a walk with Ginger down the country road like he and Jenny used to do. He hoped a meadow lark would sing him a song to appease his aching heart.

CHAPTER NINETEEN

FATHER ENGELMANN WAS up before the sun as was his usual practice. He would say the rosary as he sat in the prayer house next to the patio doors that looked out onto the pond. He would wait for the sun to come up to give him enough light to read his breviary for that day which was then followed by saying the Mass.

It was unusual for him to be still in Henry's house and it took him a few moments to get re-orientated. All the lights were off except for the family room. He made his way there and was surprised to see Henry asleep on the couch. He knew instantly what was happening; Henry wasn't going into his bedroom to sleep. He had struggled with that same issue when Anna died. The memory of sleeping with someone for years suddenly not there anymore can be overwhelming.

Father quietly walked into the room to turn off the lamp. He noticed a sheet of paper with a few sentences written on it on the rug and a pen still in Henry's hand. He wanted to pick up the letter. Father wondered if it was a love letter to Jenny. He flicked off the lamp and followed the light coming from the kitchen.

Father saw that the gas fireplace was on in the sunroom through the opening from the kitchen. He decided to go in there and say a rosary for Henry and his family. When he got there, he heard a scratching sound at the patio doors; it was

Coco. Father slid open the door and let in his companion. Together they made their way to Henry's chair. He sat down by the fire and began to pray. Coco felt cool to his feet. It was rare that it was he who would be giving warmth to Coco. It was usually the other way around.

Perhaps it was the warmth of the fire or the mesmerizing impact of the flames dancing in the fireplace which lulled both Father and Coco into a restful, contented sleep. Justin was surprised to find Father sleeping in his dad's chair. It was seven thirty and the school bus would be along in ten minutes. He decided to wake Father up.

"Father," said Justin as he gently shook Father's shoulder.

Father instantly opened his eyes and was equally surprised to see his adopted grandson towering over him.

"Oh, my, I must have fallen asleep."

"Yeah, I'm leaving for school shortly. Dad is still sleeping in the family room. I thought I would leave him."

"Yes, that is a good idea, he needs some rest."

"Would you like some cereal or something, Father?"

"No, I'm fine, Justin, perhaps some water for now. Are you ready for school? Do you need any help with anything?"

"No, I'm used to getting ready. I made my lunch but Dad will need to get some groceries. Maybe, you can mention it to him."

"Yes, yes, I will, Justin."

Just then, the phone rang. Justin was going to answer but he heard the honking of the bus.

"Geez, would you get that, Father. I wonder who could be calling so early. Tell Dad I hope he has a good day."

"Yes, I will, Justin and you, too. Say a morning prayer and I will for you as well."

"Sure thing, Father. See you later this afternoon."

The phone rang for the third time when Father picked up the receiver.

"Good morning," said Father.

"Good morning to you, too, Señor Henry. I hope my call is not too early?"

Father recognized the voice, "Is this Carlos?" Father wanted to confirm that it was Jenny's gardener.

"Si, that is correct. Is this Señor Henry?" Carlos wasn't quite sure it was Henry.

"No, this is Father Engelmann. Henry is still sleeping—"

"No, I'm awake," Henry said as he walked into the kitchen. Father turned and said, "No, Carlos, he is here, just a moment, please."

Father handed the receiver to Henry and said, "It's Carlos."

Henry nodded, "Good morning, Carlos, how are things going?"

"Very good! The garden is looking beautiful. Maria and me would like to show you what Señorita Jenny wanted to do in the backyard. It's very beautiful and we want to talk to you about our future here. Do you have time to come in this morning?"

"Yes, of course, we should talk…" Henry didn't really want to go in and yet it was not fair to talk to them about where things are at now that Jenny wasn't here anymore.

"Look Carlos, I will be in later this morning. I was thinking about coming in and seeing Jenny's place and the Angel of Thanksgiving. I should be there around eleven."

"Maria will have coffee ready and some cookies."

"I look forward to seeing you and Maria."

Henry hung up the receiver and was surprised to see Father there. Then he remembered he spent the night in the guest room after talking with Justin most of the evening.

"Can I get you some breakfast, Father?"

"I usually do not eat until after Mass. If you would like to have something and then perhaps we could go to the Poustinia for Mass. You can drive into the city after and if you want, I can come with you and we can visit Hannah in the hospital as well."

Henry thought for a minute, "No, that's fine, Father, I think I would like to go in myself, but I will take you down and stay for Mass."

"That's wonderful, Henry."

HENRY KNELT ON the kneeler all through Mass. At communion time, Henry asked for Father's blessing. He didn't feel right about receiving the host with the feelings he was harboring inside. Father asked if he wanted to go to confession but Henry declined, saying he wasn't ready. After Mass, Henry made his way to the door to leave and then stopped. He came back and sat in one of the two chairs by the patio door. He gazed out at the still pond before him. Father sat in the empty chair and waited for his hurting son to reveal what was weighing so heavily on his heart.

"Father, I am ashamed to say this, but I am so consumed by the death of Jenny, that the child she bore for me is forgotten most days. How could I forget? Jenny lived every day in the hope to give me a child and now I consider it as nothing not even worthy of my thoughts! What is wrong with me? It's as if I have shut out the most precious gift anyone could ever give to another. Jenny gave her life for this gift to me and I keep forgetting about it. I should be with Hannah day and night and here I am neglecting her through my self-preoccupation. And when I do think of the infant, I don't want the baby. I want Jenny back. If it wasn't for the baby, Jenny would still be here. Why did we have to have this child, Father? Why was it so important for Jenny to have a baby, to want to bear a child for me? Why? We were so happy and content. Our days filled with joy and now everything is gone."

Henry began weeping. He didn't look at Father, his head hung down. He raised his head and gazed out the glass doors onto the mirror like surface of the pond. The beautiful valley reflected almost perfectly in the still water. He ached to feel the serenity before him but emotions inside were too violent. So much guilt, anger and regret floated throughout his being.

Would he ever know peace again?

"It is understandable for you to have those thoughts and feelings, Henry. Perhaps, it would not be so, had Jenny lived to share the child with you."

That was all that was needed for Henry to vent more of his feelings. "Yes, if only she were here, Father. What can I do with this child? I don't know how to love it, cherish it, and look after it."

"Camilla has taken on that task, Henry. She will mother and raise the child and when you are ready, you can assist. Healing and acceptance takes time, my son. It takes a lot of little steps to come to terms with trials and challenges that come our way. It is natural for you to have these concerns, but things will fall into place."

"And that's the other thing. Camilla reminds me too much of Jenny. The other day when I saw her at the hospital, I thought for a moment, she was Jenny. When she gave me her hand, I wanted to hug her and hold her...she's my son's wife, for God's sake, I shouldn't have those feelings. What is the matter with me?"

"Yes, Jenny and Camilla look remarkably alike. In your state, Henry, once again all these things you are saying are a natural consequence of the state you are finding yourself in. You know Camilla is not Jenny, but you want to make her alive again and your daughter in-law is a perfect way to create this wish or desire of yours. If you feel you can control yourself, it is a harmless fear. Trust me, Henry, this too shall pass. Most of us, as we journey through life, may see someone other than our spouse that we may find attractive but it's just a fleeting thought. It's the second and third thought that keeps us on the straight and narrow and corrects our wishful thinking, no matter how foolish they can be at times."

Father was relieved that Henry was talking and venting his feelings. He thought he would put the attention on himself for a moment. "I remember when I owned the store there was a lady who came in that I always took a fancy to. When she came in, I changed my stance and put on an air of importance. It was when my face lit up and was more cheerful than I usually was that Anna read my thoughts. She would poke me in the ribs and say, "David, look but don't touch." That quickly brought me down to earth. So, you see, these things happen. We may be briefly attracted to certain persons but soon we see them for who they are; one of God's children who we can appreciate in a special way."

Father paused for a moment and thought he may indirectly

respond to Henry's earlier remarks about his daughter. "So, tell me about Hannah, Henry. I haven't seen her since I last visited Jenny when she was in the hospital. She was quite wrinkled and red at the time. She has grown since then and her features are different. When you saw her the other day, who does she look like, you or Jenny?"

Henry didn't respond right away and then said, "I wish she would look more like Jenny. I have to admit she does look a bit like me. She has my nose and mouth but her hair and blue eyes are like Jenny's. She's actually very pretty, Father. I wish I could accept her more and not blame her for Jenny's death."

Father was going to respond but Henry went on. "Jenny would never think like this; she was free of such thoughts. I don't want to blame a little baby for coming along and interfering with my life or be angry with God. These are terrible thoughts. All my life I have been plagued by self-defeating thoughts when things go awry. I've tried repeating Scripture passages but nothing seems to work. I even tried writing a letter last night to Jenny like I did when Julean died. It was you who advised me to do that at the time."

Henry looked up at Father, "Do you recall suggesting I do that?"

Father nodded.

"Well, it worked back then but I couldn't write more than two sentences. Nothing seems to work, Father. I just want Jenny back so badly. What can I do Father? This seems different from the time Julean died. I was able to come back. It took time, but I did. I could feel the control coming back but this time I feel helpless. I'm afraid to go up to our room; the emptiness is too overwhelming. The sight of an empty bed without Jenny there is more than I can bear. I have not endured such aloneness since Julean's death. I don't know if I will be able to handle it this time."

Henry paused and gasped for air. He felt like he was choking. "I am fearful, Father. I am sinking and feel like I am falling into a very dark hole and may not find my way out. Please help me."

Father got up, made his way to Henry, and knelt before him. His second mission clearly staring him in the face. He placed his hands on Henry's knees and said with a firm confidence, "Henry, I have never abandoned you and never will. I am here for you. Together we will see this through. This one thing I ask, do you recall what I said to you yesterday about God being here for you, too. Please, don't turn your back on Him. I encourage you to mourn and grieve over Jenny's passing; keep it pure, re-live the memories; the good times, the happy times and sad times but avoid at all costs: blame, bitterness, anger or resentment. These emotions allow impurities to mingle with sincere mourning. These emotions will quickly expand and color beautiful recollections with darkness. Turn to Him, Henry. He will help and guide you much better than I. Without His grace, we cannot even have a good thought, even say the shortest prayer, or resist from falling into despair. Together; you, me, and God will see this through. Together, God will give us victory over this sorrow. Trust in Him with all your heart and soul, Henry. Do not rely on your own understanding; it will lead you astray.

"Trust me, my son, go to the Light and do so quickly!"

CHAPTER TWENTY

---◦◦◦◦---

H ENRY'S HEART WAS not into driving to the city but he had to get groceries not only for him and Justin, but also for Father Engelmann. He would stop off at Safeway on the way out of town at the north end so that the items which needed refrigeration wouldn't be in the heat of the car for too long.

He thought he would go to the hospital first to visit Hannah. He wanted to do so alone and not in the presence of Camilla or anyone else. It was only nine thirty and Henry assumed that Camilla probably wouldn't make it up to the hospital until eleven or so. It was over two weeks since he last saw the baby and he wondered how she had changed in that time. He heard she gained weight and was doing so well. Henry felt a tiny tug of excitement to see his little daughter.

Perhaps, the reason why Henry's spirit had lifted, at least for the moment, was due to Father Engelmann's prayers. Henry knew his dear friend would be down on his knees, at this very moment, pleading for God to help him. Henry shook his head ever so slightly as he drove much slower than he usually did. How fortunate he had been during his life to have such a dear, loving friend. His words always touched his heart. Henry wished they would have longer staying power and be more effective as they usually do but the loss of Jenny seemed to overpower everything in his life. He just felt too hopeless to see any kind of life or future without his beloved wife. He knew turning to God, as Father Engelmann suggested, was for the best but he just felt helpless to do so or, perhaps, more accurately, not ready to do so.

Coming early into the city had the advantage of getting a parking space. There were several to choose from as he pulled into the parking lot in front of the Grey Nuns Hospital. He looked around at the other cars and was relieved that he didn't see Camilla's car there. He hurried to the front door to get this visit over with as soon as possible.

As soon as Henry entered the NICU, the nurse on duty recognized him.

"Hi, Mr. Pederson, it's great to see you. I was on duty when your wife was here…oh, I was so sorry to learn of her passing. She was such a delightful lady. Please accept my sincere condolences."

Henry forced a smile and nodded. He noticed her name on a tag fastened to her uniform and whispered in a low voice, "Thank you, June."

"Come, we moved Hannah to a regular crib to prepare for going home next week. I understand your daughter-in-law will be looking after Hannah."

Henry didn't answer as he followed June to the other side of the room; he simply gazed down at his daughter. June looked at him for a moment and then looked at Hannah as well. "It's truly a miracle that the baby made it and how quickly her lungs developed. We can't believe how healthy she is."

Henry didn't say a word. He forced a smile and nodded to show his appreciation as she turned towards him. He didn't want to speak or start up a conversation. He was feeling uncomfortable by her presence and wished she would leave him be.

She, on the other hand, could see Henry was still mourning and began to tell him of a similar situation that happened with her sister in the hope it would help. In that case, her sister was pregnant while her husband was fighting terminal cancer.

Unfortunately, the husband died without ever seeing the baby.

"Molly took it so badly Mr. Pederson, but eventually she knew that each time she touched her baby, she touched Bill, too. That is, her husband, Bill, if you know what I mean. If it's any consolation to you, your wife left behind a part of herself for you, too."

Tears came to both their eyes. The kindly nurse waved her hands up and down in front of her face as if trying to catch some air. Then, trying to change the subject, June added, "We have two pieces of your art work in our home; Prairie Sky and Skipping Stones. I just love the images; they remind me so much of home on the farm."

Once again, Henry simply nodded at the nurse as she turned and left. Quietly, he focused on the tiny infant. Hannah was sleeping, her little chest rising and falling so rhythmically, so peacefully. He tried to see Jenny in the baby but still saw a bit more of his own features. Her hair was the same; very fine and white with a tint of gold. Her eyes were closed; he wished they were open. He wondered if as she aged, her little nose would turn up more like Jenny's. Henry loved Jenny's nose. He reached out his hand and lifted the gown exposing her legs and feet. He counted the toes and was glad they were all there.

Momentarily he forgot himself.

He reached out for her hand and Hannah instinctively squeezed her hand around his finger. Henry was surprised by the strength of her grip.

He tried to feel Jenny.

He brushed away a tear with his other hand. He couldn't help but to weep. He tried to hold it back but the tears just kept coming. The image of Hannah blurred before him.

He began to feel self-conscious.

He pulled his hand away from Hannah but she didn't want to let go and it shook her tiny body. She opened her eyes. Henry wiped away the tears with his fingers and dried them on his sweater. He looked down and she was staring up at him; her clear blue eyes looking at him so intently.

She smiled.

It couldn't be, he thought. It must be a gas pain. He recalled Julean saying that all the time when the kids were babies.

She looked so lovely.

Henry wanted to kiss her; to feel that part of her that was Jenny. Would she cry if he did?

He ached for Jenny.

If only she could be at his side. They had moments like this together when she was in the hospital after giving birth to Hannah. Henry loved to watch Jenny more than the baby; how her eyes would light up at the sight of the infant with such happiness and joy. Jenny practically lived in this room even when Henry went home to clean up. She was still in the same room when he returned. Every possible moment she had was at Hannah's side. 'If only I could go without sleep,' Jenny would often say. Henry wondered now if maybe Jenny knew her time with her little girl would soon be up.

Henry reached out again very slowly; he didn't want to frighten Hannah. He placed his finger in her hand again and once more she grasped at it.

It felt good to be acknowledged.

He wondered if Jenny's spirit was there holding his finger through Hannah.

Henry liked that thought.

June came back from behind Henry and startled him. "How are things going here? Oh, I see your little angel is awake." She touched her finger to Hannah's tummy and said, "How is our little angel, huh? I bet you have something for me in your diaper. Have you changed her before, Mr. Pederson?"

Henry shook his head.

"Do you want to or should I do it?"

Henry forced a smile again and said, "I'll watch."

He stepped aside and watched the nurse change Hannah.

Just then, Camilla came into the room and saw Henry with the nurse. She quickly stepped back outside and peeked through the window beside the door. She didn't want to disturb Henry. It was best to leave him alone so he could bond with his daughter. It gave her such joy to just see Hannah with her daddy. The image before her blurred, as unbidden tears erupted. She quickly brushed them away not wanting to miss a moment of the two being together. Camilla wished Henry had changed the diaper rather than the nurse.

"Camilla usually comes up several times a day to feed the baby. That's your daughter-in-law, right?"

Henry nodded.

"She sure looks a lot like Mrs. Pederson."

Once again Henry nodded. He wished the nurse wouldn't have said that.

"Well, if Hannah begins crying before Camilla comes, we do have some milk in reserve. You can feed Hannah if you want."

Henry smiled and shook his head, "No, I'll leave that up to you or Camilla. I will be going soon."

"You're welcome to stay as long as you want. I think Hannah will be discharged next week. She has gained over two pounds since she was born. She is doing so well, Mr. Pederson," June added to be encouraging.

"Thank you, nurse."

"Okay, I'll leave you two then. If you need anything, call. I'm surprised how quiet she is. She usually lets us know when she's hungry in no uncertain terms!"

Henry moved closer to the crib as soon as the nurse left. He reached out to her hand again. This time she didn't grasp at his finger but instead looked a bit startled and began to cry.

"Hush, sweetie it's just, Daddy..." his words immediately trailed off. It seemed so strange for him to say that and yet it was true; he was her father! Hannah began fuss some more.

"It's okay, sweetie."

The nurse heard Hannah and began to come over but stopped when she saw Camilla come in.

"Hi, Dad, it's so good to see you,"

Henry turned sharply; he wanted to be gone before she came. Camilla came to his side and kissed him on the cheek.

"Been here long, Dad? Isn't she adorable!? I can hardly count the minutes till I come here."

Camilla bent over and picked up Hannah. "There, there, my little darling, Mommy's here."

Camilla's words jabbed at Henry. He had a hard time getting used to his daughter-in-law taking over the baby's ownership. Yet, he wouldn't have it any other way. He immediately corrected his thinking. "It's so good of you to come and do this, Camilla."

"It's a privilege, Dad. I am the luckiest girl in the world for this to have happened to. I feel Mom each time I hold Hannah. I know Jen is nursing her baby through me. That's why I keep saying, Mommy. It will always be Jenny at my side."

"What a beautiful thought, Camilla." Henry loved what she said and it felt so right. Jenny would be there, she would never abandon her little angel.

Henry felt better hearing those words. Camilla didn't claim ownership and ...yeah, it just felt right.

"Come on, Dad, there's a chair over in the corner by the window, I'm going to nurse Hannah now. You can stay if you want."

"I have to go, Camilla. I have a meeting with Carlos and Maria. They were expecting me all morning."

Henry wanted to watch Camilla nurse the baby but he thought he better go.

"I best be off, Camilla."

"We are all looking forward to seeing you Sunday, Dad. This Thursday would have been perfect to have you over but we thought Sunday would be best. Joshua and Noah can hardly wait to see you, Father, and Justin. Come early, please."

Henry nodded and forced a smile. He wanted to go over and touch Hannah once more but he just waved at Camilla. She was just beginning to open her blouse when Henry waved and left.

CHAPTER TWENTY-ONE

A N AURA OF color emanated from the front yard of Jenny's home on Hill Avenue. Neighbors from near and far came by specially to view the spectacular sight. Even cars just passing through the area immediately slowed down as their drivers were so distracted by the dazzling light. Some turned around at the corner and drove by once again just to take it all in for the second time. Even though Henry had seen the yard so many times, he never tired of it because in that amazing expression of creativity, he felt Jenny's love of nature.

In any way he could, Henry wanted to feel Jenny's love.

From a block away, he began to slow down and take it all in. The sun's rays were tinted with color as they bounced off the kaleidoscope of colorful flowers. *What a sight*, Henry thought. Jenny had orchestrated such a well-developed plan for each species of flowers to be displayed that Carlos really didn't have to change much since he and Maria came to live in the house over three years ago. He more or less maintained the magnificent garden which Jenny had created.

As soon as Henry came to a stop and opened the door, he was greeted by monarch butterflies. It often happened during past summers when Jenny came. It seemed like all of nature beckoned to his beautiful wife, but he wondered why they were in the front when the abundance of the food they liked was in the back yard. Henry barely made it up the winding path to the house when he was greeted by Jenny's friendly gardener.

"Welcome, Señor Henry, it is so good to see you," Carlos said as he hurried towards Henry with his hand extended.

Jenny always ignored a handshake and preferred a hug but Henry decided a handshake was okay.

"Hi, Carlos, it is good to see you, too. Is Maria in the house?"

"No, she is at the shrine in the back yard."

"Oh yes, that must be quite lovely at this time, Carlos."

"It is a blessing, Señor. At this time of the day the sun shines overhead on the face of the Blessed Mother almost bringing her alive. Miss Jenny frequently went there after her group sessions about this time just to say a few prayers. Come, let us go to the back and see what I have done. Señorita Jenny wanted to make a slight change to the east side where the round metal table and chairs are. It was an excellent suggestion. We are so sorry that Miss Jenny is not here to see it but we know that she is here in spirit. We feel her presence often, especially at the gazebo. Even when there isn't the slightest breeze in the air, the swing begins to move. It occurs most often when the sun, like now, is overhead, shining on the gazebo.

"Miss Jenny loved the sun."

Henry nodded in agreement.

"And look how the monarchs are flying back and forth looking for Jenny. They are so anxious for her; they hardly rest and take of the ample nectar that is so plentiful amongst the flowers and milkweed. I knew when you pulled up to the house because so many monarchs rushed to the front yard to see if their earthly angel was there."

Carlos paused, feeling Henry's sorrow over the loss of Jenny, so he added, "Perhaps the little creatures sensed Señorita Jenny through your deep love for her."

Henry forced a smile and simply nodded. He followed Carlos around the side of the home and immediately smelled the lilacs in the air.

Where was Jenny!?

His eyes widened in anticipation of his dear wife to appear at any moment.

"The aroma of the lilacs is intoxicating, no, Senor? Jenny would say so often that it has become a part of my vocabulary."

"Yes, it describes the powerful effect the strong scent of that flower has. It's my favorite, too." Henry breathed in the aroma, filling his lungs until they almost burst.

"Si, and you have another reason to enjoy the scent, it was Miss Jenny's favorite perfume. She gave Maria a bottle on her birthday. Maria and I both agreed that while the odor of the perfume came close to that of lilacs, it was only when Señorita Jenny wore it that the scent elevated far beyond the aroma of the lilacs even when in full bloom. Such was the effect of the radiance of your lovely wife!"

Henry looked at the gardener and shook his head. "Jenny often said you were a poet with words, Carlos. You have a wonderful outlook and it is true your voice does sound as if it is singing all the time."

"Ah, that is very kind of you to say, Señor Henry."

As soon as they passed the lilacs, the back yard opened up. Henry stopped and gasped at the utter beauty before him. If paradise is anything like this, he couldn't wait to get there. The festival of flowers was breathtaking. He had been here so many times yet each time it was like seeing them for the first time. Perhaps, it was because there was so much beauty, it was impossible to absorb it all at any given time. Furthermore, each time one came, the flowers were at different stages of development and thus it seemed as if the yard itself was in a constant state of growth and change!

Clearly, the landscaping was a work of art. Wherever Henry looked his eyes had an aesthetic feast of spiritual sustenance. And just when he thought he couldn't possibly absorb anything more pleasing, he gazed to the back of the yard and saw the Angel of Thanksgiving glistening in the sun. He could hardly wait to get there so he could put a flower in the basket for Jenny.

As Henry followed Carlos along the stone path, he had trouble focusing on what Carlos was saying. Henry kept thinking of that day when he and Jenny walked down this winding path together, towards the gazebo, where Father Engelmann was waiting to marry them. In just a few days it would be their third anniversary. It was such a happy, memorable, unforgettable, momentous day!

And it was just the beginning!

Each day which followed was richer and fuller with the beauty of life than the day before! It was all because of Jenny. Her charm, playfulness and spontaneity were contagious from the moment he had met her in the summer of '56 until now. Every day with Jenny was a new day. She opened him up to the fullness of life.

How could he possibly go on without her?

He recalled the day Jenny enticed him to come here to bicycle to the park. She had it all planned to make love. It was such a wonderful day and yet, perhaps he should have stopped and not made love like he did when he was a teenager. Maybe then all this would never have happened. *Henry! Stop thinking so foolishly. Stop being angry with God, with Hannah, ...with Jenny for wantin—*

"Señor...Señor Henry, is everything all right?"

Henry was so absorbed in the memory of that day at the park, he was completely disorientated. He felt foolish as he came down to earth and realized he should be listening to the changes the gardener had made and the reasons why Jenny wanted them done.

"I'm sorry, Carlos, I was momentarily distracted. Please go on. You were explaining the reason why the changes were made."

Carlos studied Henry for a moment and then went on show how under the new arrangement, each flower that grew from the earth had to be placed specifically for one reason; so, it could be seen and give joy to the beholder. So much beauty is hidden from view and Jenny wanted to maximize the spiritual nourishment which could be received by anyone who came.

"Yes, Carlos, it does express what Jenny so often thought about flowers and the wonderful lesson we can learn from them, whose only desire is to give glory to God's creation."

"Si,"

Henry's mind began to wonder again. Since his arrival, he felt at peace. Although he was reminiscing in the past, it brought him into the moment somehow.

Nature has that healing effect on God's children.

As the two men strolled along the winding path, it brought to Henry's mind the vacation he and Jenny had in Monaco, a tiny country, perched along the French Riviera. They went there to celebrate their first-year wedding anniversary and also to visit the Princess Grace Rose Garden which was planted in honor of Grace Kelly. The idea for going there was sparked by Jenny's resemblance to that of Grace. Jenny was often teased about it, especially by Henry's friend, Gary, who immediately noted the similarity in their features after seeing the movie, Rear View Mirror. They arrived the last week of May just in time, when the roses open in the Garden.

It was quickly evident to Henry that Jenny and Grace not only looked alike but also shared their affection of flowers. In so many ways, Jenny's garden and love of wild flowers reflected the beauty of that garden there and Grace Kelly's love of roses. Thousands of bushes displaying countless varieties of roses lifted the spirit for all those who came from sunrise to sunset. Henry recalled the message he read engraved in stone below the statue of Princess Grace:

"What is so special about a rose that it seems much more than a flower?

Perhaps it is the mystery it has gathered through the ages.

Perhaps it is the joy that it continues to give."

THAT SAME MESSAGE, Henry thought, could be attributed to Jenny and her love of wildflowers, especially daisies. A rose was to Grace as a white daisy with a yellow center was to Jenny. A daisy, too, was much more than a flower. It shone like the sun it resembled, freely giving of its beauty unconditionally to all of God's creatures of land or sky.

"I can see your mind is on Jenny. It is written in your eyes, Señor."

Henry smiled, "It's that obvious is it?"

"Si, but that is to be expected. It is difficult not to think of her and the love she had for all of God's creation."

"Yes, I was just thinking of that, Carlos. She loved life right down to each individual flower. She planned it so not a one would get lost or unappreciated for the beauty and uplifting spiritual sustenance flowers give to us."

"Si, that was exactly her intent and look, see how lovingly each one is seen and gives so freely. One cannot help but to be so uplifted," Carlos said as he began to walk forward again.

Henry had to agree with what the wise gardener just said. Ever since getting out of the car, he was immediately immersed in a utopia. His cares and worries were replaced by a gentle peace.

At the Angel of Thanksgiving, Henry stopped and picked a white daisy with a yellow center and placed it in the basket. It seemed to glow brighter as soon as it touched the white marble. So many miracles had occurred here; so many flowers lasting beyond their time and season.

Henry shook his head in awe.

He said a short prayer and wish to Jenny. Just as he was about to go to the gazebo and sit on the swing to take in the beauty of the garden from that perspective, Maria emerged from behind the shrubbery.

"Oh, Mr. Pederson, welcome, it is so good to see you."

"Hi, Maria and please call me, Henry."

This time, Henry hugged the tiny woman. "I see you were praying at the shrine."

"Si, it is so peaceful there. Miss Jenny enjoyed it so much too; she would say the rosary to the Blessed Mother to intercede for her…"

Maria hesitated and looked at Carlos as if she was saying something that perhaps she shouldn't be. Henry picked it up right away.

"I didn't know Jenny said the rosary here."

Carlos came over and put his hand on Henry's shoulder and said, "Si, Miss Jenny loved to say the rosary. Maria had given it to her last summer when Señorita began visiting the shrine and began praying to the Blessed Mother to intercede for a special request."

Henry's brow wrinkled, "I wasn't aware of a rosary; she never showed it to me."

Carlos looked at Maria and nodded as if to say that it was okay to disclose something important to Henry.

Maria looked up to Henry and said, "Miss Jenny desired to have a child so much, Mr... Señor Henry and she wanted to pray to Mary like I did. At the start, she asked for my rosary and so I decided to get one for her."

"I wonder why she didn't bring it home, Maria?"

Again, Maria looked at Carlos. He nodded and Maria went on. "She said that you say the rosary all the time and that it used to belong to your wife from a previous marriage. Miss Jenny was worried that if she brought it home that you may feel bad about praying to Mary with your wife's rosary and start to use hers. She didn't want to take anything away from the way you loved or remembered your wife and so thought it best to leave it here and say it when she came for her group meetings."

Henry was flabbergasted. He had to see it, to hold it. "Where is it, Maria?"

"It is laying at the shrine, at the base of the statue, Señor Henry."

Henry had to see it right away. He didn't want to be rude but he couldn't wait another moment. "I would like to see it."

Si, Señor Henry, I will take you," offered Carlos.

"No, no, that's fine, I know the way. Jenny showed me the shrine last fall when we went to the park for a bike ride."

As Henry walked towards the back of the yard, Maria said, "If you wish, you may keep the rosary,"

Henry slowly walked in behind the brush and followed the well-trodden, short path to the shrine. When he got there, he didn't have to look for the rosary. A ray of light from the sun was falling directly on the glistening beads at the foot of the statue just like Maria had said.

It sparkled in the light.

He walked slowly to the statue and knelt down on the mat. He looked at the solid beads. They appeared to be carved out of white quartz; tossed long enough to retain a smooth, yet multi-faced surface. The silver cross at the end of the silver chain was dangling over the edge of the table. It glistened each time the soft breeze moved it and caught the sun. He slowly reached for the rosary and the instant he touched it, he felt Jenny. Her warmth spread through him like a soft summer breeze caressing his entire being. He thought the beautiful garden had lifted his spirits but this went straight to his heart and soul. He suddenly felt a peace which he hadn't felt in days.

Henry shook his head. He gave Jenny, Julean's rosary and now he gets Jenny's back in return.

Unbelievable! There is such a strong connection between these two women even though they had never met! So many times he had to come to that conclusion.

"Oh Jenny, you loved and respected Julean so much, just as she had you," Henry whispered.

Henry had missed Julean's rosary. Almost every day out of habit, he would reach in his pocket and think of Julean or at night offer a prayer of love to her. At least this would begin to fill the void and emptiness he was feeling for both of his loves.

He tried to imagine Jenny here in this space, praying. It was so vivid in his mind's eye that he wanted to paint it on the spot. He could see her kneeling before the shrine, her face radiating her angelic heart.

Perhaps one day he would capture this on canvas.

He made the sign of the cross holding the crucifix between his fingers as she would have done. Instead of beginning with the Apostles Creed, Henry began by talking with Mary and revealing his broken heart. He ached and yearned for Jenny more than he could possibly imagine and didn't know how to deal with it. So much suffering and yet, to suffer is to love. *To love is to suffer.*

Jenny knew the true meaning of love. How many times was she silent and accepted others the way they were? How many times did she die to herself for the betterment of others?

How many times did she make sacrifices for others; forgive others for deep injury; to love freely without conditions…yes, *to truly love is to suffer.* But Jenny knew that what we suffer for God and others it is not lost. It is not in vain…somehow, somewhere, sometime, *God will use it for the good.*

Henry began to weep and felt uncomfortable doing so. Carlos and Maria were waiting for him. He didn't want to leave. He felt immersed in Jenny's love, perhaps it was Mary's, too. He kissed the cross and stood up. He gazed at the image of the Holy Mother and how she must have felt when her Son was crucified. She was there when He was nailed to the cross and the Father watched too…He allowed it. Yes, God turned it all into good but how, Henry wondered…*how, can He possibly turn Jenny's death into good?*

CHAPTER TWENTY-TWO

HENRY SAT OUT on the deck and reflected on the remarkable day he had spent in the city. He was glad he had seen Hannah and that she was in a regular crib without all the tubes and wires attached to her. Jenny would have been elated and counting the minutes until she came home. Henry allowed his imagination to see what that would have been like to have their baby coming home to the farm. What a day that would have been. Lauren's room was turned into a nursery. The crib was white and had decals of cherubim's at the headboard. The change table had everything on it, ready for their little angel— he quickly dispensed with that scenario, however, it was just an illusion that might give temporary joy but the letdown which would follow knowing it to be all a wishful dream would be too devastating. The room was ready for Hannah but the mother was no longer there to receive the little angel in her heart.

Henry tried to imagine a similar scenario that would now be taking place at Jeremy and Camilla's home. Camilla had told him that Joshua and Noah would now share a room together and Jacob and Hannah would share the third bedroom. Jeremy was still working on the two bedrooms in the lower level of their split-level home but they still were not completed. Eventually, all the children would have their own bedrooms.

Henry tried to visualize how Camilla described the way Jeremy had painted Jacob and Hannah's room in both blue and pink colors. Where would they put all the angel decals Camilla said she had bought? His daughter-in-law was so excited for Henry to see the room and how they had prepared it for Hannah's homecoming.

It would be such a wonderful day for everyone and yet, his heart felt so heavy without Jenny. Henry shook his head...he didn't want to go there for dinner on Sunday and he tried to think of some excuse...he just didn't want to go there without Jenny at his side to share the joy. It would all be too much... "Oh, what is wrong with me?' Henry muttered into the warm summer evening. Camilla was so excited to have him Sunday and yeah, she mentioned that it would have been better to have him there Thursday as well...

Suddenly it dawned on him why...it was their 4th year wedding anniversary this Thursday. Yeah, June 3rd, that memorable day, four years ago, Jenny and he got married. He couldn't believe how quickly time had gone by.

Henry understood now why Sunday dinner would work better than having a family meal on the day that would remind him and all of them of their marriage. It would have been difficult for all concerned to celebrate an anniversary with Jenny gone and make it a joyful event. No, too many memories for any day and especially not that one.

Looking for another source of solace, Henry reached into his pocket and pulled out Jenny's rosary. It glistened in the moonlight. He marveled at his good fortune and how when one gives away something they love and are so attached to, something else comes along which fills the void and even more so. There was now such a special connection between him and his two loves. It made him think of his guardian angel. He reached up and touched the pewter angel hanging around neck and couldn't help but feel that it was his protector who had guided him into this incredible chain of events. He could hardly begin to imagine that he was holding Jenny's rosary in his hand.

He could feel her touch as he did Julean with her rosary. Somehow, incredibly, he sensed both of his loves...or was it just his deep felt wish that they both were still here?

The growing darkness revealed more and more stars blossoming in the sky. The star of the east had now been lost amongst all the other twinkling stars. Even so, this past month he noticed a lessening of the stars ability to send rays of comfort, warmth and solace. He hungered for any way he could feel Jenny's love but it seemed blocked by the star and he wondered why. It just wasn't the same...nothing was the same.

Thoughts again of his visit to Jenny's home that afternoon provided some relief. Henry was still amazed at the symphony of fragrance and color in Jenny's back and front yard and how on a smaller scale it captured the same stunning scenery of the Princess Grace Rose Garden in Monaco. What an amazing holiday that was. They went the last week of May so they could be there when the roses opened up and also to celebrate their first-year wedding anniversary. They had never seen so many roses in one place and never would again. Thousands of rosebushes representing over a hundred different varieties of roses, feasted the eyes of tourists, from sunrise to sunset.

They stayed in Nice, a picturesque, nearby city to Monaco and bussed to the rose garden most days. They stayed at a hotel on the edge of the sea. On the day of their anniversary, they went to the Old Town and wandered the quaint cobblestone streets, with their maze of narrow alleyways visiting shops and museums and watching artists paint.

It was wonderful walking along the coast-line as that day came to a close, holding hands, watching the sun set on the Mediterranean Sea. Rather than eat out that night, they ordered in French cuisine and dined on the terrace. Later, they opened wide the balcony doors to their bedroom suite and lay in bed gazing into the heavens and making love.

Henry smiled as he immersed himself into the wonderful memory of that evening.

They had planned to go back and explore more of the beauty, culture and ambience of the French Riviera this year but then Jenny became pregnant and their plans changed. If Hannah hadn't come along, Jenny would be alive and they might very well have been once again walking along the dazzling coastline that very day. In just a few days, their fourth-year anniversary was coming...yes, he thought, we would have been there this very day basking in the sun or strolling through the vast sea of roses or making love under the stars in their suite which opened onto the terrace.

Once again, Henry shook his head, he didn't want to go into the world of 'ifs or what might have been.' He knew that Hannah could never be compared to places or things. He was annoyed with himself for even having entertained such thoughts. Hannah was Jenny's gift to him and he so much wanted to receive the precious little girl into his heart but he ached for the mother so much more.

There was no room... yet.

Perhaps, someday, he and Hannah would visit the French Riviera and walk through the rose garden and talk about Jenny and her love of flowers and how much Jenny and Grace Kelly looked alike. Henry liked that thought and it lifted his spirits. He wished the two ladies could have met; two kindred spirits so much alike and how each one was called early in life. It brought to mind the poem Grace had written about a little flower when she was just twelve years old. Henry was astonished how the words captured Jenny's spirit too, in so many ways:

Little flower you're a lucky one
you soak in all the lovely sun,
you stand and watch it all go by
and never once do bat an eye
while others have to fight and strain
against the world and its every pain of living.

But you must too, have wars to fight
the cold bleak darkness of every night
of a bigger vine which seeks to grow
and is able to stand the rain
and yet, you never let it show
on your pretty face.

Tears sat on the edge of Henry's eyelids as he recalled that poem. So many storms and cold bleak darkness came into his dear, sweet, Jenny's life and yet...

She never let it show on her pretty face!

CHAPTER TWENTY-THREE

W HEN HENRY LEFT Jenny's home that day with her rosary in his pocket, he thought for sure that he would be able to pull himself up and out of the sorrowful mood that he seemed to be trapped in. Juleans's rosary helped him to cope with her loss. Slowly over time he was able to accept his first wife's passing and to let go.

Surely, this would happen again.

That evening, when he sat out on the deck and reminisced over the day and the celebration of their first-year anniversary in Monaco, it all lifted his spirits. Even the next morning, he felt a glimmer of hope in the new day which unfolded before him. He and Ginger, at first light, began to stroll down the short cut road which led out of his property. There was more spring in his step and he was attuned to the sounds of nature and the hum of electricity in the wires. He was even hopeful that he might hear a meadowlark.

He and his sidekick turned around as they neared the main highway and headed home. Henry was beginning to be filled with an optimism that maybe things were about to turn around.

But, he was wrong.

Recovering from the loss of his dear Jenny would become more and more challenging with each passing day. As he strolled down the country road back to a broken home, he was entering into a journey which would steal his life away for a long time.

Henry never did make it to Jeremy and Camilla's home for dinner that Sunday. Justin and Father Engelmann did but Henry was immovable. He was set on staying at the farm and not wanting to go anywhere.

At first, everyone thought that Henry was just going through a very difficult grieving process. They all knew how deeply in love Henry and Jenny were; all Henry needed was time to be alone to mourn and heal.

The summer, however, passed slowly, without Henry showing any signs of his usual positive, confident self. Surely, fall would bring him out of it. Henry loved the color of the changing leaves in the valley and the smell of harvest in the air. Soon, winter would be here and he would seclude himself in his studio and paint scenes which had inspired him in the fall and listen to his favorite music. Surely, Father Engelmann's visits and talks would bring him back to the land of the living, but it was all to no avail. Henry seemed to listen to his mentor but it more or less went in one ear and out the other.

Henry didn't want to talk to or see anyone. The dark cloud surrounding him just didn't want to lift!

Henry felt guilty for being such a poor father to his son and the other children and grandchildren but he was helpless to change. He encouraged Justin to move into the city and stay with Jeremy but his son refused. He was worried about his dad and wanted to care for him. Many days, they sat side by side on the deck. It was comforting and uplifting to feel his son's love and care for him but it was not enough to pull him back to life.

The family talked to several therapists who said it was more than likely postpartum depression that Henry was suffering from and that his depression could last for months, even a year or longer. They all recommended he see a doctor and to especially watch for a serious symptom of depression; thinking about death and suicide. The doctors they spoke with were also relieved to know that the baby was not under his care with his present condition as mothers suffering from postpartum depression, at times harm the child.

All attempts to get Henry to see a psychiatrist or take anti-depressant medication failed. He strongly maintained that he was grieving and that he would take as long as needed and further, he didn't want to alter his memory in any way, shape or form of Jenny. He didn't want to forget anything and not be able to re-live each moment when Jenny was alive and they were together. Memories helped him cope but they also imprisoned him in the past.

His present moments were lost in time.

If it hadn't been for Camilla's stubborn persistence on keeping Henry in the loop, he might very well have forgotten that he was the father to this precious child that his dear sweet wife Jenny had borne for him.

But there was more, so much more that motivated and fueled Camilla's persistence. Hannah was proving to be a very special child. Her early progress in rolling over, as well as sitting up, was remarkable. Each time Hannah exhibited a new skill or trait, Camilla was beside herself and called Henry on the spot to let him know of his prodigious daughter.

"Dad! I never had brothers nor sisters; I was the only child as you know. And with just giving birth to boys I really have never had any way of comparing boys and girls but there is definitely something different about Hannah. She is way ahead of Jacob. While he is still trying to crawl, Hannah is showing signs of wanting to walk! She is saying more and more words each day: mommy, daddy, milk, bread, please and many more. I can't keep track anymore and so I started writing down the words. At four months, Dad, this is amazing!"

Camilla and Jeremy not only called often to give Henry a continuous report of Hannah's progress but also made every effort to visit Henry at the farm. At minimum they came once a week, sometimes more as they were so excited to show Henry what Hannah had mastered next.

Despite the phone calls and visits, Henry always found it very difficult to snap out of his depression. Many days, Henry even wished his enthusiastic daughter-in-law wouldn't call or bring Hannah out to the farm. He knew he should be spending time with the precious gift Jenny had given him and that he was missing out on so much of the joy and blessings a child gives to the parents, but for one thing, Camilla and Hannah reminded him too much of Jenny. He struggled with his attraction to Camilla and he could just imagine that Hannah was how Jenny was too when she was a child. Bubbly, curious, enthusiastic, spontaneous, and full of life; just like Hannah! It made him want Jenny all the more!

And the other thing which saddened him even more when Hannah came and showed how adorable she was, was that Jenny wasn't there to share in the joy. How could he possibly enjoy all this when his dear sweet Jenny should be too? He could just see in his mind's eye the sparkle of delight and sheer happiness with each new thing her little darling did. These were just some of things Henry struggled with. Oh, how many days and nights had Henry pleaded with himself to please let go of Jenny and accept life…please, please, Henry, please let go.

LATE FALL CAME and went as did the winter. His love of painting which he usually immersed himself in during the long, cold, blustery winter days was never realized. The family could not believe that he had lost interest in painting. Not once since Jenny's passing did Henry put a brush to canvas; all he could manage to do was sit in the sunroom and pretend he was reading. He had become an ally to death and many days he looked so still as he gazed into space he could be considered as no longer in the land of the living.

Winter also curtailed visits with both Camilla and Jeremy's family and Father Engelmann. Usually, Henry came down to see Father on the snowmobile but Henry had no interest in doing that. It was Justin who kept in contact with Father and took supplies down to him when needed.

At nine months, little Hannah was walking. She was speaking in sentences, starting to read, showing insatiable curiosity, was spontaneous, and had high levels of energy. She didn't seem to require as much sleep as Jacob and yet rarely fussed during the day for lack of rest. Hannah was constantly asking questions. Whereas the boys always had trouble sharing their toys, she gladly gave whatever she had easily away. Incredibly, she showed no attachment to things. And when Camilla saw the little child praying and how angelic she looked with her little hands together under her chin, her eyes closed and how fervently she prayed, it stole Camilla's heart away. On so many such occasions Camilla could not restrain tears from erupting, nor from calling Henry.

"Oh, Dad she is such a blessing. I can't wait till morning comes to be with her, around her and see what she comes up with. I don't think I will go back to work anymore. I wouldn't want to miss anything Hannah does. This experience is a once in a life time, Dad.

"You're missing out on so much!"

Henry knew he was but couldn't seem to help himself. He tried to show interest in Hannah and respond to his family's efforts to help him get back into the stream of living but it was all surface; his affection for the child lacked depth and sincere concern.

It was all so unlike Henry to be this way.

There was one event however that Henry did show some excitement over, whenever it involved angels. Anything to do with angels caught Henry's interest and attention. Many days, all he could do to survive was to clasp onto the pewter angel around his neck just to make it through another day.

It was the second week of February on a cold blustery winter day when Camilla called to let Henry know of what she considered to be a miracle. She was so excited, Henry had difficulty understanding her at first. But when it registered in Henry's mind what his daughter-in-law had just shared, the news instantly warmed Henry's spirits despite the forty degrees below zero temperature outside.

"Dad! I just had to call to let you know what your marvelous daughter did last night and again this morning. As she knelt down at her bedside like the boys do every night before going to sleep, out of the blue, Hannah recited the guardian angel prayer, verbatim just as you, Jenny, the boys, and Jeremy and I do. She doesn't pronounce a couple of the words exactly correct like 'guardian' and 'commits' but it's so close there is no mistaking it. It's so cute how she pronounces 'guardian' like 'gid-ion' and 'commits' like 'co-mets'. I asked Noah and Joshua if they had taught her the prayer and both boys said they hadn't. I recall Jenny, that is, Mom saying and singing the prayer to Hannah both before she was born and countless times after. It seems that it was recorded somehow in her little mind just waiting for the right moment when she had developed enough to just come right out and say it!

"We have never seen anything like it and the way she says it you would think she is praying directly to her guardian angel! It's as if her protector was right there in the room in her awareness and presence!"

Henry listened intently and for the first time was deeply moved by what Camilla had just told him. Tears were streaming down his cheeks as he visualized what Camilla had just shared. And, he too, had seen Jenny repeatedly say the angel prayer to Hannah. Jenny knew the little girl was special and that she would be returned back to God. Jenny was preparing her for her mission. There were so many signs...

Camilla burst into Henry's thoughts, "Are you there, Dad? Did you hear what I told you?"

In a soft low voice, somewhat drawn as if covered with cobwebs, Henry whispered, "Yes, I heard, Camilla. She truly is a gift from God. Jenny's love for Hannah was so great that I am sure we will find that everything Jenny shared, said, or sung to her little angel will come out at some point."

"I agree, Dad, and I don't want to upset you but I am astounded how Hannah's features are changing to be more like her mother's all the time. I hope this month's long stormy weather abates soon so we can come out there so you can see for yourself. Her cute adorable little nose seems to be turning up just like Jenny's and mine. It almost seems as if Jenny has come back. Hannah's heart and Jenny's seem one and the same!"

FOR AS LONG as Henry could remember, March usually came in like a lamb and out like a lion but this year was different. The deep, freezing cold, for most of February, continued right into March. Stormy, blustery winter raged on every day, with no sign of letting up. It seemed to be so complimentary to the storm in Henry's life that Henry didn't even seem to notice what everybody else was complaining about.

By mid-March, however, a Chinook came in from Alberta and almost changed everything overnight. The sun broke out of the grey gloomy clouds that had covered the sky like a heavy blanket for almost two months. The icy roads, covered with snow in so many places, quickly melted or burned off allowing traffic to once again get back to normal. A freedom and exhilaration were in the air that couldn't have come soon enough to people living on the prairies.

Everyone's disposition changed instantly except in Henry's heart. Despite the early spring, warm cheery weather and early signs of new life, Henry hung on to the past as if he was welded to it.

It would soon be a year since Jenny's passing and the family was at a loss as to what to do. They were all praying for Henry and daily, Father Engelmann offered up the Mass he celebrated for his adopted son's healing. So far, however, their prayers seemed unanswered but they never gave up hope. Father was certain he played a part in Henry's recovery and that somehow Henry's healing was related to his second mission. Father wasn't sure yet what it was he had to do to pull his beloved son out of the clutches of such deep sadness and hopelessness.

Father Engelmann was quick to see no improvements in Henry as his visits to the farm increased now that warmer weather was here and most of the snow had melted making his trek up the hill possible. Henry's lamentations still focused on the trials he had to bear, especially that there was no future without Jenny. Many days, he likened himself to Job. Although he had let go of the many challenges he had faced, he still harbored a spirit of unforgiveness toward God.

And that was his major obstacle!

It was a beautiful spring morning in late March when Father made the long trek up to the house to visit with his hurting son.

Sounding like Job, Henry began, "Life has been hard, Father, it began with the death of our first child…Julean and I were able to move forward with your help but when Julean was taken away, my faith began to falter all the more…but now with Jenny's death, it is entirely gone. The burden of life has become unbearable."

Henry could not go on and dry tears came.

"Henry, the sorrow over the loss of a loved one is natural but it is now taking on a life of its own in your case. It has cut a deep wound into your being. It will heal in time but if you allow resentment, anger, self-pity and bitterness to get into this wound it will fester and infect your entire life. Go to God and He will heal you. He will restore your soul and your wellbeing. Like Job noticed in his own life, Henry, God is going by you each day and you see Him not. He passes on love and comfort also, but you perceive Him not. You want to be healed, my Son. He is near, waiting to help you and yet, you accept Him not."

Henry heard Father's words but he felt so empty and alone, he could no longer rejoice. The dawn of each new day without the love of his life left him cold and empty. Henry wondered why neither Father, nor his family, could understand this.

"I cannot help you in this Henry, only God can breathe new life back into you. The path you are following will lead you only into further darkness. God does not promise us an easy trouble-free life. He does promise us strength and to be with us through our trials. Trust Him and He will lead you back into the light.

"What is that favorite Scripture…Trust in the Lord with all of your heart and do not lean on your own understanding…"

Henry heard Father's words but it was falling on deaf ears. Father was determined and went on, "You are walking through the valley of the shadow of death. You will fear no evil because the Lord will be with you, Henry. Come to the Poustinia and rest by the water. God will restore your soul and lead you back on the right path. As I said, life has disappointments, challenges, trials and many dark places come into life but God is here with open arms wanting to comfort and heal us.

When you decide to let go and accept Jenny's passing, you then open the door to possibilities. All the forces of the universe under the control of God can now move into your heart with new life and purpose. All of creation is just waiting for you to say "yes" to life. Where you see a dead end, God sees countless new beginnings. Where you see closed doors, God sees endless doors of opportunity open for you. Say, "yes" and God brings all sorts of new directions for your life which would not otherwise happen. Once you let go and accept and open your life again, you open your life to new possibilities.

"Soon you will feel and come to know a marvelous presence more peaceful that you have ever known—"

Henry held his hands up and shook them, gesturing for Father to stop. He hung his head and stared vacantly at the deck flooring.

Father hesitated to go on but he thought he would pose the question, "My Son, if you don't go to God, to whom shall you go? I am the first to admit it is not I who can help you, it is God. He is waiting for you to give Him your broken heart. It is He and He alone who can mend it...but you must give it to Him.

"If you continue to rely on your own strength, where has it got you? Where will it get you? We are too weak and broken and fall into despair because we know not how to neither get out of it nor have the strength to do so! In you is now an emptiness waiting to be filled. You must initiate His help, Henry. He waits for you with open arms...don't turn your back on Him a moment longer."

Father did everything to help his son begin to reach out. *He knew that the desire for God's help must exceed the depth that one hurts.* Although it seemed impossible to get Henry to that stage, Father also knew that all things are possible with Christ. His faith and trust in Jesus never wavered because as the Psalmist says in 147:3,4, "*He healeth the broken in heart.*"

It was just a matter of time.

CHAPTER TWENTY-FOUR

WITHIN DAYS AFTER that visit, Father saw a ray of hope in Henry. Memories of Jenny's love of spring and the abounding new life that spring brings, seemed to lift Henry's spirits in sympathy with his dear wife. It was true; Henry noticed the effect Jenny had on others from the first day he met her. Her spontaneity, gaiety, charm and playfulness were contagious. It opened him up to the fullness of life then and it did now just thinking of her wonderful qualities. Thoughts of Jenny bursting out of the house and running up the hill with outstretched arms to the sky thanking God for the glorious spring day and new life made him want to do the same! He could see her running through the meadow on the valley floor laden with wildflowers. He loved to run after her as she chased butterflies. So often he prayed for angel wings just to keep up to her…even in his thoughts!

Father noticed Henry's change in mood and willingness to talk and was quick to take advantage of it. The very next morning after Mass, he and Coco made the long trek up the steep hill to the farm house. Justin was off to school and Henry was sitting outside on the deck overlooking the valley. Father wondered if Henry had seen him walking in his direction.

He mustn't have as Henry was startled when Father and Coco suddenly appeared next to him.

Henry smiled and said, "Morning, Father. I am amazed that you can still walk up that steep hill. I would have come down with the truck and picked you up had I known."

"Yes, it is tiring but the Lord continues to give me strength to do His work. One day, we will hook up a telephone in the prayer house so there is an easier way of communicating with each other. Yet, it's always best to talk in person, if possible."

"Yes, that's for sure. You have always been so healthy and fit that it never occurred to me that we should have some quick way of getting a hold of one another in case of an emergency."

Father smiled and waved it off. "The Lord will figure it all out, Henry."

"So, what brings you up here, Father?"

The holy man shrugged his shoulders. "I came to see you and visit for a while. You don't come down as often anymore. So, tell me Henry, how are you doing?"

Henry was silent for a long time, then he started to talk; haltingly, hesitantly at first and then he unleashed the pain and sorrow that had congealed and took root in his heart. "You know, Father, with spring here and thinking about Jenny's love of this time of the year, it lifted my spirits but without holding her hand in mine, it just doesn't seem the same. When I was around Jenny or anyone was around her, one soon realized that what you considered fullness of life was really only half full. She quickly made us aware of all we were missing out in life. Without her here, Father, I seem to quickly slip back—"

Father was encouraged by Henry's catharsis of his mind, heart, soul and wanted him to continue and so he challenged his deeply troubled son. "But that is precisely the point of her existence, Henry; to make us aware of what we are missing and to encourage us by her example to be more alive to life!"

"But, Father—"

Once again, Father tried to get Henry to see all of his dark, old, hidden grievances; all that was keeping him from life and going to the source of all power. "Surely, her life was not in vain! We both know and hope that the way we live our lives will be a good influence upon others. We need leaders, people who are examples of how to go to the next level; we need heroes, people to model, to emulate. You had one of the best, Henry. Surely, she did not fail..."

Henry wasn't ready for this. Father's sudden assault made him reconsider his words and state in life. Before Henry could think up some vain excuse for his helplessness, Father continued with more hard love, "Would it have been Jenny's wish for you to sit here day after and day and mourn for her?"

Father paused but not long enough for Henry to rebut him and said more, "Would it not be Jenny's desire for you to continue on with life and be a beacon of light as she was? This is no life for you my son, if you continue on this path. We cannot keep the past alive. Cherish the memories and continue to live. Place your care into God's hands. Trust Him! He is waiting for you! Your family is waiting for you! Life is waiting for you! And memories of Jenny's zest for life are reminding you of that! Perhaps that is why your spirits are uplifted!"

Henry stared at his teacher directly into his eyes and tried to think of reasons to justify his pattern of living for these past months. Yes, it was sorrow over the loss of a loved one but it was more. It was self-pity, it was anger with God, it was resentment, it was blame, it was regret, it was guilt, it is all these things and more...but to what end? What good could come out of this? And, yes...the wise old mentor was right. This was not what Jenny would have wanted of him. This was the first time in months he honestly confronted himself.

A feeling of shame and waste of life began creeping up his spine.

Father wondered what his son was thinking. The light in Henry's eyes seemed to be brightening and becoming recognizable with some relief. Perhaps, thought Father Engelmann, he should reinforce his words by using himself as a further example.

"Henry, when I die, what would I want of you? Would I want a sad funeral or would I want you to celebrate my life? Would

I not want you to be happy that I am finally at home with the Father? Would I expect you to grieve and mourn and miss me? Yes, it would appease my ego to think that you would but I tell you now, my Son, do not do so any more than a minute… at the most! Otherwise my ego will burst in heaven!"

Father smiled and looked at Henry with compassionate eyes and said, "I have always tried to be a good example to you and others. Would I not want you to continue that on to others? *If not, my life was in vain.* We are called to be beacons of light. Our goal is to get ourselves and others to heaven. Isn't that what your dear wife did and wanted for you…?"

Henry nodded, unbidden tears surging to his eyes.

"Then you must do the same."

After a long silence, Henry spoke softly, "How many times did I go over your eulogy to Jenny, Father. Over and over you showed the life of an earthly angel. Over and over your words described why Jenny had the heart of an angel. Every word you said was true and described her life perfectly. I know your purpose was for us to emulate her, to continue carrying the torch she had lit and be a continuing beacon for others. Instead of doing that for me, Father, it made me aware of all the beautiful qualities and traits of my beloved that I will no longer see in the days ahead. The thought overwhelms me.

"Father, she was my life."

Father nodded. "Oh, mein lieber Gott, sprechen Sie die Wahrheit, you speak the truth my son. You have made Jenny your life. In my eulogy however, I also told of another very important part of Jenny's life and that is her commitment to God. She placed Jesus first in her life and you second, Henry. Jenny knew that without Him, she could not love you or others the way she did. Jenny knew to give her "all" she needed to be filled daily in the well spring of God's eternal love. It came from Him, Henry, not directly from you. She saw in you something that attracted you to her and it drew feelings of love from the river of divine love which flows through all of creation. That's what made Jenny so free, Henry. If you had died before Jenny, would she have felt that her life was over? That her happiness was now gone? Do you really believe that you would have had such control over the life of the one you loved? What kind of relationship would that have been? Love is a gift from God, freely given and we in turn must be free to give it to others or it is not love. Would you not want for Jenny to be free to go on and love others or would you want her to remain captive to your love as you are now?"

Father paused for a moment and gave Henry time to reflect on his words. Henry recalled that morning in the hospital room shortly after Jenny had given birth to Hannah; she expressed thoughts and words that were so similar to what Father was saying now. At the time he thought how philosophical Jenny was speaking about life and death and that all love comes from God and that we are to place Him first and foremost in our lives, over our spouse or anything. That is what helps us to go on knowing that we can always survive any calamity when we have Jesus first and foremost in our lives.

God and God alone is the source of all life and love!

Father's next words were intended to reinforce those same thoughts which Jenny was trying to prepare him for that morning should she not survive!

"When you place Jenny first and foremost in your life it is a selfish love, a self-love which does not come from the Heavenly Father. You have given control of your joy on this earth over to someone else. This is not true love, my Son. True love comes from our God. He made us so we can feel that true love for others. Cherish the memories you had with Jenny and God's gift of love you two shared with one another and move on.

"This is what I had to do when my wife died. I continued to hold dear my life with Anna and pressed forward as she would have wanted me to. Look how quickly I was blessed! God brought you and your parents into my life, whom I came to love as my own. And when I became a priest, my family increased and so did my love. It was through God that He brought you and others into my life to love through Him. It gave me new life and purpose to go on. He is the source, Henry and He and He alone must be first in your life. God has a plan in your life, too.

"So many people search for happiness in the wrong place; money, materialism, their talents, praise from others and on and on. How many times have you said to me, 'Father, I have too many masters in my life.' The good news, as I have said to you in the past is that you see the truth. That is the critical first step to healing. You see the reason why after all these years you still haven't developed a close relationship with Jesus. You are aware of your love of this world and how it continues to separate you from God! Anything which prevents or keeps us from making God first and foremost in our life is an idol or master in control of our life. If we now look into your present life, *what is it that is keeping you from God, now*?"

Father paused for but a moment, for Henry to see the reason for his continuing sorrow and then went on, "The emptiness you feel Henry is that your dear wife has become yet another idol. You must accept her passing and let her go. Jenny was a gift to you in the same way you were a gift to her. Give her back to God and turn to Him. He will fill the emptiness you feel. He must be first, Henry. He is the source of love and life and peace and contentment. In Him we are complete.

"Our sufficiency is from Him."

Once again Father Engelmann paused. He looked deeply and compassionately into his hurting son's eyes and said, "Jenny knew and understood God's plan for His children. She gave God the Father, God the Son and God the Holy Spirit her 'all' and in return, her life was filled to overflowing with divine love.

"That is why she was free to love unconditionally. That is why she was a beacon of light to us all. That is why she gave her life for her child. That is why you loved her so dearly. That is why she was a saint.

"That is why she had the heart of an angel!"

CHAPTER TWENTY-FIVE

"**H**APPY BIRTHDAY TO you, happy birthday to you, happy birthday, dear Hannah, happy birthday to you!"

Hannah rested on her knees on the dining room chair, her hands grasping the edge of the table and her pretty little face was at the same level on the table as the chocolate cake. The lone white candle stuck in the middle of the cake burned brightly, sparkling in her cerulean blue eyes. It was evident her mind was whirling as she was thinking about a birthday wish. Just a few weeks ago she had seen Jacob sit in front of his first birthday as well and he was asked to make a wish too.

Hannah closed her eyes, thought a bit more, perhaps prayed a bit more then she opened her pretty sparkling eyes and blew hard at the candle easily snuffing it out. Everyone cheered and clapped. It was Joshua that asked the question which everyone wanted to know the answer to. "What did you wish for, Hannah?"

"I prayed that Daddy gets better...soon..."

Henry had strained to keep his emotions in check. Ever since Hannah came with Camilla and her family, Henry couldn't keep his eyes off his little girl. He hadn't seen her in weeks due to the weather conditions and was amazed at how much she had grown and changed. Camilla was right; she looked more and more like Jenny!

Her heartfelt wish was all too much for Henry and tears which were sitting on the edge of his eyelids spilled over. Her prayer that he gets better was so similar to Justin when he grieved for weeks over the passing of Julean. He would never forget how Justin came home that afternoon and ran up to his art studio where he and Father Engelmann were visiting and asked him not to be sad anymore and to come out and play catch.

That scene was now being played over. His little sweetheart was now being prompted to ask him to do the same. Henry was certain that it was Julean who prompted Justin to come to Henry that warm spring day just as it was Jenny's spirit now prompting her little angel to help her daddy to snap out of it.

"Are you okay, Daddy?"

It was a question that should have come from Camilla or Father Engelmann or any of the other older children at the table but it was little Hannah. She was so perceptive and caring, it astounded everyone at the table.

Henry just nodded his head, unable to speak. His little girl looked so concerned. *For a moment there, he thought he saw Jenny.* Henry swiped the tear rolling down his cheek and then reached his hand across the table and placed it upon Hannah's hand. "Yes, I'm okay, sweetie."

Henry wasn't the only one who had tears in their eyes. Almost everyone at the table made the same motion Henry just did. Either taking a tissue from their pocket or simply brushing away drops of joy that were sliding down their cheeks too.

What happened next was just as touching. While everyone was anxious to have a piece of cake and ice-cream, Hannah made another request of Henry that got everyone's attention once more.

"Daddy, can you show me the room my Mommy got ready for me. Mommy Camilla told me how pretty it looked. Can I see it…please!?"

This time Camilla reached over and patted Hannah's hand. "Your daddy can take you up to the room after we have cake and ice-cream and open your presents. Everyone wants to celebrate your birthday, honey!"

"Okay, Mommy Camilla."

Henry was surprised how Camilla had separated herself from Hannah's real birth mother. It was clear that Camilla didn't want to mislead the child in any way. Since she was adopted, Camilla wanted to let Hannah know that in a way she was too, under the circumstances.

After dinner all the presents were opened. The very first one was from Jenny, much to everyone's surprise. It was a ceramic guardian angel that she purchased months earlier before her passing along with a birthday card with a little angel on the cover holding a white daisy with a yellow center. Perhaps it was a premonition of what was to come. She had asked Camilla to keep it at her house so it was a secret. But there was more to all this as everyone would soon find out that evening and in the days to come. The first-year birthday card was signed by Jenny but also included Henry's name as 'Daddy." It touched everyone's hearts and Jenny's presence was felt at the party.

After all the presents were opened, Hannah once again reminded Henry that she wanted to see her room. While Henry and Hannah went upstairs, Justin decided to share something which got everyone's attention just like Hannah did before.

It soon became evident how deeply Justin still missed Jenny and how dearly he had grown to love her as his second mother.

He tried to hide his broken heart to be strong for Henry, with the hope that his father would get over the loss. But when Henry's mourning over Jenny went on for days then months and now almost a year, Justin had given up and he too needed comforting just as much as Henry.

Justin looked around the table a bit shy to share what was in his heart. Father Engelmann simply smiled and nodded at his adopted grandson to go on. Everyone was staring at him except Jacob who was still eating his cake and ice-cream. More ice cream was getting on his face than in his mouth. It lightened Justin's spirit and he said, "Since Mom had bought a gift for Hannah and had a card for her, I thought I should share with you what happened two days ago when I was trying to think of a birthday present to give to my little stepsister. I thought I would check out my treasure box hidden in one of the drawers in the roll top desk to see if there was anything in there Hannah might like…"

Camilla let out a slight shriek and sat closer to the edge of her chair. She knew what Justin was about to share. They were all about to learn what Jenny had planned should something happen to her. Camilla received a cursory glance from some of the people at the table but most held their attention on Justin who went on, "After Dad and I had supper and he went outside to have a cup of tea on the deck, I sat at my roll top desk in the back office." Justin turned and motioned towards the area just before the family room. Everyone knew what he was referring to but Justin was making sure everyone at the table understood every detail of what he wanted to tell them… it was so special!

"I pulled opened the drawer, reached in and pulled on the circular ring, releasing a trap door that flipped open. When I reached in and pulled out the box I was trying to remember all that I had stored in there as I hadn't opened it in months. I was expecting to see some coins, and an old watch that belonged to Grandpa Pederson but instead, right at the top was a folded letter. I couldn't recall ever leaving a letter there. When I opened the letter, I was so surprised to see it was a letter to me from Mom!"

Everyone, present at the table, could see how his heart soared. Even Jacob stopped eating and looked at his jubilant uncle. Unbidden tears came to the young boy's eyes and he couldn't speak momentarily. Camilla got up, went to him, and put her arm around Justin softly saying, "I knew of that letter, Justin. Mom asked me to place it there, should anything happen to her. She knew you would find it at the right time when you were ready and needed it."

Justin looked up at Camilla with tear filled eyes, clearly surprised. "You knew…?"

Camilla nodded, her eyes smiling. "Jeremy and I read the letter before we followed Mom's instructions. You can share it with Father Engelmann if you want. You have already let your dad read it, haven't you?"

"That's the thing I wanted to ask you." Justin looked out to the foyer to make sure his dad and Hannah hadn't returned and then turned back to Camilla.

"I'm not sure if I should share the letter with him. That is why I brought it up. He mustn't have got a letter from Mom, otherwise he would have shared it with me or told me he had, but he didn't. I wasn't sure if I should let him see it. I don't want him to get mad at Mom for giving me a letter and not him..." Justin's words trailed off.

"Oh, Justin, you have such a beautiful heart. I think there is a letter for your dad as well but even so, yes, it would be wonderful to share your letter with him. I am sure he will be so happy for you and that will help to lift his heart as well."

After a long silence at the table, Justin got up and went to the roll top desk and got out the letter. He unfolded it and stared at it a long time. Tears welled up in his eyes once again as he just handed it to Father Engelmann because he couldn't read it.

Father took the letter and sat back in his chair. Everyone watched their dear friend, grandpa, priest, mentor, comforter... read the letter Jenny had written to her stepson. There was something very beautiful about Father Engelmann's eyes. How they could reveal compassion, joy, sorry and now a melancholy of sadness revealed what he too still felt over Jenny's passing. It was evident the old man was trying to draw out Jenny's love from a letter which she had held and written. A quiet joy was written on his face and it was only a sentence or two before Father's eyes began to redden and tears began sliding down his rosy cheeks.

He was reading and drenched in memories at the same time.

CHAPTER TWENTY-SIX

AFTER JEREMY AND his family had gone home, Henry drove Father Engelmann down to the prayer house. When he returned, he and Justin visited in the sun room and chatted about the party.

"Geez, I can't believe how smart Hannah is, Dad. Was I able to speak like that when I was one year old?"

Henry shrugged his shoulders. "I don't really recall, Justin. Probably, Julean would remember."

"Did she like her room? Is she going to start staying out at the farm, soon?" Justin asked in rapid succession.

Henry nodded, "Yes, Hannah really liked the room. She liked the angel decals I painted in the sky. She did want to stay over tonight but I told her some other time she could. As to your other question, I think it's best for her to stay with Camilla. She can care for Hannah much better than I can."

"But she can stay out every once in a while, can't she?" Justin was anxious to know.

Henry just nodded.

A long silence grew between the two men. Henry was thinking about Hannah and how fast she was maturing, not only intellectually but also physically. She was beginning to look the spitting image of Jenny. It would be easy for anyone to assume that Hannah was Camilla's daughter, too, because there was such a remarkable resemblance there as well.

Justin, on the other side of the room, was debating in his mind if he should bring up the letter he found from Jenny or wait. He thought he would do it now. His dad seemed to be in a better mood the last couple of days and perhaps this might help him even more. Besides Henry may try to look for the letter Mom had written to him as Camilla had disclosed to all at the table earlier that evening. It may lift his spirits even more, like it did mine, when I discovered my letter. Justin could see now why his dad was so elated to get a letter from his wife when she died. Justin often saw the letter from Julean, lying on top of the chest of drawers. He could tell his dad must have read it a hundred times, it looked so tattered.

Justin looked up at his dad. He was staring off into space... he took a deep breath and then began, "Dad, guess what? I just found something in the secret compartment of the roll top desk. It's a letter from Jen... I mean Mom."

Henry didn't respond.

"Dad, did you hear me. ....?"

"Oh, Justin. I thought I heard someone. ...oh... I'm sorry... what did you say, Son?"

"I found a letter from Mom in my roll top desk." Tears were filling his eyes as he handed the letter to his dad.

Henry suddenly sat up and looked straight at Justin. "This is from Jenny?"

Justin just nodded. His breath had caught as he struggled with so many mixed emotions. He was happy, he was nervous and he was...afraid. He thought his dad would react positively but he didn't know his dad lately. He had changed so much since Jenny died.

Justin handed the letter to Henry, tears filling his eyes.

"Oh, Justin...it's okay, Son," Henry softly whispered.

Henry took the letter...shaking his head in disbelief. Slowly, he unfolded the letter and sat back in his chair to fully savor this precious letter that his dear wife had written to his son. It reminded him of the note he had found attached to the fence post a week or so after Jenny had gone to Ottawa, when they were fifteen. In a way, it saved his life. He was so elated to get that note and recalled how he had read it over and over. He looked up at his son, who probably was relishing those same feelings, when he discovered the letter. Henry could tell how much his son had grown to love Jenny. Slowly, he lowered his eyes and began to read the unbelievable treasure before him...

Dear Justin

When your dad and I married, the thing I wanted most was to have a close relationship with you. I never wanted to replace your beautiful mother but in some small way to be there for you.

My prayer was answered when you opened your heart to me. I thanked God daily for the wonderful gift of your friendship.

I will never forget the day you showed me how to fly a kite. It was so much fun running on the hillside in the prairie wind. The feeling of exhilaration that swept through me when the wind caught hold of the kite and swept it up into the clear blue sky will forever be burned into my memory. I loved how it wriggled in the air. It was like a fish swimming in the blue ocean of sky! I thought for sure the strong tug of the string in my hand would pull me up and carry me over the valley.

That was such a fun day! I loved your laugh and the joy in your eyes when I got the hang of it. You have such a good heart, Justin. In a way you're like your dad. You show your feelings, your warmth, your love and your care for others.

I am so happy I was able to bear a child for Henry and a sister for you. I saw how happy you were when you saw Hannah in the hospital. She needs a big

*brother like you and I know you will look after her
and care for your dad.*

*I love you with all my heart Justin, thank you for
coming into my life and making my life complete.*

Love,
Jenny (Mom)

Justin didn't take his eyes off his dad for a minute while he
read the letter over and over. He could tell his dad was savoring
each and every word just like he did. Henry's eyes reddened
and tears surfaced up just like Father Engelmann's eyes did
earlier that evening when he read the letter too. It was a God-
send to all three men. Justin began to relax as he studied his
father. He could tell it was reviving the love and joy of Jenny's
presence. He was glad he gave the letter to him. Tears were
falling on the page, revealing what was in Henry's heart.

Each time Henry re-read the letter, he kept whispering,
"Beautiful, just beautiful, sweetheart…"

Henry couldn't speak for the longest time and then said,
"That's a wonderful letter, Son. Thanks for sharing it with me.
She loved you very much."

For the first time in a long time, Henry's thoughts over his
loss changed to Justin. He knew Justin loved Jenny too but
never gave much thought to how he was feeling.

Henry stood and the two men hugged, warmed by the fire
in the fireplace.

Before Justin turned to head off to bed he said, "I shared the
letter with Grandpa Engelmann at the supper table when you
and Hannah went upstairs. Camilla told me that she planted
the letter in the roll top desk shortly after Mom died. I guess,
Mom told Camilla to put it there for me if something should
happen to her."

Henry's eyes brightened, "Did Camilla have a letter for
me too?"

Justin shrugged his shoulders. "I asked Camilla that too.
She said Mom had written a lot of letters to Hannah that she

will get at certain birthdays. I will get a letter when I finish high school and a last one when I get married. There are also a couple of letters for Camilla's boys. She thought there might be a letter for you someplace but wasn't sure. Jenny didn't give her one to give to you, just to us kids. I hope you come across it if there is one, like I did the other day."

Henry nodded, "Yeah, just maybe there might be a letter for me. If there is, when could she have possibly written it? She wouldn't write a going away letter to me unless she knew that she was going to die."

The two men stood there staring at each other for the longest time. Finally, Justin said good night to his dad and went off to bed upstairs.

HENRY COULDN'T GET his mind off the letter Jenny had left for Justin, He wondered if Jenny had left one for him and where it might be. Chances are she didn't, unless she had the sense that she might die and wanted to say a last farewell.

The only place Henry thought Jenny might leave a letter for him was in the chest of drawers in their room. That's where Henry left his memorabilia. The top drawer was to Henry as the treasure chest which his mother stored her memories and secrets in the closet were to her.

Would Jenny have written him a letter?

The thought nagged at him as he sat in the sun room. It was getting late and he hadn't been in the bedroom for months. The memories which the room brought back were too overwhelming. Yet, he had to know. He couldn't possibly wait until morning.

He recalled after Julean died how his heart ached for her. When the nurse looking after Julean called him months after Julean's death to say she had a letter for him, it was like receiving a gift from God. Oh, how the letter comforted him. It was the same when he discovered the letter Jenny left for him before moving to Ottawa. Those letters at those moments were pure gifts of love and joy. It was like a morsel of food to a man on the verge of starvation.

He just had to go to his room!

It was shortly before eleven, when Henry made his way quietly up the stairs. He opened the door to a dark room. The blinds were shut, not allowing any moonlight into the room. The light from the hallway, stealing into the room, helped him see that the bed in the room was neatly made. He flipped on the room light. Nothing had changed. The book he was reading the day he rushed Jenny to the hospital was still there. The book Jenny was reading on her side of the bed was still there as well.

Those were his last calm thoughts before he was bombarded with a flood of memories rushing at him with incredible speed. This is what he was so worried might happen. Thoughts of the many times they had made love and whispered words of affection for each other. Their sharing of so many memories and secrets...Henry knew he better check the top drawer and get out of there before his heart broke.

The chest of drawers was against the wall, immediately to the left, as he entered the room. He stepped in front of the chest and slowly opened the top drawer. He moved over to the side, to allow more light to come inside the drawer, from the ceiling fixture. At one time, Henry had hidden Julean's letter at the bottom of other items to keep it out of view from Jenny. One day she caught him reading it and said she didn't mind at all. After that, Henry left it right at the top. There were no secrets between them. From that day forward, Henry knew when Jenny had opened the drawer and read Julean's letter too. It brought back a memory of the game he and his mom played when she, too, went into the bottom drawer of his school desk to find out if he still had planned to go to Ottawa when he finished his grade twelve to search for Jenny.

Henry quickly saw Julean's tattered letter almost in the middle of the drawer right at the top. How many times over the months and years he had opened and closed that letter. He was about to recall the words that Julean left behind for him, that were so imbedded in his mind and heart, he could recite the letter without looking. But right next to it, was a fresh letter; white and new…his heart skipped a beat.

He knew it was from Jenny.

He removed the folded letter and couldn't wait to open it. It was a brief note…it disappointed him. He wished it were pages and pages. Without further hesitation he read:

May 2, 1994

My beloved Henry whom I love more than words can say.

I was going to write you a letter but I can't think of anything that would ever express my love for you any more than the beautiful letter Julean had written for you. When you are lonely for her and I read her letter, it expresses her and my feelings. It was almost as if she knew you would one day marry me. We shared you when we were alive and now we do in our passing. We both love you and we both wait for the day we will be together in spirit in heaven.

In the same way your wonderful children were Julean's gift to you, Hannah is my gift to you. She too, is a precious child and the Lord has wonderful plans for her as He does for all of us. Somehow, I feel, she will help you with your missionary work. Thank you for the wonderful years we had together. I will take those memories as well as your love with me into eternity. I love you with all my heart.

Jenny

Henry blinked and tears overflowed and dripped on the letter. It was near the bottom and no danger of the wetness smudging Jenny's precious words. He shook his head and thought how wonderful those two women were in his life. How blessed he was to share his life with two ladies who were willing to share him with each other. They seemed to have this understanding of the situation and accepted it. Here now was

Jenny not willing to outshine Julean or take away any of the precious memories he had for his first wife.

Henry shook his head in awe of it all. They both wanted him to move forward and yet, he just seemed to be stuck. It was such a beautiful evening. He wished he could just enjoy it and move on. He knew he wasn't living in the present and yet thoughts and forces surrounding him seemed to block his movement forward. He slowly folded the letter after reading it over several times. He closed the drawer and turned to the bed. He could see Jenny laying there, waiting for him. The card dangling from the ceiling was still there. Jenny had pinned it to the ceiling after the balloon gave out. She loved the idea and the card so much when she opened her eyes to see it.

So many beautiful memories.

Henry knew his heart would explode if he didn't leave. He flipped off the light, closed the door and quietly went downstairs.

EVEN THOUGH JUSTIN was emotionally drained and very tired, he knew his dad would come up to see if there was a letter from Jenny. He was quiet but not quiet enough for his son. When Justin heard his dad open the door to their room, he got up and went to the door to his room and listened. A few minutes later, he heard Henry open the top drawer. He too had done that many times when he wanted to read the letter from his mom as well.

When he heard his dad weeping, he knew there was a letter there for him from Jenny. Justin's heart soared wondering when would she have written it and how would she know when she was going to die? Just like his dad, Justin wondered if his dad had left the letter in the top drawer. His dad would be in the sunroom and wouldn't be able to hear if he went in there and checked it out. Justin opened the door to his room as quietly as he could and tiptoed to his parents' room. He was afraid to turn on the light and yet he had to. It was just too dark to see.

Justin opened the drawer and immediately saw the new letter laying right beside the one from his mother. He was going to take it to his room but thought he better not in case his dad came up again. The thought made him nervous. He prayed that his dad wouldn't find him there now.

He took out the letter and quickly read it. It touched his heart, too, but not like the one Jenny had written to him. And then he noticed something that explained when Jenny had written that letter to dad. The date at the top of the letter was that Sunday morning she came down the stairs and fell. It was the morning she was rushed to the hospital with the ambulance. She had written the letter before she came down. *She knew she was going to die.*

Justin folded the letter and placed it back exactly the way he found it and went back to his room.

He turned out the light and thought about the letter his dad received and the one he got and the evening. It was such a great party...it would have been perfect if his dad had stayed in their room and slept in their bed.

"I hope our family is happy again and Dad is healed of his heartache."

CHAPTER TWENTY-SEVEN

D URING THE DAYS which followed, it seemed as if Father's words, the joy of spring which Jenny so loved, Jenny's letters, the beauty of little Hannah, and the Pederson family had all begun to nudge out the depths of Henry's sorrow and begin to heal his heart. It was what both Jenny and Father said about putting God first and foremost in his life which began to put a foothold into the door which he had closed for months on end. The heavy depression and self-defeating thoughts seemed to be losing their stranglehold on his mourning and grieving. Although it was all still healing at the intellectual level, at least it was a start.

Hopefully it would travel to the heart.

It was on the third day of Henry's awakening that he found himself sitting under the canopy of his front door entrance to his home. The uplifting thoughts, which had begun to blossom in his mind, filling him with new hope, however, began to be overshadowed as he watched ominous dark clouds roll in overhead and cover the sun. Within moments, the agitated clouds came nearer and lower towards him and turned as dark as night. It was the moan of the prairie wind, through the tall evergreens, which finally drew him back to the groaning ache of his spirit. Unbelievably, the tenuous respite of tranquility easily gave way to a foreboding sense of oppression, which accompanied the smell of rain and growing humidity in the air. It pressed down on him like the heavy depression he was struggling with since Jenny's death; which was one year ago that day. Insidiously, his wholesome thoughts of the past several days seemed destined to return to the ones he had tried so desperately to escape from.

He turned to the angel statue for comfort by the front door greeting visitors to the farm. He had bought the angel for his dear wife as a gift for their 3rd year anniversary. It immediately brought back thoughts of Jenny that day when she first saw the statue. He was sitting exactly where he was now when she drove up and quickly spotted the angel. He visualized her now, stopping the car, getting out and slowly walking towards the new angel. He recalled how her eyes lit up and sparkled; the smile covering her face beamed like the sun. She touched the white marble statue and ran her delicate fingers over the smooth surface and she knew instinctively that it was sculpted by the same artist who created the Angel of Thanksgiving. The image of his beloved wife was so real in his mind, he felt her tears drop on his arm. It felt warm, sweet and loving. He ached to hold her and kiss her and gaze into her cerulean blue eyes like he did on that memorable day.

Henry's thoughts chased down one memory after the other of his beloved wife. He was hoping above all hope that the more memories he caught, the better he would feel. But it betrayed him, the more he thought of Jenny and the life they shared, the more he thought that life without her was futile, hopeless and ever so dark.

Tears of sorrow and loss inched their way once more into Henry's consciousness and the full reality that he would never see his love again swept through his body, reviving anger, rather than love, towards his Creator.

Why was she taken from him? It suddenly hit him full force that it was a year ago this day that Jenny had died. He recalled those last few moments in the hospital when he rushed to hold her hand…if he had gotten there perhaps a minute or two earlier, he was certain his love could have drawn her back. But, he was no match for her guardian angel. The welcoming sight of her life-long, beloved protector was there beckoning her to come…oh, Jenny, how will I make it through another year?

The light of his life was gone, just like the light from the sky was shut out. Henry knew that the sun was grieving just like he was. The sun was Jenny's friend and missed her radiance as well. That was why the clouds were so dark and heavily laden with moisture.

The sun was crying too!

It was hard for Henry to distinguish between his tears or the droplets of rain weeping from the sky. Regardless, they were all reminding him once again of his loss. The sound of each drop exploding on the driveway was like thunder crashing his hope for a bright future without her love. The joy of his life was gone forever. All of the reasoned words of Father Engelmann and the uplifting spirit of Jenny's letter and her love of spring, which he felt earlier that week, began to fade into the pattern the rain made on the driveway before him. Henry was always so easily controlled by the inner weather of his soul. His life had no anchor to keep him from the sea of self-pity.

Henry studied the space surrounding each droplet of water that plunked onto the pavement; spaces of wet and dry. He likened the spaces to his life which lacked direction and meaning and loss…such deep loss. Spaces in his heart which would never be filled again. He saw how each drop was a decision; millions upon millions of decisions like all the drops of rain before him filling the spaces, the dry spaces which had led him astray; decisions which led him to such sorrow, time and again.

If only he had been created an angel and had to choose just once to serve his Creator. He would fly in the heavens in perfect joy, living each day blissfully in the presence of God. But for him and all of mankind it was never over. Choices must be made again and again, like the countless raindrops before him. Each decision either leading him home or distracting him…like now.

The drops were quickening as the decisions of the past were unraveling with lightning speed, playing out before him now in his present moments; should he have made love to Jenny?

Should he have given in to the desires of his heart? Should he have discouraged her more from wanting the baby? Maybe they should have travelled more and realized they were too old for a child. Why? Why? Why? Why, didn't he do this or choose that… any choice would be better than the ones which led him here.

The droplets were no more, just like all the decisions of the past. It was over; what was done was done. The spaces had all been filled in and the concrete was now saturated with rain; saturated with decisions that had played into the destiny of his present moment. A destiny, which was known from the beginning of time, had played itself out. It was too late to change the decisions of the past just like it was impossible to change the rainfall before him. It was easy to see now the different choices he could have made…if he had chosen God to be first and foremost in his life, he would be saturated with His love and washed clean like the concrete before him. The more his spirit would be renewed and refreshed like the trees and green grass surrounding the driveway, instead of only seeing the quagmire of regret before him; all the decisions which led him to this place in time.

The heavy pouring rain thundering on the pavement was nothing compared to the thoughts pounding and crashing in Henry's mind. He ached and yearned for Jenny's touch, the taste of her lips and the fragrance of lilac…*not the smell of rain.*

CHAPTER TWENTY-EIGHT

W HEN FATHER ENGELMANN saw Henry the next morning, he no longer recognized him. He expected to see Henry full of life, joyful and praising God for the gift of another day. What happened? Just when there was hope, it had quickly vanished. His son had slipped away again, deeper than before into the abyss of sorrow.

"Henry, please come down for Mass in the morning."

There was no response. Henry gazed straight ahead into space as if he was in another world. It was plain to see the man's heart was too heavily laden with sorrow. He was once again an ally of self-pity, grief and ... death.

Father pleaded with Henry once more, "Come down to Mass tomorrow morning, please my Son, listen to me."

Finally, Henry nodded. It was almost imperceptible but he acknowledged his mentor. Softly, he whispered, "Yes, I will be there..."

Father shook his head. He needed help. He wasn't seeing the problem clearly. Perhaps an outside, objective opinion on the matter was needed. He didn't return to the Poustinia right away that morning. He decided to go into the city with Justin and visit his Superior for advice.

On the way into the city, Father Engelmann talked about the difficulty Henry was having. Father was always so relieved in his talks with the young man to see how mature and understanding he was of the situation. Perhaps it was because Justin was still hurting too that he was able to understand why his father was having so much difficulty in letting go of Jenny's passing. Even still, Henry had abdicated his responsibility to his family. They needed him, especially Justin.

"It is good of you to see me, John. I know how busy a schedule you have running a large diocese."

"I am never too busy for you, David. I have been meaning to come out to your prayer house for several months now. Something always comes up to prevent me from doing so. Perhaps, later this summer or early fall it may work out. Monsignor Antonio Giuseppe, who spoke with you two years ago, planned to come back to speak with you and Henry and his wife. However, I heard of Henry's loss. Jenny was such delightful lady. I still recall speaking with her after her miraculous healing."

"She was that and more, John. I believe Jenny led a saintly life and the circumstances surrounding her passing are miraculous. Perhaps Monsignor should be considering her as a candidate. She made many sacrifices during her life journey and even at the end, she gave up her life for the child within her womb. There are also extraordinary circumstances surrounding the birth of Hannah. The infant, like her mother, is a special child of God, John. But I digress from the purpose of my visit, perhaps another time, I shall go into the details of Jenny's remarkable life."

"Yes, maybe when the emissary comes to visit you, you can share your thoughts about Jenny and her child. I did hear of her funeral and how extraordinarily beautiful it was. I wanted to attend but was away at the time at a Bishop's Conference in Toronto. In the meantime, however, I shall look into this matter at once as well. Perhaps you can document some of the facts for me and send it in to my office.

"So, when do you expect the Monsignor to come?" Father wanted to know.

"They haven't said. Hopefully it will be this summer as they want to visit with you in the Poustinia."

Father Engelmann nodded. "Are they still questioning all the miracles which took place?"

"Yes, that and he wants to know more about you as well."

Father remained silent and studied his Superior.

The Archbishop, in turn, was cautious to say too much, lest his dear friend deny meeting with the Monsignor. The truth of the matter was, David was already being considered for possible beautification and Rome wanted to know more about this holy man they kept hearing about.

"I'll come right to the point of my visit, John. You have indirectly alluded to the purpose of my wanting to meet with you. It concerns Henry's wife, Jenny's death."

"Is there something out of the ordinary, David?"

"No, other than Henry has been in the process of grieving for his loved one for over a year now and is suffering from deep depression."

"Are you concerned about Henry's safety? I have met him on several occasions and he doesn't strike me as the type to consider taking his life if that is what you are getting at."

"Not exactly, John. His will to go on is at a very low ebb but I, too, am of the opinion he is stable enough and sufficiently in control, not to resort to such a measure. It's just that he seems to be stuck in the mourning process and has become an ally to Jenny's death. He sees no hope or reason to go on. When we speak, new thoughts of hope enter his mind and along with his own catharsis, he seems to improve. However, as soon as I leave, he quickly slips back and at times, into yet, a deeper depression."

"Has he sought medical assistance and medication for his condition, David?" The Archbishop wanted to know.

"No, he is adamant that he is in the process of grieving and will take as long as needed. He absolutely refuses to see a psychologist or psychiatrist."

"Well then, David, what else can be done until he is ready?"

Father paused and then continued, "My concern is that he is perhaps under the siege of evil forces. He hasn't gone to confession in some time nor received communion. He says it would do little good to go to confession knowing that his thoughts would soon return to what they were before."

The Archbishop nodded and said, "Yes, that is a possibility. In most cases it is more or less man's wounded spirit speaking and the heart eventually heals but other times it can mean there is more at hand. Christians of all denominations don't want to think of the devil prowling around the world seeking the ruin of souls, but it is very much a reality and one of the clearest teachings of the Bible. Satan never gains so many cohorts as when, in his shrewdness, he spreads the rumor that he is long since dead. It could very well be that Henry's mourning is compounded by evil forces. The mind is where the spiritual battle takes place. Thoughts of rebellion, anger and resentment towards God for taking one's loved one, is an argument which I have heard many times over the years."

Father nodded, "It seems to me, John, that is the case with Henry. He seems to be entrenched in such deep despair and is easy prey in the clutches of Satan. As you just said, the devil aggressively works on our mind. He knows if he can control our thoughts, he can control our lives. Henry has opened himself up to so many sorrowful thoughts that his feelings towards himself, life and God can easily come under attack when fueled by thoughts that fan the flame. Henry knows in his heart what he needs to do, but his mind wars against it."

"What you are describing to me, David, sounds like your assessment of the matter may be correct. I do not know Henry as well as you do but from my meetings with him in the past, he appears to be a strong family man, self-reliant, a great artist and faithful to his family and children."

"That is the point, John. He is more mature and responsible than he appears to be now. He is a man of faith and deeply committed to his family. Yet for months now, he has all but abandoned them. It is unlike Henry to mourn so excessively. His life seems directionless and his mourning is not only anger towards God but an expression of self-centered pity. I don't like it John. I believe his excessive dwelling on the death of his wife is opening the doors to the evil one. And yet, when I talk to him, he seems to be taking my reasoned thoughts into consideration and when I leave it's as if the doors to reason, hope and family are quickly shut and the home continues to remain as a funeral parlor."

His Grace reflected on what David had just said, then responded,

"I don't believe Henry is possessed but he certainly is under the influence of the evil one. Even in normal circumstances we are, but in instances like this, he is more susceptible to the enemy. Even when one sleeps, the evil one can mix weeds into the good soil of our mind, such that during our waking hours, if we are not vigilant, those same weeds, can have harmful effects on our thoughts, words and deeds.

"Yes, yes, the things we harbor in our hearts quickly expands and if the evil one is involved, our thoughts can easily be fueled with the spirit of anger, unforgiveness and bitterness, as we are witnessing.

"Hopefully John, I can help Henry to put on the whole armor of God to withstand the forces of evil. My goal for Henry as it is with all my sheep is to bring them safely home."

"Well, David, if evil forces are at play, they know they are no match for your power and authority over them in the name of Jesus. These forces may simply leave when you are there and return when you leave because Henry leaves the door wide open since his mind is such fertile soil for them to breed in."

Father nodded, "Yes, that could very well be."

"It sounds like you are on top of the situation as best as you are able under the circumstances. I will keep him in my prayers and if you wish for me to talk to him or assist you in any way, I am here for you and your dear friend. I cannot stress enough that you keep encouraging Henry to turn to God and receive Him in his heart. That is the best way to cast out and keep Satan and all the evil spirits from interfering with our lives. We should always remember the words of the apostle John (1 John 4:1-4) 'You are of God, little children, and have overcome (the evil spirits), because He who is in you is greater than he who is in the world.'"

Father nodded, "Yes John that is at the heart of the matter. Henry has too many idols in his life which keep Jesus from being at the center of his life. He maintains Jesus is but I know it is all an intellectual commitment. His faith is stuck in the mind and has yet to travel to the heart. That is why, I believe, he is so easily swayed and oscillates from the light to the darkness. He has no anchor. He has yet to realize, that until he has Jesus in the depths of his soul, he will never know true peace. At the present moment he is easy prey to the forces of this world gaining a strong foothold in his life. He seems to want misery more than comfort, anger more than peace, death more than life…"

The Archbishop nodded, "Yes, true faith is the key and helps us deal with life's storms. Henry's belief is like so many believers; they believe but their belief is a worldly belief, an intellectual belief. It is not yet a true, deep recognition of our self-centeredness, our sinful nature and our total need and dependence on God."

"Yes, yes, John, for all too many of us, our faith is shallow. It lacks the truth and reality of what Jesus has truly done for us and His great love for us. That is at the core of our belief. Jesus, our Lord and Savior, are all too often just words-worldly words, as you say, they are not godly words. Until we reach that point, understand it and believe it in our heart, then a true faith in Jesus Christ is born…true repentance is this realization and a true turning from our worldly values, beliefs and ways."

"If it is any consolation to you David, trials are a blessing. God allows us to go through the fire to purge away obstacles that keep us from coming to Him and the heavenly home He has prepared for us. I have been in God's school of life many times during my journey. The sooner one graduates, the sooner life gets better and we realize our great need for Him. All too often we focus on the trial and fail to look at what God is trying to teach us. I believe, one day, Henry will see that the suffering and sorrow he has undergone has been for a greater good that he is blinded to now. The Lord has allowed Henry to come to a point where his talents, abilities, wealth and all the gifts he has been blessed with cannot help him. Jenny's death and his excessive grieving has taken him to his knees. He sees he can no longer depend upon himself and his great dependence on God. Without this, David, he may never deepen his faith and place his Lord at the center of his life as you so ardently are praying will happen to your dear friend. One day, David, and I expect soon, the Holy Spirit will push out all that anxiety, fear, worry, and grieving and fill Henry with the indwelling spirit of Jesus. He is at the bottom and ripe for a healing. A miracle is just around the corner, David."

"Ah, yes," Father Engelmann nodded in agreement. "Yes, that is wise, John. Your wisdom has revealed my impatience and lack of trust in the Lord to do His work. Henry will see that his dear wife was not only created by God but given to him as a gift…a gift that he must let go of and return to its Maker. It is as you have said, one day Henry will give praise and thanks for this trial."

John nodded and just as Father was getting up to leave, the Archbishop asked, "It's been quite a while since you shared with me about the two tasks which your guardian angel assigned to you during your brief stint on the other side. I believe you mentioned the first had to do with the writing of the love story between Henry and Jenny. How are you coming along with that, David?"

David smiled. "I never thought I would see the day that I would author several books let alone six! It's turned out to be a series of books and surely one that is inspired. So many of the thoughts I put on paper, I know, are not from me; they are heaven sent. It is as Zachariah said at the time; he would assist me along with the Holy Spirit. At times, it seems the pen is moving across the page by an unseen hand."

"Remarkable, David. Six books is a huge undertaking. And so, that task is complete?"

"No, there is a seventh book which I am presently working on which will bring the story to the present. However, there is more to say. One cannot end such a love story this way. Surely Henry must find himself and return to the Lord as you have foreseen and I know the Lord has work for him to do. I cannot leave this earth until I know my son's heart has been restored."

John shook his head. Father was an amazing man who still did not reflect the age he was. If it were not for his long white hair and beard, he would look to be in his seventies. Imagine, writing six books and another in the works. From speaking with him, it was clear, David's mind was as sharp as a tack. His head was clear, alert and his rapid-fire, well-reasoned thoughts and memory recollection was incredible. When would he show signs of slowing down?

It was the second task that the Archbishop was really more interested in. He recalled that Father Engelmann told him it had to do with a vision of some future occurrence which the Lord allowed him to see and why it was that the Lord saw it best that he carry out that task. Father had no memory of it when he returned to earth and John wondered if Father now knew what it was.

The Archbishop uncrossed his legs and sat forward in his chair. He planted both feet squarely on the floor and leaned forward, asking, "David, what of the second task? Have you carried it out yet?"

Father tightened his lips. "Not yet, John. I know it has to do with Henry's depression somehow over the death of his wife. But exactly what it is that I should do or what is going to happen hasn't yet been revealed to me. I sense the entire matter will unfold as my present existence catches up to the future vision I saw when I was on the other side."

John sat back in his chair but wasn't relaxed. He was clearly disappointed that he still didn't know the full details of something that only a man dear to the Lord was capable of carrying out. At least he knew it had to do with his lifelong friend's bereavement. He only hoped to be alive to see that day.

John shook his head again in awe of it all and said, "Remarkable, David. Please keep me informed. I will keep you and Henry in my prayers."

CHAPTER TWENTY-NINE

FATHER PRAYED THAT Henry would be at Mass that morning. He seemed so dismal and forlorn yesterday. The words they shared seemed to lack any power to draw his son out or give him any hope. It was the Archbishop's opinion, too, that it was imperative for Henry to reconcile with the Lord so that he was open and receptive to healing.

Henry said he would be down but there still wasn't any sign of him. Father delayed celebrating the Holy Sacrament until mid-morning but his dear son was nowhere to be seen. Several times, Father walked out onto the deck and gazed up towards the house to see any kind of life but there was no sign of anyone there. He waved and shouted for Henry but still there wasn't any response. Father strained to see if Henry was sitting on the deck but the distance was too far and Father's eyesight wasn't the best any longer. For the most part all he could see was the underneath of the deck. He hoped that Henry would come to the railing. After a few minutes, he went back inside and decided to say Mass and consecrate an extra host for Henry. He would then make the trek up to the house once more.

He felt a deep concern for Henry.

The sun was hot and shone directly on Father as he trudged up the steep hill. The heat drained his energy and he had to stop several times. Even Coco welcomed the rest breaks and lay at her master's feet. Father didn't want to sit down as it was too hard to get up. He simply stopped and looked back at the beautiful valley, ablaze with life and color. He basked in the spiritual sustenance of God's creation and then went on.

The bottle of water he had brought along was gone and he was hot and thirsty. He could hardly wait to reach the bend in the road near the top where the trees began to line the road. He welcomed the shade and decided to take a breather. This time, he had no choice but to sit down, his weary legs needed a rest.

He sat on the grass by the side of road and prayed for his dear son. A cool breeze began to flow down the length of the valley and came up the road and refreshed the holy man and renewed his energy. After a while, he picked up his cross along with his staff and continued the rest of way.

As the day before, Father found Henry sitting on the deck staring straight ahead. He wasn't aware of Father until his teacher stood right next to him. Father was holding onto a large wooden cross that was on a thick cord hanging around his neck. His mentor also wore it yesterday and blessed Henry with it before he left.

It made Henry uncomfortable.

"Oh, Father, you didn't climb the hill again in this heat?" Henry gazed at his teacher; he looked exhausted. Guilt instantly swept through Henry. He suddenly remembered that he had promised Father that he would be down there for Mass that morning. He could see his mentor's care and concern for him and felt ashamed.

He offered Father a chair next to him and also some water which was sitting on the table. "Father, I'm so sorry for not coming down. I don't know what is wrong with me. For days, I was feeling so good and uplifted, thinking about Jenny and spring time. Your words were so inspiring and then, suddenly it's all gone. The storm yesterday brought my old thoughts out from under the cover of the clouds and seemed to sneak right back into my mind. Before I knew it, thoughts of hopelessness abounded and possessed my spirit."

Henry's last three words were what Father had feared. He was certain evil forces were at work in his mind. He could feel oppressive energy emanating from his son. Father sensed it for several days but it was always overshadowed by Henry's uplifting change of mood for the better. Perhaps the Archbishop was correct; the evil spirits left when he was there and returned as soon as he went back to the Poustinia. It could all be part of a powerful deception which Satan is so good at carrying out.

A heavy silence fell between the men. They were both unaware of the low, dark clouds moving in from the north much like they did yesterday. Just an hour ago the sky was clear, not a cloud in sight. But, on the prairies, the weather can change at the drop of a hat and it looked like it was about to bear out its reputation. The land was dry and in much need of rain. Spring came early and most of the crops had been seeded. All that was needed now was the moisture to get things started. Yesterday's rainfall helped.

The smile Father had earlier left his face much like the sunlight from the sky. The developing somber mood surrounding the men was compatible with the developing storm in the heavens. Father tried to remain neutral but it could not belie his deep concern. Henry felt life deeply and his emotions were clearly evident. He was an easy read.

Henry was in a dark place.

It pained Father Engelmann's eyes to look at his son's face. Deep circles were imbedded into his swollen, red eyes. How much had he wept? How much had he slept? There were other times Father had seen such anguish there. David recalled vividly how he had felt Henry's groaning spirit when his dad had run off or when Jenny left for Ottawa. It was also clearly evident when his father and mother and Julean passed away, but Henry had always found himself and came back.

Father was so hopeful this past while that Henry was finally snapping out of it but he had sunk deeper into his anguish than ever before. Clearly, the image before him portrayed a man in a state of complete and utter despair. Henry had outdone himself in how deep he could mourn over a loss. Father had to conclude that this time, Henry's grieving was different from all the pain and suffering he endured in the past.

Henry had lost his will to live.

Father was at a loss as to what to say. He prayed for guidance. Father opened his mouth several times then closed his mouth again and continued to pray some more to the Holy Spirit in silence. This happened several times until finally he pleaded with Henry to let go. All of the arguments and reasoned thoughts he had uttered in the preceding days tumbled out again like a broken record. Father thought he would use Jenny's life as an example once again as it seemed to get Henry's attention the most.

"The utter bareness you feel Henry, is the same that Jenny and Hannah in the Bible felt. Your pain and anguish is no different. The emptiness you feel is waiting to be filled up. Perhaps, you are beginning to see that nothing which you have considered of more value than God, at the end of day, has any real value or can sustain you. When you hold on to it and make it your God and source of happiness, you keep yourself separated from God as we talked about the other day. Look what Jenny and Hannah did. They made a covenant to give back their child to Him and see how they were blessed with a child and in every aspect of their lives. It is when you give back what God gives you, your life returns and more.

"Stewardship, Henry, is not just about giving of our money and time; it's also about giving of our talents, our children, abilities and our loved ones. He is the creator. Everything belongs to God. He gives it to us as we journey through life.

"But it's all a gift.

"Jenny was a gift to you, Henry, and you must let go and give her back to God. This is what I had to do with Anna. The more we hold on, the more we separate ourselves from the Father. Jenny did this constantly! She was always thanking God for everything and see how she was blessed in return? The sooner you do this, Henry, the sooner you will find peace and know what God has in store for your life.

"When we place our lives and trust in anything of this world above God, we always find, at the end of the day, it can never fill the void in our heart or spirit as you are realizing now. It all comes together, Henry, when we place God at the center of our lives. In Him, our life has meaning, stability and purpose.

"Nothing changes.

"Our life is built on a rock and not on sand which is quickly washed away in the wake of life's challenges and trials. He is always there, Henry. He always was and He always will be. He never changes. His love for us never changes. What did Paul say in his letter to the Romans in 8:38-39, 'For I am convinced that neither death nor life, neither angels nor demons, neither the present nor future, nor any powers, neither height nor depth, nor anything else in all creation, will be able to separate us from the love of God that is in Christ Jesus our Lord.'

"Once we understand this at a depth level, our life will change.

"Henry, seek first the kingdom of God and all these things shall be added unto you. Give Jenny back to God. It is futile to continue on your present path. Death is a part of life. Yes, it is a very sorrowful time but God is there to comfort you and help you to go on. Give her back to God and He will bless you and open the doors to new life which will sustain you beyond your imaginings."

Henry continued to stare straight ahead as if he hadn't heard a word Father had said. Usually, his mentor could tell where his protégé was at by his body language but he sat there mute, as if he were a statue. His tears had dried up. If he was weeping, it was all hidden deep inside his despairing son.

"Do you recall how excited you were when you accompanied Jenny to Calgary and she forgave Peter?" Father went on. "You were so proud of how Jenny was such an example of dying to herself in forgiving a man who violated her. You finally understood what Jesus meant in John, 12:24-25 when He said, 'I say to you, unless a grain of wheat falls into the ground and dies, it remains alone. But if it dies, it produces much grain. He who loves his life will lose it, and he who hates his life in this world will keep it for eternal life.'"

"A seed has to die in order to come to life and bear fruit. You watched Jenny do this time and again. She never held back. She always gave her 'all' to God and look how she and others were blessed by it. It is now you, Henry, who must die to self. *That is the mystery of life.*

"When we lose our life then we shall find it.

"So few individuals in life find out the true meaning of this mystery. You are now in a state of joining with your dear wife, Jenny, who was blessed to live such a life, naturally. Most of us have to hit the bottom to discover its meaning. When 'all' of the 'all' within us is gone, then we are ready to fill up with the real 'all'. That was the reason why everyone perceived your precious wife, including you, as an earthly angel.

"Henry, a new life awaits you. Come to your Creator and the Lord can then bless you with untold possibilities. In fact, you will never be able to outguess or outdo God. Jenny discovered the truth in Luke's scriptural passage, 6:38, *'Give, and it will be given to you. A good measure, pressed down, shaken together and running over, will be poured into your lap. For with the measure you use, it will be measured to you.'*

"I know how much you hurt, my son, how much pain is in your heart, but give her back to God; it is the only way to life and peace."

Father's energy was expended. He took a long drink of water and sat back to regain some strength. He wanted Henry to go to confession and rid himself of guilt and renew his mind; to keep the doors closed to any outside forces. He wanted to make sure his son was using this moment to make a fresh start.

After a long silence Father said, "Henry, you haven't been to confession in a long while, nor communion. I am here for you now if you wish to do so and I also brought a Host up for you from this morning's Mass."

Henry didn't answer for a long time and finally he spoke, "Yes, I can Father but it would be in vain. I know as soon as you leave me, I will slip back. I am helpless to let go. Your words are filled with such wisdom and I know how self-defeating the way I have been living but—"

"Express what weighs on your heart, let it all out and let's see if we can deal with it. Share your burden with me..."

Henry paused before answering and then dared to say to his mentor, "I am ashamed to say this, Father, but I still resent the child. As beautiful, special and blessed the child is, I still want Jenny back more than the infant. If it were not for the baby, Jenny would still be here. I am angry with Jenny for wanting the child and angry with God for giving the child and then taking Jenny. I know that death is a part of life but it all seems so unfair. I have led a good life and worked hard for the church, helped the poor and look what God has done or allowed in return. I know your wisdom can cut through my foolish thoughts and refute all I have done but I don't want to hear it. I just want things to be the way they were. I don't see any hope. I feel guilty and ashamed for my thoughts, but no matter how hard I try to overcome them with my or your reasoned thoughts, they just keep coming back. I know I should accept the beautiful child Jenny has given birth to. I know she would want me to go on. Justin and the rest of the family are waiting every day for me to start living again and yet this heaviness overwhelms me. In the end, how can God forgive a man who continues to do what he knows he shouldn't do?"

Father reflected on his hurting son's words. The comments which followed were not judgmental, but words for Henry to contemplate on; words that he prayed would prevent Henry from slipping deeper into an abyss that he may not be able to recover from.

"No sin is greater than God's mercy. Come to Him. Don't be like Judas who didn't believe that God could possibly forgive him and took his life. Don't do the same. Peter had betrayed Jesus three times, the night before his Master was crucified. Peter was terribly ashamed and yet he trusted in God's mercy and forgiveness and returned to his Lord. The prodigal son is another example of God's mercy. God loves us unconditionally and is always waiting for us just as we are with open arms. He will heal your broken heart but you have to give Him all the pieces.

"And, yes, you are a good man, Henry. You have done great good over the years which has been stored up in heaven as treasures that will someday be rewarded. However, it is important to realize that these good acts are performed out of our love for God. We cannot buy God or control Him by good works, lest any man should boast or have God do their bidding. God's love for all of us is the same. He gives us everything freely and we, in turn, are free to give back to Him…do you understand, Henry?"

Henry simply nodded. Father went on to try and alleviate Henry's guilt. "I know your heart, my son. I know you love the child dearly that Jenny bore for you. It is natural to hurt, to feel deep pain and anger that Jenny is gone. But what you haven't realized yet, is the gift Jenny gave you and left for you. What if Hannah had died as well or there was no Hannah? Then your life would have been totally empty with just memories, which is the case with so many marriages when one of the spouses passes on. Think on this my Son, Jenny was destined to go home, but she left you part of herself and a new life! A life which you both created! Henry, wake up and enjoy this incredibly marvelous gift. Open your eyes and see how blind you have been! See your beloved Jenny in Hannah! She is there, not in the memories of the past, but here in the now, the reality of your very existence!

"Come, let us give it all to God and start fresh at this moment. If we need to do it again in an hour, so be it. Healing takes a hundred little steps. Let's take the first one. We will take it to the Lord for as long as it takes. Little by little, it will heal your heart, my Son."

Father gazed at Henry, compassionately and said, "Please, let this be an expression of your confession to me and I will give you absolution."

Tears of sorrow surfaced to Henry's eyes and he simply nodded. In a low voice, he whispered, "I am sorry, Father… you have made me see how blind I am."

"Is there anything you wish to add?"

Henry shook his head.

Father gave Henry absolution and blessed him with the cross. "In the name of the Father and the Son and the Holy Spirit." He then took out the Pyx, a small container he had placed the consecrated Host in after Mass that morning. He removed the Host and offered it to Henry saying, "The Body of Christ."

Henry gazed at the Host for a long moment and softly whispered, "Amen."

He immediately began to weep.

Father felt the presence of the Holy Spirit. He prayed for Henry to be receptive to His grace and strength. A war was waging inside Henry's mind. He hoped his son would draw upon that power now, lest he slip back. Henry was in a space that only God could reach. No words came to Father Engelmann that would offer comfort or reason. His silence was safer... *prayer and more prayer were better.*

Henry sensed that Father was getting ready to go back to the Poustinia. He looked up at his teacher with pleading eyes. "Don't leave me Father, I am afraid of what I might do."

Henry's body began to tremble. It was no longer the Henry that Father knew who spoke. Father Engelmann felt his son's words like sharp jabs to his heart and quickly sent prayer for guidance and help to the Holy Spirit. So much fear and suffering were in Henry's gaze, it overwhelmed the holy man. Father fell to his knees and reached out for Henry's hands resting on his lap. He tried to transmit his love and support to his son to calm his shaking body.

"I am here, Henry. Together, we will overcome your sorrow. I can feel it spread throughout my being. I can understand how overwhelming this is for you but together, we will share it and work through it...together we can survive."

Chapter Thirty

AN HOUR PASSED as Father continued to pray on his knees for Henry. He knew the fulfillment of his second mission was at hand. He hoped Henry was open enough to allow the Holy Spirit to flow through him, to heal the depths of his despair and pull him back to life.

The storm which had threatened the prairies earlier that day never materialized. At most, there were a few distant thunder claps and lightning streaks between the clouds and nothing more. The wind, however had broken a branch off the large elm tree at the far end of the deck, blowing it their way. Other than that, the clouds travelled south, leaving behind a clear prairie sky and scorching heat. It was good that they were in the shade on the east side of the house.

Father rested his head on his hands, which were still holding Henry's. Father just continued to pray, at times in tongues and at times, in words which Henry could understand.

It calmed Henry's spirit.

Night approached and the twinkling stars and solitude of the evening offered some relief from the heat and tranquility for both men but only for brief moments until both fell asleep, exhausted. Henry sat slouched in his chair and Father slid to Henry's feet beside Coco.

Neither of the men heard the phone ring several times. Jeremy and Camilla wanted to come out with the boys and Hannah but Justin suggested that this wouldn't be a good night since Father and Henry were sleeping and seemed over-tired. They decided it was best to leave them alone.

Before Justin went to sleep, he went to check on his dad and Father only to find that they were still asleep on the deck. Coco raised her head and was torn to stay or come to the young man. Coco chose to stay.

Justin went back to the kitchen and got some food and water for Coco. He knew the dog wouldn't leave her master. He set the food and drink next to Coco and she stood and ate. Justin shook his dad several times and offered to bring out some food, but he declined. The darkness could not hide Henry's heart from his son. His eyes were full of tears and in the moonlight, glittered with fear and hopelessness. The few words he uttered were hoarse and filled with pain. Justin's heart went out to his dad; he began to tremble. Father was so exhausted physically and emotionally by the day's happenings; he slept through all the commotion.

Justin went in, returned with blankets, and placed one on his dad's shoulders and the other on Father. The air was still warm from the heat of the day but by mid-night the temperature would cool considerably. Justin hoped they would soon get up and go to bed. Henry held that same thought especially to get Father to a bed but Henry was so drained by his self-inflicted mental torment; he was quickly overtaken by sleep.

BOTH HENRY AND Father were awakened by the dawning of a new day. They couldn't believe that they had fallen asleep on the deck. The brisk morning was cool to their skin but the light of the glorious sun rising above the hills soon began to warm their spirits.

Every bone in Father Engelmann's body pained as he slowly rose. Coco's nose kept constant touch against Father's legs as if trying to help her beloved master stand. Father held his hand slightly on the dog's back for support. He stood before Henry and gazed into his son's lack-luster eyes.

Father left Henry's side and went into the house. When he returned, he was carrying a towel and basin of water. As soon as Henry saw him, he knew what Father was planning to do, "Oh, no, Father...no, please, don't, I am shamed enough."

"I come not to shame you, Henry, but to lift you back into the stream of life. We are here to serve; you must humble yourself to be a servant to all. You must take up your cross and follow Him. God has created you to do Him some definite service. He has prepared some work for you which He has not assigned to another. Soon you will know your mission."

With that Father knelt down, washed Henry's feet and kissed them. While he was doing so, Henry wept deeply. It made him think of the Scripture, John 12:24, "...Unless a grain of wheat falls into the earth and dies, it remains alone; but if it dies, it bears much fruit."

What fruit had he borne this past year?

Father's act of humility took Henry's mind off himself. The fear seemed to have subsided...his senses had returned but not sufficient to overcome his lingering despair of the day before. Father felt Henry slipping back again. Within seconds, Henry's eyes flashed with anguish; his voice was dry and hoarse. Father expected to hear a loud piercing cry or outburst of anger but the sound was so faint it was barely audible.

"Why? Why Father Engelmann? For what purpose does God take a mother from a child, a wife from a husband...why?"

Father stood in front of Henry and spoke softly and gently to his hurting son. "My words and thoughts have entered your ears, Henry. It is my prayer that they will travel inside of you if not today, then in the days which follow until they reach your heart. I've spoken all that the Lord has asked me, and now the rest is up to Him. Prayer, prayer and more prayer is all I can do for you my Son."

Henry could see the love and compassion in his lifelong friend. Father's smile was always so radiant because his thoughts were always filled with God. For a moment there, he saw Jenny; they were so much alike. It gave Henry comfort and yet there was something in the holy man's gaze that was similar to the look in Jenny's eyes just before her passing. The aura that Henry had seen surround Father Engelmann for as long as he could remember seemed to be growing brighter the last few days just like it did for Jenny.

An unknown premonition sent a chill throughout Henry's body.

Tears blurred Father's image of his broken son. He looked compassionately into Henry's eyes and said, "Come unto me, all ye that labour and are heavy laden, and I will give you rest. Take my yoke upon you, and learn of me; for I am meek and lowly in the heart: and ye shall find rest unto your soul.

"Come down for Mass, my Son, God is waiting for you."

A spiritual energy travelled the length of the gaze they shared. Henry got up and in the next moment, the two men warmly hugged one another. It was plain that his words of wisdom and understanding had failed to reach his hurting son. Henry was filled with fear for the future without his beloved and he lacked faith and trust in God to turn it all into good. Henry was so filled with hurt and anger, he resisted the work of the Holy Spirit within him and was more open to harmful forces. The very power and strength he needed, he fought and rebelled against. Father sensed what was going on inside. Henry believed in God at an intellectual level but a belief in the mind is not sufficient; it must touch the heart.

That is where faith is born.

Father noticed the branch which had broken off the tree and blown their way on the deck by the short-lived storm yesterday. How quickly the leaves began to shrivel up overnight and look dead. It reminded him of the Scripture, "I am the vine and you are the branches..." When we fall away from the vine we too die and shrivel up. The flow of living waters is impeded and stops. Father could see his dearly beloved Henry was broken and could feel his life shrivel before him. The source of life was gone and he was dying.

As a last effort to liberate his son, it came to Father to lay hands on Henry for the power of the Holy Spirit to be released. Without further thought, Father reached out both hands and laid them on Henry's head. He slightly bowed and began to pray that Henry be filled now. Father Engelmann's plea was so deep and strong that the prayers, which erupted from the holy man, groaned. As he prayed in tongues, Henry began to weep and shake. Perhaps it was a sign that the depression was leaving but Henry lifted his hands and grasped Father's wrists with a mighty force releasing the hold that Father Engelmann had on his head and cried, "Enough, Father. Enough, it is no use, my spirit resists too much…"

Father staggered back. He knew the force within his son did not belong to Henry's spirit. He could see in Henry's eyes, a spiritual battle for his very soul was at hand. This would require measures beyond what the holy man was able to offer. Father simply nodded, patted Henry's slumped shoulders, turned and walked slowly away down the deck.

Henry's eyes followed his mentor, teacher and friend as he trudged steadily along. Coco's nose touched Father's knee with each step he took. What a loyal, comforting companion the dog turned out to be for Father. The sight gave a momentary respite for Henry.

At the end of the deck, just before he disappeared around the corner of the house which led to the road leading down to the valley, Father turned and waved. He smiled once more at Henry and personalized the Scripture, Ezekiel 36:26 to offer hope to his lost son:

"Today, Henry, the Lord will give you a new heart, and a new spirit, He will put within you. And He will remove the heart of stone from your flesh and give you a heart of flesh."

Chapter Thirty-One

After Father Left, Henry plunged with a vengeance even deeper into his despair. It was plain that a battle was waging for his soul. Deep within, Henry knew Father Engelmann was right, yet, he couldn't let go. His thoughts confused him. He was bound by forces he didn't understand and completely unable to break free of them. He felt repulsion towards himself, for his actions towards his beloved friend. That was the first time he showed such utter disrespect for Father. He felt ashamed, frustrated and so powerless to break the chains which held him so captive. So many conflicting thoughts swarmed about in his head. It was as if a beehive had burst within his mind, setting hundreds of angry bees in all directions. He felt sting after sting with each self-defeating thought.

Somehow, he reasoned that by tormenting himself with the loss of his dearly beloved, he was punishing God by not accepting His will. To let go would be to accept what God had allowed. No! He must let God know how deeply He was hurting him. Yes, Henry would make God feel guilty and sorry for him. He knew God wanted him to come to Him and by refusing, it hurt God's heart.

Henry wanted to punish God, too.

A heavy cloud weighed on his broken heart; he felt internally oppressed. He couldn't keep his troubled mind on the Lord.

He began to rely on his own understanding while his faith and trust faded as quickly, as the mist that covered the valley floor.

Just how long should he hold onto his anger against the Lord until it was enough? He didn't know. All he knew was that he had to punish himself for his thoughts and indirectly keep hurting God as well for being the cause of it all.

Rather than learn from Father's act of humility, it made Henry angrier at God. If Jenny had lived, he wouldn't be in this situation and Father wouldn't have had to be so concerned about him. Father's acts were twisted in his mind as shameful and made him feel more guilt.

With each destructive thought, Henry opened the door to the forces of evil, allowing them to feed and expand in his agitated mind. He could no longer sit. Henry got up and looked down into the valley. The rising sun was burning off a low mist which covered the pond and parts of the road. He wondered what it would be like to see Father walk in and out of the cloud and if it would confuse the old man. He looked for his teacher but he was still nowhere in sight. Twinges of guilt stabbed at him for not driving his friend back to the prayer house. He shook his head in shame.

FATHER PRAYED FIERCELY for his son as he left the farmhouse and began his long walk back down to the Poustinia. He knew Henry was in the clutches of evil spirits so Father was preparing himself to battle for his son's soul. This would be the last time he could come up to the house. His body was too weak and frail from days of fasting to make that journey again. Even Coco sensed Father's lassitude and for the first time moved her nose away from her master's knees to prevent him from falling over her.

Though the trek was downhill, it seemed to Father like he was carrying a heavy cross. His deep concern for his son weighed like a huge stone on his heart.

Henry was imprisoned.

He had opened the door to darkness and had shut out the light. Father desperately wanted to free his son in the Lord before his remaining days on earth came to a close. He cried out to St. Michael the Archangel to defend him and Henry in battle. "Be our defense against the wickedness and snares of the devil. May God rebuke him, I humbly pray, and do thou, O Prince of the heavenly hosts, by the power of God, thrust into hell Satan, and all the evil spirits, who prowl about the world, seeking the ruin of souls."

Father Engelmann said the prayer so powerfully; a rush of adrenalin swept through him and revived his spirit. He could feel the warmth of Zachariah's hand on his shoulder gently leading him on.

THOUGHTS OF HIS mentor's words of hope drifted into Henry's awareness like a healing balm. He could feel his teacher's love ascending in the air like rising incense trying to wedge its way into his despairing heart. Henry struggled to accept Father's light, he felt it radiating up to him.

It was growing brighter.

Suddenly, Father appeared from around the side of the hill. He had made his way down the road to the valley bottom. At first, Henry didn't see Coco hidden in Father's shadow, just like his guardian angel would be. However, they would both soon disappear into the mist at the valley bottom. The fog was denser in some areas, more-so than others. It appeared as if Father was walking into another world. The aura surrounding the holy man was so glowing, it seemed to burn off the mist more than the rising sun!

No sooner had Father turned onto the bridge crossing the stream, the mist vanished and the morning light struck Coco, her nose still brushing Father's knee with every step. It should be him next to Father, being led back to God. He envied Coco and how near she had grown to her new master; so obedient, so accepting, so loving…It was all so laid out before him what he needed to do…what was holding him back?

How would he ever rise above his sorrow and return to the light?

Just before the prayer house, a thick mist, like a heavy cloud, hovered over the valley floor. Father and Coco entered the foggy air and disappeared. Henry would not be able to see when they got to the prayer house as only the roof of the Poustinia was visible.

With Father no longer in sight, the seed of hope his mentor had planted began to vanish. The holy scene before him blurred as tears surfaced once again and thoughts of sorrow flooded back into his tormented mind. Almost instantly, despair cast out all hope of a future without Jenny.

Henry thrust his arms high up toward the prairie blue sky and uttered a heart wrenching cry as if summoning God to appear.

"Why, Lord? Why...?"

His legs weakened and he fell back into the chair and stared hopelessly into the dawning of another day.

WHEN FATHER RETURNED to the prayer house, he could just make out one of the chairs on the deck through the thick fog. It was a welcoming sight. He climbed the step onto the deck and made his way to the chair and collapsed into it. Father was exhausted. It was not the downhill trek which drained him, it was Henry's burden. He tried to take on his son's sorrow to give him relief and rest when he should have given it all to the Lord. His yoke is easy and burden light. Father shook his head at his impatience to wait on the Lord.

Although his prayers seemed unanswered, he knew God had listened. Father knew he had to trust in his Lord and not on his understanding lest his faith and life fall apart. He had prayed, offered Masses, fasted, counseled and prayed over his son for the release of evil spirits but so far nothing seemed to help draw Henry back to life.

What else was he to do?

David took a deep breath and let it out slowly. The ethereal atmosphere began to soothe his troubled spirit. It was like he was resting in a cloud. Coco licked his dangling hand from the arm rest of the chair before lying down at her master's feet. It was quiet, still and calm save the rippling sound of the creek flowing steadily over the beaver dam.

A thought floated into his mind. He recalled the time he had felt a similar weariness, when Jenny lay dying in palliative care. After a powerful prayer session in the chapel, with his prayer warriors requesting God to heal Jenny, so she may be united with Henry, he went to the care home sunroom where he further pleaded with the Lord to take his life, in exchange for Jenny. He began by reading the 23rd Psalm and before he finished, his spirit had left him at that time. The words came to him once again, now...

"The Lord is my shepherd; I shall not want.

"He maketh me to lie down in green pastures: He leadeth me beside the still waters.

"He restoreth my soul: He leadeth me in the paths of righteousness for his name's sake.

"Yea, though I walk through the valley of the shadow of death, I will fear no evil: for Thou art with me; Thy rod and Thy staff they comfort me.

"Thou preparest a table before me in the presence of mine enemies: Thou anointest my head with oil; my cup runneth over.

"Surely goodness and mercy shall follow me all the days of my life: and I will dwell in the house of the Lord forever.

THE BEAUTIFUL PRAYER soothed Father's spirit along with the scene unfolding before him. The mist was slowly burning off in the rising sun, revealing what it had hidden. Out of seemingly nothing emerged the image of water and translucent trees in the distance. The lingering fog over the water softened the reflection of the hills in the mirrored surface of the pond. It gave him a feeling of mystery, space and peace. It brought him into the present moment which further quieted his mind and made it receptive to God's whisperings to His host of angels.

Father could hear the soft flutter of unseen wings.

As he watched the morning sun continue to burn off thousands and thousands of moisture diamonds glistening in the air, the thought occurred to him that the reason why the Lord hadn't taken his life for Jenny when she was terminally ill was because that offering was needed at another time. Perhaps, this was the main reason for his return. It had always grieved the holy man as to why his life wasn't taken at that time. Could it be possible that the Lord would give him the honor of laying his life down for his dear, son!?

Instantly, the words of John 15:12-13, came to his mind:

"This is My commandment, that you love one another as I have loved you. Greater love has no one than this, than to lay down one's life for his friends."

David's eyes brightened as a part of the vision into the future which he saw when on the other side was coming into his present awareness. It seemed to confirm that he would be given the opportunity to exemplify that same kind of sacrificial giving toward another that his Master had shown on the cross.

Rejoicing filled his heart! A great inner joy began to sweep through Father Engelmann as he rose and made his way into the Poustinia. Little did David know, however that God had much more planned for His faithful servant. Father would be blessed and honored with the highest gift given to man. Soon, Father's joy in serving his Lord on this earth would find complete fulfillment.

The final hour of his second mission that he was assigned at the doorstep to heaven had begun.

Chapter Thirty-Two

F ATHER'S LIFE WAS now purpose driven as he entered the
Poustinia. After taking a shower, he put on his black
trousers, black shirt and white collar. He loved the collar, so
proud to let the world know that he was the Lord's shepherd,
charged with looking after His flock. To Father, the collar
was like a wedding ring; his marriage to Christ and to the
Church. He belonged to Christ and gave full control of his
life over to Him.

David turned around in the small bedroom and pulled out
the chair from the desk next to the bed and sat down. He gazed
out the picture window at the creek that meandered between
the hills, which fed the large pond in front of the Poustinia.
He loved this view of the valley. Many times, he envisioned
it as the Sea of Galilee and Jesus on the hillside teaching the
crowds who came to Him. What a blessing the prayer house
had been for him. It was the perfect place for him to carry out
his first mission; to write a love story.

It would also be the perfect place for him to complete his
second mission.

On the far-right corner of the desk sat a pile of manuscripts.
He never dreamed that the story about Henry and Jenny's lives
would fill up six books and even more so, that he would be the
author of them. He reached over and pulled the stack in front
of him and examined each one in turn. The first book was

Pewter Angels; how it all got started. How Henry and Jenny met in his store and it was love at first sight. Father could still recall the aura of light that surrounded the two young lovebirds as their guardian angels sent a spiritual energy along the gaze they shared joining their very souls. But alas, they got separated and an adventure began to re-unite them, the likes of which we have never seen. Then in book two, *Another Angel of Love,* Julean came along and swept Henry off his feet. Jenny, too, met another but her marriage wasn't as fortunate as Henry's, yet Jenny survived. Despite their marriages, the flames in Jenny and Henry's hearts for one another never went out. Book three, *Angel of Thanksgiving* shows Jenny's grateful heart and commitment to be thankful in all things, even her failed marriage. Henry, too, suffered a great loss when his dear wife, Julean, passed on. It was incredible in book four, *The Angelic Occurrence,* how Jenny moved back to Regina and the house she had lived in was purchased by Henry when she got terminally ill! It was amazing how their guardian angels helped to bring them back together in book five. It was truly *Angel Promises Fulfilled.*

And finally, there was book six, which he still hadn't given a title to. It described Henry and Jenny's first years of marriage together and Jenny's prayer to give Henry a child. It gave an accounting of all the amazing events leading up to Jenny's pregnancy and the resulting complications. By the time Father had written the story up to that point however, the manuscript had grown too large. It was already another book unto itself. He had already started yet another and final book which would give some kind of satisfactory ending to this amazing epic saga!

Father shook his head in disbelief. He acknowledged that he could never have written such a detailed account of their lives, in the first five books, had he not died and was allowed to see all that transpired in Henry and Jenny's lives. During those precious moments, Zachariah made it possible for him to see all the events and circumstances which conspired to keep them apart and bring them back together again.

Once again, David shook his head as he pushed the pile of six manuscripts back to the corner of the desk. What an assignment that was from Zachariah and it was not over. There was still the final book to be finished. "Ah, yes, yes, of course, only the Lord would have arranged the circumstances so this epic story would require seven books." Father smiled as he thought about it. "Seven is a favorite number with the Lord and accounts for many situations and circumstances throughout the history of man. The first of course being the creation of the world in seven days. The Lord was pleased then and He is pleased now. Yes, seven novels it is; the perfect and most complete way to conclude this wonderful journey."

Father pulled the seventh manuscript he had been working on from the left corner of his desk and opened it to where he had last left off. David tried to give an accurate accounting of all that had transpired since that eventful day when Jenny, Henry and he had died and were all miraculously brought back to the land of the living. So, everything which Father had written since then was based upon what he had personally witnessed of their lives until two days ago when he last wrote in the final and seventh manuscript. It wasn't as clear as the memory of events Zachariah allowed him to see on the other side but David did his best to make daily notes of their lives so he wouldn't forget any important detail of the closing part of this epic story.

Father opened the manuscript and quickly scanned what he had written so far. Jenny was in a coma and Henry was struggling with the decision whether or not to abort the child within Jenny's womb to save his dear wife's life. Due to God's Divine Providence, Henry's father-in-law came along and guided his troubled son-in-law to make the decision to deliver the baby. Hannah was born but damage to Jenny's various organs had taken its toll, especially on her angelic heart causing her heart to give out. Henry was devastated and went into a deep depression and so far, all attempts to bring Henry back from the darkness he entered have failed.

Father picked up a pen and wrote for over a half hour on book seven to bring the story to its final hour. His first mission was now completed up to this moment in time.

Who would finish book seven and bring the story to a close?

The readers of this captivating story would want to know what happened to all the characters, especially Henry and Jenny. They would be heartbroken to learn of Jenny's death. The readers, like Henry, would have to accept the passing of their dear heroine, but the full story must be told...

Father took out a fresh sheet of paper from the top drawer of the desk, and put his pen to the paper once more:

Saturday. May, 14, 1994,

My dear Henry,
Someday soon, the Lord will take me home and you will be left to deal with the matter of this story. What an ....
..
..
....
Someday, we will all be together again in heaven with the angels and saints giving honor and praise to our Lord.
With deep love and affection, yours in Christ,
David Engelmann.

A few tears fell on the page. He laid the pen down on the desk and then brushed a tear away which was sliding down his cheek. He placed the letter on top of the last book so Henry would notice it. He got up and as he turned towards the closet, he noticed the painting on the opposite wall. It was the poignant scene Henry had painted when Anna died. It not only captured Anna's passing but even more so, the deep love which they shared. Father loved the way Henry had also painted in the cross, hanging above the head of their bed, depicting Jesus, who was at the center of their lives and marriage. Father was so happy when Henry brought the painting and the cross from his bedroom in the care home last fall, since he was now spending most of his time at the Poustinia. Father loved the scene and recalled so many memories of his dear Anna. Tears surfaced in his eyes...

"Soon I will be home, Anna," Father whispered.

He went to the closet and brought out his liturgical vestments that he would wear for the celebration of what might be his last Mass.

Father loved the ritual of getting ready for the Holy Sacrament. On the bed he laid out the amice, alb, cincture, stole and chasuble in the order they would be worn. All garments were white.

As David picked up the amice, a rectangular piece of white linen with two long cloth ribbons, he said, "Make me white, O Lord, and purify my heart so that being made white in the Blood of the Lamb, I may deserve an eternal reward."

He placed the cloth around his neck, covering the clerical collar and tied it by crisscrossing the ribbons in his front, bringing them around the back, around the waist and tying them in a bow.

The alb was next. Father picked up the long, white garment and placed the opening over his head. It fell from his shoulders to his ankles. He slid his arms into the long sleeves extending to the wrists. His daily clothes were now completely covered. A rush of excitement swept through Father as he prepared to offer the Mass with purity of body and soul. When he put on this garment, it always reminded him of his baptism when his parents clothed him in white, to signify his freedom from sin, purity of new life and part of the Christian community.

Father picked up the cincture and tied the long, thick cord with tassels at the end, around his waist to secure the alb. He slid the cord slightly to the left, so the tassels hung to the side and he said, "Gird me, O Lord, with the cincture of purity and extinguish in my heart, the fire of all desire, so that the virtue of self-restraint and chastity is always abiding in my heart."

David took the stole off the bed, kissed the long, narrow, white cloth and placed it around his neck like a scarf. He crisscrossed the ends of the stole across his chest to symbolize the cross and tucked the ends in the cincture to keep it in place. Each time Father wore the stole, it reminded him of his authority and dignity as a priest, but also of his duty to preach the Word of God with courage and conviction. He prayed now for the Holy Spirit to convict him of these virtues so that in all his words, thoughts and deeds he would reflect Christ.

Finally, Father picked up the chasuble, the outer garment worn over the alb and stole. The aura of white surrounding the holy priest was so brilliant it was as if the sun had entered the room. Father gazed upwards and said, "Over all these virtues put on love. Let the charity of Christ forever dwell within me. It is love which binds everything together and makes them perfect."

Father Engelmann was ready. The words of Isaiah 1:18 came to him, "'Come now, let us reason together,' says the Lord: 'though your sins are like scarlet, they shall be as white as snow; though they are red like crimson, they shall become like wool.'"

He brought his hands together in prayer in front of his chest and crossed his thumbs and slowly made his way to the living room which housed the small chapel. At the doorway, he stopped and gazed at the altar as he had done so many times before.

It was all set up for what might be his last celebration. Everything was prepared before he took his shower. He had lit the two candles on each side of the altar, set out the hosts on the paten as well as the chalice, ciborium, cruets containing wine and water, bowl of water and linen cloths.

Slowly, he walked to the altar. David always maintained no one could walk into God's holiness on hurried feet. At the altar, he stopped, kissed it and began.

Chapter Thirty-Three

"In the name of the Father, and the Son and the Holy Spirit. Oh Lord, I offer this Mass for Henry and his family. Grant them peace and healing of heart, mind and soul."

Father was no longer concerned about Henry; a confidence was building within him. Just going through the ritual of getting dressed to celebrate Mass always excited him.

David knew that his second mission had to do with helping Henry recover from his loss of Jenny and free him of his despair but there was more…something else awaited the holy man. He had seen it in the vision he was granted when on the other side and knew it was just a matter of time that what he had seen in the future would come into his present moment.

Father had a strong premonition that the moment of revelation was very near.

To Father, the Holy Mass was like going to Calvary. Each time he said the Mass, the sacrifice of Jesus' crucifixion was renewed at the altar. Imagine, the body and blood of Jesus hidden under the appearances of bread and wine; really present as God and Man sacrificing himself for us on the altar just as He sacrificed Himself on the cross!

The Holy Eucharist was the highlight of Father Engelmann's priesthood. It was the central act of his faith which he tried to instill into his parishioners. Without faith, his sheep would miss so much. All they would see is bread and wine being offered and nothing more. With faith, they would see the reenactment of Christ's sacrifice for them! And along with the offering of that sacrifice, they could bring their own petitions to God as David had planned to do this morning. Father Engelmann felt a rush of excitement sweep through his being as he thought of his offering. Soon, his beloved son would be free from his prison. Uplifted with that thought, Father continued with the Mass filled with hope, love and immense gratitude!

Today, more than any other, Father could hardly wait to get to the moment of consecration when the bread and wine are changed into the body and blood of Jesus Christ, yet he wanted to savor this Mass; not rush it.

When he came to the readings, David decided to sit in one of the chairs by the window. His legs were still weary from the downhill trek. He picked up the lectionary, which included a three-year cycle for the weekday Mass readings and sat in his usual wicker chair, by the window. He pinched the red tassel between his fingers and flipped open the book to the readings of that day. After reading them very slowly, he made the sign of the cross and read the Gospel. He closed the holy book and quietly meditated upon the teachings of Jesus. He knew them so thoroughly; it was as if he had swallowed the Word and it had become so much a part of him. He could recite the Bible without opening it! It was no longer required to instruct him to follow the will of his Lord, as he had given his will and entire life over to Jesus years ago.

He had become like the Word!

David gazed out the patio doors at the still pond before him. Such restful repose he derived from that setting. It brought back to mind the 23rd Psalm and slowly he said it again. *"The Lord is my shepherd; there is nothing I shall want. Fresh and green are the pastures where He gives me repose, near restful waters He leads me…"* Tears of joy slid down his cheeks as he whispered,

"This is the day the Lord hath made, I shall be glad and rejoice in it." And then he added again, "Soon, I will be home, Anna."

He stood up and made his way back to the altar. He turned some of the pages in the Missal resting on the altar lectern to the Nicene Creed. He gazed up at the large cross above the altar and said his profession of faith:

"I believe in one God, the Father Almighty, Maker of heaven and earth, and of all things visible and invisible. And in one Lord Jesus Christ, the only-begotten Son of God. Born of the Father before all ages. God of God. Begotten not made; of one being with the Father; by Whom all things were made. Who for us men, and for our salvation, came down from heaven. And was made Flesh by the Holy Spirit of the Virgin Mary; And was made Man. He was also crucified for us, suffered under Pontius Pilate and was buried. And on the third day He rose again, according to the Scriptures. And ascending into heaven, He sits at the right hand of the Father. And He shall come again in glory to judge the living and the dead; and of His kingdom there shall be no end. And I believe in the Holy Spirit, Lord and Giver of life, who proceeds from the Father and the Son. Who together with the Father and the Son is no less adored, and glorified; Who spoke by the prophets. And I believe in the One, Holy, Catholic and Apostolic Church. I confess one Baptism for the remission of sins. And I look for the resurrection of the dead. And the life of the world to come, Amen."

David turned back to the Missal, opened it and began the Offertory.

Father had forty-one hosts on the paten and the wine was already poured in the chalice. These are the gifts which are brought to the altar. These small gifts at this point have practically no value and represent us along with any personal offerings we wish to further make.

Father took the jar filled with water and carefully spilt a few drops into the chalice with the wine; this too, represents us as we intermingle with the wine which will soon be turned into the blood of Jesus.

After offering the bread and wine, Father Engelmann gazed up at Henry and invited him to make his personal offering.

Even though Henry was not there in the chapel, Father believed that his adopted son would somehow be present to make the right offering along with the sacrifice of Jesus Christ.

Father prayed, "…so that our sacrifice, may be acceptable to God the Father Almighty." The instant Father made this offering, the vision he was allowed to see when he was on the other side, began to further unfold. He had already seen part of the vision when Jenny died and Henry's heart was broken. He knew that part of the reason he came back was to help his beloved son recover from his loss.

But more of the vision was still unfolding.

He had made a covenant with the Lord that when he returned to the land of the living, that at his last Mass in the Poustinia, the Lord would honor Father by accepting the offering of his life for his life-long friend; that Henry would not only be freed from the possession of his depression and all evil spirits but also from all idols of this world which kept God from being his sole Master. Before David now, was the vision of him making this offering which was represented by the few drops of water and bit of host in the chalice of wine.

But there was more to the vision he had seen…there was still more to the covenant he had made and in the next few moments, the entire vision would finally play out…

HENRY FOUND HIMSELF caught in a web of utter despair. Ever since Father had left him early that morning, his anguish seemed to spread like wildfire throughout his being. There was a raging spiritual battle going on for his soul. He wished that his life would be over. He knew in this state, he couldn't go on. Life without his beloved wife was completely empty.

The sunshine was gone.

Despite all the reasoned words of his mentor, Henry was locked in a prison of darkness and could not see any light or hope…he was possessed by his illness.

Suddenly, Henry felt a stirring in the deep recesses of his soul. He opened his eyes and gazed down at the prayer house. An aura of light surrounded the Poustinia and it was becoming brighter and brighter. Henry stood, as if lifted and walked to the railing to see better what was going on...

FATHER KNEW THAT Jesus was going to come to the altar within minutes. "Oh God, deign to bless what we offer, and make it approved, effective, right, and wholly pleasing in every way, that it may become for our good, the Body and Blood of Your dearly beloved Son, Jesus Christ our Lord."

Father's vision which he had on the other side was slowly coming to pass. He could see that in the covenant he had made, he did offer his life just as he was doing now. "Let Your will, not mine, be done," Father whispered as he anxiously awaited upon the Lord to accept his life for his beloved adopted son.

HENRY DIDN'T SEE the tall angel of the Lord who was standing next to him. He was so intrigued by the growing light emanating from the prayer house. A vision of untold beauty was unfolding before Henry's eyes. The walls of the prayer house seemed to disappear as if made of glass. There in front of the altar, Henry saw his beloved teacher. As he gazed on this sublime sight, the stirring he felt within, moments ago, turned into an unexplainable peace which began to rise from his feet restoring his entire body as it ascended. The heavy cloud which had enveloped him since Jenny's death began to lift...

FATHER WAS JUST moments away from the consecration when God the Creator of heaven and earth would change the ordinary bread and wine before him into the Body and Blood of Christ, true God and true Man! A rush of adrenalin swept through Father. Soon, his offering which had such little value on its own would become divine and have infinite value when combined with Jesus' sacrifice.

HENRY COULD SEE Father was about to begin the consecration. His despair was lifting... Henry could not hear Father's words but from all the times he had celebrated Mass with his teacher, Henry could imagine Father's words rising up to the Lord now with such fervor, belief and commitment of heart.

Henry could see that his suffering is nothing compared to the sacrifice Jesus made. Yet, if offered, it could give such glory to God. Up to that point, Henry's despair had shut out this immense offering he could have placed on the paten with the bread and in the chalice with the wine. But now the gates to freedom were open!

Henry felt compelled to make his offering along with Father Engelmann's.

THE MOST SOLEMN moment of the Holy Mass was here. Father took the host and said, "Who, the day before He suffered, took bread into His holy and venerable hands, and having raised His eyes to heaven, to You, O God, His Almighty Father, giving thanks to You, He blessed it, broke it, and gave it to His disciples, saying:

"All of you take and eat of this: *For this is My body.*"

Father elevated the Host. It was like Father was raising the sun. The image of Christ almost blinded the holy man. The risen Jesus was present in the Eucharist. Father dared to whisper, "*My Lord and my God.*"

David then picked up the chalice and continued with the consecration, "In like manner, when the supper was done, taking also this godly chalice into His holy and venerable hands, again giving thanks to You, He blessed it, and gave it to His disciples, saying: All of you take and drink of this:

"For this is the Chalice of My Blood of the new and eternal covenant: the mystery of faith: which shall be shed for you and for many unto the forgiveness of sins.

Father set the chalice down and said, "*As often as you shall do these things, in memory of me shall you do them.*"

David paused to savor the miracle which just took place before him. He stared with love and adoration at the bread and the wine which was now the Body and Blood of his Lord which he offered up to God the Father along with his and Henry's offering.

Tears, like beads of light, glistened down his cheeks as he continued, "Mindful, therefore, O Lord, not only of the blessed Passion of the same Christ, Your Son, our Lord, but also of His Resurrection from the dead, and finally His glorious Ascension into heaven, we, Your ministers, as also Your holy people, offer to Your supreme majesty, of the gifts bestowed upon us, the pure Victim, the holy Victim, the all perfect Victim; the holy Bread of life eternal and the Chalice of unending salvation."

The moment was here when Father asked God to accept his offering which is combined with Jesus' sacrifice...

Raising his head and hands towards heaven, Father uttered a heartrending cry, "Oh, heavenly Father, You commanded us to love one another as You have loved us. You said there is no greater love than to lay down one's life for his friend. I now come to you, Father, through Your Son Jesus, my Lord and Savior, to grant my heart's prayer and offering. Take my life and restore Henry's. Free him from his depression. Cleanse him of all unclean spirits and purify his heart and purpose. Give him the grace to lay down his life for You and to do Your will for the rest of his days. Grant him peace oh Lord. Oh, Father! Thank You for allowing me to give You glory in Your presence now to fulfill Your command. Give me the honor to lay down my life for Henry as Your Son did for us."

Father lowered his hands and looked down at the Missal and continued to read, "And this deign to regard with gracious and kindly attention and hold acceptable, as You deigned to accept the offerings of Abel, Your just servant, and the sacrifice of Abraham our patriarch, and that which Your chief priest Melchisedec offered to You, a holy sacrifice and a spotless victim."

Finally, Father asked for the blessing that God accept his offering and Henry's. *Father firmly believed that Henry had made an offering.* Every word which followed was said more with the heart than from the mouth. Every word radiated light and was vibrant with great joy.

"Most humbly we implore You, Almighty God, bid these offerings to be brought by the hands of Your holy angel to

Your altar above; before the face of Your Divine Majesty; that those of us who, by sharing in the Sacrifice of this altar, shall receive the most sacred Body and Blood of Your Son, may be filled with every grace and heavenly blessing. Through the same Christ our Lord. Amen"

Father paused, somewhat surprised that his offering still was not accepted by the Lord. In the next moment he would know why. The vision he had seen on the other side was about to play itself out completely before him. The present moments of his life had finally caught up to the future vision he had seen. In the next instant, David recalled the complete covenant he had made with the Lord. God had granted David's plea to not only accept his life for Henry but to bestow upon his faithful servant, the honor to feel the suffering and passion of Jesus in his body and soul. David was about to receive his greatest joy. His love for God would be complete. He would receive the highest honor bestowed to man...*to feel the weight of the sins of mankind*...so it seemed.

No, it was not for his honor and glory; it was all for the sake of his beloved son's faith and love for Jesus.

It was to give all glory to God.

CHAPTER THIRTY-FOUR

A N INDESCRIBABLE STILLNESS pervaded the valley. Henry had never, in all the years he owned the acreage, been surrounded and invaded within and without, by such an absolute silence. The peace which Henry had felt inching its way throughout his body suddenly overtook him in a flash. The heaviness of his anguish and despair vanished from his mind and heart, leaving in its wake, an incredible lull in the turmoil he had endured for months and months.

And then…the Holy Spirit flooded his being, like a tsunami, transforming his mind and renewing his spirit. He was a new creature in Christ: old things were passed away; behold all things within Henry had become new! The presence of God had again blossomed in Henry's soul. Henry felt life as never before; greater than all the sunsets or all the springtime's he had seen in all his days. It was greater than his love of Jenny, Julean, his family or anything he had idolized in his entire life.

His true Master was before him and within him!

Being renewed in spirit, Henry suddenly became aware of the Archangel next to him. He was tall and shimmered with a brilliant white light. Henry recognized him as the Archangel who had emerged from the tunnel of light just as he, Jenny and

Father Engelmann were about to cross over to the other side. He was the angel of high rank who had delivered the message to their guardian angels that the three of them would all be healed and restored to life. Henry no longer feared him as he and the others did at that time. Henry knew he had a message for him and he was right.

The Archangel gazed at Henry and said, "Your beloved friend's covenant with the Lord has restored your spirit and shall deepen your faith...come and see."

Henry knew that Father had given his life for him. He didn't want to leave the vision he was seeing but Henry only hoped and prayed his beloved friend would still be alive.

Reluctantly, Henry followed the angel just as Father was stretching out his arms. A nimbus of light crowned Father's flowing white hair. His face was radiant; completely transformed. Henry began to run to the prayer house. He had to return to the Father, he had to go home.

He felt like the prodigal son.

FATHER RAISED HIS arms and spread them out like a cross to receive his blessings. He lifted his head upwards as the heavens opened releasing a dazzling light. Father's face shone with a supernatural radiance as the blinding light flashed down towards him. Angels fluttered all about the prayer house in jubilant expectation of another saint. It was as if David's hands were struck by lightning as he felt the sharp pain of steel spikes penetrating his palms. He cried out in agony. Instantly, blood began to spill out from the wounds to each of his hands. Father staggered back, not so much overcome with the pain as he was with intense joy!

Zachariah was holding Father from behind. In the next instant, David felt another sharp, agonizing pain in his feet. His legs gave way and he collapsed to his knees. Glistening tears of radiant joy covered the holy man's face. The love for his Lord was so strong it overshadowed the immense agony blitzing throughout his body.

There was immense joy in Father's suffering.

There was nothing that could shut out the love for Jesus in his heart. As he knelt there feeling the weight of the sins of man, he cried, "Not for me Oh Lord, not for me but that Your name be glorified!"

David's heartfelt prayer was heard and the covenant fulfilled. Suddenly, the glowing white outer garment Father was wearing was stained with blood on his side. The lance had pierced his heart. With his last breath, Father Engelmann cried, "Thank you, my Lord, my God, my Savior for this blessing, my life has been made complete."

Zachariah laid the holy man down before the altar.

Father Engelmann's spirit had left him.

CHAPTER THIRTY-FIVE

H ENRY FELT AS if he had wings as he raced down the hill. There was an incredible sweetness in the air. When he turned the bend in the road leading down to the valley, the prayer house came into view in a way he would never see again. Henry was utterly stunned by what he saw. The aura he had seen surrounding the prayer house from the deck was dim in comparison to the dazzling light he saw now. It was as though the heavens had exploded a glorious, dazzling light on the Poustinia. Angels were excitedly flying all about the prayer house.

Amidst the holy scene, Henry saw Father's spirit rising. He was cradled in Zachariah's arms and being taken up to the heavenly Father. David was filled with a light so brilliant, Henry was unable to look at it. It was as if ten suns were shining in his face. Choirs of angels were chanting the most beautiful melody he had ever heard. The valley was filled with wonderment. Henry never thought he would hear himself saying or thinking this but he envied Father for being home.

Unbelievably, he was happy for Jenny to be there, too!

A Scripture verse Father quoted so many times came to mind. "Eye hath not seen, nor ear heard, neither have entered into the heart of man the things which God hath prepared for them that love Him."

Henry couldn't even begin to imagine all the treasures Father had stored up in heaven but one thing Henry knew for sure was that the heavenly Father was waiting with open arms for his teacher. He could hear the good Lord greet Father Engelmann now, "Well done, good and faithful servant! You have been faithful with a few things; I will put you in charge of many things. Come and share your Master's happiness!"

The rush of adrenalin since seeing the vision and racing down the hill took Henry's breath away. He now knew what he would find when he got to the Poustinia. He began to slow and fill his lungs with the cool fresh air of the valley.

The aura of immense light and the vision he was allowed to see was gone. It gradually disappeared just like the mist that covered the valley that morning. A peace and serenity pervaded the valley as if all of nature was still in awe of what had transpired. Henry had missed so much. For so many months, he had lived in the past that he had forgotten the beauty of the present moment. The valley looked alive with color; the butterflies abounded in the air. How long were the monarchs back? Jenny would be ecstatic to see them. Julean, too, loved this time of year.

It made Henry think of his two loves.

And with that thought, he could feel their presence on either side of him as if they were there! In his state of depression, he had blocked out God, and in so doing he had blocked out His love and all the joy associated with that love! The door was opened again and the immense rush of his two loves was restored! He was living in the now of life: the moment!

Henry could also feel his guardian angel behind him gently leading him on. And suddenly he became aware of Ginger strolling ahead of him.

In blind faith, Henry reached out both of his hands for Julean and Jenny. He knew Jenny was to his left; lilac scented the air. He wasn't disappointed; he felt their warm hands intertwine with his as he continued his stroll towards the prayer house filled with new, jubilant life.

An electrifying power was surrounding the prayer house; it felt to Henry like the deck he stepped onto was holy ground. He heard the flutter of wings.

The air was saturated with the odor of sanctity. It reeked of holiness.

Even Ginger seemed affected by the surrounding atmosphere and simply lay down on her belly with her legs stretched out in front of her. Henry commanded her to stay.

When he opened the door, the sweet fragrance grew ever stronger. He had smelled it before during his visits to see Father in the Poustinia but never was the aroma so pungent; so utterly heavenly.

Henry walked in through the kitchen rather than the foyer entrance. Mainly because from that vantage point the altar and cross came immediately into view. It was all right there fully in one's awareness; *the heart and soul of Christianity.* The story was instantly told; the immense sacrifice Jesus has done out of love to save the soul for all humanity.

Father was not yet in Henry's view; he was hidden behind the kitchen counter and partially behind one the kneelers. Within moments, Henry would come across his beloved friend. He felt the soft touch of his angel's hand on his shoulder and the tender squeeze of his hands of support from his loved ones...

It was very quiet except for the faint sound of a liquid softly trickling. Henry's heart began to race. It was like that morning when he climbed the stairs to the Engelmann's living quarters above the store to see why Mr. Engelmann hadn't come down yet. It was the morning Anna had died. Henry felt perspiration roll down his back now just like then. The image he saw of Mr. Engelmann holding Anna's hand when he walked into their bedroom that morning was forever imprinted in his mind and heart but what he saw now, utterly and completely overwhelmed him.

His knees grew weak as he saw his teacher's arm on the floor, sticking out from behind the kneeler. Blood was gushing out of his hand.

What on earth was going on?

Henry rushed into the living room and saw his dearest friend lying there with blood oozing out of the palms of both his hands! Coco was standing at his side, her nose nudging

Father's shoulder. Henry's eyes swept to Father's feet and blood was spilling out from wounds to both of his feet running over his ankles to the floor.

Suddenly, Henry realized what had happened. Father Engelmann had received the Stigmata. He remembered reading about St. Francis having received the wounds of Christ's crucifixion as well.

Was Father still alive?

He saw his spirit rising into the heavens in the vision he had earlier but perhaps he is still alive; the blood is still flowing. His heart must be pumping the blood.

He rushed to Father's side and knelt down in a state of semi shock. Henry placed his finger on David's neck trying to feel a pulse.

There was none...

He reached for Father's hand and placed his finger on Father's wrist but there was no sign of life there either.

Then, Henry saw the blood stain on the outer garment of Father's side; it was growing. Yes, Henry remembered, that's where the lance pierced Jesus' side when he was hanging on the cross. *Father had received all five wounds as Jesus had!*

How could the blood keep flowing from all of his wounds without the heart pumping? Then Henry realized Father's deep affection for his Lord. The blood is driven by sheer love. Father Engelmann loved Jesus with his whole heart and soul... he was giving his 'all;' his last ounce of himself for his Lord and Savior.

Henry recalled what the Archangel said to him on the deck. The full impact of Father's offering of his life to set him free from the prison of his depression hit Henry like a loud clap of thunder that reverberated throughout his being. He was overcome by such an ultimate act of love and began to weep.

As Henry knelt there filled with deep gratitude to his beloved friend and the honor God had bestowed upon the holy priest he recalled once again the words the Archangel said to him, "Your beloved friend's covenant with the Lord has restored your spirit and shall deepen your faith...come and see."

Henry pondered over the angel's message. He could only imagine Father making a covenant with God at the doorstep to heaven that he would come back if his life would be accepted for his. Henry understood that but what puzzled him now was that Father wouldn't have wanted to be blessed with the stigmata for doing so. Father did so out of love and always strived for humility and quickly gave all honor he received to the Lord.

Then, the rest of the Archangel's message came to him...that Father not only wanted to restore his spirit but *to strengthen his faith...come and see.*

Suddenly a light went on in Henry's mind and heart! Yes, of course that was Father's motive; he did not want to receive the stigmata just to be like his beloved Jesus; it was not to appear holy, it was so that he could bring Calvary to me and show me beyond a doubt Jesus' sacrifice and love for me! Yes! As the Archangel said, Father wanted to strengthen my faith! *He wanted to take my faith from the head to the heart!* By receiving the wounds of Christ, he wanted to take my weak faith which I struggled with all of my life from the unseen to the seen!

"Come and see..." was the message. Yes, Henry, come and see what Father did for you so that your belief would be strengthened. Henry, he brought the very wounds of Jesus back for you to see!! *How much more real could Father have made it for you!?*

Oh Father, thank you, thank you.

From that moment on there were no more doubts. There were no more idols.

There was only Jesus.

Henry stared at the blood flowing from Father's wounds. *There is no greater love than to lay down one's life for a friend.* Henry could not begin to imagine the pain, suffering and love that was there before him. The full impact of what Jesus had done for him pierced his heart.

From the deepest recesses of his being erupted a gratitude and love beyond anything Henry had ever felt before. Henry raised his head and gazed at the cross above the altar and cried, *"My Lord and my God."*

He bent over and kissed his teacher on the forehead, knowing he was kissing Jesus. "Yes Father, you have become like Jesus." How often had Henry heard his mentor say that the only thing he wanted to own when he died was Jesus in his heart. Henry nodded, filled with love for his friend. Softly he whispered again, "Your lifelong prayer has been realized."

Instantly, he felt his mentor's love for him in return.

Henry's head fell towards Father's chest and with deep groaning sounds... he wept deeply.

CHAPTER THIRTY-SIX

H ENRY SPENT OVER an hour staring at the cross in total adoration of Jesus. The love of Christ was so strong in his heart, he could have knelt there the entire day but he knew he had to deal with Father's death. And what about Coco? He knew she wouldn't leave Father and come with him. He decided to put the confused dog in the bedroom and close the sliding doors. Henry was concerned that she might lick Father's wounds.

It was a struggle getting Coco to leave Father's side and confine her in the bedroom. She immediately began whining as he closed the doors. Henry turned to look at Father again lying there and didn't want to leave his dear friend.

Reluctantly, Henry tore himself away from the incredible rapture he was caught in and ran back to the house. He would have carried Father up with him but then realized that he shouldn't move the body and yet, what should he do? Father's death was so unusual, he wasn't sure who to call first; the RCMP, a coroner or the Archbishop to let him know that Father Engelmann received the Stigmata and passed away.

He had to catch his breath as he stood by the phone; his heart was racing so hard. Henry thought it would explode through his chest any moment. Under the circumstances, he thought it best to call the Archbishop first.

"Archdiocese of Regina, this is Bernadette, how may I help you?"

"Hi, Bernadette, this is Henry Pederson, I hope Archbishop O'Neil is in."

"Oh, hello, Mr. Pederson, Yes, His Grace is in but he is in a meeting. Can I have him call you back when he is free?"

Henry paused and then with a tone of urgency said, "Bernadette, please inform the Archbishop that this is an emergency and I need to speak with him right away. Tell him it has to do with Father Engelmann."

This time, Bernadette paused and then replied, "Just a moment please."

Within less than a minute, Archbishop John O'Neil was on the phone.

"What is it, Henry? Has David gone to the Lord?"

"Yes, but a miracle has happened. He received the Stigmata and is lying before the altar in the Poustinia. I don't know what to do. Do you want to come out here and see Father before I call the police and a coroner to examine the body? It will be difficult to explain what has happened."

There was a momentary silence on the line as John immediately thought of Father Engelmann's second mission and what it was all about. He had the feeling that before the day was out; he would know what his good friend and the Lord had arranged.

"I understand," John said, as he pulled himself back to Henry's concern. "Perhaps wait fifteen minutes and then call the police so we all arrive about the same time. You may need some assistance to explain what has occurred. I will leave at once for your acreage." The Archbishop paused and then added, "Do you have a good camera?"

"Yes."

"Very well then, as soon as I get there, we will decide what further action is required."

Henry hung up the phone. He was anxious to get back to the prayer house and be with Father Engelmann but now he had to wait for the Archbishop. He wondered if Father was still bleeding and how much pain he felt before he died. He should have been there with his friend.

The adrenalin was racing through his body. He could hardly contain himself. When he felt like this before on other occasions he always called Father but his mentor was now gone. Henry knew this would be the beginning of many such circumstances he would now have to deal with alone.

The next person he could call would be Camilla. She would be at home and she was a good person to talk to. He picked up the phone and dialed the number.

"Hello."

"Hi Camilla, it's Dad. I need to tell you something…"

Camilla was shocked by the call. It was so unexpected. Henry hadn't called in months and he sounded so different; full of life and excited.

"What's up, Dad?"

"I was just down at the prayer house and Father Engelmann has passed away."

There was a long pause. "Oh, I'm so sorry to hear that. I will miss him terribly. Was it a heart attack?" Camilla wanted to know.

"It wasn't heart failure, Camilla. His death is surrounded by extraordinary circumstances. His offering at Mass is part of it and the Stigmata is the other."

"Stigmata!? What on earth is that? And what offering did Father make that would take his life?"

Henry didn't want to get into the offering Father made at this time but he would explain about the wounds of Christ. "When Christ was crucified, nails were driven into His hands and feet to hold Him on the cross. Later when He died, a Roman soldier thrust a spear through Jesus' side, piercing both the lungs and the heart, blood and water came from His side just as the apostle John recorded in his Gospel. The re-occurrence of these wounds, the mark of the passions of Christ on a person, is called Stigmata. It's a miracle which happens to very holy people close to Jesus."

"Oh, Dad, that must have been so painful for Father...did blood actually come out of his wounds?"

"Yes, when I left to come back to the house and make phone calls, Father was still bleeding from all five wounds. I can only imagine how painful it must have been and yet, I know how fervently Father wanted it. He wanted to experience the sufferings of Christ so that he could not only associate with Jesus' suffering but also that his suffering benefits others."

Henry suddenly realized that, that may have been another part of the offering his mentor made on his behalf. Henry shook his head in awe of what Father did for him.

"That's unbelievable, Dad. I think I read once that something like that happened to St. Francis."

"Yeah, that's right. He did receive the Stigmata, too, shortly before he died. In any case, it's a miracle. Not too many people are close enough to Jesus to receive such an honor and blessing. It's a sign of sainthood."

Before Camilla could ask another question, Henry said, "Listen, dear, call Jeremy and tell him to come home and get you. See if your neighbor can watch the boys as I don't think it's best for them to see this. I'll call Justin at school to come home."

Henry paused and said, "Would you mind bringing Hannah? I would like to see her...to hold her."

Camilla couldn't believe her ears. She was stunned. Clearly, another miracle had occurred. She wondered if Father's death was connected to this somehow.

Her father-in-law was healed.

Henry called the local RCMP in Lumsden and informed them that Father Engelmann passed away in a prayer house he was staying at down in the valley. Henry advised that they call a coroner to examine the body. He didn't go into details but did indicate there were special circumstances surrounding the priest's passing.

CONSTABLE COLT McGREGOR had been assigned to the Lumsden RCMP detachment for the last five years and knew of Henry's acreage. At least twice during that time, he was discharged to the site due to calls from the security company which monitored the home. In both cases they were false alarms.

Colt also knew of Father Engelmann as his mother lived in the same care home as Father. Unbeknownst to the constable, his mother along with Father Engelmann, had prayed for years that her son's faith in God be restored and that he would come back to the Church.

The RCMP officer had just issued a speeding ticket and was returning to his patrol car when the dispatcher called, "Colt, we need you to go to Henry Pederson's acreage. A priest by the name of Engelmann passed away and Mr. Pederson said there were unusual circumstances. We have requested a coroner to meet you at the site."

"I know Father Engelmann. I met him once at the care home my mom stays at. She will be very sad to learn of his passing. He is very revered by the residents at the home and apparently all over Regina and the province. I'm not too far from the property and will head over right away. Relatives of mine wanted to visit Mr. Pederson's studio a couple of weeks ago to look at some of his paintings but he said he didn't have any and to call back in six months."

"That's good to know. My wife really likes a print he produced called, 'Sliding Down Church Hill.' I was thinking of getting it for her, for her birthday."

"Is that the scene of kids sliding down the hill beside the United Church?"

"Yeah, that's the one."

Colt took the exit off the main highway and headed north down the graveled grid road. He thought about his mother who had been pleading with him for years to come back to church. His nine-year-old son was killed when they were coming home late one evening after a fishing trip up north. A drunk driver crossed the center line and hit them straight on. His son flew out of the front windshield and was killed instantly. Colt and his wife only suffered a few scratches and the drunk walked away unscathed.

This changed Colt's life in two ways: First, he joined the RCMP to do everything he could to keep drunk drivers off the highway. He was very diligent in carrying out that duty. The second aftermath was not as positive and had a very detrimental effect on him and his family. Colt never got over his anger and hatred for the man responsible for the fatal accident and also developed a deep anger at God for allowing the death of his son over that of the drunk driver. He vowed never to go back into the church again.

When the constable pulled into the farm yard, he saw a Buick in the driveway and Henry Pederson speaking to two clergy and a woman. He parked the patrol car behind the shiny black car and got out. Henry and his guests stopped talking and looked at the approaching officer. Henry recognized him from a couple of years ago when he came to check out a false alarm.

"Morning, I'm Constable Colt McGregor."

"Yes, I remember you from a few years ago. Thank you for coming. This is Archbishop O'Neil, his assistant, Joseph Tomkin, also known as the Chancellor, and Bernadette, the Archbishop's secretary. I was about to take them down to the Poustinia where Father Engelmann is."

"What is the Poustinia?" Colt wanted to know.

"It's a prayer house. Father has been coming out here for years to do personal retreats. So, if you want to follow me down—"

"A coroner is coming out here. I'll wait until he comes and then bring him along. Where is the road to get down there?"

"Come, I'll show you."

Henry excused himself from the others and took the officer to the deck and pointed to the prayer house.

Colt was shocked, "That's really something, Mr. Pederson. What a beautiful cottage by the stream. Very picturesque. So, that's where Father is?"

"Yes, I will take the Archbishop and the others down there and you can bring the coroner. See the road crossing the bridge down there?"

Colt followed Henry's hand pointing to the road and nodded.

"That's the road you will come down on. It starts up at the barn and switches back down around the hill over there and that leads to the bottom." Henry pointed to the hill.

"When I go down, you can watch for the road I take. It's the only one and there is no turning back as it's too narrow and a deep gorge runs alongside the road all the way to the bottom."

Colt nodded, "I'm looking forward to getting down there. I wish it were under better circumstances."

Henry nodded. So much had been happening; he somehow forgot his sorrow over Father's passing. The officer brought him back to the present.

As Henry drove his passengers down around the hill, they gasped at the view of the valley and how the prayer house was nestled beside the pond. Bernadette seemed to capture the feelings of all of them, "Oh, my, that is so beautiful, Mr. Pederson. The reflection is majestic. I can see why Father loved to spend time here."

As soon as Henry got to the prayer house and they all got out of the car, it was immediately evident that the valley still seemed to be reeling from what had transpired earlier. They were overcome by the aura of sanctity that permeated the air. Like Henry, before, they too, could feel that they were on holy ground. The Archbishop made the sign of the cross. So did the others.

Henry led them into the Poustinia through the kitchen entrance so they could see the chapel and Father Engelmann as he did. As soon as they entered the house, each one gasped after the other. The odor of sweetness hit their nostrils preparing them for the miracle they were about to see.

Slowly, they walked into the small chapel and shuffled around so they could all see Father Engelmann lying there. Blood was still oozing from his wounds. Tears surfaced in all of their eyes. Bernadette brought her hands up to her mouth as if to scream. The Archbishop shook his head, clearly overwhelmed by the sight of his holy friend lying there blessed with the Stigmata. The Archbishop fell to his knees and was immediately followed by all the others. Not a sound was heard or a word spoken. The image of Father Engelmann lying there in a growing pool of blood was horrific, yet it was the holiness of the scene which touched the minds and hearts of those present.

They knew a saint was in their midst. It was as if they were at Calvary and Christ was just taken down from the cross and laid there.

Coco was so agitated in the bedroom that Henry opened the door and let her out. She immediately went to Father's side, laid down and rested her head on his shoulder as if she was mourning Father's passing like everyone else in the room.

A good fifteen minutes elapsed without a word being spoken. The Archbishop reached into his pocket and took out a small bottle of holy oil and while still on his knees, made his way to Father's side. He opened the bottle and began to anoint the holy man; first, the forehead, lips, hands, feet and side. He turned to the Chancellor who handed him a book of prayers. He turned to the page which is said after someone has passed away. The Archbishop made the sign of the cross and read the prayer.

Just as the Archbishop finished, a car pulled up to the house. They heard car doors slam and talking. Henry got up and went to the front door and greeted the constable and coroner. He held the door open and motioned with his hand for them to come in. The Archbishop, Chancellor and Bernadette looked at the officer who was the first to enter the living room.

Colt McGregor had seen many things in his life but there wasn't anything that could have prepared him for this. He stopped in his tracks and his face turned white as a sheet. The odor of sanctity and the image stunned him. He fell to his knees. All those present thought the officer was having a heart attack. And then something unexplainable happened. It was as if everyone there was in a state of suspended animation except for Colt and the Archbishop.

Time stood still.

Colt burst into tears and cried, "Forgive me, Father, for I have sinned. It has been eight years since my last confession and these are my sins: I have blasphemed against God for allowing the death of my son. I have harbored anger, hatred and unforgiveness..."

For over ten minutes, the forlorn officer spouted out one transgression after the other. Sins he had long forgotten since his youth came back to his mind. Incredibly, only the Archbishop could hear the officer's confession. As soon as the Archbishop blessed Colt and gave him absolution, life returned to the room. Henry, however, could sense a healing had taken place. The officer immediately exuded a freedom similar to how he was feeling, too!

The coroner still was at the doorway to the front entrance. He seemed confused and disorientated as a result of what just had happened. He shook his head and walked in to see Colt still on his knees in a spirit of prayer. Father Engelmann still wasn't visible to him. Not sure of what to do, the coroner stepped around Colt and was shocked by what he saw. He had to brace himself at the doorway to the living room as his legs were about to collapse, too.

Colt got up and wiped his tears. Normally, he would have been highly embarrassed but he didn't think anything of what happened to be out of the ordinary in lieu of the circumstances. He felt incredibly at peace and free as if he could fly. Everyone seemed to be in a different state of mind and focused on Father Engelmann and not on Colt whatsoever, except for the Archbishop.

Collecting himself and his thoughts, Colt introduced the coroner to all the people in the room. Since the coroner seemed in a state of shock and not sure what to make of it all, the Archbishop explained what had happened to Father Engelmann solely on the basis of what he had read about other saints having received the Stigmata. This was a sight which none of them had ever seen before and probably would never again.

Accepting what the Archbishop said, as it seemed to be the only logical explanation, the coroner made his way to Father's side and knelt down for a closer examination. As soon as he touched Father's wrist, he immediately withdrew his hand. The coroner fully expected to feel a cold stiff hand and instead a warm electrifying sensation swept through him. He never had felt anything like it before. He opened his bag and took out a stethoscope and listened to Father's heart. It was silent and yet blood was still coming out of the wounds seemingly driven by some unknown force. The coroner seemed dumfounded by it all. He didn't suspect foul play and yet...

The Archbishop sensed the coroner's concern and explained further the miracle of the Stigmata and the wounds which Christ endured when he was crucified. He pointed to the blood still forming on the chasuble and said, "There is no tear or puncture to the cloth. No object has pierced the garment. If we lift the cloth we will see a wound in his side similar to the wounds in Father Engelmann's hands and feet. These wounds are all the same as those received by Jesus when he died. The wound to the side reflects the wound inflicted upon Christ when a soldier pierced his lance through Jesus' side and blood and water gushed out as it is doing now. If you want, we can lift the garments and you will see the wound has miraculously occurred."

The coroner reflected upon what the Archbishop said and examined the garment more closely. He lifted the chasuble and looked to see if the alb had been penetrated in any way but there was nothing except blood still forming and expanding on the inner garment. Clearly, the blood was coming from the top and not out the back.

The coroner nodded and furrowed his brow, obviously very puzzled by the entire matter. He reached into his bag again and took out a camera and began to take several photos. The Chancellor also took photos with his camera at the same time. Henry had his camera too but decided he would wait until later if more were needed.

"Well, I'll write up my report and put down the cause as you have said. I would like to fully examine the body once again at the morgue before I finalize my report. You can go ahead and call the funeral home or ambulance to pick up the body."

Henry nodded, "Yes, I will call Speers as soon as we are done saying prayers." Henry shook the coroner's hand and the constable's as well and they left.

Just as the patrol car was leaving, Jeremy pulled up along with Justin and Camilla. Camilla got out of the car first carrying Hannah. When she and the child entered the house, Camilla seemed oblivious to Henry and the others in the room. She passed Henry at the front door and stepped into the chapel and gasped when she saw Father Engelmann lying there. She held Hannah in one arm and brought the hand of her other arm to her mouth to cover a cry. "Oh, my good Lord—Oh, Father!"

Camilla stepped in and knelt before Father. She didn't hear the similar reactions which Jeremy and Justin made as they stepped into the room. What happened next stunned everyone. Hannah struggled to get free of Camilla's hold. Reluctantly, Camilla set her down on the floor. Unbelievably, no one made any attempt to shield the child from the scene. Somehow it never entered into their mind. It was all so natural for Hannah to be part of this...

The little girl went to Father Engelmann and said as clear as a bell, "Grandpa, I love you." Hannah bent over and kissed Father's cheek. Tears instantly filled everyone's eyes. It was as if Jenny was working through her daughter.

It was what Jenny would have done.

Hannah remained squatting in front of Father and stroked his white flowing, long hair. Neither Henry, Camilla nor Jeremy made any attempt to remove the child. She seemed to be expressing her farewell to the holy man like everyone else. Justin seemed to require the attention more-so than anyone else.

Henry put his arm around Justin and explained to his son what happened. Justin was so close to Father. The young man began to weep all the more. He wanted to hug Father but didn't know what to do about the blood still flowing form Father's wounds. He gently broke loose of Henry's arm and knelt next to Camilla. Justin reached out and touched Father's wrist.

Camilla put her arm around Justin and they both wept, deeply. Jeremy stood at the doorway transfixed by the unbelievable scene before him.

Henry couldn't take his eyes off his little angel. He imagined what Jenny would have looked like as a child. Camilla had combed Hannah's wheat colored hair into a pony tail at the back. Her blue eyes sparkled just like her mother and her guardian mother, too! As he clearly recognized at Hannah's first birthday party how much little Hannah resembled Camilla and could easily be mistaken for being her birth mother. It was truly amazing how the two girls before him looked just like their mother.

He was surprised that Father's death hadn't overwhelmed him yet. Henry was still reeling in a state of freedom and awe over what Father had done for him. His heart was filled with both sorrow and gratitude. He had to be strong for his family. Henry knelt next to Hannah and reached in his pocket and took out Jenny's rosary. He made the sign of the cross and began to lead everyone in prayer.

Hannah was immediately drawn to the sparkling beads. She knew the rosary belonged to her mother!

CHAPTER THIRTY-SEVEN

THE ARCHBISHOP HAD a hundred and one questions to ask Henry. He knew it wasn't the best time to interrogate Father's close friend but it was vital that a thorough accounting of this entire matter be recorded for future reference while everything was fresh in the minds of those involved. Surely, a delegation from Rome would be sent to investigate what transpired and it was his duty as head of the diocese to make certain all the facts were accurately written down.

If the truth be known, John had another motive still closer to his heart for wanting to know the facts of all that had transpired. Ever since Father Engelmann had told him of the second mission he was assigned during his stint on the other side, John dreamed and prayed for the day he would eventually know what that task was. With the death of his dear friend at hand, surely Father's final assignment was accomplished that day. He could hardly wait to hear what it was.

Before Henry went outside to the deck to meet with the Archbishop and his staff, Henry asked Jeremy to drive up to the house to call Speers Funeral Home and wait for them until they arrived and bring them down. He also instructed his son to take Coco with him and lock her up in the garage with Ginger as she would be very upset when the ambulance took Father's body away.

Henry then went over to Justin and Camilla who were still

kneeling in front of Father Engelmann. Justin was taking the death of his grandfather very hard. The young lad couldn't stop crying. Henry rubbed his son's shoulder, trying to console him. He picked up Hannah who was still squatting in front of her grandpa. He kissed the child and held her in his arms and walked out to the deck.

Henry sat next to the Archbishop. It was obvious that he couldn't wait to learn what happened from Henry's point of view. The Chancellor sat next to the Archbishop and Bernadette sat off to the side ready to transcribe verbatim every word exactly in the way it was spoken. She had years of experience and training learning how to listen with complete attention and with the uncanny ability to remain as inconspicuous as possible.

"Henry, I know this is a very difficult time for you and the family and that you would rather be with Father, yet for the purposes of future beatification of David Engelmann, it is imperative that all the facts surrounding Father's passing and his receiving the Stigmata is recorded as accurately as possible."

The Archbishop paused for a moment. Henry nodded, "I understand, Your Grace."

"When did you last see David alive, Henry? Take your time and try to recall every detail...don't rush. Father Engelmann never spoke much of himself so it is imperative we learn of his life from others who have witnessed his holiness. The Church, people of the Church, historians and writers will want to know all they can. I have already started an accounting of his life many years ago as I anticipated for some time he would be considered for canonization. What has happened today only confirms my previous judgment to be accurate."

Henry sat back in his chair. He was surprised how calm and patient Hannah was. Her head lay quietly on Henry's chest as he reflected on how best to begin. He told the Archbishop of his struggle with depression since his wife's death and how it continued to get worse over the past year. "I caused Father Engelmann great concern and over the past months, Father did his best to counsel me and offer Masses and prayers for my recovery."

The Archbishop nodded. He knew of Henry's struggle and recalled Father Engelmann's concern that perhaps evil forces were involved as well.

"About two days ago," Henry continued, "my deep sorrow over Jenny's passing seemed to peak. Father sensed my need for help and made the long, steep uphill trek to visit me. Yesterday, when he came again, his counsel and wisdom was so insightful and sharp, I felt as if I was being cut in several places. I felt some relief but was afraid to be alone. Father spent the night with me and shortly after we awoke on the deck this morning, he decided to go back to the prayer house. He pleaded with me to come down this morning for Mass. When he walked away, I had the sense it would be the last time I would see him alive."

Henry stopped and wiped a tear rolling down his cheek. He kissed Hannah on the forehead and continued, "No sooner had Father left, then my sadness and anguish returned like I had never experienced it before. Despite his sound advice, my depression had such a stronghold that nothing seemed to lift the dark cloud enveloping me. Father suspected that I had opened the doors to evil forces and he was right. I so much wanted to go down to the prayer house but I seemed immobilized to do so. I felt my life was finished. If my lifelong mentor was unable to help me, my future held no hope...I saw no solution...only death."

Hannah opened her eyes and put her arms around Henry's neck and hugged him. Henry responded and kissed her on the cheek; once again tears surfaced in his eyes. This time it was Hannah who brushed away the tear rolling down his cheek. It was as if Jenny was cradled in his arms. Henry gazed lovingly at his daughter and then at the Archbishop. "This little girl is part of the story John, but let me finish what I was saying."

Henry pointed up to his home on the side of the hill. "I was watching from the deck up there for Father to come down the road after he left me. As you can see from here, I wasn't able to see Father from the deck until he got close to the bridge crossing the creek. As soon as I saw him, I leaned forward in my chair and watched as he crossed the bridge. There was a heavy mist on the valley floor this morning. It wasn't all over but interspersed. It began at the bridge and continued all the way to the prayer house. When Father crossed the bridge, I saw him enter the fog. It was like he was disappearing into a cloud...like heaven. It was the last time I saw him alive until I saw a vision from the deck where I was sitting."

The Archbishop leaned forward and seemed to freeze in time. The Chancellor mimicked his superior and Bernadette stopped writing. They were all eager to know what Henry had seen.

"While I was in my deepest moment of despair, I suddenly saw the sky brighten. What could possibly be causing the air to brighten more than the sun already has? I looked closer and there before me, the light was emanating from the Poustinia... this house!

"It was shimmering in light.

"I don't remember standing up. It was more like I was lifted out of my chair and set down in front of the deck glass railing. I felt as if I was in another space and time. Thoughts of despair, depression, death were all suspended...the furthest thing from my mind.

"As I gazed at the prayer house, the walls and roof became transparent somehow. I was able to see right through to the chapel. Incredibly, I could see what was going on as if I were standing right inside the prayer house participating in the Mass. Father Engelmann was about to consecrate the bread and wine into the body and blood of Jesus. He was at the part where Father and those present make their offering to God along with the sacrifice of Jesus. He broke off a piece of the host and dropped it into the chalice filled with wine. As you know, both the bread and wine represent our offering. But we can also put on the paten beside the hosts and on the chalice with the wine our personal offerings as well!

"At that moment, Father Engelmann stopped and looked straight up at me as if the house were made of glass, convicting me to make an offering along with his."

Henry paused and the Archbishop asked, "Can you share with us what personal offering you made?"

Henry nodded, "I offered back to God my dear wife. At that moment, I knew she was a gift from Him to me and I had to let go and give her back to Him. At that same moment, I intuitively knew the offering my beloved teacher and friend was making as well. Both our offerings, although insignificant in comparison to the sacrifice of our Lord, when combined with His, at that moment of consecration becomes a divine offering!"

The Archbishop stared at Henry in wonderment and simply nodded.

Tears instantly surfaced in Henry's eyes. His words caught in his throat unable to go on. Hannah sensed her daddy's emotional struggle and reached out for his hand and tenderly grasped it. The Archbishop noticed the child's gentle, consoling touch and almost imperceptibly shook his head. It was as if the child understood and empathized with her grieving father.

After a brief pause, his gaze returned to Henry, gesturing him to take his time and yet, just as imperceptibly he leaned closer to Henry uncovering his impatience. He couldn't wait for Henry to reveal Father's offering even though he suspected what it was.

"He had given his life, for me, Your Grace. At the moment the offering was made, along with Jesus' sacrifice and the miraculous process of transubstantiation took place, I was instantly healed. An incredible peace swept through me and the heavy cloud weighing over me since Jenny's death vanished in a flash. All the anger, bitterness and sadness I felt...is gone!"

Henry paused and looked down at Hannah sleeping in his arms. "Jenny gave birth to this little girl a couple of weeks before she died. I haven't been able to hold her since that time until now!"

The Archbishop wanted to discuss Henry's relationship with his child but didn't want to be distracted and so he tried to get Henry back to the moment he felt healed. "So, you felt your depression leave you the moment Father made the offering..."

"Yes, and it was at that moment I became aware of a tall Archangel beside me. He said that Father Engelmann made an offering for me and that I was to come. I was reluctant to leave as the vision was so beautiful but I felt prompted to obey. The last thing I saw before I stepped off the deck was to see Father Engelmann stretch out his arms. He looked as if he was about to be hung on a cross. He was so full of Jesus, it looked as if light was shining through his entire body!"

"Remarkable," muttered the Archbishop.

"I hurried to the road; I so wanted to see Father before he went Home. When I got to the bend in the road which opened the view to the valley and the prayer house, the vision was gone and so was the angel. When I came down here, I immediately smelled that wonderful sweet odor and saw what you saw."

"Utterly remarkable," The Archbishop said again. "We are already seeing miracles: your healing and Father's offering and his receiving the Stigmata are all testimony to Father's holiness. The officer also was healed; I haven't heard such a heartfelt confession in all my days as a priest."

"When did the constable say confession, John?" Henry wanted to know.

The Archbishop furrowed his brow, "As soon as he entered the living room and saw Father Engelmann, he fell to his knees and made a confession of all his transgressions for over ten minutes. Surely you heard him...?"

Henry shook his head, "No I didn't. I was wondering why you gave him absolution."

The Archbishop turned sharply to the Chancellor and his secretary. They too shook their heads. "Remarkable, this is all absolutely, remarkable. Another miracle has occurred! The man's privacy was honored. It was between him and the Lord."

The Archbishop paused for a moment and then said, "David is well on his way to becoming a saint. In my assessment, he has already passed the first two steps."

"What are the steps to sainthood, Your Grace?"

"Before a person can be considered for that holy rank, he or she must have been dead for at least five years. In David's case this requirement may be waived. As I said, he has already passed the first two steps out of the four to becoming a saint.

The first is to be called a 'Servant of God.' Over the years I have received enough documentation and testimony to fill twenty files. Six years ago, when David, you and your wife were all healed and brought back to life, numerous miracles were recorded at that time as well. You may recall a delegation was formed which collected even more documentation that proved David lived heroic virtues. And now that he has been blessed with the stigmata, I am certain that if all this were presented to the Congregation for the Causes of Saints in Rome, this would more than meet the second requirement which earns David the title of 'Venerable.'"

"The third and fourth steps have to do with miracles, don't they?"

"That is correct, Henry. The third step is to be *beautified* and recognized as *'Blessed.'* This requires one miracle through the candidate's intercession. The fourth and final step towards canonization requires a second miracle after beautification. Once this second miracle has been received through the candidate's intercession, the Pope declares the person a 'Saint.'"

"What an honor that would be for Father Engelmann to be included in the official catalogue of saints!" the Chancellor said, suddenly chiming in.

"Yes, it certainly would be," confirmed the Archbishop.

Henry wanted to make a comment on what the two men just said but Hannah began to squirm in Henry's arms and asked for her mommy. It sounded out of the ordinary to Henry and yet he understood that under the circumstances, Jeremy and Camilla had been the parents to the child. Henry was surprised how well Hannah related to him. Camilla did such a wonderful job to keep Henry in the loop by coming out so often to see her daddy.

"Excuse me, Your Grace. I will be right back."

When Henry returned, he was shaking his head as if he had been further awestruck. "This is an amazing day, Your Grace. Camilla just reminded me that today is our fifth anniversary. It was June 3, 1989 that Father Engelmann married Jenny and I. Today he gave me the greatest gift one can give: his life. What an anniversary gift! For over a year, I was unable to love nor receive love. Today, I was free again to feel the presence and love of my dear Jenny through the love of God."

The Archbishop looked at Henry and nodded, "What a blessing, Henry. What a blessing this day has been for you..."

Henry sat down and after a long silence considering another amazing part of this memorable day, the men resumed their discussion. The matter of the funeral came up, where it should be held and what Father should wear. Father Engelmann would not want much fanfare and yet, he was revered by so many people not only all over the city but the country as well. They had a right to know that their beloved priest and friend had died and be given an opportunity for them to pay their last respects to him. So, it was decided that the funeral be held at the Cathedral rather than the parish he presided over. Furthermore, they would have an open coffin on display for a three-day, twenty-four-hour vigil and then he would be buried on the third day.

Although Father had arranged for a plot beside Anna, the Archbishop wanted to check into the possibility of placing David's body in a crypt in the church basement. They did agree however, to place Father's body in a pine box he had purchased years ago when his wife, Anna was buried. It clearly reflected Father's humility, poverty and freedom from any form of worldly attachment.

After moments of reflection, the Archbishop added, "This will have quite an impact upon the diocese. Father Engelmann's outreach went well beyond the city. He has lived a long life and touched countless people. I hope having a three-day open vigil will be long enough."

Henry was beginning to see this was no longer a simple matter or funeral. He knew this would be only one of the many interrogations he would face. Father would not want such ado and yet, his holiness touched so many hearts and his example should not be taken lightly or hidden. After all, this is the purpose of sainthood to inspire and motivate others that they, too, can lead holy lives and like David Engelmann become a 'Servant of the Lord."

Henry also brought up Father's wish to be buried in his tan suit. However, once again under the circumstances, it was best for Father to wear church garments. At the time he had made that request, he was married to Anna, but now he was married to the Church and belonged to the people of God. In the end it was decided to leave on the garments he was wearing. "Change nothing," the Chancellor said, "It shows along with his other wounds the gift the Lord bestowed upon the holy man. It will bring great honor to Father Engelmann."

Henry, however, had a different perspective of the matter. He wanted to respond to a similar comment the Chancellor had made before he took Hannah in to Camilla. Slowly, he began, "You know, Joseph, Father's motive to receive the Stigmata was not to receive honor or to be glorified in any way. He shunned praise and honor and strived for humility. I believe his real motive was to restore my faith in Jesus."

The Chancellor nodded and said, "Go on, Henry."

"Father knew that my greatest difficulty was not dealing with depression but to place Jesus at the center of my life above everything. He knew my struggles with the idols of the world, including Jenny. That is why he made a covenant with God when he was on the other side to come back if God would accept his life for mine to set me free from the forces of oppression and the Stigmata was to bring Christ to me before the altar. Father wanted me to see firsthand the suffering and wounds Christ incurred on my behalf through his offering of his life for me."

The Archbishop sat up and exclaimed, "Ah, now the detail is coming out! And yes, it is as you say, David was an extremely humble man and his motive would not have been to be blessed with the Stigmata for honor."

"That's right, Your Grace. Whenever Father received praise, he would immediately mutter to himself, 'Not for me Oh Lord, not for me but glory to Your name.'" Henry paused for but a moment. His eyes lit up as another detail came into his mind. He added with further conviction, "In fact, Your Grace, just as I was about to leave the deck to come down here, I saw him stretch out his arms as I mentioned to you earlier but what I forgot to tell you was that moments later when I left, I heard him cry that same mantra; 'Not for me Oh Lord, not for me but glory to Your name.' It reverberated throughout the valley, sending chills up my spine at the time. You see, he didn't want the Stigmata for honor but to show me, in no uncertain terms, the immense love Jesus has for me to the point of being crucified. If by showing me the wounds of Christ, he could bring me home to the Savior, then that, would give honor and glory to God."

A silence hung in the air as they considered Henry's observations.

It was clearly evident in the Archbishop's eyes that his investigative mind was carefully weighing the facts. It was just as evident that perhaps he found a flaw in Henry's well-reasoned analysis thus far. Slowly, the Archbishop nodded and leaning closer to Henry he said, "Yes, Henry, that all fits into David's way of thinking...but how are you so certain David made such a covenant?"

Henry thought for a moment and reflected carefully on the Archbishop's astute question and replied, "One day, when Jenny and I were down here with Father, we briefly talked about his second mission. It was then he made a slip of the tongue and said that he still did not know what the covenant was he had made with the Lord. Over the six years since his near-death experience, we had discussed the two tasks he was assigned by his guardian angel, Zachariah many times. But that was the first time Father had said that. When I questioned him on it, he acknowledged that he couldn't really remember if he had made a covenant or if it was just a slip of the tongue and that he was really referring to the vision he saw which still hadn't been revealed to him yet."

Henry paused; he knew what he shared was not enough to support his conclusion that Father had made a covenant but perhaps it gave further credence to what he remembered about what the Archangel had said to him. "The slip of tongue that Father made may very well have been what did in fact happen, Your Grace. To support my conclusion that Father made a covenant on my behalf when he saw the vision is what the Archangel said to me this morning on the deck."

The Archbishop immediately sat up again and leaned towards Henry. "See, how important detail is? And why the need to discuss all of this while the memory is still fresh. This important detail may have been lost otherwise! Please go on, Henry. What did God's messenger have to say?"

"I remember his words clearly; the Archangel said, 'Your beloved friend's covenant with the Lord has restored your spirit and shall deepen your faith…come and see."

Henry paused for a moment and added, "And when I came to the prayer house and saw what Father had done out of love for me fueled by the love of Jesus in his heart, I finally knew who my sole Master was. At that moment, Your Grace, my gratitude to Father Engelmann was so great and yet, it was so small in comparison to the gratitude I could now feel for what Jesus had done for me. Father brought Jesus to my very doorstep…visible to my mind and heart. He had taken my faith from the unseen to the seen!"

"Remarkable! Truly remarkable, Henry. It is as you have said; such a covenant was truly made between God and His faithful servant. We have witnessed a divine miracle of God today."

John nodded his head and thankfully concluded that he had finally become aware of Father Engelmann's extraordinary second mission. Satisfied, he leaned back and relaxed. As he gazed at Henry, he recalled his last discussion with David Engelmann in which he had foresaw that Henry was going through one of God's trials to bring the struggling man back to the faith; that a miracle would soon be at hand. What the Archbishop could never have foreseen, however, was the amazingly creative way in which the Lord brought this all about. Imagine, six years ago, God's divine Providence was at work when David Engelmann had died and then brought back to life. During that time on the other side, he was given two missions; one, was to write the love story about Henry and Jenny and the other was based upon a vision he was allowed to see. We now know what that vision was. Father Engelmann had made a covenant with God that he would come back if he were allowed to offer his life for his adopted son, but also to receive the Stigmata not for his glory and honor but to bring the full reality of Jesus' love to Henry and what He had done for Henry and all of us.

Remarkable, truly remarkable, thought John, *that I have been so blessed to witness this! Truly, there is no greater love than to lay down one's life for a friend.*

The sweet odor of sanctity permeated the still air as Henry and his guests contemplated the miraculous happenings of the day. Often, there was a silence between the sounds of nature in which they heard the jubilant flutter of unseen wings.

CHAPTER THIRTY-EIGHT

As THE ARCHBISHOP foresaw, people came for all three days to the Cathedral to see Father Engelmann. The news had spread quickly that the holy man had received the Stigmata. Many came just out of curiosity. The church was open around the clock and even into the late hours of the evening or early hours of the morning, the church was filled.

Many people suffering from various ailments claimed to be healed; cancer patients, arthritis victims, hip and knee problems, kidney failure, the list was endless. All who made the claim that they were healed had to be thoroughly investigated. A heavy rope cordoned off Father's coffin but still people reached over or under to touch his body. Finally, a full-time commissionaire had to be employed to keep mourners from touching the body or coffin.

The Archbishop was also correct that David's body would not decay. The odor emanating from the corpse seemed to grow sweeter with each passing day. Henry spent as much time as he could at the church in prayer. A re-occurring theme that played itself out in Henry's mind was the similarity between Jenny and Father. There was talk that Jenny, too, could be considered a candidate for sainthood because of the sacrifice she made for the life of her child. She, too, offered up her life in the same way Father Engelmann did for Henry.

The Archbishop had asked Henry to give the eulogy for Father Engelmann. He, too, would speak but felt it only fitting that Henry's lifelong friendship with Father should say the parting words.

Gary and John were both coming. Henry had called Gary the night Father died and told him. Gary wept and his first response was that another Saint Francis had gone to the Lord. So many lives from all over and of so many denominations were touched by the holy man. Judging by the number of people who came to the vigil to pay their last respects to Father, the Church anticipated an overflow attendance. Speakers were already in place in the large foyer to the church but they also thought it best to install temporary speakers outside to the front and to the side of church as well. This would prove to be a wise decision.

Henry was feeling somewhat nervous about the eulogy and yet his main concern was that he said everything that needed to be said about the holy life his mentor and teacher lived.

ON THE DAY of the funeral, Henry, his two oldest daughters and Justin got into one car and drove to the city. The funeral would begin at ten o'clock and a High Mass would be said in Father Engelmann's honor. The Archbishop would be the main celebrant of the Mass accompanied by several other priests one of which was Father Knuka. He, too, would be saying a few words about his association with David at St. Mary's Parish.

It seemed like something very dear and special was missing without Father Engelmann in the car or around the house these last few days. Henry and all the children noticed a light had been dimmed at the farm and Father's kind benevolent smile that lit up the room was absent. "Where is Father?" or "When is Grandpa coming?" someone would say or they would catch themselves looking here or there fully expecting Father to be there out of habit before realizing he was gone. *He was family.* With Jenny and now Father no longer present in their physical lives, it was going to be a huge adjustment for all of them to make, especially Henry and Justin.

All of the Pederson children were so happy and relieved that their father was healed. If Father hadn't freed Henry of

Jenny's passing, the death of his closest friend whom he loved with all his heart as well, would have thrust Henry into an abyss he would never have recovered from. He was already in such a dark place that the chasm he had to cross to come back to the land of the living would have been insurmountable.

Henry would have to make every effort now to help his son recover as well. Not just from Father Engelmann passing but also Jenny's, too. He was finally starting to realize his family's needs above his own.

All the residents at the care home were taking Father's passing very hard. Special needs had to be met to get some of them that were no longer mobile to the Cathedral. Several rows of seats had been cordoned off especially for them. Henry was glad to hear Johnny, who was making a record in Toronto, flew in for the funeral. It was also great that J.J. and his family and all the staff who knew Father Engelmann were coming. They were flying in on J.J.'s private jet that morning and leaving later that afternoon. Matti and Thomas took the news of Father's death very hard. Henry was surprised by the deep impact Father had made on others whom he didn't know that well. And yet, when one wears Jesus in their heart, even being around them for a few moments is enough for others to be drawn into the Light.

It was a good hour before the ceremony would begin when Henry and his family pulled up to Speers Funeral Home. From there, the immediate family and close friends would be driven to the Cathedral in limos. Jeremy and Camilla and the boys were already there and right next to them was Matti, Thomas, J.J. and his family.

The funeral director was busy giving final instructions to his staff. After Communion, the casket would simply be closed and left there at the foot of the altar. A home for Father's body still hadn't been decided upon; most likely a crypt in the church basement was being arranged. Henry and his family would go in the first limousine and the rest in the second. No hearse was necessary.

At precisely nine thirty, the limos drove away from Speers Funeral Home. It would take no more than ten minutes to drive to the Cathedral, however, they wanted to be early and it was reassuring for all concerned that they were where they were supposed to be at the time assigned for the ceremony. At nine forty-two, the entourage pulled up in front of the crowded Cathedral. The Speers' staff had anticipated this might happen and several men dressed smartly in black were directing people to the sides to make room for the funeral party. The foyer was so packed however; the men were finding it more difficult than usual to direct the crowd. Finally, the man in charge came to the limo with Henry in it and suggested that the Pederson party enter into the church through the back. Even then, the cars had difficulty in maneuvering out of the growing crowds.

As Henry made his way to the pew, he immediately spotted John sitting tall above all the other people. His eyes drifted down to his friend, Gary sitting next to him. Gary nodded, his eyes filled with compassion. Gary knew the great bond of friendship and love which existed between Father and Henry. Gary and John had flown in from India two days earlier. Henry had spoken with Gary over the phone. They wanted to speak with him about missionary work. They were coming out to the farm tomorrow.

Before Henry sat down, he noticed Doctor Kreake sitting beside a woman he didn't know, probably his wife. Henry recalled Father telling him about the friendship he struck with the doctor when visiting Jenny in the Santa Maria home. Henry nodded to his in-laws, Jack and Valerie Carter, who were sitting in the pew behind theirs.

At five minutes before ten, Henry and the others were finally seated in the front rows. He never realized the maze of halls and passage ways in the old church to enter from the rear to get to the sacristy which was crowded with clergy and altar boys. In any case, they were here and seated. They probably couldn't have made it through the front of the Cathedral. Henry noticed that the church was packed. Extra chairs were placed down the aisles and wherever possible without violating the safety regulations.

Father Engelmann's casket was still open and the odor of sanctity still permeated the air. In fact, Henry thought the sweet fragrance of sainthood had grown stronger. An aura of light surrounded Father as he lay there in peaceful repose.

Henry could picture his dear friend now in his mind's eye as he had viewed the open casket last evening with Alison. How peacefully he laid there like most people who pass away but how many have known true inner peace in their lives? Henry knew that Father Engelmann was one of the few who had. Father chose the road less travelled. Father took the narrow road and that made all the difference.

Henry was pulled from his reverie as he became aware of the entire choir singing a Gregorian chant from the loft at the back of the church. It created an atmosphere of solemnity, preparing the parishioners for a Pontifical High Mass.

At exactly ten o'clock, the choir began singing the introit of the Mass, a fragment of a psalm, as an altar boy carrying a crucifix attached to the end of a long pole led a large entourage of more altar boys, priests and the Archbishop.

A pamphlet at each pew was distributed prior to the Mass explaining what was happening in the High Mass and also inviting the parishioners to participate along with the choir. The entire Mass would be sung.

When the Archbishop and his assisting celebrants arrived at the foot of the altar, one of the priests gave the Archbishop the censer, a gold metal container on a chain which contained a piece of burning charcoal. From another covered container, the incense boat, a heaping spoon full of incense was taken and placed in the censer. Immediately smoke began to rise and with it the prayers of God's people.

The Archbishop proceeded to incense the altar and sanctuary, symbolic of purification and sanctification. All the while the choir, like a group of angelic singers, was chanting Psalm 50, the 'Miserere,' invoking the mercy of God. Normally at funeral Masses, incense is used at the final commendation, in this case however, the Archbishop made his way to the coffin and incensed it all around as a sign of honor to the body of the deceased which became the temple of the Holy Spirit at Baptism and as a sign of the faithful's prayers for Father Engelmann rising to God.

Henry could just visualize Father looking down at the beautiful ceremony taking place on his behalf. It took almost thirty minutes longer than the regular Mass to get to the readings and Gospel because of all the pomp and ceremony and because all the prayers were sung. Father loved the traditional Mass and the flavor of Latin interspersed thus far. Henry wished Father was present to see the twinkle of delight in his eyes.

Nervousness began to inch its way throughout Henry's body. He had never spoken in front of such a large audience before. He could feel his mentor beside him patting his knee and whispering, "You will do fine."

Father Knuka spoke so highly of his beloved brother in Christ. He was not surprised that Father had received the Stigmata. Father Engelmann was the holiest person he knew and was such an inspiration to him. The one thing Father Knuka said which clearly identified Father Engelmann was his authenticity as a man of God. He walked the talk. After Father Knuka spoke, it was time for Henry to give the eulogy. Just as Henry rose, Justin patted his hand. Henry turned and smiled at his son and whispered, "Thank you, Son."

On the way to the podium, Henry stopped in front of the coffin, bowed and said a short prayer. When he got to the podium, he took out his notes and flattened the paper and then began to imitate his teacher. He slowly swept his eyes from one side of the church to the other making eye contact with as many people there as he could. As he did so, Henry prayed for strength to speak calmly and clearly and hoped his words would be from the Holy Spirit and inspire others to emulate Father Engelmann's example. Henry's eyes came to rest on a space just next to where Justin sat in the front row. He visualized Father's arm around his son, wearing his usual kind, benevolent smile. It was so real in Henry's vivid imagination that he was momentarily distracted from giving his speech. The parishioners were beginning to wonder when he would start or if he was too nervous to speak.

Father Engelmann nodded to his protégé, signaling that he had everyone's attention and so, Henry began:

"Your Grace, Archbishop O'Neil, Reverent Fathers, and everyone present.

"'This is the day the Lord hath made, I shall rejoice and be glad in it.' This was the refrain Father Engelmann said every morning upon rising because regardless what the day brought him, he completely trusted in God's divine Providence. Over the years, Father Engelmann had commended his body, his soul, his mind, his 'all' to God. He yielded his will fully to God's will. Everything which came to him in all circumstances he accepted as God's will and trusted in Him to turn it into good whether it was for him, for others, or for some circumstance that he may never know of or live to know of.

"In the same way Jesus was obedient to God the Father, in all things even unto death, so too, was Father Engelmann obedient to Jesus even unto death. Like Saint Paul who said in his letter to the Galatians, 'It is no longer I who live, but Christ lives in me,' was also reflected in Father Engelmann's life. He was free of all worldly attachments and was profoundly meek and humble of heart. Each day he would come to the Lord in brokenness and pray for guidance:

"*O Holy Spirit, blood of my soul, I adore You. Enlighten me, guide me, strengthen me, console me, tell me what I should do. Give me Your orders. I promise to submit myself to all that You desire of me and to accept all that You permit to happen to me. Let me only know Your will.*'

"Most of you here today who have known Father Engelmann can attest to the aura of light and peace he emanated. One knew immediately they were in the presence of Jesus. Cardinal Newman captures the spirit of Father Engelmann perfectly in the first two paragraphs of his Fragrance Prayer:

"*Dear Jesus, help me to spread Your fragrance everywhere I go.*
Flood my soul with Your Spirit and life.

Penetrate and possess my whole being so utterly,
That my life may only be a radiance of Yours.

"Shine through me, and be so in me
That every soul I come in contact with
May feel Your presence in my soul.
Let them look up and see no longer me, but only Jesus!

"Of all the beatitudes which Father lived out and reflected, the one that touched my heart the most was his purity of heart. In that regard, he was like a heavenly angel as angels constantly see the face of God. And what does the beatitude say? 'Blessed are the pure in heart for they shall see God.' The light which radiated from Father's countenance tells me that it is so, as could all those who came into his presence. He lived in the present moment; fully alive to the world around him and ready to serve with his 'all,' others and his Lord.

"The sweet odor of sanctity that we all smell in the church is evidence of the fragrance of Jesus which he spread. He had swallowed the Word which became flesh and dwelt amongst us. Every cell within the holy man dripped of Jesus. He was closer to his beloved Lord than he was to his own skin.

"It was inevitable that Father Engelmann, so passionate to be just like Jesus, would at the end of his life receive the blessing of the Stigmata to make his earthly life complete. Such was the holy life of Father Engelmann and there is no doubt in my mind that one day, he will be canonized a saint.

"When one looks at the life of Father Engelmann in the wake of such a legacy, one may feel daunted and say that it is impossible to live such a life. Yet, sainthood is within the reach of all of us and should be our top priority. God would not make such a request of us if He hadn't given us the abilities or made His help available to achieve such holiness. Father Engelmann was no different from us and faced many of the same challenges of pride and self-centeredness which we do.

"Mr. Engelmann and his wife, Anna came to Canada from Austria during the Second World War. Although he was an educated man who taught at the university level, his degrees were not recognized here. Since they could not afford to go back to university and upgrade his degrees, they purchased a grocery store in the east end of Regina and settled in to make a life here.

"In the summer of 1956 as a young boy of fifteen, I began to work for the Engelmann's. At first, I was reluctant to do so but I soon realized it was the best decision of my life. Mr. Engelmann was a warm-hearted man, wise and insightful, who along with Anna, created such an atmosphere of trust, acceptance and unconditional love, there was nothing neither I, nor anyone in the neighborhood was afraid to share with them.

"I will never forget when my friend Gary who also worked for the Engelmann's said the store was a church in disguise in which so many people were healed. Selling groceries was more of a front for their real purpose. Daily, neighbors came just to talk or share their troubled hearts and be prayed with. So many miracles occurred in that store and my life was changed, shaped and formed for the better, forever.

"I loved working for the Engelmann's and couldn't wait for Saturdays and the summer holidays when I could work for them every day. In a sense, they adopted me as the son which they could never have. He was like a father to me just as Anna was my second mother.

"What a blessing it was for me to start out in life as a young person to have such a wonderful, godly man as my personal teacher and mentor. Not just for a day, a season, but there for me as I journeyed through life. I have been greatly blessed and daily I thank the Lord for the honor and privilege to have had him as my closest friend. Although I could talk to my parents about trials and challenges which came into my life, I just found it so easy to share my concerns with Mr. Engelmann.

"Whenever we could, we would go out back of the store and sit on two old weathered crates and talk. This was the 'school of life,' he would often say. People passing by would never know the advice and knowledge that was being passed down. He was wise and spoke only after thoroughly listening to my concerns.

Often, he would simply nod, rephrase or clarify my feelings. At times, I had so many conflicting emotions, I didn't know what I was feeling or thinking. Carefully and thoughtfully, he brought clarity and order into my life and always related it to the teachings in the Bible. Mr. Engelmann firmly believed that the spiritual side of our lives was more important than our emotional and mental side. If we are obedient to God and take time to pray and meditate on God's word, our life will always be in order.

"Years later when I studied to be a counselor, I quickly realized that I had learned more about behavioral psychology and counseling skills from Mr. Engelmann than any class offered at the university. He was a natural counselor and to this day, I have never come across anyone with greater understanding, empathy, and insight into life and how to live it than David Engelmann.

"At the beginning of summer holidays, after completing grade eleven, Anna died. It was a time for deep mourning. The entire neighborhood felt the loss of a loved one and friend. For days on end, it seemed like the heart of the store was gone. But in the days and weeks which followed, Mr. Engelmann picked up his cross and once again followed the Lord but this time, into a new calling. He entered the Priesthood and embraced a life of total service and self-giving sacrifice to the Lord and to His flock.

"I will never forget the Sunday when Mr. Engelmann came to our home and told us of his decision to sell the store and become a priest. I knew straight away, he would make a wonderful priest. He was perfect for the job!

"The day he closed his store and I drove him to St. Mary's Parish before he left to go to the seminary at Gravelbourg to study for priesthood, I became aware of just how detached Mr. Engelmann was from worldly materialism. All he had was a small suitcase which contained, his wedding suit, the cross which was above the bed in his bedroom, a wedding picture of he and Anna and his Bible. Those were his possessions. Some of the money he made from the sale of the store, he gave to me as a gift to pay for my university and all the rest, he gave to the poor.

"Clearly, Father was more interested in storing up treasures in heaven than he was on earth.

"Over twenty-five years later, when Father retired from parish work and I drove him to the care home, the small suitcase filled with the same articles was still all he owned except for his Bible which he gave to me. Like St. Francis of Assisi, his patron saint, Father was committed to living a life of poverty, obedience, chastity and love of God and service to others.

"I don't have to tell you about the latter as most of you know the life Father Engelmann led. He was guided by the Holy Spirit and since he had yielded his will to Jesus, he was always in the light. Everywhere he went, people rejoiced because they were filled with the light. When a person leads a sanctified life, it sanctifies another. On his lips were always the words, 'Feed my Lamb, feed my sheep.' He was always there for his sheep in good times and bad, sorrowful times and happy times. His homilies were inspired on all occasions; whether it was at Mass, or when he married us, baptized our children or buried our loved ones. It was his constant goal to bring each and every one of his flock home to the Father.

"He was a servant to all.

"When Father retired from parish work, the care home he moved into was never the same again. Once a convent for Sisters of the Precious Blood, Father Engelmann re-opened the chapel to celebrate Mass and carry on Bible study sessions. Soon the chapel was bursting at the seams. Residents and nearby neighbors of all denominations and friends and relatives of the residents came just to celebrate Mass with Father Engelmann. Many times, the singing and praising was louder and more fervent than one of the packed Sunday Masses at the Cathedral!

"Father might have freed himself from most of his parish responsibilities but almost daily, he seemed to be expanding his outreach to another flock. Wherever he felt there was a need, Father worked tirelessly to fill it. He visited all the hospitals and care homes and made himself available at any time day or night to hear confession or tend to the dying. One would have thought at his age he'd be exhausted and would need to slow down and take more time to rest. Amazingly however, the more he gave of himself, the younger he grew, the more energy he received to do God's work.

"He even started a newsletter which was distributed to all of the care homes and to friends and relatives of the residents. He encouraged the elderly to write of their wisdom and describe their needs so their children could have a better understanding of them in the care homes. He encouraged the children to visit their parent or parents more often and to attend church. New life and responsibility swept through many of the care homes and the families of the residents there.

"Over time, Father Engelmann began to withdraw from the care home to spend more time at the prayer house which I had built years ago on our acreage down in the valley. It was situated next to a large pond fed by the stream which meandered through the valley floor. The prayer house which we often referred to as the Poustinia, the Russian name for prayer house, has a chapel inside as well as a bedroom, washroom and kitchenette. Compared to most one room Poustinias, this one would be considered a five-star prayer house."

The congregation laughed.

Henry smiled and went on. "The chapel consists of a small altar with a tabernacle and backs against one of the living room walls. A large wooden cross hangs on the wall just above the altar. Father loved the house and the way it sat in front of the pond. It reminded him of the twenty third Psalm as he rested by the still water. Every day, when Father Engelmann was there, he would say Mass. He loved the Eucharist. It was his source of spiritual nourishment and strength. Often Jenny and I would go down early in the morning and celebrate Mass with Father Engelmann.

"It was here at the prayer house that Father received the Stigmata. In my closing remarks, I thought I would share with you how that happened.

"What many of you know or may not know, is that six years ago, Father Engelmann had a near death experience. While he was on the other side, he was allowed to see a vision of what was going to happen in my life at some time in the future. He made a covenant with God to return so that he could offer his life for me in order that I be totally healed and brought back to Jesus. When he returned to the land of the living, the vision he had was removed from his memory and would be recalled to him when his present existence would catch up to that future event. Last week, Father and I learned what that event was. Before I share that with you, let me back up in time.

"Over a year ago, my wife gave birth to our little girl, Hannah. The pregnancy was a difficult one surrounded by serious complications. At the risk of her own life, Jenny carried the child longer than she should have to help it grow and develop so it would survive when born. Unfortunately, doing so was at the peril of her own health; shortly after the birth, Jenny developed a heart condition and died.

"I could easily have been buried with Jenny as my life died along with hers. For over a year, I went into a deep depression, trapped by forces I could no longer overcome. Father Engelmann tried daily to help me and offered countless Masses for my recovery, all to no avail.

"Then, just over a week ago, Father Engelmann came up from the prayer house to visit me at the farm. He spoke such words of wisdom and prayed over me but again nothing seemed to be able to penetrate the mental prison I had built and was trapped in. I was so afraid that day of what I might do, Father spent the night with me on the deck. In the morning, he tried once again to reason with me but again to no avail. Finally, he pleaded that I come down for morning Mass. He blessed me and left. I had the sense when he walked away, I would not see him alive again.

"Later that morning as I sat on my deck which overlooked the valley and the Poustinia, the prayer house suddenly began to glow with a bright light. I stood up at the railing and looked down. Incredibly, I was able to see right through the walls of the Poustinia as if they were glass and see Father Engelmann saying Mass. It was as if I were there attending Mass, too! At the consecration of the bread and wine into the body and blood of Jesus, Father Engelmann offered Jesus' sacrifice up to God along with his offering to give up his life for mine. At that moment, I too, felt prompted to make my offering along with Father Engelmann's. I offered to give Jenny back to God. As I let her go, a peace surged through me that surpassed all my understanding. In a flash I was set free.

"I wanted to see Father Engelmann again before he died and so, reluctantly, I left my vision and hurried down to the prayer house only to discover Father's spirit had left him and he had received the Stigmata…"

Henry struggled to go on and wept. After composing himself he said,

"There is no greater love than to lay down one's life for a friend. I was deeply moved by what Father had done for me. So many times, during my life, Father Engelmann was there for me as a teacher, mentor, friend and comforter and now he even offered his life for me!"

Henry stopped and could no longer go on. He wept some more. Once again, after gaining composure, Henry continued, "Father Engelmann knew me inside out. My life was an open book to Father. One of the things he knew I struggled with all my life was making Jesus my one and only master. Although I knew intellectually what Jesus had done for me on the cross, I never really was grateful to Him from the heart.

"How could I see God hanging on the cross for me and not be affected!?

"Father understood my spiritual blindness. He knew of the darkness that separated me from God. For years, my faith was weakened by the many idols before me; money, recognition, possessions and even my wife Jenny. I had no real need of God. As I said, I was grateful from the head but not the heart. But when I saw Father, so full of Jesus, saying his final Mass in the Poustinia offering his life for me alongside the re-enactment of Jesus' sacrifice for me, my spiritual blindness was removed and my faith restored! That was the covenant he had made with God when he saw the vision to free me totally from: my depression, my lack of faith, my ingratitude, my idols, myself and to bring me back to Jesus. He wanted to make real for me the Scripture which I took so lightly; 'There is no greater love than to lay down one's life for one's friends.' Father Engelmann, so full of Jesus, did exactly that for me. He took my weak faith from the unseen to the seen. Through the Stigmata, he brought the very wounds of Jesus back for me to see. How much more real could Father make it for me or for you!?"

Henry paused and shook his head. "When I saw Father laying there with the wounds of Jesus, I could no longer look at the crucifixion of my Lord and not be affected or thankful from the core of my being. At that moment, all my doubts were gone. There are no more idols. *There is only Jesus.*"

Henry pointed to the coffin and said, "Father Engelmann is not laying there to receive honor or praise rather, he wants to increase our faith. Look at the wounds and see Christ! See His immense love for us. How can our faith not be elevated to new heights as we see the wounds exactly as they happened to Jesus? What we see hidden at consecration during the Mass, under the appearance of bread and wine is truly the Body and Blood of Jesus; Father Engelmann made Jesus' sacrifice visible for us to see so our faith may grow in our hearts. What a blessing he has given us to see the very wounds of Christ so that we might believe and be saved. Even unto death, yes, his very death, Father wanted to use his life to lead his sheep home."

Henry shook his head and said, "It is all about love, my dear brothers and sisters in Christ. It is the light of true love which can bring heaven to earth. It is this kind of love that will bring peace and salvation to the world!"

"If there is a message Father Engelmann would want me to leave with you it is this: come to the Lord each day to pray and read and meditate on His Word. We will never grow in faith or our love for Him if we don't take the time to know Him. Ask the Holy Spirit to open your eyes, ears and heart and convict you of the Word. Go as often as you can to Holy Communion and receive His nourishment and strength to be obedient to His Word. It is in the celebration of the Eucharist that the Scriptures find their fulfillment. Keep eternity ever in mind as you seek His will in all circumstances and you will know peace in this world and the next.

Henry looked over to Father's coffin and said, "I will never forget the last words you said to me in the Scripture Ezekiel 36:26 which you quoted: 'Today, Henry, the Lord will give you a new heart, and a new spirit He will put within you. And He will remove the heart of stone from your flesh and give you a heart of flesh.'"

Tears surfaced in Henry's eyes as he nodded and said, "Yes, that day I did receive a heart of flesh. You gave me your heart which I know was the heart of Jesus. Thank you, my dear beloved friend, thank you for our lifelong friendship even unto death you gave of yourself so that I might see the Word with my eyes, hear the Word with my ears, and understand the Word with my heart…thank you from all of us, Father David Engelmann…

When Henry finished his eulogy, he invited Margaret Tearhorst to come and sing the St. Francis Prayer of Peace. He felt that only Margaret with the voice of an angel could capture the essence and beauty of the prayer which Father not only so dearly loved but said and put into practice each and every day of his life. Margaret loved Father and as she stood there, she gazed at the open casket and smiled as if to say, "This is for you, Father. I love you…

Make me a channel of Your peace
Where there is hatred let me bring Your love,
Where there is injury, Your pardon, Lord
And where there's doubt true faith in You

Make me a channel of Your peace
Where there's despair in life let me bring hope
Where there is darkness only light
And where there's sadness ever joy

Oh, Master grant that I may never seek
So much to be consoled as to console
To be understood as to understand
To be loved as to love with all my soul

Make me a channel of Your peace
It is in pardoning that we are pardoned
In giving of ourselves that we receive
And in dying that we are born to eternal life.

It took another two hours for the High Mass to be finished. Even though priests and lay people were stationed at each aisle in the front and back of the church, considerable time was spent distributing the Host and Wine to the massive crowd that had come to pay their respects to Father Engelmann. The choir singing and the mingling of Father's odor of sanctity with the incense lingering in the air lifted the atmosphere in the Cathedral to a heavenly state. Henry was certain he felt the presence of his dearly beloved friend along with a fleet of angels during the entire time.

When the High Mass was over, Margaret sang the processional hymn, *Whatsoever You Do**, which once again captured Father's spirit of love for his brothers and sisters and his Lord...

What soever you do to the least of my brothers, that you
*   do unto me.*
When I was hungry you gave me to eat,
When I was thirsty you gave me to drink,
Now enter into the home of my Father.

What soever you do to the least of my brothers, that you
*   do unto me.*
When I was homeless and strange in this land,
Searching for kindness, you held out your hand.
Now enter into the home of my Father...

---

* By Willard F. Jabusch

Chapter Thirty-Nine

T HE DAY AFTER Father Engelmann's funeral, Henry felt prompted to go down to the prayer house. He knew it wouldn't be the same. With each passing of a family member or close friend, a void is created which can never be filled. Yet, Henry felt surprisingly at peace. Father's sacrifice had freed him from the clutches of darkness and brought back his life and Lord.

Henry decided to walk down and slowly take in the peace of the valley. It was a beautiful summer morning and the prairie wind had decided to take the day off. There was just enough of a breeze in the air to carry the crispness in the valley as he descended.

Coco was already down at the prayer house. As soon as Henry opened the garage door, she bolted out and headed straight for the valley hoping her master would be at the Poustinia. Ever since Father passed away and she was removed from the prayer house, every evening she had to be picked up and brought back to the farm house for her meals and also to protect her from a pack of coyotes. Even still, she had hardly eaten anything as she so deeply missed Father. Justin and Henry were hoping that she would get over Father Engelmann's absence but so far, she hadn't shown any sign of her grieving lessening; in fact, it seemed to be increasing. In a way Coco's grieving was similar to the way Henry missed his dear sweet Jenny.

Gary and John were coming out later and he wanted to prepare the prayer house for their visit. He was so focused on Father's death and his wounds that he hadn't paid much attention to the state Father had left the house in. Henry also remembered there was some blood on the floor and wondered what to do with it. Perhaps he should check with the Archbishop. Maybe, he shouldn't touch anything in case the Archbishop wanted to look everything over again.

When Henry opened the door on the kitchen side, Coco rushed in ahead of him. The sweet odor of holiness was still in the air. He walked in slowly, trying to adjust and accept the fact his beloved friend would no longer be there to greet him with his open arms and warm, benevolent smile.

Many times, when he came, he would catch Father in the act of adoration of the Holy Eucharist on display on the altar. He would be in such deep communion with Jesus, he wasn't aware of Henry's presence. Henry almost had to shout for Father to notice he was there. The Holy Eucharist was a mystery of faith that many people struggle with. Yet, it was Father's faith that the white Host on display was the Christ Lord. He shared once with Henry that the wooden carving of Jesus hanging on the cross above the altar came to life. Henry gazed at the cross and his heart went out to Jesus. Father had made the crucifixion so real to Henry.

Henry could still visualize Father laying the floor; it was forever burnt into the memory of his mind. The five spots on the floor where the blood had oozed out of Father's wounds still attested to that incredible unforgettable morning. He noticed that the blood had dried. Henry thought he would scrape it off the floor and save it in a metal container and store it as a relic underneath the altar some place. He had read that all church altars have a relic of a saint imbedded somewhere in its structure. He wondered if the one he had did too.

Coco was beside herself. She kept sniffing the floor where Father had lain. Henry held her by the collar to prevent her from licking at the blood. She struggled free and dashed into the bedroom and circled all around. She jumped up and off the bed and finally, she settled on the mat by the bed and rested her head on Father Engelmann's sandals. Henry's heart went out to the faithful dog. If only there was a way to communicate to her what had happened to her beloved master.

Henry made his way to the altar, careful not to step on the blood. This was where Father was just before he died. Henry had seen Father here in the vision he had from the deck. It was an amazing sight to be able to see right through the Poustinia. Father must have known he was going to receive the Stigmata, the way he stretched out his arms to receive the wounds. Henry now wished he had stayed a little longer on the deck to see it happen.

Henry recalled all the hosts Father had consecrated that day. Henry wondered why. The archbishop put them into a ciborium and locked them in the small tabernacle at the back of the small altar. There were forty hosts in all. It was symbolic of the forty days Jesus fasted and prayed before he began his ministry. Surely, Father Engelmann didn't have anything else planned for his life, did he?

We may never know, thought Henry.

Henry bowed his head and prayed. Tears came to his eyes as so many memories flashed through his mind. He was so grateful to Father for freeing him from his bondage. He could very well be still sitting on deck moping about, spinning his wheels, going nowhere. "Thank you, Father," Henry whispered into the silent room, his words echoing off the walls. "Thank you for all the times we shared here. The times Jenny and I sat by the window or out on the deck, discussing so many meaningful topics." Henry wished it was the same now but knew they were both here in spirit.

He made the sign of the cross and decided to check out the bedroom. Father's brown Franciscan habit was lying on the bed. It was the one he had on when he last came to see Henry. Father loved that habit as he tried to emulate his beloved St. Francis. They would have made quite the pair.

Henry bent down and patted Coco's head, "Good girl, Coco, I miss him dearly, too.

As he stood back up and his eyes swept to Father's desk, a sudden excitement surged through him. He suddenly remembered the story Father was writing. "Oh, my," Henry muttered. He couldn't believe the pile of manuscripts on the desk. His gaze rested on the high pile on the right side of the table. There were six manuscripts.

Henry picked up one at a time and read the title and the order which they followed. As he read each one off, he recalled Father telling him the titles of each book; *Pewter Angels* was book one and *Another Angel of Love* was book two. He remembered those two but what did Father title the other ones? Book three, was *Angel of Thanksgiving*. That was a great title. Henry could already imagine what the cover would look like; The Angel of Thanksgiving standing next to the gazebo either on Jenny's estate or her back yard on Hill Avenue.

Book four was titled *The Angelic Occurrence*. Henry remembered now that it had to do with buying Jenny's house. The hair on the back of his neck rose just thinking on that.

Henry picked up the fifth manuscript on the pile; *Angel Promises Fulfilled*. Since the story was about Jenny and him, it probably had to do with them finally getting back together again. It was their angels that did it all. He felt sudden warmth of the pewter angel hanging on the end of the silver chain against his chest.

The sixth manuscript was untitled. He briefly read the prologue which was about the Holy Spirit and then flipped to the back which took the story to Jenny being in the hospital, faced with the decision to terminate the pregnancy or face inevitable death. Henry held the manuscript by the back edge in one hand and with the other fanned the pages with his thumb occasionally stopping to scan its contents. What he could ascertain was that Father was giving an account of their lives from the time they got married, Jenny becoming pregnant and the subsequent complications which occurred.

He could hardly wait to read the entire story up to that point but there was more to tell, wasn't there?

Henry placed the books back on the pile in the order in which he found them. He pulled out the chair and sat down. He noticed another manuscript or something which Father must have been writing on. Henry recalled Father telling him that he was working on the last book in the series which would tie it all together and bring the story to an end. "Yes," Henry muttered, this is probably the manuscript which would bring the story up to the point Father passed away.

As he pulled the manuscript over, he noticed a letter on top. It was addressed to him. An eerie feeling inched its way up his spine. It was as if Father were there saying his last words to him:

Saturday. May, 14, 1994
My dear Henry,

Someday soon, the Lord will take me home and you will be left to deal with the matter of this story. What an absolute blessing this has been to write about the love story between you and Jenny. My, my, such a story; so many trials and tribulations, so many twists and turns, yet in the end true love is always victorious.

You will notice there are six manuscripts on the right side of the table. I never imagined there would be so many. But through the direction of Zachariah and the Holy Spirit guiding my pen it flowed along like a leaf drifting slowly in the pond in front of the prayer house.

To the left, below this letter is a seventh book. It is necessary Henry for several reasons. First there is still so much of this story which must be told; what happens to Jenny? What was my second mission? And what happens to you?

The other reason I should have expected. Seven is the perfect way to end this project. Seven is the number of days it took the Lord to create the universe and has significance in countless other circumstances

in the Bible. In any case, God communicates the idea
of divine completeness, perfection and wholeness by
means of the number 7. Apparently, the Lord wants
both you and I to finish this one. Hopefully, all the
important things about life and our reason why we
are on earth express the will of the Father. You will
be inspired to write the final chapters just as I was
inspired to begin and write the story. I'm certain your
skill at writing will take the story to new heights. I
am also confident that with your artistic abilities you
will design a fine cover for each book. I will ask Saint
Theresa, the little flower to pick a heavenly rose for you
and send it to you the day you get book one off the press.

Now, there is the matter of the second mission that
the good Lord wants me to do. As you know, I was
allowed to see a vision of what it was and instantly
agreed to come back. I feel it has to do with you and
Jenny and also some covenant which I made with the
Lord at that time. When I returned to the land of the
living, as you also know, memory of that vision was
removed from my conscious mind only to be revealed
as the future of that event comes into the reality of
the present moment. I have the sense I shall know
what the vision was all about before this day is over.
The past is rapidly catching up with the future.

Henry, you have been blessed with many gifts
and talents which must be used for the Lord. In the
discussions which you have had with Gary and John,
it seems that the Lord has plans for you in missionary
work. But there may be other areas He wants you to
work in. For this reason, it is very essential that you
make a retreat here in the Poustinia. I highly recommend a forty-day retreat for you. During this time
the Lord will reveal many things to you. You need to
stop and take time to listen to His voice.

Over the years you have expressed again and
again your desire to draw closer to God. When we

seek Him with all of our hearts, He will come to you, Henry. You will know the greatest joy there is in this world and that is to know your God. I am conse-crating forty hosts for you at today's Mass to provide spiritual nourishment for you as you make this jour-ney. God will richly reward you for doing this as He has to all who have made similar journeys in the past.

There is no greater joy for me, as you know, than to pray and fast for the Lord.

Henry, my time on this earth is drawing to close, I have the sense that it is very soon. Should the Lord take me before I see you again, I don't need to tell you how much you have meant to me over the years. You have been Anna's and my son from the moment you came into our lives at the grocery store. Every day I am thankful to the Lord for such a blessing. I love you with all my heart.

Someday, we will all be together again in heaven with the angels and saints giving honor and praise to our Lord.

With deep love and affection, yours in Christ,

David Engelmann.

Henry wiped the tears from his eyes. He now knew why Father had forty hosts there for him. He smiled at the part that he would share in the writing of this story. He had always wanted to write a self-help book when he was a counselor. Maybe, just maybe his dream to write a book or two will still come true!

CHAPTER FORTY

JUST THEN, HENRY heard a car pulling up to the prayer house. Coco stood before Henry did and ran to the door. Henry knew she was looking for Father and would be greatly disappointed. Henry got up and looked out the window. He recognized Gary's sister's car. His friends were here.

"What a beautiful odor, Hank," were the first words that both Gary and John said as they walked into the Poustinia.

"It's very similar to the sweet fragrance that was in the church at Father Engelmann's funeral," remarked John after he gave Henry a warm hug.

"Yeah, I think it's called the 'odor of sanctity'. The Archbishop said it's common when a very holy person dies. He had smelled it before once in another diocese."

As soon as Gary entered the chapel in the living room, he fell to his knees.

"Is this Father's blood from his wounds?" Gary wanted to know.

"Yes, I was just thinking about what to do with it. I thought about scraping it all up into a crucible or container of some kind and saving it as a relic."

Gary nodded, "Yes, that is a good thought, Hank."

"I'll ask the Archbishop if that's best and perhaps save it under the altar here. I know most churches, if not all, have a relic stored in their altars. Usually a bone fragment of the saint the church is named after."

Gary nodded in agreement but remained silent and looked down. "What an incredible event that has occurred here, Hank."

"He was such a wonderful, holy man," said John, tears surfacing in his eyes.

Henry simply nodded. The three men remained silent for over fifteen minutes without speaking. Each was captured in their own thoughts and memories of Father Engelmann.

Coco finally grew tired of waiting at the door for Father to walk in and returned to the bedroom and settled down on the mat beside the bed. Once again, she rested her nose on Father's sandals.

Finally, Henry said, "I have water in the fridge, but no food. I can make coffee or tea."

"Water is just fine," said Gary.

"Works for me, too, Hank," echoed John.

Henry got the water and suggested that they go outside on the deck and enjoy the morning.

"So, Hank, have you given any more thought to doing some kind of missionary work?" asked Gary coming right to the point of their visit.

Henry nodded, "I definitely feel called to do that, Gary. I don't feel prompted to do what you and John are doing but more to travel from church to church across North America and let people know about the wonderful work that you and John are doing along with others and how we might help through prayer and financial support."

"That's exactly what we need. We talked about this before. It's not so much a matter of bringing people over from the west to do missionary work as it is to train people already there who are part of the culture and called to do this ministry. They know the language, the conditions, the food and water hazards and how to get from one region to the other."

"Yeah, I can definitely see the logic and reasoning behind that approach."

"What we need though is volunteer doctors, nurses, engineers and teachers who can work there and also train the educated people there how to help their own people in such dire conditions."

"You know, Hank," said John, "it would be good for you to visit India and even other parts of Asia to see firsthand the poverty, disease and conditions. It touched my heart like nothing else. Reading about it just isn't the same as actually being there. With your vivid imagination as an artist, you would come back and paint pictures with words of what you saw and put a passion into your heart for this work."

Henry smiled and nodded in agreement. "I know I should go there, I would find it very hard to live under those conditions. My sanitation training running a restaurant made me into a clean freak. It's a miracle how you two can do it alongside Mother Theresa and all her help. It's a gift you all have been given to live and work under such intolerable conditions."

"It took me a long time to adjust and accept it too, Hank. I was ill much of the time at the beginning but slowly, God gives you the grace and strength to cope and do His work. The joy in helping people and being with them in their last moments before they die, more than compensates for the hardships. That is what we are there for, to help and teach them a better way whenever we can and it's possible to do so."

"And in doing so to bring Jesus to their hearts," added John.

As Gary took a sip and drank the clean water from his bottle, he said, "I see children and adults scooping muddy, filthy water from the lake and rivers and drinking it. It's amazing the immunity they have developed over the years to all the possible diseases they can contract. Eventually it catches up to them and many die."

"So many are just skin and bones," added John once again. He, too, was an example of what he just said. It was clear to Henry that John was living right along with his brothers and sisters in so many ways.

A silence fell among the men. A deep peace permeated the air and their spirits. It was as if Father Engelmann were there with them discussing how to help the poor and impoverished. They all kept their heads down not wanting to show their deep sadness that their dear friend was gone. However, they were part of his legacy. It was now up to them to carry on the good which he taught them to do by his example.

"You know," said Henry, "should I decide to make such a tour, another thing we need to talk about are the many people in the western world who are poor and impoverished in so many ways." Before Gary or John could respond, Henry added, "And there is the growing problem of many people who have stopped going to church, especially the young people. It seems contradictory to try and bring Jesus to people abroad in the east when so many people here who know of Jesus and have every opportunity to come to Him are turning their backs on Him."

Both John and Gary nodded. John was the first to speak, "It's just

that people of the west are so blessed with all of the essentials of life and more. We spoke of this before when we were here last year. People have no need of God."

"That's right," added Gary, "poverty, no attachments, terrible housing conditions and on and on leads to God in thanks for any little blessing. Here, blessings abound. My sister is in a fret trying to decide what color to paint the living room when millions are starving. It's not that we should feel guilty about doing this; it's just that we should and can do more to help our brothers and sisters here and abroad. Our priorities are backwards."

This time, John took a deep breath and continued much the same as Father Engelmann would have if he were there. "When times are good, people get caught up in the secular culture to get ahead, amass wealth and materialism. They seek happiness and importance and identity from it. Each accumulation offers some joy and increases their feeling of worth but it's just temporary and never fills the void in their lives.

"But, when a trial comes along such as a death or a terminal disease, we soon learn that all the wealth or whatever we have isn't worth much. We are forced to stop and examine our lives and it doesn't matter much whether we are old or young, we realize that we may be prepared for this world but not the next. Somehow, people need to see their real spiritual poverty and the impermanence of life. Countless people in India for example, face death every day. They know the value of the present moment and to be prepared."

Gary paused and gazed at Henry, "Well, hopefully what you are thinking about doing will get people to examine their lives and why we are here and restore core values. Children need to be taught this in the home as to a large degree they emulate their parents."

Henry nodded and said, "Yeah, that's a major part of the problem, for sure. Before Jenny passed away, I was supposed to give a presentation to her ladies' groups along with their husbands at a scheduled social event. But when Jenny died, I lost interest in everything but recently it's been on my mind again to consider doing it. My talk would be mainly directed to the men and the great need for them to become more active in all aspects of the operation of their home; examine their role as fathers, husbands and as leaders in the spiritual development of the family. Like you said, Gary, children learn from their parents. If they see their mom and dad concerned about justice in the world and our responsibility towards the poor and impoverished, hopefully when they grow up they will do the same.

"Young people are very questioning and easily see the double standards and worldly values so many of us live by. If parents don't go church, then neither can they tell their children to go or expect them to. If parents go to church on Sunday but do not live out the teachings which are taught during the rest of week, God really isn't in their lives nor connected to how they live out each day with their children. If the home reflects worldly values of just trying to get ahead and amass more and more and neglect the spiritual side of their lives, then these values are hollow and lack substance. Simply put, all too many mothers and fathers have failed to engage themselves and their children in a way that gives purpose and meaning to life. Young people see this disconnect and don't see the value in going to church nor are they motivated to develop their spiritual lives."

Gary sat up and said, "What you are saying gets me excited, Hank. It is not just about trying to get money for missionary work out of a sense of obligation or guilt but out of real care and concern and love for our brother and sister. Giving should be a result of the way we live our lives and not just an isolated act such as writing out a cheque. Children can be taught to give part of their allowance for a charity they want to support. They can become pen pals with another child abroad, learning that their brothers and sisters should be included in their prayers. It's all part of a bigger picture. A home has to operate in such a way that a child comes to know their true identity. As you said, Hank, men have to step up to the plate and see the critical role they play as head of the home."

"And they must start by putting Jesus at the center of their life," John quickly chimed in. "He is the source of their strength; He is their mentor, an example of how to be and the sacrifices they have to make to bring their families home to God. I can't thank Father Engelmann enough for showing me my true identity; that I am a child of God, a part of His family to which we all belong." John paused for a moment then added, "Even though a lot of young people didn't have the best example in their home, many of them have questioned what life is all about. Some even come to India to help serve the poor but do not really know Jesus in their hearts. It's more of an effort to try to find meaning in their lives which they didn't find in their upbringing."

"That's a great observation, John. So many young question their parent's values and lives and are looking for deeper meaning and purpose in their own lives but have failed to see the necessity for Jesus and the Holy Spirit to anchor them in their search for meaning. Just think what would happen if more and more parents began to develop the spiritual side of their lives and connect it to the way we live and how it all fits together."

"Yeah, that's right, Hank. Many young people come and are so fervent to help change the world but soon they are bogged down with the everyday turmoil, suffering and poverty. They lose heart and feel their efforts are in vain. Those that turn to Jesus and the necessity of His Spirit to fill them with grace and strength eventually are able to stick it out."

Henry nodded, excitement filling his eyes, "That's the key. When the goal in the family is to put God first and live with eternity in mind, everything falls into place. When parents walk the talk, then their children will accept what they are trying to pass on to them. The key is for parents to understand this and believe that they must change to see the fruit of that change in their children and eventually in society at large. And as you said, it's the Holy Spirit which convicts us and gives us the wisdom and strength to change."

"Yeah, Hank, Father Engelmann often said in our discussions that the day of Pentecost has to return to the church and its people. When this happens, people will once again be on fire for the Lord like the early Christians were."

Henry nodded again, "Imagine fathers releasing the Holy Spirit in their lives. Would they not then set their child's heart on fire!?"

Gary and John gazed at Henry trying to read where he was at in all this. Clearly, Henry had the vision of what needed to be done and the ability to do it.

And as Henry returned his friends gazes, he knew the devoted men of God in front of him were looking for some kind of commitment to help them. After a long silence, he said, "I plan to make a long overdue prayer and fast retreat here in the Poustinia. I'm ashamed to say, I built this place years ago for exactly that purpose. It's about time I use it to find out what God wants me to do for the rest of my life. In fact, it was Father Engelmann's last request in a letter he wrote to me that I make a forty-day fast retreat here.

"I'll let you know what He says."

CHAPTER FORTY-ONE

IT WAS OVER nine months since Henry had been to Jeremy and Camilla's home. He felt a twinge of guilt over being so preoccupied with Jenny's passing that he had neglected his family.

Henry put his arm around Justin as they walked up the sidewalk leading to his eldest son's home. It seemed odd that Father Engelmann wasn't beside them as he usually was. The smell of fresh baked bread hit their nostrils as soon as they opened the door. Henry had forgotten the terrific bread Camilla was taught how to bake.

Before he could comment on it, the kids came running; all four of them including Hannah, his little Jenny. Henry couldn't pick them up fast enough and acknowledge each one. Jeremy came out of the living room and hugged his dad. "It's so good to have you here, Dad." And then, Camilla appeared at the kitchen door just like his mother, Mary used to. "Oh, Dad, it's so good to see you. We missed not having you here so much."

"Hi, Camilla, the bread smells great and you look wonderful." Henry hesitated and then got it out in the open. "You look so much like Jenny standing there."

"Yes, I know…I hope it's just a nice reminder of her for both of us."

Henry walked over and gave Camilla a warm hug. "Between you and Hannah, I'll never be able to forget my dear wife."

And turning to Justin, he added, "Justin has Julean's features and so I'm blessed all around!"

"Come, Grandpa, I want to show you what I painted. Daddy made an easel for me and said one day I'll be as good an artist as you!"

"You will be better, Noah. Let's go see what my little Rembrandt painted." Henry picked up Hannah and took Noah's hand. Jacob, Joshua and Justin followed.

"Supper will be in twenty minutes," hollered Camilla.

Jeremy went back to watching a BC-Roughrider game on TV. The Riders were just about at the BC goal line when Camilla ordered everyone to the table. Father Engelmann usually said grace and at times Henry did but tonight was going to be different. When everyone was settled, Camilla bowed her head and made the sign of the cross and said, "Dear Lord, this is going to be a difficult mealtime for us without Mom or Grandpa Engelmann, so please help us to accept their passing and absence. We know they are here in spirit. Help us Lord to move on and enjoy the family we have just as we all did when our parents went home to You. We all made it then and we will all make it again now. So, dear Lord, bless us all and help us to not be afraid to talk about our loved ones. They would be the first to want us to celebrate their lives and be a part of this beautiful family. And yes, bless this absolutely delicious food I prepared! Amen!"

"Now that, was a Father Engelmann prayer if I ever heard one."

"Amen, to that, Dad. Well, done, honey!"

And then, Hannah looked at Henry and said, "I have a prayer, too. Thank you for my Daddy!"

"Ah, that was nice, Hannah. And I say that about you and all my grandchildren every night!"

There was only a pause for a moment when Jeremy said, "Please pass the potatoes; boy am I hungry!"

"Pass the butter, please Joshua," said Henry, "I want it to melt in all the little holes of that fresh baked bread. Did I ever tell you when I was your age I ran home from school and couldn't wait to open the door and smell what was cooking or baking? My favorite was bread and fried potatoes with onions. Mmmm good!"

Turning to Joshua, Henry asked, "Did you know my Mom was your daddy's Grandma?"

"I remember Grandma Pederson, and I remember her bread, too," replied Joshua."

"By golly, you're right! You were about four when grandma passed away. Sometime, I'll bring over the photo album and we will have to look at the pictures of all our grandparents."

A brief silence fell over the dining room as everyone enjoyed the great food Camilla had prepared. Between mouthfuls, Henry shared that he was going to begin a forty-day retreat at the prayer house next Monday. He said he wanted all the kids to come and visit him on Saturday and he would like to keep Hannah for the day. Henry didn't mention the 'fasting' part since he didn't want to worry the kids. He had already gone in to see Dr. Kreake last Thursday to make sure he was in good enough health to do a juice fast.

"Well, perhaps come to the shop for a day before you begin your retreat," said Jeremy. "A lot of customers are asking about you at the café and gallery. They miss seeing you there."

Joshua was so excited about his science project that he kept interrupting his dad to share what it was all about.

"That sounds great, Josh," said Justin. I remember when Dad helped me make a robot out of cardboard boxes. Maybe in your project we can make a space-suit out of cardboard boxes too. Let's go to the basement and you can show me what you have done so far."

The two boys excused themselves and Henry continued to talk to Jeremy about coming in to the café on the weekend.

Camilla shared about two of her students and told a couple of jokes to cheer things up at bit. All in all, the dinner went over well. What Camilla didn't mention was that one of the girls in her care at the Tutorial School had developed preeclampsia and was deciding whether or not to terminate her pregnancy. It was similar to Jenny's condition as the medication wasn't working either for the girl in question. Camilla had advised her student to pray to Jenny to intercede on her behalf to be cured of the condition. Within a week, the girl's blood pressure had returned to normal and she decided to continue on with her pregnancy. The doctors were astounded how the condition was eliminated almost overnight. Camilla decided to report the incidence to the Archbishop.

They were a family in mourning and healing. It would never be the same again and yet as the freshness of memory begins to fade and the new life experiences of those left behind come into the fore, life moves on and continues the cycle they were seeing now.

Henry stayed until all the kids went to bed. He visited with all of them in their bedrooms and kissed each one goodnight. He had to admit, seeing his little girl go to bed and the prayer ritual she developed tore at his heart. He loved how adorable and angelic she looked kneeling at her bedside and reciting the guardian angel prayer and asking Jesus to bless each member of the family. Unbidden tears kept filling his eyes. Thank you, Jenny for this wonderful gift was all he kept repeating as he closed to the door to Hannah and Jacob's bedroom.

Justin and Henry visited for about an hour longer with Jeremy and Camilla after the kids went to bed. Henry reminded Jeremy that he wouldn't be able to come to the café for over a month as he was going to begin his forty-day fasting retreat that upcoming Monday. As soon as the word 'fasting' slipped out, Camilla immediately questioned it.

"Are you serious, Dad? Are you really going to stop eating for forty days?"

Henry wished he hadn't said what he did but tried to soften what he was planning to do by saying, "Well, it's not a total fast, I will be doing a juice fast; that is drinking water and different juices…"

"But no food whatsoever?" Jeremy chimed in.

Henry shook his head. "No, but I checked with the doctor, and he says that I am fine. I already did lose some weight this past year but it wouldn't hurt to lose a bit more. He cautioned me to look for some symptoms and how to come off the fast."

"Yes, that's very important Dad," advised Camilla. "But still to go for forty days without food is…is…crazy!"

"A juice fast is very healthy. A lot of people do a week or ten-day juice fast just to clean out all the toxins that build up in the body."

"A week juice fast is quite different from a forty day one, nonetheless," countered Camilla once again.

Justin spoke next in defense of his dad. "Look at Grandpa though, he fasted all the time. He looked thin and yet he was healthy…and Jen…I mean Mom did too. She started out by not eating one day of the week and then I remember her going for several days, didn't she Dad?"

"Yes, that's right Son. Jenny fasted for seven days. She prayed during that time for God to grant her a child. And her prayer for many years was granted."

After a long pause, Henry added, "The fasts which Father and Jenny did were not to lose weight or clean out the toxins but more of a spiritual purpose; to make a retreat and fast. I've thought about doing this for years but never considered to make one for forty days. The main reason though why I am doing a forty day fast is because Father Engelmann left me a letter recommending that I do. He even consecrated forty hosts for me to have one each day of the fast. He wants me to do what he had done many times over the years. It's also what Jesus did before he started his ministry."

Once again no-one spoke. Henry didn't want to draw attention to himself or appear holy by what he was about to do. He wished he hadn't brought it up and so he decided to change the topic and asked Camilla how her tutorial classes with the girls were going. She decided to only work two days out of the week because she was needed at home and she didn't want to miss out on the growth and development of the children; especially Hannah and Jacob.

"Oh, Dad, it's so interesting to see how Hannah is developing ahead of Jacob. As you can see, Jacob is just starting to walk and only has a few words in his vocabulary. I don't mind at all that he is so far behind Hannah as his development is very normal for his age. In fact, he is starting to walk early, too. However, it's just that Hannah is so special and far advanced that I can't stop interacting with her. She is more like a five-year-old than just over one. I could just spend the entire day answering her questions. She is so curious about everything! It begins the moment she wakes up until bedtime. And she is so well mannered; if one of the other boys interrupts her she just allows them to say what they want. Or if Jacob wants attention or is crying, she goes over to him and tries to appease him by stroking him or offering him a toy. She is so tiny and yet, so grown up for her age!"

Henry didn't want to make a fuss about it over the other children and so he more or less took what Camilla was saying in stride. But he knew that Hannah was God's child; Jenny gave her to Him and there was a special purpose for her.

But then Camilla said something which touched his heart and the others in the room as well.

"You know, having Jacob and Hannah makes me realize how the gift of life is such a wonderful miracle. How it all starts from a single cell and keeps dividing into a human being! We take life for granted; so many miracles right under our nose and they are so quiet and silent that we don't even notice them." Camilla paused to wipe a tear rolling down her cheek, her blue eyes sparkling in the dim light of the living room. She reminded everyone of Jenny, especially Henry. He immediately empathized with his daughter-in-law and unbidden tears surfaced in his eyes, too.

What Camilla shared next brought tears into everyone's eyes. "As I went into Jacob and Hannah's room this morning both were still sleeping so peacefully. I thought how Jacob was born full term and Hannah born two months premature struggling for her life. Her lungs were not developed. She was so malnourished her skin was transparent, her oxygen supply so limited that the doctors and even I suspected that she would suffer from so many complications or be mentally challenged and yet she beat all the odds and has made an amazing recovery, even surpassing my Jacob! Truly, so many miracles have occurred with that little girl. Jenny would be so ecstatic, she would be rushing to the Angel of Thanksgiving daily, giving thanks and praise to God."

Camilla paused; her voice trailed off and she looked down. Tears of joy fell on her lap as she calmly wept. Jeremy got up and put his arm around his dear wife and said, "You are a miracle I thank God for every day, I love you, Camilla."

It felt odd when Henry and Justin left to leave Hannah behind. She was Henry's daughter and yet it just seemed right for Hannah to be raised by Camilla. Hannah needed a mother and father and Camilla and Jeremy were perfect. They both loved Hannah as their own and in no way restricted Henry from coming or taking Hannah for a while. Henry had learned that Jenny had spoken to Camilla of this possible eventuality and this was Jenny's wish too. Jenny knew that Henry would not be able to raise the little girl and if Camilla and Jeremy agreed to such a scenario, it would be best for all concerned. Fortunately, this is the way it just seemed to naturally work out.

"Praise the Lord," was all Henry could say as he and his young son got into the SUV and drove home to the farm.

CHAPTER FORTY-TWO

IT WAS MONDAY morning, June 20, 1994 when Henry spent his first day of his forty-day retreat in the prayer house. He put a big X on that day in the calendar hanging on the kitchen wall. Yesterday, he and Justin spent the day bringing down carrots, spinach and other greens and vegetables which he would juice twice a day. The rest of the time it would be just water. The fridge was full with two cases of bottled water. Otherwise, the cupboards were bare; no cookies, crackers, or snacks of any kind. He was hungry already and the day was just beginning.

Before Henry had come down that morning he weighed himself at the house. He came in at two hundred and fifteen pounds give or take a few ounces. Even though he didn't eat that much the past year since Jenny's passing, he actually gained almost eleven pounds from being so listless and just moping around. Since his healing, his appetite returned and so did another four pounds. He anticipated losing that weight gain in short order. He said a prayer with his son, left some instructions and chores that needed to be done and then waved goodbye. "Come down whenever you want Son."

It was just past eight o'clock in the morning when Henry walked into the prayer house. He had left Coco inside overnight knowing that he would be here first thing in the morning. She didn't come to greet him. Henry knew she would be lying on the mat by the bed.

Father Engelmann would have said his breviary and Mass by now. He would either be going for a walk with Coco or writing his story. Around mid-morning, he liked to take a nap and then again during the afternoon.

Slowly, he would get into his own routine as well and focus on why he was doing this. He wanted direction in his life and to be certain that it was God's will. Even though Father Engelmann asked him to do this, Henry felt prompted for years; he was more than ready. He envied Father and his friends, Gary and John for the close relationship they had with Jesus and he wanted that for his life, too.

It was true what Father had told him shortly after he started to work for him at the store when he was a young teenager. His words somehow imbedded themselves into his mind and they came back to him now: "Henry, this world so desperately needs people who have thought things through and don't go through life like a leaf tossed by the wind. We need, more than ever, strong people whom others will want to emulate because of the wholesome way they live."

It was as if Father were there beside him now; he always spoke such truths. Henry remembered when Father said those words it was the day after he and Gary went to see the movie 'Rear Window.' They were walking home after the show and Gary told him he wanted to become a priest. Wow, Gary knew then what he wanted to do with his life and here he was still floundering. Well anyway, he was developing and using the gifts God gave him. But like Father said, we need heroes in our lives to look up to and want to be like. His friends definitely had influenced him in that regard. He probably never would be here if it wasn't for them.

Henry walked into the bedroom and his heart went out to Coco lying on the mat beside the bed with her head resting on Father's sandals. She was waiting for Father to come back. No matter how hard Justin tried to coax her to come back home with him, she wouldn't budge. He literally had to lift her up every evening and lock her in the garage overnight. As soon as the garage opened in the morning she made a dash for the prayer house. Her eyes looked so sad and forlorn as she looked up at Henry. Her head remained stationary on the mat, clearly showing that she had no intention of getting up for anyone other than Father. Just the way her eyes rolled up to gaze at Henry revealed how much she missed her master.

Henry came to her and knelt down. He began to pat his old sidekick and softly said, "I miss him, too, Coco. I'm afraid he isn't going to come back. I hope we become friends again while I'm down here. You're a good faithful dog, Coco. I know how dearly you loved Father."

Henry patted her head a couple of times, stood and made his way back out to the living room. He went to one of the wicker chairs by the patio doors and gazed at the pond through the windows. Such a peaceful scene. His mind drifted back to his friends trying to rationalize why it was easier for them to come to the Lord than for him. They didn't have any attachments, no wealth, no possessions and basically were free from worldly values. Whereas he had amassed a small fortune, large enough to easily live comfortably for the rest of his life. Yet, if they hadn't chosen long ago to make that commitment, they might have also been in the same boat and maybe possess even more wealth than he did. At the end of the day however, who was the richer?

The path he had chosen made it very difficult to come to God. Jesus recognized this when He said that it was easier for a camel to go through the eye of a needle than for a rich man to come to God. And, as he examined his life, he was independent, gifted with many abilities and talents and very capable of doing anything which needed to be done or that he set his mind to doing. He really had no need of God, so he thought, until his world came crashing down on him. This past year since Jenny's passing and the ensuing sorrow and depression clearly showed him his utter need and dependence upon God. If Father hadn't sacrificed his life for him, he would more than likely be sitting up top on the deck immersed in self-pity and grief.

It was clear to Henry what Father did for him. Father gave him his life back. He set him free from the darkness he was trapped under as well as all of the idols of the world but it was now up to him to choose to take the final step. All of his life he struggled with that issue; to be for God all the way or, lukewarm for Him. Father always said it was easier to convert a man who hits the bottom than a lukewarm Christian who sits on the fence.

Right now, Henry had such a love for the Lord but it wouldn't last if it wasn't nurtured. Henry knew he was in a honeymoon period with the Lord. He had seen it many times before with other Christians. However, eventually it would fade into the hard trials and challenges of daily living. Soon the choices and decisions would confront him; he would be free to choose one way or the other; to follow in the footsteps of his mentor who in turn gave his life for Jesus or to slip back and once again choose the idols of the world who were constantly in the forefront of his life.

"Yes, this is why you are here," Henry muttered to himself. "To get to know Jesus ever more deeply from the heart and no longer from just the head." He needed to love Jesus like his mentor did. To come to Jesus in brokenness and humility. He needed that kind of attitude but from the heart. In the same way Father loved Jesus first and foremost in his life even above his Anna, Henry too, needed to continue on with that kind of love. Father's sacrifice had given him a taste of that kind of love. A love for his Lord that was greater than the love he held for anything else...even his Jenny. Hopefully, the next forty days would continue to deepen, solidify and further unlock his heart for Jesus. He needed to stay rooted in the freedom he had now in Christ. "Thank You, Father. Thank You...thank You for bringing me into the light. Please pray for me, intercede for me...pray I stay in the light."

Henry went over to the kneeler in front of the altar and began to pray, "Okay, Jesus, here I am. Please release the Holy Spirit within me if He is not already with my spirit and help me to get to know You and love You with all of my heart and soul. I know You are alive and real and exist...it's just that I want to know You to be more real in my life than Jenny was. I don't want to slip back...I am weak and so in need of Your mercy and love. I know You love me. Father helped me to see and feel Your love but now I want it to be directly from You. There is a favorite Scripture of mine in which You said, 'Whoever loves Me will keep My word, and My Father will love him, and We will come to him and make Our dwelling in him.'

"Before this retreat is over, dear Jesus let me know You from the heart. Make Your dwelling within me."

Henry gazed at the cross above the altar and prayed silently for a while longer. He then got up and sat in one of the wicker chairs again by the window. He picked up Father's Bible and read Scriptures for another half hour. His goal was to read the entire New Testament during his retreat.

Hunger began to preoccupy his thoughts. By now, if he were at the house, he would have visited the fridge several times and poured at least two cups of coffee. He got up and went to the altar, unlocked the tabernacle and took out the ciborium. He lifted the lid and took out one of the Hosts. He asked for God to forgive his doubts and for all the times he had turned his back on Him and for any sins which he forgot. He recalled going to confession that day Father came up and gave him communion, so, he felt free of sin and able to receive the Eucharist. Yet, he softly whispered an act of contrition:

"Oh my God, I am heartily sorry for having offended You and I detest all my sins, because I dread the loss of heaven and the pains of hell, but most of all because they offend you, my God, who art all good and deserving of all my love. I firmly resolve, with the help of Your grace, to confess my sins, to do penance and to amend my life."

He stared at the consecrated Host for a long time and said, "Jesus, strengthen my belief that You are here in the flesh. Strengthen it like Father Engelmann's belief." Henry visualized the wounds of Jesus' sacrifice which Father had shown him. Tears surfaced in Henry's eyes. He took the Host in his mouth and ate it.

Henry decided to take a walk. He wished now, Ginger were there with him. He had decided to leave the dog with Justin and to guard the house. He called out to Coco. He went over to the doorway, bent over and patted his knee trying to entice her to come, but she didn't budge. "Come on, Coco...Come..."

Henry stood, turned and went outside. He decided to follow the route Father usually took. He had watched him from the deck hundreds of times. Today, he would begin to follow his teacher's footsteps, hopefully, in more ways than one.

It was a hot summer day. The wind in the air made it seem cooler. That was one thing one can usually rely on in the summer, even on the warmest days, for the prairie wind to keep one cool. The valley floor was cooler; he could feel it. The trees leaves were still young and looked fresh. Henry loved the color of spring and early summer. It was to his eyes like a fresh drink of juice made of spinach and celery. He could smell the celery in his nostrils, despite the brisk breeze that suddenly came down the valley. It stirred his hunger.

It was mid-afternoon when Henry got back to the prayer house. His walk was longer than he intended but he was so engrossed with the subtle change of the tree colors, he wished he had brought his outdoor easel down with him. But then again, if he got involved in his painting, he could easily spend the entire day doing that and defeat the purpose for being here. No, it was best he left his paints in his studio for the time being anyway.

He made himself a glass of juice. This was the first bit of food he had since the day started. He was pleased with himself. He picked up Father's Bible and went outside and sat on the deck chair and read. He was into the eighth chapter of Matthew when he dozed off. The cool air, as the sun began to sink lower in the western sky, woke him. A deer standing next to the deck startled him more than he did the animal. He wondered if the deer was looking for Father Engelmann.

The deer stood there much longer than Henry thought she would before she slowly moved along. On many occasions he watched Father from the deck actually feed the deer from his hand. Perhaps that was one of them waiting for Father to come to her just like Coco wished for Father to come to her, too.

The cool air began to chill him to the point he had to get up and get a sweater. He returned as he wanted to watch the sun set from that perspective. It was from an entirely different view than when he was at the top. He was amazed how quickly the shadows raced across the valley floor as the sun began to sink. He was fascinated with how the light was pushed out by the growing darkness. *Always studying the light, he mused; just couldn't let go of that painterly part of him.* And yet, his purpose here had to do with the *light*.

The darkness was spreading; it felt eerie and cold. The air cooled so much quicker down here than from the deck.

He felt alone.

Hunger pangs began to gnaw away in his stomach. He thought of drinking water to squelch the hunger but knew it would make him cooler than he already was. He debated whether he should go in. When he looked up however, his hunger and coldness suddenly left him. The twilight was taking over and along with it came that special serene time when everything stood still. Henry felt a growing peace…the creation of God was filling his void. The air seemed to grow warmer.

He stayed on the deck for another hour watching the growing darkness and the ever blossoming of the stars in the heavens. The moon reflected perfectly in the pond in front of him. It was so much different from down here than up at the top, too. It was as if the moon was sinking in the pond.

The sounds of nature at night became louder, nearer and more alive; the crickets chirping, frogs croaking and an owl hooting in the distance. The sound of the rushing water sounded like a rapid much more than usual. Perhaps now that he was alone, everything is far more apparent. Yet, it seemed so loud…why hadn't he noticed the sound of the water like that when he visited with Father? The answer came back again…It was because he was now alone. *All alone.*

The sound of coyotes howling nearby startled him. He expected to see one any moment to come onto the deck. He wondered if any ever did when Father was here. With Coco to defend him or at least bark to scare them off, he probably was okay. The thought of being alone with all kinds of animals around began to unsettle him. Every sound got his attention.

He wondered how many animals were watching him now. He wished Coco were here with him.

But Father Engelmann was never alone.

Several times he saw angels surround the prayer house. At times when he was down here visiting Father, he was certain during the times they didn't speak, he heard the flutter of wings. And then Father had Jesus in his heart and the Holy Spirit indwelling in his being. Perhaps that was why he was so unafraid to be here for days on end. Henry looked all around looking for an angel but one never appeared. Instead, he whispered the angel prayer:

Angel of God, my guardian dear,
To whom His love commits me here,
Ever this day be at my side
To light and guard, to rule and guide
My life…and Jenny's and Justin's and Hannah's and all
*   the others…*
Forever and ever.
Amen

He hadn't said the angel prayer in a long time. It filled him with peace. He wished Jenny were there next to him. They had often said that prayer together as they held hands. He wanted to reach out to her but instead reached inside his shirt and felt the pewter angel. He could hear her whisper the words of the inscription, 'Watch over my beloved.' Often at night before she went to sleep she would murmur that phrase to his protector.

The star of the east seemed to shine brighter just then. Perhaps it was because it's so much darker in the valley. And yet, he could feel her love in the shimmering rays of the star. He was certain, Jenny was near…

The wind had gone to sleep about an hour ago. Perhaps he should, too. Since the wind abated, it didn't feel so cool anymore, but he was tired and hungry and decided to call it a day. Father Engelmann was in sync with the daily cycle; rise with the sun and sleep after it sets. Maybe he should too.

When he got into the bedroom, he noticed Coco drank her water but didn't touch her food. She slightly wagged her tail when he came in. It looked hopeful. Henry bent over and patted her head and then stroked it. "It will get better, Coco."

When he stood up, he noticed the manuscripts on the table. He just had to start reading the story; a rush of excitement took away his fatigue and hunger. He sat at the desk and opened up book one, *Pewter Angels*.

It was three-thirty and he was still wide awake. Henry couldn't put the book down. "How could Father Engelmann have seen how I first saw Jenny from our house when she walked by on July 6, 1956!?" Henry was flabbergasted. "How would Father know exactly my thoughts, how I felt and what happened in the store when Jenny and I looked into each other's eyes?" In fact, Father knew more what had happened than he did!

"It's absolutely amazing! "Henry exclaimed, waking up Coco.

But then, Henry recalled Father telling him and Jenny when he had that near-death experience, how he was granted a vision of their lives and all of humanity right up until the time Jenny was healed and they all returned back to earth. "That's right," Henry recalled. "Father was able to take in the knowing of ages in a single thought! That's right," Henry repeated again into silence of the room as a feeling of great exhilaration swept through him. He was having one 'aha' moment after the other. "That's right," Henry said for the third time. Father was able to remember everything while he and Jenny didn't. Father needed to remember and see everything in order to write the story which he was assigned by Zachariah!

Incredibly, Henry was reading his life story from age fifteen on! It was the most remarkable feeling he ever had! He wished Jenny were here reading along with him. He could just imagine her excitement. Surely, she must be fluttering about more than her guardian angel, who was like a hummingbird all the time, at least according to Father Engelmann.

The sun was just beginning to give light to the valley when Henry finally fell asleep. He had read over one hundred and fifty pages and was just at the scene where he and Jenny were going to the park the day before high school started. They were lying on the grass looking up at all the clouds in the sky. Henry could feel his desire for Jenny. His eyes were beginning to droop and they closed. Henry began to dream of them making love…he dreamt of another day they fulfilled their desire to give themselves to one another. It was the day Jenny conceived…it was the day Hannah was given life.

CHAPTER FORTY-THREE

THREE HOURS LATER, Henry woke up. The rising sun from the east blazed in through the large picture window in the bedroom. It was impossible to sleep in that light. For a moment there he thought he was having another vision. How could Father sleep in such intense light?

Henry's second thought on the matter quickly solved that mystery. Father went to sleep when the sun went down and was up before the sun. He was usually in the living room area sitting in one of the chairs by the patio doors which faced the pond. Henry recalled one other time when he went down to the Poustinia and sat by the window discussing Jenny and her life with James. Henry recalled the soft light chasing away the shadows in the valley and faintly stealing into the house through the glass patio doors. He recalled vividly how the tint of yellow and orange light struck the walls. Henry rarely forgot the light. It was at the heart of all his art.

Now he was seeking the 'light' of Jesus in his heart.

Henry was still tired but he couldn't wait to get back to the story. It was the most incredible thing to see his life on paper describing his inner most feelings and thoughts. It was like re-living his life with Jenny and the Engelmann's. He almost felt omnipotent because he could predict what would happen next with amazing accuracy! Father's vision and his ability which he received to remember everything with such detail was all so true to life!

Henry yawned and stretched at the same time and walked out into the living room. He was surprised to see Coco standing by the patio door. She needed to go out. Henry opened the door and stepped out along with Coco. "Wow!" Henry gasped at the perfectly still pond and the serenity of the scene before him. A slight mist hovered over the water. This was close to what heaven must be like. The ethereal atmosphere was filled with peace.

It was near twenty-four hours since he had anything to eat except for water and two glasses of juice. He didn't feel hungry…yet. Without having to digest solid food, Henry's energy level was higher than usual. Perhaps, that was why he wasn't overly tired with only three hours of sleep. As he entered the room again, he noticed Coco had already returned and lay down on the mat in the bedroom. Her head rested on Father Engelmann's sandals. Henry wondered what she was thinking of and where she thought Father might be.

Henry tried to follow the same routine as yesterday. He wanted to continue reading *Pewter Angels* but he had to delay it. It was secondary to why he was there. He went to the living room and knelt down. He made the sign of the cross at the same time as he gazed at the large cross hanging above the altar. He thought about Jesus and how He died for us. All the suffering, torture and pain He endured; Father had made it real for him. He could vividly see the blood gushing out of the wounds. Henry wanted to cry out with great gratitude for what Jesus had done for him and humanity. He recalled how Jenny described the time she was dying in the hospital and how she, too, felt such a close relationship with Jesus. She experienced His suffering along with hers. She understood the pain and anguish the Lord suffered for her and all of us. He would never forget the talk she gave to the congregation that day Father Engelmann invited her to share the vision she had and how she was filled with sadness and yet such joy despite her pain. She had found meaning in her suffering and seemed to understand the mystery of it all as well.

Henry was happy that Father had brought him closer to the Lord, yet still felt twinges of guilt for all the years he had an unappreciative heart. He prayed for the Holy Spirit to come and convict him and fill his heart and entire being with love and gratitude. *He never wanted to go back to his old self again.*

Henry gazed at the cross and cried out, "Jesus, strengthen my faith, my belief!" He said it with such conviction that the echo of his cry returned with such strength, tears surfaced and shivers ran up and down his spine. Coco suddenly jumped up and came to the doorway. Maybe Father expressed such outbursts too from time to time and she thought it was her master. Coco almost came to Henry but then stopped and went back to her mat beside the bed.

Henry got up and read some more of the Bible rather than follow the readings in the Lectionary. He read for almost an hour and finished more than half of the Gospel of Matthew. He was reading too fast and he was beginning to feel very tired and hungry. He was no longer concentrating on what he was reading. He went to the altar and took out another Host. He stared at the round disc of unleavened bread for the longest time and tried to visualize the Host as actually being Jesus. Father often said celebrating Mass was like walking with Jesus to Calvary. He held up the Host so that he could see the Host and Jesus hanging on the cross above the altar at the same time. Through Father Engelmann having received the Stigmata, Henry saw it; Jesus nailed to the cross and his side pierced at the same time. There on the floor was living proof what Jesus had done for the human race. Henry looked down and once again saw the wounds of Christ through his beloved friend. Henry fell to his knees, filled with such deep feelings of gratitude and sorrow.

He was beginning to see what Father saw; what Jenny saw; what his friends, Gary and John saw. Tears of thankfulness poured out of him...

Over and over, Henry asked for mercy and forgiveness. He wanted his heart to be convicted and he cried for more, "Convict me oh, Holy Spirit; increase my faith, strengthen and deepen my belief."

Henry gazed adoringly at the Host and ate it. A warm feeling swept through his body. He was so hungry he wanted to eat all of the hosts. He was disappointed at himself for such a thought...the Host was not meant as food, but as spiritual nourishment. He could see now that he would need strength to fast and endure the next thirty-nine days. His motive for coming here had to be right.

He was here to seek God's will for his life. He was here to draw near to God and claim His promise that He will draw near to him. Fasting and praying were the channels to God's heart; this was the way to open the portals of heaven. His desire to come to God freely and openly without any ulterior motive had to be sincere. Father Engelmann's sacrifice to him had made Henry deeply realize just how much God and Jesus loved him. It was done freely as a gift. Henry finally got it; that he could never have done enough to deserve God's favor or love. No! There was nothing on earth that he could ever do to repay Father and His Son, Jesus Christ.

Jesus loved him unconditionally. While he was yet a sinner, Jesus suffered and died for him; freely given as a gift to him and others. Henry could never earn that. No amount of good works could ever earn what God had done for him out of love. He could see the error of his ways by trying to manipulate and control God by his good works.

Henry shook his head in sorrow. "Oh, Lord, keep my motive pure. I come to you, Father, to You, Jesus and to You the Holy Spirit out of gratitude, love and praise. Oh, help me, Lord, to develop such a deep, close relationship with You so I know Your will for my life from moment to moment. So that others will see You in me as they saw You in my beloved Father Engelmann.

Henry wept.

AROUND NOON, HENRY went to the fridge and took out a bottle of water and drank half of it. He hoped it would help to fill him and reduce his raging hunger. Fatigue, from not having enough sleep, also began to have its toll on him. Perhaps that was a blessing. He would sleep the hunger away. He went into the bedroom and the sun was no longer coming in directly as it was earlier. He stepped over Coco and lay down and faced the west wall. Within minutes, he was fast asleep.

Around two in the afternoon, he heard a whimpering and scratching sound at the door. Surely, that couldn't be Coco coming back to life! He got up and went to the door. It was Ginger. "Ah, Ginger, you miss me, do you? I guess with Justin at the gallery and Coco down here, it's lonely up there." Henry bent down and patted her head. "Come, come in, Ginger." She immediately went into the bedroom and lay next to Coco.

Hunger returned with a vengeance. He considered some of Coco's dog food that he noticed in the cupboard. He went into the living room and knelt down.

"Please help me with my fast. I am doing this for You, Jesus. I want to know You, to love You, to be grateful and praise You with a cheerful and sincere heart. Help me. Help me to develop a close relationship with You. Help me to show my gratitude and love for You for all You have done for me. Let my praise and thanks be forever on my lips!"

Henry was beginning to feel his dependence on God. He also began to realize how much he thought of food and all the time he spent satisfying his body; especially keeping his belly full. He decided to go for a walk. He hoped with Ginger there, Coco would be encouraged to come along but she stayed. Henry wondered why she was still so loyal, not being able to see her beloved master. He stepped outside and took a deep breath of fresh air and seeped in the beautiful summer afternoon. He couldn't get over the rich greens. He almost wanted to go to the nearby trees and eat the leaves.

"Come, Ginger," he said as he stepped off the deck and walked the trail which Father usually took. He felt more rested but his hunger would not leave him. He was amazed how

Father Engelmann was twice his age and the stamina he had to fast and walk the hills like he did. Many times, he thought Father looked like Moses as he walked along. Henry felt like that now, too.

He reached into his pocket and took out Jenny's rosary. He decided to pray to Mary, to intercede for him to her Son for help. She knew how men got hungry and the joy she must have had in feeding Jesus and Joseph. Henry loved the name, 'Mary.' It had such a beautiful, pure sound. It reminded him of his mother who also had the same name. Henry wished he was walking home, he could already smell the bread baking in the oven as he opened the door! *His desire for food overwhelmed him.*

When he returned to the prayer house, it was dinner time. His hunger never left him the entire time he was walking. All he could think about was food. He went to the fridge and decided to have a tall glass of orange juice. He had cranberry that morning. He drank it all without stopping. He got some dog food and water out for Ginger and Coco and fed them. Coco finally had some food. Ginger eating next to her must have stimulated her appetite.

It was still warm outside, so he decided to go out on the deck and read more of Pewter Angels. Once again, he was flabbergasted how well Father had written the story and how it captured his and Jenny's love for each other. He was so absorbed in the story, he hadn't noticed the sun was setting and the reason why he was finding it harder to read the writing. He was just at the part when Jenny was leaving with her parents to catch a plane to Ottawa. Tears spilled down his cheeks as he relived that heartbreaking moment. Jenny had rushed over to him and they were about to have their farewell kiss when suddenly Jenny was torn from his arms. All he saw was the angry flash of Jenny's mother's eyes…he wanted to see Jenny's though. He ran to the taxi and tried to see his beloved one last time but she was whisked away and his world came crashing down. The story was so real, Henry felt the deep pain of loss once again and then…he felt the soft touch of his mother's hand on his shoulder like an angel trying to comforting him... "Oh, Jenny, despite all trials and tribulations our love brought us back together but this time..." Henry couldn't finish.

He lifted his head just in time to watch the last glimmer of the sun sink behind his house on top of the hill. He thought once more of the story and of Jenny leaving and it would be decades before he would see her again. The thought should have filled him with hope but Henry knew her return would be short lived. In five short years, she would be gone again and never to return. The hurt and sadness he felt at that moment overshadowed his hunger...

He longed to fill the void left with the loss of Jenny and his beloved friend, Father Engelmann. But he was in Jesus' care now, comforted by the creator of the universe Himself.

Chapter Forty-Four

H ENRY HAD TO say, the second to the sixth day were the most difficult to deal with. Not only did the hunger and desire for food overwhelm him, he also began to experience violent symptoms of detoxification. He recalled the doctor telling him he was fit to do the fast but to expect headaches, dizziness, fatigue and even fever to name a few. It was the headaches which Henry rarely had that were the most painful symptoms so far.

For years, he had been taking in food and drink which were not good for him and now that he stopped and began fasting, the body was cleaning, sanitizing and renewing itself. The liver had stored and neutralized many poisons and so had the colon held years of polluted materials but fasting began the cleaning, by opening up all those dark and dingy corners, exposing their muck, dirt and mire.

The dreary cloud cover and muddy conditions from the pouring rain outside seemed to compliment what was going on inside his body. He could just imagine the countless bottles of water he was drinking, forming rivulets inside his intestines and stomach, washing out the crevices of muck, just as the rivulets in the road outside was carrying away the mud.

It was the first Saturday of his fast and the kids were supposed to come for a visit but the steep hill was too slippery and dangerous for Jeremy's SUV to come down. It was just as well as Henry wasn't in any shape for company as much as he wanted to see them.

On the seventh day, however, something happened. Henry not only woke up to a beautiful blue sky but he got a reprieve and perhaps a reward for sticking it out. Both his hunger and headaches seemed to go away and a peace fell on him. It was like the time he was into jogging. It was so difficult to keep running and after four or five miles it seemed he broke free of his effort and fatigue and felt like he could run forever.

He felt like that now.

He felt like running and shouting up and down the hills of the valley. A weight was lifting both physically and emotionally. He felt like he was getting in control over his body. He felt his will power and self-discipline which to a large degree, had been dormant for years. Instead of stuffing himself unthinkably with snacks and drinks and food whenever, he now directed his body to get their calories from internal stored sources. Even more so was the strength he was feeling to look after his body which was the temple of the indwelling presence of Jesus. He wanted to care for it now like never before!

The benefits were not only great but divine!

As Henry walked with Ginger that morning, the sun shone brighter, summer was more glorious, the wind on his face more refreshing, and the sound of the birds and meadowlarks overhead more beautiful.

In the evening, the stars twinkled with intensity; the moon was lower and brighter in the sky. Henry felt like he could fly like the countless butterflies all around in the meadows. He wondered if the angels surrounding the house would lift him.

He knew they were all around there.

The euphoria of getting over that initial hump when one begins fasting began to spread to Henry's prayer life. He was more grateful and appreciative of his blessings. He wondered if he was drawing nearer to God. While Father Engelmann helped to free him of his depression and increase his love for the Lord, it still seemed to Henry, however, that it felt much like he did when life was good and everything was fine. He would soon find that everything was not what it appeared to be. His spiritual growth to the next level was yet to come. *And it had to come from Him.*

It wasn't until the eleventh day, as Henry was reading the Gospel of John, that he became convicted of his pride, his judgmental, critical and condemning attitude, his independent spirit, self-centeredness and lack of obedience to the Father. The more he read of Jesus' life, the more he realized that Jesus, even though He himself was God, was totally humble and submissive to the Father. He always sought the will of the Father before doing anything. Henry rarely sought the will of Jesus in making any decision. In fact, he could not even begin to count the number of times he had turned his back on Jesus and did what he wanted.

Just like all the junk and dirt Henry had fed into his body over the years, he also did many things which he wasn't proud of and was ashamed of and sorry for. In the days which followed, he became conscious of his own nothingness and of all the weakness of his flesh. Henry's sins and character flaws began to surface.

Detoxification of the heart and soul had begun.

He found a growing need to repent and be free of all the poisons he had allowed into his body and soul. His body was a gift like everything he had. His body was the temple in which the Holy Spirit resided! He felt deep shame and sorrow for how inconsiderate and sinful he was at times, desecrating the temple which housed the Spirit of God! How he had ignored and turned his back on God just to satisfy his every whim and pleasure.

And despite his sinful nature, God was always there to forgive and receive him like the prodigal son. A growing gratefulness for all of his blessings brought Henry to his knees time and again. He went into extended periods of weeping and sorrow. God was honoring him with His presence as Henry began in earnest and real sincerity to seek Him. Yes, the Scripture James 4:8 is true; "Draw near to God and He will draw near to you." And just that morning it was confirmed again in Jeremiah 29:13; "You will seek Me and find Me; when you seek Me with all your heart."

Henry's physical hunger was completely replaced by a hunger for the Lord and more of His presence and His Word. He couldn't get enough of Scripture. Each passing day, Henry fell to his knees as sins and transgressions of his past life kept coming to mind. The Light of Jesus was exposing his hidden sins, shortcomings and self-centeredness. Nothing could hide in the shadows any longer. Henry could see that the closer he drew to Him, the more he saw his true self and how far short he was from being the child of God he should be.

The light of the Word was transforming Henry. Over and over, he pleaded for forgiveness before taking another of the consecrated Hosts his mentor had left for him. His gratefulness to Father Engelmann for suggesting he do this fast couldn't be expressed enough. Henry began to appreciate what his mentor had done and practiced for years and the immense benefits his beloved teacher had derived from doing so.

No wonder Father was so holy; prayer and fasting humbles the spirit. No wonder his mind was so sharp, his body so youthful and radiant with health; prayer and fasting cleanses the body of toxins and releases untold energy. It leads to an amazing longevity of life! No wonder he was so holy and Spirit filled and showered daily with blessings from the Lord overflowing all the days of his life. Prayer and fasting opens the portals of heaven and brings God so close, we can feel the warmth of His breath! No wonder he was able to resist Satan and all evil spirits; they would never dare touch or come near to a soul so completely filled with light. No wonder he was so free and detached from the secular world. Prayer and fasting led him to the source of life; he knew Jesus was the way, the truth and the life. Yes, Father Engelmann knew the benefits of prayer and fasting and relinquishing his will to the Lord and obeying God in all respects.

It is little wonder that David Engelmann was a saint!

How foolish Henry was to think that Father Engelmann was missing out in so many pleasures in life when it was really himself who was missing out on the real joys of life and living! Each passing day was filled with insights; the true meaning and purpose of life was unfolding before him. He was prompted to get up and pray at all times during the day or night. The Scriptures were not just idle words but his life! *They were the blueprint of how he should live!*

With the healing of his body, his mind became clearer and he could see what was really important and what mattered in life. Fasting was releasing his spirituality and expanding his consciousness of life beyond his imaginings. The Holy Spirit was convicting him, giving him strength and wisdom.

Often, Henry was so grateful, he would go out onto the deck and raise his hands heavenward and shout, "Thank You, Lord! Thank You for all my blessings, my cup runneth over!" He now knew why he had seen Father Engelmann do that very thing when he walked the hills surrounding the prayer house. *When one begins to fall in love with the Lord, you want to shout it from the roof tops!*

CHAPTER FORTY-FIVE

Incredibly, Henry had just completed twenty-six days of fasting in the prayer house. Almost four weeks! He never dreamt that he could make it this far. The kids were concerned about him but he just re-assured them that he was okay and highly recommended that they try it, too. Every Saturday, Jeremy and Camilla along with the children, came to visit for an hour or so and then left Hannah behind for the day with her dad. It was the perfect way to offer Henry a break from the intensity of the struggles he was going through during the week. The visits assuaged his feelings and offered him a respite from his hunger. But even more so, he was growing closer to the little girl he so truly loved and reminded him more and more of his dear sweet Jenny each time he saw her.

Today was Saturday and Henry was expecting them later that morning around nine-thirty.

He had been up for two hours and already read the Scriptures and had communion. He had trouble reading any more as he was so anxious to see the kids come and he loved spending the day with Hannah.

He stepped out onto the deck and took in a deep breath of fresh air. He felt the brisk breeze flow across the pond. The ripples sparkled in the sun but the peaceful repose and reflection of the hills on the water surface wasn't there that morning. Henry raised his hands upward to praise God for the gift of another day and as he did so, he saw a blue object zig-zagging in the sky just above his house on top of the hill.

"Was that a kite?" he muttered under his breath. He focused his gaze in earnest and from that vantage point; he was certain that it was the blue kite that he and Justin had made years ago. It was the same kite Jenny and Justin had flown that memorable day on the hill just outside his studio. In fact, Henry surmised, that whoever was flying the kite would be on that same hill.

"It must be Justin! But why is he flying the kite this early? It's not even eight o'clock." From that view looking up the hillside, Henry could not see the hill as it was hidden behind the farm house. And yet, what on earth motivated his son to get up so early and fly his kite? Henry wondered how long Justin had been out there.

The wind was perfect for flying a kite. But there had to be more to it…

It came to him in a flash that Justin missed Jenny so much that his son, like he himself had done so many times that past year, was trying to revive precious memories of their time together. He probably missed Father Engelmann too and was finding a way to free himself from his loneliness…to draw upon memories of what once gave him so much joy. Tears came to Henry's eyes and he softly whispered thanks to God for reminding him of the sorrow that his son may still be experiencing.

Henry wished he could see his son and the happiness in his eyes as he re-lived those moments in time. *He should be up there with him, helping him to heal, too.* For all too long, he had neglected his son and the entire family by being so pre-occupied since Jenny's death and now Father Engelmann's. He would have to make every effort to be there for Justin.

The kite flew behind the house and hid from view. Henry held his gaze steadfast in the sky, waiting for the kite to whip back into the cerulean blue sky, but after five minutes and then ten, it never re-appeared. What Henry did see however, was Jeremy's SUV coming into view as the vehicle wound its way around the turn in the bend.

My, my, Henry thought, *everyone's so early. Perhaps they were as excited as he was to see them!* Henry's heart raced as he watched the truck cautiously make its way down the hill, cross the bridge, slowly making its way towards the prayer house. The car windows were open and he heard the kids jumping up and down yelling in excitement. Joshua stuck his head out the window along with his right arm waving.

As soon as the car parked, the back doors flew open and out ran Joshua and Noah followed by Hannah and Jacob. They ran to Henry, each wanting to be first to give him a hug. Henry held his arms open as they all rushed into them.

"Hi Grandpa," they yelled. The bigger boys were greeted first and then Henry picked up Jacob and last his little girl. "Daddy, Daddy, I'm here to visit again!" cried Hannah. "Are we going to walk along the stream and see the fish?"

"Yup, we sure are, sweetie and so are the boys. First, let me give Camilla and Jeremy a hug." Henry sat Jacob and Hannah down and gave Justin, Jeremy and Camilla a warm greeting.

"How are you doing, Dad? Geez it's been four weeks since you've eaten. You're going to starve and get sick."

The expressions on Camilla's and Jeremy's face seemed to echo Justin's sentiments.

"I'm fine, in fact, I never felt better. Look at the weight I've lost. My belt has moved up three notches and I had to drive a nail into the belt to make a fourth hole this morning! The doctor told me I would know when to stop. He said that I will begin to feel a real hunger coming on and when that happens, I should slowly start to take in food again over a one to two-week period. So far, I'm just fine and the energy and freedom I feel is incredible! I am beginning to know the wonderful gift of will power and self-discipline which the Lord gave me."

Henry's positive words didn't wipe the concerned look away on their faces so, Henry added, "Trust me, if one is healthy enough to fast, the benefits are amazing. Not only from a health point but spiritually it's...it's just so incredible. It's hard to describe but prayer and fasting, simply stated, opens the doors to heaven. It puts God on alert that you are serious in coming to Him. It opens the doors to God's heart and His whispers; we feel His love for us and begin to know His plan for us.

He becomes real in our lives ...

Henry had to pause; he was so overwhelmed with love for the Lord. Tears surfaced in his eyes.

Justin shook his head, trying to understand what his father was saying and doing by all this. Though he had to admit, his father looked so much better than he did this past year. Still, Justin more or less ignored all his dad had said so passionately. "I brought down more water and also some snacks for you."

"No, I'm fine, Justin. Just leave the water, although Hannah may want some snacks."

"Actually, Dad, I have a few plastic containers filled with vegetable sticks and a light lunch for you to give to her," Camilla said and then hollered to Justin, "bring the bag in the front seat, please and thank you!"

"Can we go on the paddle boat, Grandpa?"

"Yeah, that's a good idea, Noah." Hannah and Jacob clapped their hands in anticipation of the boat ride. Joshua ran ahead and began to push the boat into the water.

"Yea, yea!" All the kids yelled with excitement as off they went. Jeremy and Camilla sat on the deck, watching and enjoying the peace and quiet. Shortly, the children were in the paddle boat. Hannah sat on Henry's lap while Jacob sat on Justin's knees in the front and Joshua and Noah sat in the back. They alternated paddling and using the battery-operated propeller. Within minutes, they were out of sight as they slowly went down stream which meandered in and out of the valley floor.

"I saw you had the kite out early this morning," Henry said, without looking at Justin.

"Yeah, I woke up early and saw the trees swaying in the wind and it remin...it would be a good day to fly the kite."

Henry knew it wasn't just the wind and his son almost revealed his true motive. He decided to bring up the topic. "Yeah, when I saw the kite it immediately reminded me of the day you and Jenny tried out the kite on the hillside. I'll never forget that day I saw you two from the studio window."

Justin's response was swift. "It was so cool seeing the kite fly up on Jen— I mean, Mom's first try. Boy, she sure looked excited."

"You miss her, Son?"

Justin didn't speak, he just nodded his head.

"I miss her too and also Father. They were so much alike in so many ways."

Justin just nodded again.

"Are you crying, Justin?" Hannah wanted to know.

Justin turned beet red. He took a quick swipe at a tear rolling down his cheek. "Nah, just the wind watering my eyes, Hannah."

A silence fell as Henry and all the children just seemed to enjoy the paddle boat, silently gliding through the water.

It came to Henry once more, the freedom and joy of those precious moments, when Justin saw the jewel inside of Jenny. The wind had stolen his defensiveness and the young boy was helpless in the midst and beauty of his stepmother. How they had tried for years, through words and actions, to convince Justin that Jenny was not there to ever replace Julean but all these demonstrations of love were always shunned by Justin.

And then, without trying or even thinking about it, in the freedom of the moment, God is there and touches lives! He is now free to intervene without our interference! Love simply flows like the wind, lifting the kite into the heavens. He allows us to see into the hearts of each other and see the love which is always there.

It is this love and beauty which unites us.

Henry will never forget that moment and the lesson of just being and living and enjoying fully, the precious moments God gives us to love; to simply live freely in the moment without manipulations or attempting to change and control others. Yes, it is God's love which heals perfectly and creates miracles.

That day Henry saw such a miracle happen.

Tears that welled up inside him then, welled up inside of him now...*love always does this when it touches home.*

Henry squeezed his little girl a bit tighter and reached across to Justin and patted his knee. The Lord was healing them both...Henry was getting outside of himself...he was now ministering to others just as he saw his mentor do a million times and more. He was learning once again to live and love in the moment of life...*the present moments*...when God creates miracles in our lives.

About an hour later, they returned. Jeremy and Camilla could hear the children before they saw them from behind all the brush lining the stream.

"Mommy, I'm here!" yelled Jacob as soon as he saw her on the deck.

When they got back, they visited for a while and then got ready to leave except for Hannah. They would pick her up later that afternoon. But before Justin got into the car, Henry asked, "Is the kite still up at the house, Justin?"

"No, when Jeremy came up the lane to the house and saw me this morning, he stopped at the hillside. I reeled the kite in and threw it into the back of the SUV."

"If it's here why don't you bring it out and maybe the three of us can try out the kite down here in the valley. The wind is still up. I think Hannah would enjoy seeing the kite fly into the sky and so would I."

Justin thought a bit and said, "Yeah, okay." He reached into the back area of the SUV and pulled out the blue kite. Camilla's children wanted to stay too and see the kite flying but Jeremy had to get back to the city to get to work. The kids looked so disappointed. Henry really wanted to visit with just Justin and Hannah but his heart went out to Camilla's children.

"Justin can drive the children back to the city in a couple of hours if that's okay with you and Jeremy. It might be fun for all of them to take turns flying the kite."

Henry looked at Justin and asked if that was okay with him.

"Yeah, sure, I can drive the kids back, Camilla."

Jeremy nodded that was okay with him and the children jumped up and down with glee.

In no time, Justin took the kids out into the meadow and had the kite flying high into the sky. Joshua got the hang of it right away and so did Noah. Justin just had Hannah and Jacob hold part of the string and together they would tug away at it. Henry loved to watch the kids and took special note of Hannah running through the field of flowers. The monarch butterflies seemed to follow her just like they did her mother. Every now and then Hannah stopped to pick a white daisy with the yellow center and wave it in the air as she tried to follow the kite.

Just before noon, Justin took the boys back into the city. The only way he got them to agree was to take them to McDonalds for lunch!

After Justin and the boys left, Henry and Hannah made their way back to the deck.

"So, let's see what Mom put in the bag for you. Did she bring your favorite book? What have we got here…a book about angels!?"

"We all have a guardian angel, Daddy."

"Yes, I know. I'm excited to read it, Hannah."

Henry picked her up and sat her on his knees and together they read the book. He was surprised that she could read much of the book by herself. He liked the part which told how angels protect us and keep us from harm.

"And they pray for us all the time, too," Hannah added.

After Henry finished, he said, "Did you know that angels see God all the time?"

Hannah, nodded, "Uh, huh. I see my angel, too. As soon as I say my prayers and go to bed, my angel sometimes tucks me in and sings to me."

"Really, what does your angel look like?" Henry wanted to know.

"She is very pretty in her long white gown. It's so shiny and bright and her wings are like a butterfly. See, look how many were following us when we went on the paddle boat!" Hannah reached out her hand for a monarch butterfly to land on it.

Henry shook his head and asked, "I loved how you said the guardian angel prayer before you went to bed when I was over for dinner.

Hannah looked up at him, her golden wheat colored hair fluttered in front of Henry's face as his little girl once again nodded and said, "Mommy and Daddy say it with me all the time."

"Can you say it for me now, Hannah?"

Hannah looked at her Daddy and said:

"Angel of God, my guardian dear,
  To whom His love commits me here,
  Ever this day be at my side
  to light and guard, to rule and guide.
  Amen."

"Oh, Hannah that's beautiful. When I say it, I sometimes add on the end for my angel to look after Jenny, too." Henry didn't know if he should have said that. Hannah may not understand. He was shocked by how she responded though.

"Oh, that's my other Mommy. She is in heaven. You were married to her just like my daddy is married to my mommy."

Henry looked at Hannah, amazed at her understanding. "That's wonderful that you know that, Hannah."

Hannah nodded and added, "My mommy said that I am very special to have two mommies and two daddies. Someday, I will meet my other mommy."

"Oh Hannah, you are very special. I love you so much."

"I love you too, Daddy," said Hannah, her sparkling blue eyes glistening in the noonday sun.

Tears surfaced in Henry's eyes as he gazed at his beautiful little girl and gave her a warm hug.

She was Jenny, all over again.

CHAPTER FORTY-SIX

ON THE TWENTY-EIGHT-DAY, Henry woke just as the sun was rising over the eastern hills of the valley. He loved how the rays of the sun seemed to burn into the top edge of the hill. On rare occasions like this, that scene always reminded him as if the sun was having breakfast and took a huge bite out of the hill top. The shape of the view left behind seemed to smile at him.

He stood on the deck and greeted the dawning of a new day. What an incredible peace pervaded him; within and without. The pond in front of him was calm and so still he wouldn't have known it was silently moving if it were not for the sound of the water wriggling through the twigs and rocks of the beaver dam.

What a picture of serenity and peace the early morning and nature offers to anyone who rises early enough to welcome the sun come up above the horizon. An amazing gift is given to us by the good Lord if we come to Him at this hour. His Word comes alive and we are open to His whispers.

"Oh, thank You, Lord. Thank You!" Henry softly cried as he looked at the sun now rising above the hill and its full power shining so gloriously in the clear blue sky. The valley was becoming alive as the shadows scampered and no longer had anywhere to hide. The power of the light does that…it destroys the darkness. And that was his job now, *to be such a light.* His dear friend and teacher brought him to this point and now it was up to him to carry the torch.

Decisions and choices, we make moment by moment as we journey through life are at the heart of the matter. His mentor had taught him that right from the start when he began working at the grocery store. The values and principles we develop in our lives by the choices we make determine who we are and the life we make for ourselves. His teacher taught him this over and over and despite that he had the best model to follow, it took him over fifty years to get it; to free himself from the idols and values of the world and adopt the teachings of Jesus Christ. If it had not been for his friend's offering, he might never have realized just how shallow his faith was. It may have taken more of his life and the workings of God's divine Providence to finally bring him to this point. Or perhaps never!

The inner peace he was feeling now he could have enjoyed for years. He saw it in his teacher almost daily; as close as the air he breathed and, yet he was blind to it. His mind and intellect helped him to believe he was a man of faith but in reality, it was the evil one who initiated such thoughts. The *mind* is Satan's territory; where he works day and night. He helps us to believe such shallow thoughts and quickly expands them thus blocking the truth from travelling to our hearts.

As Father Engelmann always said, the Truth and the Word must travel from the mind to the heart for the light to come on. Otherwise it remains dim and ineffective. We cannot do God's work effectively until this happens as others are always on the lookout for phonies, hypocrites and Pharisees who expound Christian truths but don't live it.

Walk the talk, that was Father Engelmann; authentic and true to himself inside and out. That's what the world needs so desperately; people who have thought things through; people who see the need for the Comforter, Healer and Advocate to help them swallow the truth of Jesus' teachings and live it.

The sun was now rising higher into the morning sky. More and more color and beauty of the valley was being exposed and reflected in the pond before him. The warmth of the sun's rays on his skin was warmed even further by the glory of God's creation for His children. The blessings abound daily if we but stop and see; *His works are all around.*

God's love surged through Henry lifting his spirits. He slid out of his chair and fell to his knees. With his eyes closed, he lifted his face up to the morning sun just like he and his mentor did so many times as they sat out back of the store on the old grey crates. So many truths were being passed down and continued to do so throughout his journey in life.

"Thank You, God the Father, for the gift of such a loving caring friend. Thank You for all the trials that You have allowed in my life. Thank You, too Jesus, thank You my Lord, my Savior, my all." How fortunate Henry was to have made the decision to do this forty-day fast and prayer retreat. He knew he had to do this, despite his miraculous healing. His friend had offered his life for his healing but Henry had to step out and accept it and use that gift as the basis for further growth and strengthening.

It was true, as we seek Him with our heart we will find Him. Henry knew in these past few weeks he had drawn nearer to God and his Lord had drawn nearer to Him. Fasting definitely had helped him to detach from the world and be more focused on God. His faith and prayer life were blossoming more each day and he could see his lifelong aspirations to be more like his friends and mentor being finally realized.

Like his mentor said, God wants us to step out in prayer to develop strength of character and purpose. He wants us to be warriors and build our faith on a rock. This is what he had done these past four weeks, yet in spite of the peace he felt as he knelt there under the warmth of the heavens, a quiet voice inside of him whispered that he had still not let go of his worldly ways. He still was too much attached to the things of this life and took them too much to heart.

How could that be? For days now, he had looked directly into the obstacles which prevented a closer relationship with the Lord and thought he had dealt with them, hadn't he? Wondered Henry.

Did this uneasiness have something to do with the image he kept seeing daily of that last day when Father Engelman was with him on the deck and Father washed his feet? It was such an act of humility and mimicked what Jesus had done the night before he died. Cleary, it was a message for him to follow his mentor and serve others.

But, ...but, there was more...Henry could sense it...

As happened so often when Father and Henry sat on the old crates and faced the rays of the sun, insights seemed to illuminate their minds and discussions. Henry felt certain, his mentor was kneeling beside him helping him to see that he was still attached to the world; it's ways, it's thinking and how it loves. Despite his recognition of his continuous struggles with breaking away from seeking the approval of others, equating his worth with what he owned, his love of the flow of accolades...he still wasn't free of these lifelong insecurities.

At the heart of this common malady was the way the world teaches us to love one another; conditionally.

So often, Henry had seen that in others and himself during his counselling years. We put conditions on others to determine if they are worthy of our love. So often in our relationships, we are critical and judgmental. Many times, too, we apply conditions on ourselves as well, determining how we feel about ourselves. However, in God's world, love is unconditional; a gift freely given. Henry saw firsthand the wounds of his friend revealing in no uncertain terms the complete giving and sacrifice Jesus had made for him. Jesus didn't place conditions on him! Or judge him or ask him to beg for mercy or pay for his transgressions before Jesus would make such a huge sacrifice and undergo such horrendous torture and suffering. No! Jesus' sacrifice was freely given out of a love which Henry felt the day Father died for him but it still was for the most part in his head and had not yet completely travelled to his heart!

Suddenly though, it happened with blitzing speed. His heart was illuminated and insights flashed before him like lightning! "Yes, yes," Henry muttered, sounding like his teacher, "Father,

Jenny, Gary and John knew all about conditional and unconditional love! That was the secret to their peace and why they were always so centered in the storms of life. They knew they were children of God, loved immeasurably. There was no competitive spirit within them. They didn't compete with others to win or appear better. They didn't seek or live for the approval of others or pursue riches or fame to be worthy and feel loved. They didn't stew over guilt when they sinned. And look, how people gravitated towards them and felt so at ease in their presence.

No! No! No, Henry! He cried in his mind. They had no need for the values of the world and he didn't have to either! Why on earth would he choose to derive his worth from the opinion and approval of others?

Henry suddenly realized that seeking the approval of others was just another idol in his life. He placed what people thought of him on such a high pedestal as if they were god! This is sinful. It goes against the first commandment! I am the Lord thy God, thou shall not have any gods before me. It was all in the mind, the result of years and years of conditioning; faulty thinking and the result of conditional love. And because we love this way, we think that God loves us conditionally too!

God loves you Henry just as you are!

The creator of the universe freely gives you His love so completely that He had His only begotten Son die for you!! In God's eyes, you have incalculable value and worth. Simply claim your inheritance and follow Jesus!!

"How foolish we are to live and love conditionally! Henry could see it was this kind of love that makes us so critical and judgmental of each other. What did Jesus say; don't judge lest ye be judged, and another; take the log out of your own eye before you try to remove the splinter out of others." Henry looked down and saw his finger pointing and the lesson Father taught him so long ago. When we point our finger at others, note that three, point back to you. Yes, in the end we are no better or worse than most people.

It is this way of loving and relating to others which separates us. It is as if we get up and step into an elevator each day. If we do this and that, we get praise and glory and move up. If we say this or that or fail to prove ourselves, we go down. Up and down, up and down all depending how the wind of approval blows our way. What a highly insecure and destructive way to live, when heaven could be on earth each day if we chose to place Jesus at the center of our lives.

Why are we so blind to this? Why do we turn our backs to what Jesus did for us and offered us when we could have such freedom in Him?! Henry recalled the analogy which Father often said to help people understand their indifference to Jesus' sacrifice. If someone gave us a million dollars as a free gift, wouldn't we be indebted to that person for life!? Wouldn't we go out of our way to obey him, love him and be ever so grateful? Wouldn't we want to do good for him to return our deep appreciation!?

Yet, this is nothing compared to what Jesus gives us and has done for us. He not only gives us in sense, a million dollars once but He does so again and again! He is always there ready to forgive and open the doors to heaven!

Henry normally would be feeling exhilaration at this insight and still he remained kneeling in the rising sun. There was more he had to put together.

There was more *'mind'* knowledge that had to travel to the *heart*!

The image of Father Engelmann washing his feet returned stronger and more convicting than ever. Somehow this was all related and connected together.

Once again, his heart was illuminated stronger than before! Credit may have been given to the powerful rays of the sun for this, but to one who understands the divine Providence of God, he would know that the Lord had just showered Henry with grace and wisdom; *the seed to abundant life, my son, means dying to oneself!*

It all comes down to humility warring against one's pride.

Yes, that's right… Father, Jenny and his friends had learned that the path to total freedom from the values of the world and deriving one's worth and value from others was to serve them! They simply lived to love their Lord and to be obedient to Him. They knew that in Jesus Christ, their lives were sufficient. *They needed nothing else.*

Yes, submitting to others is the path to take; loving them when they fail to love you; being kind when unkindness is shown; where there is injury, forgiveness; seeking to console rather than to be consoled, to understand rather than to be understood; to be a peacemaker...

Yes, being a servant to others is key in God's kingdom.

Loving others unconditionally requires suffering at times, requires pain at times, requires tears at times, requires being hurt at times and requires dying to oneself *all the time.* To be a light, to trust in God to turn it all into good, is to choose the narrow path, but it is the path to freedom, to peace, and to eternal life.

How beautifully simple it is *but comes at a cost.*

The journey to holiness is the journey to humility. It is the journey which Jesus took and if we choose to follow Him, we must take this path, too. It's the journey few travel but at the end of our journey in life, it's the ones who have picked up their cross daily and followed him who shall inherit unimaginable treasures in heaven and know true love and peace on earth.

Yes, Henry thought, *help me oh Lord to love like You. Help me to see others as my brothers and sisters. To love them as the child which You created. Yes, we fail and sin but we are not the sin. We are Your children who have chosen an act or thought or word that was harmful. That is the sin which we hate but we still love the sinner just as You have loved us.*

Henry began to see how it all fit together. When we love Jesus' way; unconditionally, we begin to do away with our critical, judgmental attitudes and accept ourselves and others. We no longer compete with one another or seek the approval of the world. We no longer equate our worth with what we own and possess. We are God's children loved immensely. In Him we are completely, totally and thoroughly sufficient!

Father Engelmann, in spirit, was leading Henry to see a glimpse of God's overall plan as he did so often when he was alive. But Henry was now ready to understand. God's plan is always there for all to see and know if we but stop and take the time to come to Him. How beautiful and plain it all is; how each piece of the puzzle fits together. How God created a universe for us out of love so that we may share the wonders and glory of heaven with Him. He knew when He created us that we would be imperfect by giving us free will. He knew we would sin and separate ourselves from Him. He knew his Son would agree to restore our relationship with Him by becoming man and paying for our sins. He knew Jesus would teach us how to live before His immense sacrifice. He knew when His Son returned to heaven to claim His place at the right hand of the Father, that the Holy Spirit would now come so that the spirit of Jesus in His glorified state would continue down through the ages and indwell in the hearts of all those who believed in Him! Yes, the Holy Spirit would now come and give mankind the grace and strength to live the way Jesus taught us.

But there was still more to His plan which would convict Henry deeper and deeper in the coming days. Not only did God have His Son become man and die for us, to restore our relationship with Him and open the doors to heaven for us, but He also included us to be an incredibly important part of the world's salvation! Imagine, God, who is almighty and could have done all things Himself, willed to bring about His purposes by the beings He has created! *We are co-workers with Him to carry out and continue the redemption His Son began!*

Imagine, God entrusted us to help Him spread the Gospel and save the souls of others!

He gave us three great commandments. To love Him first and foremost with all of our hearts, mind and soul, to love our neighbor as our self and to go out and spread the Good News and bring Jesus to the world. We must be in the world but no longer of the world. We no longer can have the mind of the world but possess the mind, heart and spirit of Jesus. We are His eyes, ears, feet, legs, hands and mind. Others can no longer see our dark side, only the light of Jesus!

This is our purpose on earth. This gives true meaning to our lives.

"Oh, heavenly Father, thank You for helping me to see, for opening my eyes to the truth, the way and the life. Thank You for letting me understand Your nature; three persons in one God. Thank You for allowing my finite mind to understand a glimpse of Your wonderful plan for our salvation so that we may have eternal life with You.

Unbelievable, incredible, stupendous.

Words failed to describe how awesome our heavenly Father is. He created us knowing that we would need help. He didn't abandon us but gave us a way back to Him. It is ours for the taking. *We are free to decide.*

Thank You, Lord. Thank You, thank You, thank You!

Henry could see so plainly now his great need of God. Had he placed the Lord first in his life and come to Him when Jenny died, he would have avoided months and months of pain and anguish. How foolish he had been for turning his back on God. He would have been on the road to recovery, healing and acceptance of Jenny's passing and would already be doing work for God which Jenny and Julean would have wanted him to do!

Henry fell forward and lay prostrate on the deck and began to cry out to the lord to free him from himself and to see the world through the heart of Jesus.

"Oh Lord Jesus Christ, Son of God, have mercy on me a sinner. You promised Lord that You would set the captives free. I confess, Jesus, that I am a slave and only You can break the chains that bind me. I repent of relying on my own strength. Without You, Jesus, I can do nothing. I ask You, Lord Jesus, to set me free from seeking glory and fame and praise for myself. Set me free from all the idols of the world: money, praise, possessions, people and any obstacle which keeps me from You. Help me to always place You first and foremost in my life. Free me from all my insecurities, false thinking and worldly ways. Help me to build my life upon a Rock. Please, oh Holy Spirit, give me the wisdom and common sense to always see through how self-defeating and foolish my thinking is when I fail to use Your wisdom. Help me always to see that to live for You and obey your commands and teachings is the perfect way to live. It brings light to the world and to our own heart and lives! It never harms others like our thinking does and can.

"*It is perfect for all!*

"How utterly foolish it is for me not to trust in God and follow His Son. It opens the doors to freedom, to life and constantly prepares me for eternity! How foolish it is to live for myself and seek my own glory. This could very well be my last day and I am not ready! Everything I strive for is here today and gone tomorrow. Free me from my critical and judgmental attitude, free me from loving conditionally. Help me to remove the blinders from my eyes and mind so my heart can see the beauty of Your love.

"Come now Holy Spirit and clothe me with power from on High. Help me live by Father Engelmann's mantra that all I do is not for me but to give all praise and glory to You who are deserving of all my love. Give me the grace, Lord Jesus, to walk in faith today, confident in Your love and mercy. Amen."

Henry lay there in brokenness and weeping. The love of God flowing through him. He could feel the loving presence of his mentor beside him; comforting him. Henry recalled that morning before Father died when he last visited Henry on the deck. Father had laid hands on him to receive the Holy Spirit but he wasn't yet ready to receive the gift which God wants to give all of His children.

Suddenly, Henry felt the warm loving touch of Father Engelmann's hands touch his head as he lay there on the deck. His dear mentor knelt right next to him praying for him to receive the ultimate gift of love.

In the next instance, Henry saw himself for who he really was; a sinner and his total emptiness and great dependence upon the heavenly Father. "Oh, Lord, have mercy upon me a sinner. Have, mercy, oh Lord, have mercy. Into Your holy hands I commend my spirit, my soul, my body and "all" that I have. I am here to serve You completely..."

Deep yearnings of love began to bubble up and words unknown to him came from his lips with a taste of sweetness that he had never experienced before. A well spring of living waters from the core... the very essence of his being gushed up and through his 'all.' It was as if he were huddled with the disciples in the upper room on the day of Pentecost. The very same Spirit which filled the room that day; which filled the hearts of all those present was here in the Poustinia now, too. An aura of light filled the room and entered Henrys' heart... he had finally come home.

In the stillness of that beautiful moment, the soft reassuring words of his mentor said, "A new heart God has given you, Henry, and a new spirit, God has put within you: He has taken out of your flesh the heart of stone and given you a heart of flesh.

"Today, my son, these Words are no longer just in your head, you have claimed this promise of the Lord...*in your heart.*"

Chapter Forty-Seven

THE NEXT MORNING, Henry woke praying in tongues. If someone had been in the bedroom, they would have heard him praying all night long with the gift he had received from the Holy Spirit. The words expressed for Henry his deep gratitude and praise to God more adequately than he ever could. The sound of the strange words were so beautiful, Henry didn't know if he ever wanted to stop.

Coco had got up and rested her head on the edge of the bed, curious to see if that was her master praying. Father Engelmann must have also woken up many times in that glorious state.

It was as if Henry had wings as he flew out of bed. He literally floated into the living room. At the sight of the cross above the altar, Henry fell prostrate upon the floor of the chapel and wept tears of joy and utter freedom. At a depth level, he realized that he was a child of God. He fully accepted Jesus Christ as his Lord and Savior and he had been blessed to receive the Holy Spirit.

It all made sense to him now. Father Engelman could see in him what St. Paul saw in the early church. He saw that those who had received the Holy Spirit had a passion for the Lord and those, who hadn't been anointed, lacked that inner fire and real commitment to Jesus. Henry could see now, as the strength and power of the Spirit flowed through him, what gave the early Christians that spirit of love and courage to lay down their lives for Jesus. Henry could see now what was truly lacking in so many churches and Christians.

The power of the Holy Spirit was lacking.

Henry vowed that this would be his mission for the rest of his days…to encourage people and the church to revive the Pentecost. "Unless we do so," Henry said aloud, "the commitment, power and love to bring us all to Jesus will always be lacking. There is no passion for the Lord or for serving Him. Their minds and hearts have not been touched and transformed by the Holy Spirit which gives that fire for Jesus!"

Jesus told His disciples before He ascended into heaven that He must go and assume His place in heaven and the Father would send the Holy spirit to help them. Jesus would plead for them in Heaven to the Father and the Holy Spirit would be their advocate and comforter and guide on earth. But perhaps most important was that Jesus could now, in His glorified state, be able to indwell in the hearts of men through the power of the Holy Spirit.

While Jesus walked the earth, He was present to the disciples from the outside in the flesh and tried to teach them, be an example to them how to live and how to evangelize but now that He was no longer with them in the flesh but would now indwell within them! Yes, Jesus Christ can live through all mankind by the grace and power of the Holy Spirit!

Henry realized that it was not enough to simply say the Jesus prayer to be saved. To accept Jesus as your Lord and Savior is the first crucial step, but it must be followed up with a change of heart; a honest submissiveness to His will and willingness to follow His ways. Slowly, Henry could see his relationship with Jesus was developing on new ground; a deep trust was developing and a firm resolve was emerging to follow Jesus wherever He leads.

A personal relationship is a good start but if it does not grow into a deep spiritual commitment and relationship it is not enough. To say we are for the Lord is not the same as living out our daily lives for the Lord.

Actions speak louder than words.

"Yes," Henry said, "a real change of heart is necessary; I really mean what I say. I really am willing to change my ways. I am willing to give up my sins, my temptations, my worldly desires and ways and come to Him and His son. It is true that the Holy Spirit urges and prompts one in this direction but unless one is truly ready to yield to the Holy Spirits urgings and say "yes, Lord," here I am, help me. Then and only then, are we ready to receive Jesus and His spirit. Only then are we open to receive His grace and blessings and strengths to really and truly follow Him." Henry gazed at the cross above the altar and continued to speak as if talking to Jesus...

"Faith, love and belief without works is dead.

"When we pray and search for God, He will draw near to us. The more we seek Him in our hearts the more He will give us His blessings and grace to continue to grow. He wants us to develop character and deep commitment to Him and His purposes. Unless we do this, how else will we become mature strong Christians? A simple prayer and desire for a personal relationship, followed up without commitment and good works has no life."

EVER SINCE HENRY received the anointing of the Holy Spirit, insights kept popping into his mind. The one he really found helpful came to him as he was out walking later that afternoon. He was thinking that in just a few days he would be finished with his fast, returning to the world and all its ways. One concern he had was dealing with his judgmental attitudes and tendencies towards being critical of himself and others. It came to him that this wasn't something to fear but rather a blessing.

Each time a situation came along in which someone was doing something which he thought wasn't right or acceptable, his first obligation was to talk to that person if appropriate. God wants us to respectfully correct others and ourselves if our behavior is unacceptable or what we are doing is not best. It was the second thought, however, which Henry didn't often do which was an inspired insight. If it was not appropriate, or the situation did not lend itself to talking it out, then we should immediately pray for that person. It diffuses the resentment, bitterness or anger and brings God into the equation by helping that person overcome the things which hurt or irritate others.

Keep the divine love of God always flowing.

Isn't this far better than running someone down in your mind or to openly gossip about them?

"Of course, that's the key! Every time we are critical or judgmental of someone, pray for them. Yes, turn a negative action into a positive one which brings praise to God and His grace and blessings upon us and the other person to change our hearts for the good of all."

Henry was elated by the thought! It was as much the path to freedom as it was a way to remove a common stumbling block to fullness of life. The moment we allow our mind to dwell on the injury, it quickly festers and soon it expands so much it controls and imprisons us for the day and sometimes for years. Be quick to close the doors to Satan!

And then the Holy Spirit sent Henry another thought. It's always good to keep in mind that we too are sinners and have failed or fallen short of others' expectations. The situation may be different, the gravity many be different but still during our journey in life, we have sinned against God and man. Once again, Henry looked at his hand and smiled as he saw how his three fingers pointed back at him when he pointed his one finger at others.

And remember too, my son, God loves that person as much as he loves you! Yes, we are all God's children! Be quick to separate the act from the person and forgive. Like God, we are to love the sinner but hate the sin. The act, thought or deed is what is wrong but the person whom God created is okay and wonderful. We must always try to separate the person from the sin.

It was as if Father Engelmann was next to Henry still guiding him towards the Light. Jesus not only helps us not to judge others lest we be judged but also tells us to pray for our enemies, to pray for others who have hurt us or exhibit character traits which are self-defeating or harmful. Yes, Lord, it is best to pray that you can accept that person and be a light to that person? If they are unkind, return kindness. If they are grumpy, return friendliness and if they show anger, be a peacemaker. As Father so often said, the blind cannot lead the blind, lest both fall in the ditch. It is clear to see which approach is beneficial to both the transgressor and to you? Does this not keep you free from being controlled by the shortcomings of others? To think you are better than them by putting them down is nothing more than trying to puff ourselves up. This is the same when we gossip about others. It's just pride and very sinful.

And just when Henry thought he had found the key to overcoming his critical, judgmental attitude, he was cautioned and reminded what the goal should always be. To keep in mind that these are not techniques to use to accept others and their shortcomings, but rather a path to an inner transformation from death to oneself and service to God and others. It is to open our hearts; to crucify our pride and strive for humility. To have a genuine care and concern for others and their welfare and salvation.

To truly be a light, we must love like Jesus loved; unconditionally. This is our ultimate goal and to do so we need to acknowledge our complete dependence on God for the strength and grace to live this way.

Henry nodded, and muttered, "Yes, Jesus, without You we can do nothing but with You and Your Spirit within our hearts we can do all things, even thank God for whatever comes our way. Yes, to return kindness when unkindness is shown, is to offer the sacrifice of praise. By praying for others from the heart, our praise bears genuine fruit which gives honor and glory to God. When we can weep for others, seek no revenge or retaliation but love them, then the seeds of true humility are growing in our hearts; we are rooting out our pride and loving like Jesus. Now the light of Jesus is flowing out of us from an authentic purpose and motive.

Yes, it's plain to see the 'whole' path we must take.

Henry felt so buoyant as he strolled along the well-worn path which Father had trodden over the years. He climbed the hill on the south eastern side of the prayer house. No wonder this was Father's favorite look-out.

From there, he looked down the length of the valley. In a small way it wasn't the Alps, but it was a beautiful site from prairie standards. In any case, the day had gone by so wonderfully for Henry with the anointing of tongues and all the new insights the Holy Spirit was showering on him, he couldn't help but do what he had seen Father do so many times when he reached this spot during his walks.

He raised his hands to the heavens and shouted at the top of his voice, "Praise God, for all the blessing He showers on us daily!"

A poem he had read on praise came to mind and he shouted it all the more. It made such good sense to praise and give thanks. There is such power in praise! Henry savored each word contained in the wisdom of every sentence as he sweetly sung the lyrics heavenward:

Praise opens heavens portals
Praise causes doubts to cease
Praise brings special blessings
Praise leaves the sweetest peace.
Praise breaks all bands asunder
Praise sets the captives free
Praise lightens every burden
Praise is the master key

Praise changes circumstances,
Praise establishes the heart
When praise comes perpetual
*Praise is a holy art!**

---

*   Poem by Frances Metcalfe

Chapter Forty-Eight

WHEN HENRY FIRST started his fast, forty days seemed like an awfully long time to go without food. Yet, compelled to do it by Father Engelmann's urging and his desire to know God's plan for his life, Henry committed to do it. He was almost there!

Today, was the thirty-third day and Henry felt elated that he came this far. Thirty-three days was significant to Henry as it was Jesus' age when He finished His ministry on earth. He, too, went into the desert for forty days to fast and pray. Henry was proud of himself that he was in some small way doing what his Lord had done. Looking back Henry could see how important it was to pray and fast when facing major decisions and how Biblical in nature it was to do so.

Although he felt hunger, it wasn't a screaming feeling that would signal he had to begin eating again. The juices he drank regularly had sustained him enough. He could only imagine the trial Jesus went through to live only on water and as did others, like Father Engelmann who wanted to emulate Him.

In the remaining seven days, Henry wanted to finish reading the books Father had written and also add to book seven to bring it up to date. Henry was absolutely amazed how Father was so blessed that he could recall and relate such an accurate accounting of what had transpired in their lives over all those years. Truly, he was guided by the Spirit and the incredible vision he was allowed to see. Henry hoped that what he would be writing could emulate the warmth and style of his mentor.

Henry was three quarters finished with book four, *The Angelic Occurrence*. He had purchased Jenny's home. No wonder he immediately felt her spirit as soon as the realtor showed him and Jeremy the home on Hill Avenue that cold blustery December day. What an incredible story to read; how their guardian angels brought them back together in that unlikely way! And to read Father's sermons which he gave over the years, Henry had to admit Father's homilies touched his heart more the second time around. Perhaps it was because his mind was clearer now and more receptive to the Word of God.

Henry sat back in his chair, his mind once again returning to the story. He began to think of how Jenny's and his guardian angels brought them back together once more. Henry felt somehow it all had to do with the last two letters they had written to one another with the pewter angels tucked inside. It was a miracle how they each received their respective letters after Mr. Sarsky's secretary had mailed them. They had escaped being lost, burnt and hidden in each of their mother's treasure chests and still the letters found their way home to each of them. It had filled their hearts with hope once again that perhaps they might still get together one day.

Henry shook his head. "Unbelievable," he thought. "The letters were truly angelic." And then, like a thunderbolt, that last thought was immediately followed by another.

The Angelic Letters series!

"That's it! That will be the name of the series which Father Engelmann wrote!"

Henry felt not only the presence of Jenny and Julean but also Father Engelmann as well. He could just imagine his mentor being so pleased with his student. So often when working in the grocery store and he had come up with a new idea, Father would be so delighted. In the silence of the prayer house, Henry could almost hear Father say, *"That is a good title for the series, Henry!"*

Later that afternoon when Henry had finished reading book four, he decided to go for a walk. He had almost forgotten about Coco who never moved off the mat. She was so quiet and listless, he almost tripped over her. He bent down and stroked her head. She opened her eyes and looked up at him; so forlorn and filled with sadness. She reminded him so much of what he had felt after Jenny's passing that it felt eerie to Henry; how animals can have that same sense of loss.

Henry was concerned about her but there was nothing more he could do. If only she would eat. She looked as thin and frail as Father did before he died. "Come, Coco, let's go for a walk. Come,..." Henry patted his knees but there was no convincing the grieving dog from leaving the only attachment which reminded her of her dearly beloved master. Henry thought about putting on Father's sandals but they were too small.

When he got to the patio doors, he turned once more and tried to entice Coco to come but she just lay there. Henry knew she would soon pass on if she didn't start to eat. Fortunately, she did drink water from time to time.

ON DAY THIRTY-FIVE, Henry woke just as the sun was nearing the horizon. He had finally got in sync with nature's timetable like Father Engelmann did for most of his adult life. It's a wonderful habit to develop. For the past week, just like his mentor, Henry started to go to bed shortly after the sun set and was ready and fresh to begin the day when God's whispers were most audible. On occasions, he was sure that he heard the flutter of wings, too. It comforted him to know that he was never alone.

There was a lot Henry wanted to do today, so he got right to it. Right after prayers and Scripture reading, he wanted to finish book five, *Angel Promises Fulfilled*. Henry loved Father's writing style. How each word came from the heart and seemed to be wrapped with affection. And how he captured the emotions that the characters were feeling was truly amazing. It was almost as if he were inside the person he was writing about. Henry loved Father's way of describing nature and setting the scene in which the characters were situated; it was as if you were there. Father was truly inspired to write this epic story and he prayed now that that inspiration would pass onto him. Henry was just at the part where he took Jenny up into a hot air balloon and proposed to her. That was such a great moment in time! Father Engelmann couldn't have written it better; it was so real. Henry felt like he was rising in his chair along with the balloon soaring into the heavens while gazing into Jenny's sparkling blue eyes!

"Incredible," Henry said, after he finished reading the last page. "After all those years since 1956, we were finally married." The title Father had selected was perfect. Their angels had fulfilled their promises. The pewter angels were instrumental in bringing Jenny back to Regina and also reviving hope in his heart when he discovered the angel in his mother's hope chest that they could possibly get back together again. *And they did!*

Even though Henry had closed the manuscript to book five over an hour ago, he still couldn't let go of the final chapter. What a day that was, getting married in Jenny's back yard; such a wonderful happy moment. The flowers, butterflies, friends, Margaret's beautiful singing and to make it all perfect, Father Engelmann was brought back to life to perform the wedding!

Henry shook his head as he thought of that day and their wedding night and all the wonderful days which followed. He knew if he deliberated too much longer, he might slip back into his former state of despair to which he no longer wanted to go. He was on a new journey now but he would always cherish the precious memories.

The sixth manuscript laid within arm's reach on the end of the desk. He wondered if Father had written this book right up until Jenny's death or was her passing in the last manuscript which Father was working on when he died. Henry didn't want to relive that scene again but he had to know how Father handled that part as it was written from real life. Father was no longer writing from what he had seen on the other side but in the reality of the present moment.

Henry picked up the thick handwritten document. He glanced at the prologue and then skimmed through some of the beginning chapters describing Jenny's desire to bear a child for him. He took a deep breath of air and went to the end of the manuscript to see how it ended. As soon as he started to read the last chapter, he knew that this was not the book when Jenny would pass on. It described when Jenny was in a coma and he was deciding whether or not to abort the child within his dearly beloved wife's womb.

It all started to flood back to him; how happy they were to know she was with child but then complications set in. She became ill, and refused to abort the child, even when she knew the danger to her health by prolonging the pregnancy. It was all too much for Henry to re-live. He wanted to go back to the ending of book five when they got married and were to live happily ever after! Wasn't that how good stories end!?

Decisions, decisions…What a struggle that was that day trying to decide what to do. He didn't want to lose Jenny and yet Hannah had the right to live too. He was so relieved when his father-in-law came to the hospital that day and guided him to make the right decision. It was amazing how God's divine Providence is always at work and how He works through people to minister to one another.

Henry felt relieved that he could read book six knowing that his Jenny would still be alive when he got to the end. It would be in the last book, book seven, which would be the most difficult of all to read. Henry wondered how Father dealt with it and if he wrote about the yearlong depression he had gone through. Father would have written it all in such detail right up until his own death. Henry knew that Jenny had died in that part of the story. He didn't know, however, if he would ever be able to read the last book.

The readers of this story too, would be devastated by the loss of their heroine. It's just too sad of an ending. How will they and I cope? And yet, he finally recovered, didn't he? He finally accepted the reality of life on earth. We are all born to die one day. Some sooner than later. Our true joy and happiness is not of this world but in the next…

Chapter Forty-Nine

In the three days which followed, the Lord gave Henry a different dream for each night. The first dream was so real that he was relieved to wake up and realize that it was just a dream. He had flown by Air Canada and then Air India, finally landing in Calcutta, thirty-five hours later. The long trip and layovers were exhausting but Henry was so excited to see Calcutta first hand, that the fatigue hadn't hit him yet.

Gary was there to meet him and they took a taxi back to the Mother House. Henry was overwhelmed by the sights, sounds and unbelievable masses of people. He was amazed how the opulence of the city changed as they drove further and further into the impoverished areas. Within a matter of miles, Henry saw amazing buildings, welcoming cafes and beautiful parks; the complete antithesis of utter poverty. Even the air changed from the sweet smell of flowers and opulence to the odor of sewage and death. Little wonder Calcutta was often referred to as the world's slum! Henry just kept shaking his head; it was like landing on another planet which had been ravaged by a great war and this was the end result.

Normally, visitors stayed in a residence about ten minutes away but because of the mission Henry was doing, he was allowed to stay in the main residence with Gary. He was immediately greeted and welcomed with warmth and friendliness by the other volunteers and sisters. For the first time, Henry felt accepted for who he was and not what he did and owned.

In the days which followed, Henry got into the daily routine of sharing the prayer life and the apostolate of the sisters. He was up at five for morning prayers and then out on the streets. Mother Teresa was away at another Mother House and so Henry didn't get a chance to meet her. Gary was his personal guide into the slums of Calcutta. It was a day Henry would never forget. What he had seen the other day during his drive from the airport to Mother House was nothing in comparison to what he saw firsthand today. So many people suffering and dying, with no place to live except cardboard houses on the street. Many didn't even have that. The smell of excrement, urine combined with beggar's cries for alms overwhelmed him. So many of God's children abandoned, rejected and despised.

How could this be?

Henry watched as Gary knelt down on the crumbly pavement and held people covered with grime and dirt as they passed on. They had nothing; no family at their side, rejected, unwanted. Gary's reaching out and loving them may very well have been the first experience of being accepted and loved by anyone. Henry's heart was breaking at the sight. He couldn't stop the tears from surfacing.

In the afternoon, Gary gave Henry a tour through the makeshift hospital. It was heartwarming to see so many sisters and volunteers helping the sick and dying. Henry thought how fortunate it was for these people to at least have a bed to sleep on and someone to clean them and feed them in their dying days and hours.

The day ended in the chapel with adoration of the Holy Eucharist. Sisters and volunteers praying to Jesus for the sick and dying; for all the homeless and poverty-stricken people. Henry was certain they were also praying for strength and grace to deal with the day ahead in service of the Lord. He couldn't stop the tears from flowing and by bedtime he was exhausted.

For the first week, Henry mainly volunteered in the hospital where the patients had been cleaned and tended to. In the second week when he went out with Gary again, Henry's heart was tested beyond his limits when he reached out to an aging man lying in the filthy gutter. The stench, the dirt and filthy rags the man was wearing overwhelmed Henry.

Henry was filled with a deep emotional revulsion. How could he touch the man before him, hold him and show love when filled with such repugnance...? Saint Francis felt the same about the lepers, recalled Henry. Francis, too, was filled with disgust and loathing for the sores which covered their bodies and yet, Francis embraced and kissed the leper. How did he do it? How did Gary and John do it? How could they show such love in the face of such conditions and utter repugnance?

How can God allow this?

And then just before he woke up, the answer came to him in the words of the song which Margaret Tearhorst sang at the closing processional hymn of the Mass for Father Engelmann:

What soever you do to the least of my brothers, that you
do unto me.
When I was hungry you gave me to eat,
When I was thirsty you gave me to drink,
Now enter into the home of my Father.

What soever you do to the least of my brothers, that you
do unto me.
When I was homeless and strange in this land,
Searching for kindness, you held out your hand.
Now enter into the home of my Father...

When Henry awoke, he knew what his mission was. He knew in his heart that this was the work he was meant to do. He understood now what motivated Gary and John and Father. He, too, could feel deeply, the love of the Lord, the source through which he could love his brothers and sisters.

Jesus had called him by name. He was in the world and yet no longer part of it. He was no longer seeking the treasures of this world but now bent on storing treasures for the eternal world. That was where his heart belonged now! Yes, he now belonged to Jesus and like the apostles who went before him; Henry was now a fisherman of men and charitable hearts.

The Lord had opened up a window for Henry to experience his first taste of when the west meets the east; to see his brothers and sisters and share in their humanity. But as he lay there, he also realized it was not only in Calcutta or Peru or wherever, be it abroad or here, there were needs to be met. It was easy to love in Calcutta, where the physical poverty is so great, but as Mother Teresa said, *"You will find Calcutta all over the world if you have the eyes to see."*

He tried to go back to sleep but the vacant eyes of the people in his dream haunted him; so sad, so forlorn, so empty. He had to reach the hearts of people in the western world. A fire was growing in Henry's heart; the needs were so great and urgent. He began to weep and his heart was soothed, once again by Margaret's clear, angelic voice singing, that heart rendering song. Each word came to life as it fluttered so melodically and soothingly from her lips...

> *What soever you do to the least of my brothers, that you*
> *do unto me.*
> *When I was hungry, you gave me to eat,*
> *When I was thirst,y you gave me to drink,*
> *Now enter into the home of my Father...*
>
> *What soever you do to the least of my brothers, that you*
> *do unto me...*

THE NEXT NIGHT, Henry had his second dream. In a way, it was a continuation of what he had dreamt the night before. It was the sisters and volunteers swarming into the chapel at the end of the day. They were tired, yet anxious to kneel before the Holy Eucharist in adoration. They knew that the consecrated host in the monstrance was the physical presence of Jesus; Body, Blood, Soul and Divinity.

The dream never went any further than displaying the Host. When Henry woke up it came to him what the dream meant. The sisters and volunteers were going into the chapel to be replenished and nourished by Jesus. Henry had done the same during his fast. He couldn't wait from one day to the next, to receive Jesus in the hosts which Father Engelmann had consecrated. Daily, Henry felt his faith deepen.

Henry clearly understood that in order to pick up our cross daily, the resurrected Christ must be at the center of our lives. It is His immense love and sacrifice for us which gives us the strength to go on and continue His redemption. Daily, we are to die to ourselves and resurrect with Him filled with new life of service and love for others. To do so, we must be nourished and replenished by Him daily.

That was what had changed his friends, Gary and John into such warriors for the Lord.

Henry could only imagine them getting up and working in the slums of Calcutta every day. The stench of human misery all around, the cry of the poor and rejected and forgotten. The homeless and children abandoned because their parents could not support them. What kind of life awaited them from day to day? The pain that one feels to see such utter suffering and desolation. The heat and exhaustion of carrying the dying to the shelter. The stones and hurts and angry shouts of so many rejecting their help.

Yes, Henry understood...*true love without pain and suffering is no love at all.*

Henry recalled how his dear friends praised and gave thanks in all their trials and challenges, how their attitude was filled with understanding and wisdom of the Holy Spirit. Henry could now see how they responded so lovingly and accepting of all this hardship. They were filled with gifts and fruits of the Spirit. They were lifted up by their love of the Lord. The indwelling Christ yielded by the Holy Spirit sustained them to face what was untenable, unbearable and intolerable. Imagine what would happen without the Spirit of God living through them. Within a day they would be lost and forlorn.

Sadness, anger, frustration... they would throw up their hands and say, "This is impossible," and turn away as so many of their very brothers did that lived there. They would be forgotten and rejected and abandoned. It was only through the infilling of the Spirit and indwelling of Jesus that sustained them!!!

No wonder they rushed into the chapel each and every evening to gaze upon Jesus in the host! They needed the nourishment of Jesus to continue their work!

Yes, it was all making sense to Henry now as his new life flowed through him. He was being renewed by the transformation of his mind as living waters flowed through him. He raised his head towards the cross and words so sweet and beautiful flowed from his lips praising his Lord on high!

That is what was at the heart and soul of Father Engelmann holiness, too! That is what gave Jenny the strength and grace to deal with the many challenges and trials she faced in her life. This is what makes a marriage work and transforms one's life. It is when Jesus is at the center. It is when we are led by the Holy Spirit to convict our hearts to come to Jesus daily in adoration and love and to receive Him in the Eucharist; Body, Blood, Soul and Divinity.

People must see that they will never rest until they rest in Jesus.

Henry knew that his message when he went on tour, would not be just to raise money for the poor, but to change the hearts of those he would speak to. For us all to realize that we, too, are poor in spirit and have great need of Jesus and to receive Him in our hearts so we have new life within us. We must see that we are all God's children. When we give, it is not a matter of just writing out a cheque; it is out of love for God and for all He did for us. It is out of love for our brothers and sisters in Jesus. It is because we have placed Jesus at the center of our lives.

ON THE THIRTY-NINTH night, Henry had his final dream. It was about Hannah. He wished this dream could have gone on forever. It started out with Jenny making a covenant with the Lord to give back the child which He had blessed her with. Jenny was elated beyond words when she knew that day in the park that she was with child. He wished the dream would have shown how happy Jenny was to give birth to her little girl but instead it went on to show what the Lord had in store for their little angel.

In many ways, it was a vision similar to that which Father Engelmann had when he was on the other side. He, too, saw into the future but when Father returned back to life, memory of that vision was taken away. And so it was with Henry. When he woke, a scene of thousands of people flashed through his mind and then it vanished. He struggled to recall more of the dream but it was gone from memory except for a feeling of overwhelming wonderment and hope for the future.

CHAPTER FIFTY

I T WAS THE last day. He did it! Forty days and nights in the Poustinia. What a wonderful, wonderful experience!

Henry felt he had achieved his purpose for being there. He wanted to draw nearer to God and rid himself of all obstacles that prevented him from making God first and foremost in his life. He knew there would always be temptations but he now knew how to handle them and get the strength for doing so. He knew he had to be broken and realize his dependence on God in order to grow in humility and faith.

Father Engelmann continually stressed that in his life. Henry recalled when Father shared with Jenny and him, how he too, struggled with pride and being independent and self-righteous. He too, was quick to judge and be critical, but when he gave himself over to the Lord, the old self was gone and a new creature was born.

Henry felt like that now; more genuine, authentic, and real. He didn't need to put on a front in order to gain people's approval or worry about what they thought. He could see how foolish and self-defeating it was to give all this power over to others to control how he felt and thought of himself.

No! All that matters is what God thinks.

Henry realized at a deep, heart level now that Jesus laid down his life for him and paid for his sins. Jesus opened the door for him to come to the Father and accept his inheritance as a child of God. He was part of God's family! That was where his identity was! He would no longer derive his worth from what he does or owns or achieves. Father Engelmann, Gary, and John understood this but even more so, they knew that it was not about them. It was all about serving God and others. And that was the key which opened Henry's understanding of what life was all about.

How many times over the years did his mentor say when he received accolades, "Not for me, oh, Lord, not for me, but glory to Your name."

Those were the last words Henry heard his beloved friend say when he was blessed with the Stigmata. He could still hear Father's mantra reverberate throughout the valley that unforgettable morning, "Not for me, oh, Lord, not for me, but glory to Your name."

What a wonderful insight!

"When we fully realize what Jesus did out of love for us, we carry on the redemption which He started by serving Him, dying to oneself, obeying Him and loving Him. That is all that is important; living only for the approval of the Father. If we fail or stumble or fall, Jesus is ready to pick us up and forgive; His love is constant; He never rejects us…"

His merciful heart has no bounds.

A rush of freedom swept through Henry as he gazed at the cross above the altar and said, "I am no longer bound to myself or to men! Oh, Lord, help me to follow in Your footsteps as my mentor did. Help me, too, to press on toward the goal to win the prize for which God has called me heavenward in Jesus Christ. Help me, too, so that I can say, "I have been crucified with Christ. It is no longer I who live, but resurrected Christ who lives in me."

Henry was so excited to work with Gary and John to serve the Lord, he could hardly contain himself. He would talk to the Archbishop this week about his mission. He would travel to India first and upon his return he would begin his tour of the churches in Regina. If it was well received, he would expand it to the rest of the province and beyond. If it was the will of the good Lord, Henry was prepared to travel into the United States as well.

The big concern he had was Justin and Hannah. Justin was seventeen and was growing up fast. He was mature and could be left alone but Henry wasn't sure if he should be put in charge of the farm for several weeks at a time. However, no sooner had such thoughts entered his mind, it was overpowered by positive thoughts. Things have a way of working themselves out and he shouldn't put obstacles in front of his mission and trust God to work it out.

During the fast, his time spent with Hannah every Saturday was a God send. Just two days ago, when the kids were here, he felt so sad when Hannah was picked up by Jeremy later that day. He regretted not spending more time with her since Jenny's death. He loved that little girl more and more each time he saw her. She is so much like her mother. "So spontaneous, charming, full of life and surprises," he added.

He recalled reading in book two, Another Angel of Love, where Father Engelmann described how Jenny felt about Camilla as being a wildflower and growing to be the most beautiful of all.

Henry thought that of Hannah, too. He knew Hannah had a special purpose and definitely Jenny's heart; the heart of an angel.

Henry sat down at the desk and picked up the last manuscript that Father Engelmann was working on. He knew that it was in this book when Jenny died. He silently prayed to the Holy Spirit to help him, to give him the courage and strength to face Jenny's passing. Sure, it was a story but Father's writing is so real and after all it is a true story. Hopefully, though, he had grown beyond his grief and had the power of the Holy Spirit to prevent him from slipping back.

He opened the book and began to read. Tears streamed down Henry's face as he read how Father Engelmann had written it with such passion and feeling and empathy and understanding. It was as if Father were living the loss through his adopted son. It was plain that Father loved Jenny so dearly too. It was the way the old man described every joy, sadness, anguish and deep mourning that exposed his heart.

Father had captured in words so realistically and powerfully Henry's pain and grieving... he stopped reading; the memories were too vivid...perhaps some other time...not now.

Henry skipped several chapters and began reading again when spring came and his feelings and sadness seemed to lift, just thinking on Jenny's buoyant love of that season. He recalled those few days when his spirits seemed to revive but it didn't last long. His depression came back with a vengeance. The words jumped off the pages as Henry relived in the story, the depths of sorrow and yearning he had for his beloved. All hope was gone and then, just when he thought that only death would end it all, his dearly beloved friend came to his rescue. Once again, Henry began to weep as he read that part of the story only a few weeks ago when Father would say his last Mass and offer himself up to free Henry from his bondage.

What a powerful moment that was!

The feeling of being released from his bondage was gone in a flash. In a heartbeat, the forces which held him captive vanished. Tears surfaced in Henry's eyes as he read on about that eventful day. What a sacrifice his teacher did for him. There is no greater love than to lay down one's life for a friend. What an act of love for him and for God!

Henry shook his head. What precious, amazing, moments in time that must have been when the covenant, which Father had made with Lord, began to finally play out in the present! Imagine! What Father had seen over five years earlier in a vision finally came back to him just over a month ago in the reality of Father's present moments of living! What an incredible event that must have been for Father to finally see the covenant between him and the Lord come to pass. Father received the Stigmata!

Even though Henry knew this had happened, just reading about it now, touched his heart profoundly. It was now up to him to complete the story.

Henry picked up Father Engelmann's pen and began writing from the point where Father Engelmann had gotten ready to say his last Mass. It was now Henry who could write what happened at the Mass because he was allowed to see a vision of it from his deck! Incredibly, Henry could see Father celebrating the Mass, offering his life for him. He remembered Father stopping and looking up directly at him waiting for his offering. He would never forget that moment when he offered to let Jenny go. Their offering was offered up together with Jesus' sacrifice and was accepted by God.

Father received the wounds of Christ and he, his healing and freedom!

Henry couldn't write fast enough. The scene of that morning was so real as it flashed across the screen of his mind. The words spilled onto the pages like a gusher. It was a miracle how it all happened so fast...he wished he could have seen Father receiving the Stigmata...it was seconds away when he left the deck with the Archangel to run down to Father.

Henry felt shivers racing up and down his spine.

He composed himself and slowed down. He wanted to capture every detail of those unforgettable, momentous moments in time... what he saw and felt when he got to the prayer house. Never would Henry have thought he would be sitting there describing Father lying before the altar bearing the five wounds of Jesus and trying to describe in words the incredible odor of sanctity and the aura of such holiness surrounding the Poustinia!

Henry was amazed how writing about what stirred him so powerfully was so similar to that of painting. Every image of that day could have been a painting! Only now he was painting with words rather than a brush! It's the same creative energy... all a gift from the Lord!

"Thank You, thank You, Lord for this ability to share our hearts."

Once again, Henry stopped writing for a moment to collect himself. Tears were blurring the page in front of him. He was so overwhelmed by what Father had done and now he was gone. For all the years they had known one another,

Father was always there for him; ready to help and lead him back to God.

Henry looked up and gazed out the picture window at the beautiful valley before him. Softly he whispered, "Thank you, Father for bringing me back into the Light. Thank you for restoring my soul."

How many times did Father gaze out this window to the beauty before him? The valley was so alive with summer. So many colors of green painted before him by the hand of God and dotted with the color of wild flowers. "Unbelievable, Lord, how magnificently you created nature to give us such daily spiritual sustenance. How often we take your handy work for granted!"

Just then, Henry noticed a monarch butterfly sitting on the window sill. Henry studied the color and shape of the wings. He tried to see if it was a male or female but it flew away before he could tell. It was startled by a barn swallow zooming in to land on the brick molding surrounding the window. Even though the swallows made such a mess on the window and deck in the early summer, when they would make a nest above the window frame, he made no attempt to shoo them away. He loved to watch them fly and noticed how protective they were of their nests.

Henry brushed away a tear rolling down his check and began writing again about phoning the Archbishop and the RCMP to tell them of Father's passing. He wrote about the miracle which happened to the constable and the reactions of the Archbishop, Chancellor and secretary when they saw the five wounds of Christ on Father Engelmann. It was almost a chapter in itself when Henry described the interview which followed outside on the deck. The Archbishop wanted to make certain every detail was recorded.

What Henry loved most about that time was holding Hannah. It was like holding Jenny in his arms. "Oh Jenny, thank you for leaving part of yourself behind. Hannah is such a special gift. I love you so…"

It took Henry a long time to write about Father's funeral. Several times he had to lay the pen down and collect himself.

There were moments when he could not stop weeping for his beloved friend. He decided to take a break and pray and thank God for all of his blessings, especially for his dear mentor.

Henry made his way out to the living room area. Before he knelt down at the kneeler, he went to the altar and opened the ciborium and took out the last host. Henry gazed at it for a long time and then raised it up so that the image of host and Jesus hanging on the cross above the altar were viewed at the same time. He had seen Father Engelmann do this hundreds of times. "Thank You Lord for all You have done for me. Thank You for the miracle of being present in this Holy Eucharist and the strength and spiritual sustenance you continue to give us. "What an amazing gift of Your presence to us." Henry ate the host and whispered, "I love You Jesus. I worship You"

By late afternoon, Henry had the story caught up to the present. He wrote about the success of his forty day fast and how it helped him draw nearer to God. He wrote about his dreams and his decision to go to India and then make a tour of all the churches in the city. He felt great! A feeling of elation swept through him over his accomplishments. He would try in the days ahead to exert his will power and self-discipline more often and be careful what he ate and how much he ate. He could readily see that putting a reign on the flesh had amazing results. The control, energy and freedom roaring through his being was so strong at that moment, he thought he could fly like the angels he knew were surrounding the Poustinia.

Henry needed some fresh air. He had been so absorbed in getting the manuscript up to date he forgot to take his usual afternoon walk in the valley. It would be wonderful if Coco would come today, too.

He turned his chair so he could see Coco lying on the mat but...she wasn't there. He looked through the bedroom doorway and couldn't see her at the patio doors in the chapel area. "Perhaps she wants out and is at the kitchen door."

When Henry got up and passed the foot of the bed, he stopped dead in his tracks. Coco was lying in the closet, her head resting on Father's sandals. He had moved the sandals there last evening, hoping and thinking that maybe removing Father's shoes from the mat would help Coco to not be so conscious of her master, but she found where they were.

She lay very still…

"Oh, Coco…"

Henry knew before he touched Coco, she was gone. Her rib cage was clearly visible from losing so much weight. She was skin and bones. In the last few days, Henry noticed that her food was totally untouched, despite his efforts to make her eat. He went down on his knees and stroked her head. She must have been dead a long time as she felt stiff. He was so engrossed with the story and writing, he hadn't noticed.

"Oh, Coco, you were such a faithful and loyal dog; such a dear friend and companion to Father."

Henry marveled at how the grief-stricken animal had so dearly missed her master. It touched his heart how she laid her head on Father's shoes trying to be so close to him. Henry could understand how she died of a broken heart. He missed his friend so dearly, too.

Tears blurred the image of the loving animal longing so deeply for her master. "Well, Coco," Henry's words echoed softly on the walls of the bedroom, "You are now at peace and so happy up there with Father, walking by his side with your nose lovingly touching his knee, as you stroll together in the meadows of heaven."

LATER THAT EVENING, Henry decided to stay out on the deck a while longer and take in the beautiful valley filled with the hush of evening time. As he stood there is the stillness, his artistic mind began to analyze the moment… In so many ways, he thought, it is similar to the peace of early morning, yet it is at twilight that nature reaches its own unique quiescence. The day is coming to a close and just a hint of soft light remains for a short period of time as the sun slowly sinks below the horizon and then vanishes. In the morning, the light lifts our spirits and prepares us for the day, but it is the all -pervading atmosphere of twilight time that soothes and arrests the scars, troubles and cares of the day. Whereas the morning light exposes the details of life which keeps the mind busy and preoccupied from all around, it is now, ever so slowly, obscured by the growing shadows of the night.

Earlier that afternoon Henry had studied the trees and shrubs on the hillside storing into memory their colors, shape, size and how they grew. All is now hidden in the darkness. The reflection of the distant hills in the silvery water of the pond is reduced to a simple shape of rich darkness contrasting sharply with the light of the rising moon. All the clutter of life disappears; gently pushed aside by an omnipresence of timelessness, simple clarity and oneness. Whether it is early morning or early evening the message is the same...

Come to Me and rest a while.

Henry had to admit that over the past forty days he had come to love this time of day even more than he already did if that was possible. This was the last evening of his forty-day fast and he had come to know his Savior and Lord so much more intimately. It was the relationship he had sought all of his life. It was always right there, just waiting for him to open the door and allow his Master into his heart. Although we blame God at times for being so distant, it is never Him, but always us who create the obstacles that separate us, not only from God, but also from others.

He thought again about his mission to help encourage people of the western world to help their brothers and sisters in the east. It was so deeply burned into his heart during this fast. Tears surfaced in his eyes just thinking on it. So much healing, distribution of resources and help was needed. Henry now knew why his mentor wept so many times and prayed and fasted for healing in the world and for God to have mercy on us.

Father was so holy, caring, loving and compassionate. He was so close to the light that any blemish, even the slightest venial sin he felt so deeply. Where all too many of us become accustomed to living in the darkness, within the light of world, Father so lived in the light that any darkness instantly affected his soul. Clearly, it was no longer Father Engelmann who lived but Jesus. All thoughts, words or deeds that did not reflect Jesus' thinking or teachings instantly stabbed his heart like a knife.

"Oh, Lord, help me to follow in the footsteps of Father Engelmann." Jesus was the Word and Father strived daily to become one with the Word. To become the very message and teaching of the scriptures. Like Father, dear Lord, I pray to put my flesh on the Word, crucify it and become one with the Word like my teacher did.

A buoyant energy of spirit filled him as he got up and walked to the edge of the deck. He breathed in the crisp, cool air; the odor of an impending fall was in the air. He knew that August was just around the corner.

"Aha, this is Father's secret to renewed strength and vitality; to be the Word! This is a wonderful place for a retreat. I shall miss these quiet moments."

Henry gazed at the water and studied the moon's reflection deep below the surface of the pond. The brilliant disc received its light from the sun just like he would receive the light from Jesus. And just like man can learn to live on the moon without air or food, so too, he could learn to live in this world with the nourishment of Jesus' Word.

Just then the peaceful image of the almost perfect reflection of the moon was disturbed by the V-shaped ripples created by a beaver cutting silently through the water. It made him think how his peace and the reflection he has of Jesus in his heart will soon to be disrupted as he enters back into the real world of living tomorrow. It frightened Henry somewhat because he knew the potential for a hundred and one things that can go wrong or create distractions from the Lord. Yet, if he continued to do what he had done these past forty-days; to come to the Lord each morning and evening and pray, meditate and give praise and thanks to the Lord, he will remain in the Light like his dear mentor. The babbling water trickling through the nearby beaver dam seemed to concur with Henry's reflections.

Henry felt his mentor's presence now. He was so close, Henry felt the warmth of his loving arm around his shoulder.

He would never be alone; his teacher would be ever near just like Jenny and Julean would be too.

As he stared into the heavens, Henry could picture Father having dinner with Anna and Jesus and the rest of the saints in heaven. He would never forget the day when Father died and he saw his guardian angel lift him up to God who was waiting there to receive him with open arms.

It made Henry think of another song Margaret sang at Father's funeral:

> *I call you to my Father's house. A lovely dwelling place.*
> *He comes to meet you on the road, arms ready to embrace*
> *Lay down your sorrow, calm your fear. The Father bids*
>   *you come,*
> *With open arms he welcomes you to your eternal home...**

Henry gazed into the star studied sky. The stars twinkled just like Father Engelmann's friendly eyes sparkled with a quiet gentleness and peace.

Henry was no longer afraid.

"Goodnight my dear friend, thank you for leading me home..."

---

*   by Delores Dufner

CHAPTER FIFTY-ONE

A T SEVEN THIRTY the next morning, Henry's family came down to congratulate him. He had been up so late last evening reading and writing that he was still in bed when they barged into the prayer house. Jacob and Hannah were the first ones to come in and jump on his bed scaring the wits out of him.

Everyone laughed.

"Hey, Dad, you did it! Way to go!" said Justin, standing at the doorway.

"Yeah," echoed Jeremy, "What an incredible feat! No solids for forty days and just drinking juice and water is amazing, Dad. I bet you are in for a big steak tonight."

"Oh, no," Camilla cautioned, "that is the last thing to do. Dad has to be very careful in what he eats for the next week or two. I have been reading up on it and solids have to be introduced much like an infant is introduced to solids."

"That's a good way of putting it, Camilla. Dr. Kreake instructed me to eat soup to start with and then salads until my digestive system adjusts again. Actually, I have decided to keep my meat consumption to a minimum. I have never felt better in my life. I am excited to see how much weight I have lost."

"I have never seen you look this good, Dad. Your skin color and weight loss has dropped years off your appearance. That was a major undertaking. We are very proud of you," said Camilla.

"This experience has been a great reminder to me of two great gifts the Lord has given us; will power and self-discipline. With that and strength from Him, I have gained control over my body once again. The long walks coupled with fasting, praying and drinking juice has detoxified my body. I feel great mentally, emotionally and spiritually."

"That's for sure, as Matti would say," remarked Camilla and then added, "So, how was the spiritual side of it, Dad?"

"All I can say is unbelievable! This is the closest I have felt to God, ever. And I have come to a decision about doing missionary work with Gary and John."

"Oh, Dad, that's wonderful!" Camilla was so glad to see her step-father getting back into the stream of life again.

"Will it mean you are going away?" Justin asked cautiously.

Henry anticipated that this might be of a concern for Justin and tried to answer reassuringly.

"Yes, Justin it will mean a little travelling and for the first while it will be in the city and surrounding small towns. If it works out and is well received, it may continue in other provinces. I thought when I'm gone for a week or so, you might come along and take in a hockey game or football game or whatever is in season or going on at the time."

Justin's face brightened, "Yeah, that sounds great, Dad."

"Well, that's not in the immediate agenda. I'd like to get back home and get caught up on a few things."

"Oh, yeah, the Archbishop called yesterday and wants to meet with you as soon as you are done your fast," said Justin.

"That's good, I want to see him about something, too," and before Henry could say what it was, the kids started to beg him to go on a paddle boat ride.

"It's a little early to be out on the water. It's cold out there and you're not dressed warm enough. How about we go up to the house and Mom will make some pancakes and after we will come back."

"No, we want to go now."

"No, Jacob, it's too cold and I didn't bring a sweater for you or Hannah. Grandpa's right, let's have breakfast first."

As they were leaving the prayer house, Justin asked, "Where's Coco, Dad?"

Henry looked at Justin and tightened his lips, "Coco passed away yesterday, Son. She just wouldn't eat and missed Father so much. She died of a broken heart."

"Oh, no," said Jeremy. Camilla expressed the same sentiment.

"Where is she, Dad?" Justin wanted to know.

"I buried her out behind the Poustinia yesterday afternoon."

"Can you show us, Grandpa?" asked Joshua.

"Yes, come. I said a prayer for her, but let's all say our good-byes to her now. I think she and Father are looking down on us right now as they prepare to take their morning walk somewhere in heaven."

No sooner had they got back up to the house when the phone rang. It was the Archbishop.

"Hello, Henry, I heard you were completing your forty-day fast today."

"Hi, Your Grace, yes, I did it! It was an amazing experience. Have you done one?"

"Yes, several over the years. It has many spiritual benefits which I am sure you experienced."

"You can say that again. Now I know why Father Engelmann did it all the time."

"There are two reasons for my call, Henry. The first, an emissary from Rome is presently in Ottawa doing an investigation and was inquiring if on such short notice he would be able to fly to Regina and meet with you at the prayer house before he returns to the Vatican? Would that be possible, Henry?"

"Yes, of course. Would he be here just for a day or the entire week?"

"I will call him as soon as I return to the city and find out when he plans to come and how long his visit will be. I'm certain he will want to talk to me about Father Engelmann and others as well. He did mention that he is interested in knowing more facts surrounding the death of your wife, Jenny as well."

"Has it to do with her miraculous healing of cancer four years ago? We went over that quite extensively with a delegation from Rome at the time."

"Yes, I am sure he wants to see how that miracle fits into the circumstances surrounding Jenny's pregnancy and her refusal to abort the child at risk to her own life. I do not know of all the details. We shall soon find out.

"The second reason for my call is somewhat related to the Monsignor's visit. He and I will be discussing David Engelmann's passing and all the circumstances surrounding his death. Although the Vatican has read my report describing the events, they have asked more questions and I would like to go over what happened with you again…and, I do have some further queries. I thought it best to be there at the scene to help refresh your memory of the event."

"Yes, we could meet. I also made a decision during my fast concerning my future which I want to discuss with you. The family is here for the entire morning but later this afternoon might work or tomorrow."

"This afternoon would be wonderful, Henry. I have meetings all day tomorrow and the next and I don't want to put this off until next week. How does two-thirty sound?"

"That will be fine, Your Grace. I'll be waiting for you."

Just as Henry placed the receiver back on the phone it rang again startling him.

"Hello," Henry said

"Ah, Señor, Henry, I was hoping you would answer. Jeremy told me you completed your fast yesterday and would be back up at the house today. How was the retreat?"

"Just great, Carlos, in all respects. I have never felt better, am closer to the Lord and He showered me with so many blessings my mind is still reeling. I highly recommend it."

"Si, I too have fasted many times but they are short; one day, two…the longest so far has been five days. The benefits as you say are well worth the effort."

"And how are Maria and the children?"

"Maria is fine and so are the children. My oldest son and his family are coming for a visit in the middle of August for a week before school starts. We are very excited to see them. But I know you are busy and have many things to do so the reason for my call is to ask you to be our guest speaker to kick off the new season of the ladies' groups which Señorita Jenny started. We missed your talk last year due to Jenny's passing. If you do not feel up to it yet, we understand, but it would be so wonderful if you could."

"Yes, I was planning to speak about the role of men in the home and community. I started to make notes almost two years ago…my, my, how time passes. In any case, Carlos, sure, I will be happy to do it. So, when is date for the social event?"

"It is September the sixteenth, a Friday evening at 7:30. Would that work into your schedule, Señor?"

"Yes, I'm sure it will, Carlos. I am pretty well fully retired now and ready to do the Lord's work. When I see you in the next while, I will share with you what my plans are in the days ahead."

"I am sure the Lord has many things planned for a man of all your talents."

Henry simply thanked his friend for his nice comments but immediately said in his mind and heart, Not for me oh, Lord but glory to Your name.

After breakfast with the family, Justin found some old clothes of his to put on the kids and they all went down to the pond for a boat ride. When they got back up to the house, it was shortly before noon and much to the kids delight, they decided to go to McDonalds for lunch. Justin went with them and agreed to take the kids to a movie later that afternoon. That would give Henry just enough time to take a shower and have a nap before his visitors were scheduled to come.

When Henry entered the bedroom, the first thing he looked at was the empty bed. The last time he saw it was months ago. Someone had made the bed and tidied up the room. His last memories were of the room being in such disarray. The day after Jenny died, he slept in the bed with his clothes on and after that day, he had never gone back into the room... until now.

Henry wanted to start sleeping in the bedroom again and get back to normal. It was only one o'clock and during the past forty days at the Poustinia, he got used to taking a nap. He walked over to the bed and brought the covers back exposing the pillows; his and Jenny's. He easily visualized her laying there like the sleeping beauty.

Unbidden tears surfaced.

He reached into his pocket and took out Jenny's rosary and tossed the sparkling beads on his pillow just like he did with Julean's before he gave them to Jenny when he last viewed her at the funeral home. He stared at the beads glistening in the soft light and whispered a prayer to the two loves of his life.

He took off his clothes and had a shower. When he returned with just his shorts on, he slipped into bed and took hold of the rosary. He pulled Jenny's pillow next to him and rested his arm over the top. The rosary dangled from his hand as he began to pray. He was just starting the second decade when he drifted off into a deep sleep.

At precisely two thirty, the doorbell woke him up. At first, he didn't know where he was after spending the last forty days in the Poustinia. He quickly got dressed and ran downstairs.

The Archbishop was accompanied by the Chancellor and his secretary, Bernadette, as before. Rather than go directly down to the prayer house, the Archbishop wanted Henry to retrace his steps starting with the day Father Engelmann came up to the deck and when he left to go back down to the Poustinia the next morning. His Grace also wanted Henry to go over the vision he had from the deck of Father celebrating the Mass and also where the Archangel stood beside him that morning.

When they got to the east side of the house where Henry sat that morning, he went over it again but this time he added. "It's a good thing I saw the vision of Father Engelmann saying the Mass at the altar and the offer we both made."

"Why is that, Henry?"

"So, the story would be complete and accurate in every detail."

Before Henry could explain, the Archbishop revealed his impatience similar to that of his former mentor. "What story?"

"The story which Father Engelmann was writing. You recall all of the manuscripts on Father's desk in his bedroom?"

"Yes, yes, that is one of the things which I also want to talk to you about." I knew Father Engelmann was writing a story...I believe it was about you and Jenny, is that correct?"

"Yes, but, let's wait until we get down to the prayer house and I will show you what I mean. It will be clearer to see what Father had written and where he left off and what he wanted me to do."

As they walked to the car, the Archbishop asked Henry if there was one thing he learned from his fast or message he would want to share, what would that be?

Henry didn't have to think long, "First of all, I have to confirm what Father Engelmann has told me for years in suggesting I do such a retreat. Fasting detaches us from the world of daily living and helps us to focus on God and what is truly important in our lives. I have learned how deeply God and Jesus and the Holy Spirit loves each and every one of us. God through His divine Providence is always at work to use any situation, trial or joy to bring us back to Him. I am amazed how He never ceases to work in our hearts to draw us out of ourselves, out of our pursuit of vain and perishable things, so that we can receive His grace and give ourselves wholly to Him.

"When I look back, I see so many times when His hand was involved in my life especially through my dear teacher and friend, Father Engelmann. But more directly to your question, Your Grace, the message that we all need to hear is to come to prayer each and every day and ask God to release the Holy Spirit in our hearts. He plants the seed in our hearts to take the path towards dying to ourselves; to begin the journey towards humility. Jesus was the perfect example of this. He was the servant to all and obedient to the Father even unto death. And as the Bible teaches, even Jesus, in His humanity, needed the strength and power of the Holy Spirit as man to do all He did during His ministry.

"This is the age of the Holy Spirit, this is His time in the history of mankind to convict us of Jesus' sacrifice and all the teachings He gave to us how to live when he walked the earth during his three-year ministry. I am convinced, Your Excellency that this power and strength which we all need so desperately to live for our Lord and be prepared for eternity is all but lost or hidden from the lives of all too many Christians and even in our churches.

"It's not mentioned and stressed enough.

"We need this power in our lives. Even Jesus, before He began His ministry, in His humanity, He had to receive the Holy Spirit to empower Him to do all He did. The climax to His ministry was His promise to send the Holy Spirit to the disciples after He returned to heaven which He did on the day of Pentecost. There must be a great revival of the Pentecost in our churches and our lives if we are to live for Christ from our hearts with true passion, commitment, humility and believe. To love as Jesus commanded us to do, we need the power and strength of the Holy Spirit!"

The Archbishop nodded... "Well said, Henry."

Chapter Fifty-Two

THE MOMENT HENRY and the Archbishop walked into the prayer house, the Archbishop said, "I can still smell the odor of sanctity. My, what a holy man David was. I recall so well the day he visited me shortly after Anna passed away with his request to become a priest. For two days, I struggled with his request. He was on in age and would require study at the seminary and he had been out of school for thirty years or more. I had made up my mind to decline David for reasons I have shared, but that night I had a dream. An angel appeared in my dream and said that the Lord has special plans for David Engelmann and that his request should be honored. I called David first thing the next morning and accepted him as a candidate for the priesthood."

"Wow, we can all see the special plans he had for Father Engelmann. He turned out to be a saint!"

"It goes to show that decisions should always be run by the Lord. I would have made a poor decision, had not one of his messengers interceded. I mention this as I wanted to know if the angel I saw was the same as you did. I can still recall every detail: he was tall and had a kindly face much like David's. His hair was long and flowing and so was his beard. His eyes were brown and had great depth. He wore a long brown robe and his voice was soft and mellow."

"No, the angel I saw was shimmering in a long white garment. The aura of light was so bright; I could not make out his features. He was definitely an angel of high rank, I would say an archangel. The one which you saw in your dream sounds like Zachariah, Father's guardian angel. When Jenny, Father and I returned miraculously from the dead, Jenny and I did not remember our stint on the other side but Father recalled everything and I now think I know why. But what I wanted to say was Father shared with us as much as he could what he had seen on the other side. He described Jenny's and my guardian angel as well as his. What you described, Your Grace, was Father's guardian angel."

Henry wanted to share with the Archbishop the dream he had about Hannah having a special calling like Father Engelmann but decided to leave it for another time.

"Hmm, yes, it could very well have been David's guardian at that time." The Archbishop paused and then said, "Now, what about the manuscripts you were going to show me. This was Father's first task his angel requested of him and the second we now know; it was to deliver you from your depression through his offering."

Henry nodded. "Yes, Father had made a covenant with the Lord to do that by offering up his life and also to receive the Stigmata to bring me back to the faith. It's the first mission, however, to write the story about Jenny and me that still has to be worked out and that is why I suggested we come down here as it will be easier to explain."

Henry's visitors followed him into the bedroom where he showed his guests the pile of manuscripts containing books one to six and then pointed to the last manuscript on the other side of the table which Father was working on before he died.

"Before we review that, here is a letter Father wrote to me that very morning of his death. He instructed me to finish the story. And this," Henry pointed to the seventh manuscript, "is where Father finished that morning and where I continued to write, during my forty-day fast retreat. I have now brought the story up to yesterday."

The Archbishop studied Henry and remained silent. His eyes told Henry to go on.

"Now, as I was saying when we were on the deck of my house, about the vision I saw. First, it was necessary for me to see Father so that I could make my offering along with Father's offering, but it was also to see what happened, so I could continue to write the story! In a way, I was allowed to see a vision in the same way Father had when he was on the other side, in order to write so accurately and vividly, the love story of Jenny and I."

The Archbishop's eyes brightened. "Yes, that is precisely what David told me when he was questioned after his stint on the other side. His guardian allowed him to see everything up to the point prior to his return.

Henry nodded and quickly added, "And the writing of this story corroborates what he said. He could have only done so with supernatural help. There is no way a person could write every detail like that and at his age, it's,… it's mindboggling!"

The two men gazed at one another in awe.

"Your Grace, you must read this story, I couldn't put it down. It's not because the story is about Jenny and I, but also includes my life with my first wife, Julean. It's about Father Engelmann when he owned the store and his wife, too. But the real essence of the story, Your Grace, are the life lessons throughout. What Father did was weave teachings into this captivating love story of how Jenny and I met at age fifteen, parted and four decades later miraculously came back together again. Within this epic saga he touched on all the major issues we encounter as we journey through life.

"In a way, it's a self-help book series. This is what I wanted to do when I was a counselor. The big difference though in what I would have written and what Father did was that I would have listed a set of do's and don'ts which would have quickly been forgotten. However, to write about the challenges and trials of life that we all face, through the lives of the characters, allows the readers to identify with the characters and the difficulties which they had to deal with; death, terminal illness, forgiveness, integrity, unconditional love, why God allows suffering and pain, these are just a few of the issues

Father deals with. And what is even more amazing is how Father shows the readers that the key to deal with all of these life challenges is by placing Jesus at the center of your life! He leads people back from a dead-end secular way of life, to their Christian heritage.

"It's remarkable what Father was inspired to do!

"It's a spiritual journey, intended to lead the reader home to our heavenly Father!"

"Amazing...we will definitely review these books," commented the Chancellor.

The Archbishop nodded. "Yes, we certainly must do that, Joseph."

"Oh, I can't wait to read them," Bernadette piped in excitedly.

The Archbishop ignored his secretary's comment and asked Henry, "Are the books all titled and does the series have a name?"

"Yes, the first five are all titled. Henry reached over to the pile of manuscripts and named each one as he went through them.

"And as for the title of the series, it came to me during my fast, The Angelic Letters Series."

Henry unbuttoned the top two buttons of his shirt and pulled out the pewter angel.

"Ah, yes, I recall you sharing with me the story behind the pewter angels when I interviewed you shortly after your miraculous healing. Your wife, Jenny had an identical one which you sent to each other when separated way back in 1956."

"That's right, John. You have a good memory. I had written ten countless letters to Jenny and she did to me as well, I later learned when we got back together. But those two letters with the angels tucked inside were the only two which were not destroyed. It was our guardian angels who protected the letters and it was also them who brought Jenny and me back together after four decades. I thought it only fitting that the series would be aptly titled with a theme related to the letters somehow."

"So...The Angelic Letters Series! I love the title!" exclaimed Bernadette not able to contain her excitement.

Henry nodded. "Thanks, Bernadette. There is this book six though which is also still untitled and of course the last and seventh book is not titled yet either. I thought the other day about a title related to the Poustinia since much of the story in book six takes place here.

"Yes," nodded the Archbishop, "involving the prayer house that's surrounded with angels does have a lot to do with the story—"

"That's it, John!" Henry said excitedly. "I recall telling Jenny that I often saw angels flying around the prayer house at night and she said Father Engelmann is well protected by angels... and then she added, 'It could very well be that the Poustinia is the house where angels dwell.' I remember telling her that was such a nice way of capturing the vision I had of angels flying all around."

Henry paused for a moment, "Yes, that's the perfect title for the sixth book; 'The House Where Angels Dwell,' and the credit to the sixth book in the series goes to Jenny!"

"Oh, I love that title, Henry. I can hardly wait to read this love story!" Bernadette said as she just had to chime in again.

"I have to admit, I am very intrigued to read it as well," concurred the Archbishop.

The Chancellor nodded and added, "All you have to do now is find a publisher to publish the series."

"I think that's already taken care of, Joseph. In Father Engelmann's letter to me, he suggests that I pray often to Padre Pio and Father Francis Xavier Seelos to intercede for the success of the books. They were Father's favorite holy people besides Saint Francis of Assisi, of course."

"David, spoke of them often with me. Father Seelos was from his home land who immigrated to the United States in 1800. Father prayed that Father Seelos would be canonized someday like Padre Pio was...Oh, forgive me Henry, I shouldn't have interrupted you. You were saying that your publishing is taken care of...does, Father Seelos and Padre Pio have something to do with that?"

Henry's eyes brightened; he wished his mentor were here. Father always loved it when Henry came up with another idea. "Yes, with my business experience, I thought I would try to publish the books myself under the publisher name, Pio-Seelos Books. Indirectly, they would become the publishers! If anyone can make the books reach readers with this important message, they can through their intercession!"

"Remarkable idea," said the Chancellor.

"This all fits in with what the Lord wants me to do. I have already mentioned to you about my calling to do mission-ary work. Well, two nights ago I had a dream that I went to Calcutta and worked with my friend, Gary, in Mother Teresa's Mother House. It was so real, I was glad I woke up. The poverty there is inconceivable. Well, I won't get into that but I just want to say that since this story is the result of a vision from heaven, it is destined to reach millions of readers. It has always been Father Engelmann's prayer that we help the poor, our brothers and sisters in need all over the world."

Henry's eyes brightened once more as the Archbishop, just like Father Engelmann used to, leaned forward with anxious anticipation of what Henry was about to say next.

"The money made from the sale of these books will go to the missions; to dig water wells, build schools for children, hospitals for the sick and on and on. The Angelic Letters Series, Your Grace, is going to touch the hearts of countless people. It will bring many back to the faith, inspire them, help them with trials they face, teach them about God's Word and how we should live!"

Henry was so excited he was running out of breath. "This is an inspired story, Your Grace! It's a gift from God! The Lord will work countless miracles through these books with His Divine Providence. Just imagine, Your Excellency, the lives of so many people and their circumstances all turning into such tremendous good!"

Chapter Fifty-Three

Henry checked his watch; it was almost two o'clock. That's when the Chancellor was going to drive the Monsignor to the farm. Henry felt a little nervous, not knowing what to expect. He recalled when a delegation came from Rome to investigate Jenny's death and miraculous recovery and healing. He and Father Engelmann were also interviewed extensively as well in regards to their near-death experiences. Some of the individuals on the panel were very abrupt. One person in particular seemed to play the Devil's Advocate and often his questions and statements seemed to suggest that what they said was doubtful or not totally the truth. But then, Henry surmised, they have to be absolutely certain that what they are dealing with is in fact a miracle and involved the hand of God.

In any case, Henry was relieved though that only one emissary was coming and wished to interview him in private. He was also certain that Monsignor Antonio Giuseppe was not the Devil's Advocate back then but remembered him as being gentle and open to what had happened. Father Engelmann had many private discussions with the Monsignor and developed a rather fond relationship with the man from Rome.

At precisely two o'clock a shiny black car came around the bend and within seconds was in full view. Henry opened the front door and stepped out under the canopy to greet the two dignitaries. The car stopped just short of the driveway and the Chancellor was the first to get out of the car. "Hello, Henry." Joseph called out.

"Hello, Joseph," Henry replied, "nice to see you again."

The Chancellor rushed to the other side of the car to open the door but Monsignor had already opened it and was getting out. He wore a black cassock with a wide purple fascia which was a sash worn high on his waist. The ends hung down on his left side. He wore a white roman collar. Henry expected a skull cap or beanie on his head but then remembered Monsignors do not usually wear them: Cardinals do. It was just as well as the prairie wind was in full force and the cap would be long gone by now.

The bottom of the cassock waved in the wind as the Monsignor approached Henry with his right hand extended.

Henry approached the emissary in same manner. "Welcome to our home, Monsignor Antonio Giuseppe. It's a pleasure to meet you again."

The Monsignor took Henry's hand and replied, "Yes, it's been over five years I believe, if my memory serves me corretly. And yes, it's a pleasure to see you again as well. You have a nice setting here, Henry. You are somewhat secluded and I was surprised to suddenly see the valley as we were coming down the lane."

"It surprises most people to suddenly come upon a valley in the flat prairie, but millions of years ago, glaciers were here and grooved out these pockets of beauty. This is also why we call this acreage, Sudden Valley Ranch."

The Monsignor smiled and then said, "I am excited to see the prayer house. The Archbishop keeps talking about it so fondly, as has the Chancellor on the way out. First let me thank you for meeting with me on such short notice."

"No problem at all, Monsignor, I didn't have anything planned for this week so this is working out just fine. Perhaps, before we go down to the prayer house in the valley, we should visit the deck on the east side of the house. It overlooks the valley and the Poustinia..."

"Ah, yes, the Russian name for prayer house. In Russia it is considered more of a hermitage. But you were going to say..."

"Yes, Your Grace, a lot of what happened the day of Father Engelmann's death took place up here on the deck. I suppose you are interested in hearing about the circumstances surrounding Father's passing and how the holy man received the stigmata."

"John has prepared an extensive and highly detailed report of what has transpired but I would like to hear it from you as well."

Henry turned and led the way. Rather than go through the house, Henry took them around the south side, the way Father Engelmann usually came to the deck when he came up from the prayer house to visit.

The Monsignor didn't exude any air of sophistication and his very personable manner so far relaxed Henry. He surmised the senior man was in his seventies. Henry didn't recall his hair being so snow white the last time he saw Monsignor, but Henry did remember his round spectacles, which seemed to compliment perfectly, his round friendly face.

When they got on the deck, Henry led the Chancellor and the Monsignor to the spot where most of the action took place. Then, Henry began to tell the story of what happened. Since he had just written all about this in the seventh book, it was all fresh in his mind.

Suddenly, their discussion was interrupted by the sound of the patio door opening. Camilla came out and introduced herself and the two young children; Hannah and Jacob. Camilla made particular reference to Hannah and that she was Jenny's child."

Monsignor bent over and extended his hand to Hannah, "So, you are Jennifer's little girl. I am pleased to meet you, Hannah."

"It's nice to meet you, too." Hannah replied as she gave her little hand to the Monsignor. "Mommy Camilla, said you came very far from a place called Rome."

"Yes, that is where I live. It is far away but I came to see you and your mommy and daddy." And then turning to Jacob, the monsignor once again extended his hand to the little boy. Jacob, however hugged Camilla's leg and just looked at the strange man. Rather than pursue shaking Jacob's hand, the Monsignor straightened out and reached out to pat Jacob's head but he shied even further away behind Camilla's dress. The Monsignor simply smiled and said, "Such a handsome little boy."

"I have made some iced tea and dainties if you wish for something to nibble on?" Camilla said, taking away the attention from the children.

"Some iced tea would be delightful, but no sandwiches for me. And I look forward to our meeting tomorrow."

Camilla gave a cursory glance at Henry and then back to the Monsignor and said, "Yes, I look forward to our meeting as well."

The Chancellor, who had more or less just stayed in the background so far, declined Camilla's offer and said, "I must be getting back as I have a meeting this afternoon. I will return about four-thirty to pick up Antonio. It's very nice seeing you again, Camilla."

After the Chancellor had gone, Camilla took the children back into the house and left Henry and Monsignor alone. For over an hour, Henry shared how he first met Father Engelmann and began to work for the Engelmann's back in 1956. He described the deep friendship they had developed over the years right up to the day Father gave his life for him and received the Stigmata.

"So, Mr. Pederso—"

"Please continue to call me Henry..."

"Yes, thank you, Henry. So, you say you saw an angel standing beside you. Can you describe him to me?"

Henry reflected for a moment and then said, "He wore a shimmering pure white robe; his hair was long and flowing... its color as well as the features of his face were impossible to tell because of the brilliant light. He definitely was an angel of high rank. I say that because over four years ago when Jenny, Father Engelmann and I passed on, we all saw the same angel coming through the tunnel of light to bring the message to our guardian angels, the decision of the Lord, to heal all three of us and return us to earth. He was of such high stature, much more so than the angels who were assigned to protect us. That is why I say it was an angel of high rank when compared to ours."

"I see. And the words he spoke confirmed that David had made a prior covenant with God when he had his near-death experience."

Henry nodded.

The Monsignor gazed at Henry for a long time as if he had forgotten what his next question was. But Henry was soon to learn as the interview went on for the afternoon, that this was the holy man's way of ascertaining if what he said was accurate and truthful. It was as if the Monsignor was checking it out with the Holy Spirit and getting His input on the matter at hand.

"The second question I have has to do with what you saw from this vantage point. From the report I read, the Archbishop recorded that you saw the sky brightening and the walls of the prayer house fall away…"

"Yes, not necessarily fall away but more so turned into glass. I could see right through the house and saw Father saying Mass as if he was standing right here. It's a miracle, Monsignor. It seems impossible and yet it's what had transpired."

Once again, Monsignor studied Henry's face for a long time and nodded. "Well, perhaps we shall go down to the Poustinia. I may wish to come back up here after."

Chapter Fifty-Four

WHEN THEY GOT to the prayer house, Monsignor commented on the quaint setting of the chapel, nestled down in the valley. He admired the simplicity of the house next to the pond and vista of hills, all around providing a sense of seclusion.

Henry led Monsignor in through the kitchen door, the same entrance he used when he first found Father laying on the floor at the foot of the altar. The Monsignor kept muttering something as Henry described every detail where Father had lain, where he usually sat, where he slept and where he wrote the epic story by candlelight. The Monsignor paused at the table and shook his head at the sight of all the transcripts. He reached forward and passed several pages in his hand by flipping them past his thumb and occasionally stopping to read a few lines.

"That was quite an assignment by his guardian angel to write such an epic story. And I understand that you have taken over and are charged with finishing it at some point."

"Yes, I have already started to complete book seven. And yes, I do have to bring it to some conclusion. I have read all the books Father Engelmann had written and I am astounded by the story and life teachings Father wove into the saga. Truly, an incredible work."

"I will definitely read them as soon as they are published."

Henry went to the fridge and offered Monsignor a bottle of water, then the two men went outside and sat down on the chairs facing the pond. After a brief pause, to collect their thoughts, Henry began describing Father Engelmann's virtues and holiness and why he should be canonized as a saint. The Monsignor however surprised Henry by interrupting him.

"We are all aware of Father's exceptional holiness, Henry. The Archbishop has been documenting David's life for some time, even before he went into the priesthood, considering him a saint long ago. No, we are way past that step in the process. It's all so well documented what this wonderful holy man has accomplished. I was assigned to read and keep track of the Archbishop's logs for years now. The Engelmann's were exceptional people in their community. It's unfortunate more was not recorded of Anna, Father Engelmann's wife, as she, too, by all accounts was very holy as well.

"In any case, the Diocese of Regina is very fortunate to have an Archbishop who saw what was happening and had the foresight to keep very accurate records of Father's virtues and heroic deeds. Perhaps, I know just as much and even more than you of all the holy man has done and accomplished over the years. There is no question in my mind or the mind of anyone else in the Congregation for the Causes of Saints in Rome."

Monsignor paused, allowing Henry to take in what he had just said and then went on again.

"Many miracles have already been investigated by the Archbishop and verified and attributed to Father's intercession and prayers prior to his death. Since his death, many people have reported healings through the intercessory prayers to Father Engelmann. At least nine cases of healing have been investigated that doctors cannot attribute to any medical application or related to scientific proof. The only logical explanation in these cases so far seem to be attributed to the persons touching Father while he was on view at the Cathedral prior to his funeral service. And…there are still thirty-six other cases still to be investigated.

"It is clear, Father Engelmann has already passed the requirement of two miracles following the death of the candidate, for consideration of sainthood. But even so, Father Engelman's case is exceptional in that he has received the Stigmata. A sign from God Himself of his holiness!"

Henry was not aware of all these miracles and recordings by the Archbishop. He just shook his head and was speechless. Furthermore, he had anticipated that this meeting with the Monsignor would be mainly one of answering questions and defending the holiness of his beloved teacher but this was not the case at all. In fact, what was yet to come would astound Henry all the more!

The Monsignor went on, "In my mind, I too, am convinced Father Engelmann is a saint and that the Pope will waive the five-year waiting period that would traditionally be required before launch of proceedings. So, you can see, Henry, I am not here to in any way to attack the evidence in favor of your dearly beloved friend from canonization."

Henry was flabbergasted. "Well then what brings you here?"

"Several reasons. I am here out of curiosity to see where and how the holy man lived." Monsignor turned around and gazed at the valley before him as he had done earlier when they came. After a long silence, he said, "The setting is very peaceful. The view is not like the French Rivera but in a way, even more beautiful. As I observed when we came down, it is simple and quiet; it is serene and so fitting for a man of such humble needs to be so blessed by the Lord. I can smell the holiness in the air and know we are surrounded by a choir of many angels. This is holy ground and I would encourage you to declare it as such. There is great healing power here. The presence of the Holy Spirit is very strong."

Monsignor turned back to Henry and said something which puzzled Henry even more than he already was. "I am also here, more so, to talk about your wife, Jennifer."

"My wife Jenny? If it has to do with her miraculous healing of cancer four years ago, that has been proven to be a miracle. That case was investigated thoroughly and even you were a part of the team at that time."

"Yes, that is true, Henry. I am thoroughly familiar with her file as well. But I have read an extensive report over and above the huge file which documents her miraculous healing from cancer. That has officially been accepted as miraculous. The body of physicians associated with that case have all agreed; there was no medical or scientific explanation for what had transpired there, other than the hand of God. But that is not what I have to share with you about your wife…"

Henry wondered where this was going. As he watched the man from the Vatican sit back and relax more in his chair, Henry sensed that this was going to be a lengthy sharing. He could hardly wait for what Monsignor was going to say next.

"As you may know, Henry, when someone exhibits a virtuous life within a community, the Bishop of that Dioceses is placed in charge of the initial investigation of that person's life. If it is determined that the candidate is deemed worthy of further consideration, the Vatican grants a 'Nihil Obstat.' This is a Latin phrase which means, "nothing hinders." Henceforth the candidate is called a 'Servant of God.'"

Henry sat at the edge of his chair and asked pointedly, "Are you considering Jenny a saint, too?"

The Monsignor shrugged his shoulders and waved his hands at the same time to suggest the possibility.

"Yes!" Henry blurted, "she was so much like Father Engelmann, I cannot say the number of times I thought how holy she was. Although I never considered her to be a saint, but now that you bring up the matter, I could all day and night talk about her virtues—"

The Monsignor raised his hand and waved it as if shooing off an annoying fly that seemed to take turns bothering both of them.

"That is not necessary, Henry, I know all about your wife's life and attributes."

"Do you mean about her medical files?"

"No, about her life from her earliest years. How angels visited her in the form of butterflies. How she talked to them every night. How she grew as such a special child, so spontaneous, loving and free. She was born with the heart of an angel!"

The blood drained from Henry's face. "But how do you know such things? Not even The Archbishop would have known that."

"Yes, that is true. It would take a very special person to know every detail of Jennifer's life besides her guardian angel of course. But no one has that kind of communication with the supernatural. It would have to be ...let us say, an earthly angel."

The Monsignor smiled and went on. "Let me first say by way of explanation, when a Bishop or in this case, the Archbishop, sends in the initial report of a person who lives an exemplary life and is considered 'a Servant of God,' a Church Official, known as a Postulator is appointed to coordinate the process and serves as an advocate and must prove that the candidate lived heroic virtues. This is achieved through the collection of documents and testimonies that are collected and presented to the Congregation for the Causes of Saints in Rome. When a candidate is approved, he or she earns the title of 'Venerable.'"

"But Your Excellency," Henry interrupted, "I don't know of any one ever doing that for Jenny and certainly no Postulator has been appointed so far..."

It was plain that the holy man from Rome knew a secret by the way his eye's brightened. Monsignor knew something incredibly astounding and was about to share it with the man before him. It would lift his heart and make his faith in life, in God and Jesus even deeper, if that were possible.

"This is where it gets quite interesting, Henry. Once again, the Archbishop had the instinct and foresight to keep track of Jennifer, following her miraculous healing and recovery. The more he followed her life and all that was spoken of her, especially by Father Engelmann, when they met on a scheduled basis, the more the Archbishop felt guided to document Jennifer's life, too. He not only followed the work Jennifer did in the community with her ladies' groups but kept an accurate report of the many ladies she counselled who came back to the church with their faith restored. Your wife, Henry was the cause of many miracles, which would have gone unnoticed if it were not for the Archbishop. However, these are outward signs and to an extent, reveal the heart of that individual, but it is not the same as one who is capable of seeing into the heart of a person."

"Only God can do that!" Henry blurted.

"Yes, but there are occasions when circumstances allow for a person who is also very holy to be granted such visions and insights into the hearts of mankind."

The Monsignor crossed his legs and went on, "As you may know, Father Engelmann has prayed over many people and through his intercessory prayers to Saint Padre Pio and Father Xavier Seelos many miraculous healings have occurred. Father had also gained the reputation over the years of seeing into the hearts of people who went to him for confession. Occasionally, he even refused to give absolution to someone who had not forgiven a transgressor or repaid a debt."

"Yes, yes, Father had that uncanny ability to see into the hearts of people. I can attest to that 100 percent. He knew me like an open book. There was nothing I could hide from him. I often wondered why I even bothered to confess my sins to him because he already knew what they were and even told me many times of sins I had forgotten. But what has this to do with Jenny? And who is the Postulator that knew of Jenny's earlier years growing up?" Henry wanted to know.

"This will be hard for you to believe. It always amazes me how God's divine Providence works in our lives. The Vatican made a special concession on their choice of Postulator when once again, your Archbishop had the keen perception to suggest that Father Engelmann be Jenny's advocate."

"What! Father Engelmann, Jenny's Postulator!?"

"Yes, who better knew Jennifer from the moment she was born than Father Engelmann…"

Then it hit Henry like a ten-ton truck. "Oh my…oh my good Lord. When Father Engelman died and went on the other side, he was allowed to see into the lives of all humanity, especially into our lives; Jenny's and mine so he could write the epic story he was assigned!"

The look on Henry's face was so hard to describe but the Monsignor would have given anything to be able to capture it on film.

"Yes, Henry, who better than a man who was allowed to see into the heart and lives of others from a heavenly perspective. Such a person would make a perfect Postulator; he would know another person inside and out. There would be no need to really do further investigation, or seek further testimonies, as the truth of the person is all there in the knowing knowledge of that person who was allowed such an incredible vision. The Archbishop was quick to realize that although he did some investigations and logs of your wife's life that it wasn't necessary as Father Engelmann's knowledge and insight into Jennifer's life went way beyond anything that could ever be recorded on her behalf. What impressed me the most in reading Father's documentation was when Father shared the homily he had written in one the books he had written. It centered around the theme that Jennifer had the heart of an angel. That homily was all I needed to know of this holy woman which you were fortunate enough to marry."

Tears spilled form Henry's eyes. He was emotionally affected by the Monsignor's sharing. He hadn't known that Father was assigned to be witness to Jenny's life in this capacity. He struggled to speak. He sat back and tried to compose himself.

The Monsignor simply sat back and waited. Every now and then, he surveyed the pond and shook his head. Henry assumed he was taken by the simple beauty of the scene before him but he, too, was astounded by this entire matter.

Henry broke the silence, "Does this mean that you are also considering her to be a saint as well?"

"Yes, in part it is because of the way she lived and was such a light to others but what received our attention even more so was the circumstances that surrounded her pregnancy and how she died. In Father Engelmann's last documentation, he strongly supported Jenny to be a candidate for sainthood. She sacrificed her own life for the child within her womb. She was against abortion and had given her life. The doctor, I believe your father-in-law, also stated when interviewed, that prior to her delivery, Jennifer said that if it should come down to her life or the child's, he had to promise that it must be the child's…yes, the Vatican is considering her for sainthood—"

"But, as you said earlier, doesn't it stipulate that a person cannot be considered for Sainthood, until he or she has been dead for at least five years?"

"That is the case, but the Pope can waive that requirement as he feels in this day when the sanctity of life is considered so shallow, it would serve as an example of persons who do and show divine love to support their belief. Jennifer did so at the peril of her own health and eventually her life."

"But doesn't it require some miracle for beatification? I think that is the third step isn't it?"

"Yes, to be beatified and recognized as 'Blessed,' one miracle is required through the candidate's intercession, in addition to recognition of her heroic virtue. And there is final step which we have already discussed; Canonization requires a second miracle after beatification."

"So that may take some time for miracles to be associated through Jenny's intercession?"

Once again, the Monsignor smiled, revealing that same look as if he were the cat who swallowed the canary.

"One miracle has already been attributed to your wife, Henry—"

"But where, how, who… when!?"

"Once again, I am amazed at God's divine workings as you may be too when I share what transpired. When I was in Ottawa at a conference, I knew I was planning to come and visit you before winter set in but I shortened that plan and decided to come sooner because of what happened in Ottawa when I was there."

Henry's eyes grew large…what on earth was he about to hear…?

"In Ottawa? That is where Jenny lived. Did Jenny perform a miracle there?"

The Monsignor nodded. "On the last day of the conference, I was sitting next to the Bishop who looked after the Ottawa

Diocese. He shared with me that he had just witnessed an unusual healing and that it was through some person who he was not familiar with. When he mentioned the name of the person involved in the miraculous healing and described the extraordinary circumstances surrounding it all, I immediately sat up because that was the person whom I wanted to talk to the Archbishop here in Regina about."

"Was it Jenny!?" Henry was so close to the edge of his seat that he threatened to fall off.

Monsignor Antonio Giuseppe smiled and nodded at the same time. Henry got the sense the man across from him was enjoying the suspense and dragging this out for all it was worth.

"Tell me, Monsignor, what on earth happened?"

"Apparently a woman from Jamaica was visiting her sister in Ottawa along with her ailing husband whose lungs were ravished by cancer. He was given just weeks to live. Incredibly, the man smoked, even though it was that very habit which brought him to that point in life. The woman's sister suggested that they pray for her husband—"

Once again, the blood drained from Henry's face; this time even more so. He looked as white as a candle. He kept shaking his head and simply had to ask the question without a further second delay... "Did you visit this man?"

"Yes, yes, I did and the rest of the family too."

"Tell me straight away, was his name Eddy?"

Monsignor nodded, "Yes, Eddy Ziegler and his delightful wife's name is Coreena."

Henry raised his hands to his head in total disbelief. "This can't be possible! Eddy is my best friend, Monsignor and the woman's sister is Mattilda who was Jenny's best friend...And I suppose you are going to tell me next that somehow Jenny healed Eddy."

"Yes, I made all these connections the second last day I was there in my discussions with the family. That is why I wanted to stop off in Regina before heading back to Rome to share all this with you. You will be getting a call from Ottawa in the next day or so. I told them to give me the opportunity to share this with you. It's not every day we get a chance to give such great joy to a widower about his wife and the circumstances, as you can see, are so extraordinary, but there is more to come."

Henry's eyes widened again and he couldn't stop shaking his head. "I don't think there is anything that can top what you have already shared with me."

"Well, let me try! First, you are correct, Eddy has been miraculously healed of all of his cancer and smoking habit too, I must add—"

"But how did Jenny get involved?"

"Well, I was just about to tell you..." The Monsignor sat back, enjoying every minute he could drag this out. He reminded Henry of the times Father Engelmann had done the very same thing to him.

"Please, Monsignor, the suspense is killing me!"

The elderly man smiled and went on. "Apparently when Mattilda, her friends and their employer, Mr. Hamilton, came to Jennifer's funeral, Mattilda took back with her to Ottawa, one of the daisies from an angel's basket that was situated in the back yard of her home here in Regina. It was one of several flowers which Jenny had placed in the basket that never seemed to fade or shrivel up. The flowers seemed to survive on their own as if they were planted in soil and watered every day. In fact, I saw the flower and must admit, it seemed as fresh as if it were picked that very day. In any case, Mattilda had Eddy hold the flower and the entire family and staff of Mr. Hamilton's household began to pray for a healing and asked Jennifer to intercede on Eddy's behalf.

"Well, by nightfall, Eddy had stopped coughing and by the next morning, he said he never felt better in his life. When he reached for a cigarette, he found it so distasteful that he immediately threw it away and to the best of my knowledge, has never touched them again. After a week of thorough examination by the staff doctors in the hospital, they were all dumfounded and reported that this man who was destined to die within weeks, if not days, had miraculously been healed. I examined the x-rays myself which had been taken just two days before and compared them to the x-rays after the healing. Eddy's lungs were as healthy as a new-born child. I will be taking some documentation of this back with me to the Vatican for further consideration, but by the looks of it, Jennifer just passed the first miracle required for beatification!"

Henry's tears turned into elation and then laughter. It hit Henry so incredibly unbelievable how God works, that he couldn't stop laughing. Once again, he had to stand and try to dissipate what he just heard racing through his mind.

"I'm so sorry, Monsignor, please forgive my rudeness. Earlier you mentioned that you were always amazed how God works through his Divine Providence. You may not believe what I am going to share with you. Eddy Zeigler was one of the boys back in 1956 who was involved with the rape of Jenny. He and three of his friends attacked us one late summer evening when Jenny and I were on our way home after attending a movie, at a downtown theatre. We had missed our bus. While walking home, we met up with the boys just as Eddy was being dropped off at his home. They roughed us up but stopped when a couple driving by stopped once they saw what was happening. Eddy went home and the other three boys left but later on, as Jenny and I continued on our way home, we ran into the three boys again. This time they knocked me semi unconscious and took Jenny to the park where one of the boys raped her."

This time it was the Monsignor who interrupted Henry. "Did Jennifer become pregnant?"

Henry nodded and decided to play out his secret this time. "And guess who the child was that Jenny bore?"

Monsignor's eyes told Henry to please go on…quickly.

"It was Camilla, who later met my son and they got married! It's a long story, Monsignor but that is how Jenny and I got back together after being apart for over four decades. Truly amazing!"

A smile grew on Henry's face. He thought he had news too which the Monsignor didn't know of but Henry would soon find out that Monsignor still didn't reveal all of his secrets.

Henry could see the man's mind working as if trying to see how these happenings were all related.

"Imagine Monsignor, that one of the very boys who Jenny hated back then, she learned to forgive and love. This same boy ended up marrying the sister of her best friend, Mattilda! It is truly incredible how God's Divine Providence works and how it takes, at times, years to play out.

"Think on this.

"As I said, Jenny didn't like Eddy for what he and his friends did to her. Yet, not only did she forgive him but not long after her death, incredibly, she is responsible for his miraculous healing! I'm sure she must be up there chuckling over this as well!"

This time, the Monsignor uncrossed his legs and leaned forward, "Now you think on this, Henry. If Jennifer had not forgiven Eddy during her life time, this flow of divine love may not have happened because Jennifer would not have been open to it, since she would have harbored unforgiveness in her heart during her lifetime. Can you not see how important it is to forgive and be open to allow God to work such amazing miracles in our lives!?"

The Monsignor got him again! Henry couldn't help himself; he raised his hands heaven-ward and began praising God. Suddenly, his praise and prayers were so thankful that the Holy Spirit took over and said what he was incapable of expressing to God.

In the silence of the prayer house, both men began weeping and the Monsignor joined in with Henry speaking in tongues as well.

After twenty minutes or so, the men stopped and sat down. For the longest time, they just looked at one another and every now and then laughed at the Lord's workings. The Monsignor was also blessed to interpret what was said in tongues and said to Henry, "The Lord wants you to know Henry, that He is so pleased that you have come back to Him and that He has important work for you to do."

Henry just nodded. He wiped a tear away that was sliding down his cheek. It was more from laughter and joy than any sadness. Finally, Henry asked, "So tell me, for Jenny to be considered for sainthood, a second miracle is required. That could take some time, if ever."

The Monsignor smiled at Henry with that same look that he was about to reveal yet something else which would send Henry off, once again reeling. "Not so, Henry. That is another reason for my visit. The Archbishop has informed me that another miracle has been attributed to Jennifer's intercession here in Regina."

"What!? How can that be? Who...why haven't I heard of it?"

"Yes, I am surprised that you haven't heard as it involves someone very close to you. Apparently, she didn't know whether or not to tell you as she didn't want to upset you or revive any memories of your wife's passing."

"What... what is going on here...who are you talking about?"

"It is the very person you just mentioned who so incredibly came into your life which you and I know is also part of God's Divine Providence. It's your daughter-in-law, Camilla."

"What...this is all too much! Has this got something to do with what you and she exchanged up at the house about meeting together tomorrow? Was it because of this?"

Monsignor Antonio simply nodded.

Once again, Henry got up and walked around the deck trying to compose himself... "This can't be happening...how on earth is Camilla involved with a miracle that involves her mother!?"

"Well, your daughter-in-law works at a school for unwed mothers. Apparently, one of the students under her care developed a very severe case of eclampsia. Three specialists upon thorough examination said she must have an abortion immediately, otherwise she would be dead within hours. The young mother was very distraught, as she didn't want to abort the child but everyone said she must. She had recovered from two seizures and was warned that a third seizure was on the way which would be fatal. This is when Camilla suggested to the distraught young woman to pray to Jennifer to intercede or somehow give the troubled young lady a sign of what to do.

"Now, according to the reports, all medication had failed at this point. The girl's blood pressure was over 200/95 and she was only in her 24th week of pregnancy. Far too early for the infant to survive; the lungs are not sufficiently developed and severe complications were definitely impending should the infant be born."

"What happened?" Henry could hardly wait to know.

"Well, no sooner had they prayed for Jennifer to intercede, then the amniotic sac broke and the young lady went into immediate labor. Within two hours, the tiny infant was born. All reports are that both the mother and infant daughter are doing fine. The mother recovered remarkably well and within hours, her blood pressure was back to 120/80. Once again, the doctors were dumfounded and all admitted that there was no scientific or medical explanation to explain what had happened. So, Henry, if this miracle bears out, Jennifer has passed the fourth step and is an eligible candidate for canonization.

"I have been involved with this case for over twenty-five years. I have come to know Father Engelmann's heart and the love he had for the Lord. And through his documentation as Postulator for Jennifer, I have come to know her as well. Father loved your wife very much and wrote extensively of her virtues and how many times she was an inspiration to him."

Henry silently wept as he listened to Monsignor relate all this amazingly, wonderful news. He felt so blessed to have been a part of the lives of these two extraordinarily holy people who both had the heart of an angel.

The Monsignor, also emotionally drained, filled with compassion and understanding, reached forward and patted Henry's knee and said, "It would be the highlight of my career as a servant of God to see that the Pope considers Jennifer and Father Engelmann as saints and declares them both as such in the very near future!"

CHAPTER FIFTY-FIVE

"**H**EY, DAD, MATTI is on the phone and wants to talk to you about your fast. She says she has some exciting news to tell you."

"Okay, thanks, Justin. I'll get it out here in the sunroom. Hello, Matti?"

"That be me, Henry. So, tell me, how that 'fast' be for you? Your boy tell me you be so holy you ain't talking to him no more."

Henry laughed, "Oh, no Matti. The good Lord showed me time and again how far I fall short of His mercy and grace. But I have to say, it's a wonderful experience and truly does help one to draw closer to God, His son, Jesus and the Holy Spirit."

"That be a good t'ing' you doin', Henry. You be an inspiration to me and maybe the Lord help me to lose a little weight, too."

"Yes, that's for sure, Matti. I lost over thirty pounds and I have never felt better. The first few days are tough but after that, you have so much energy, it feels as if you have wings and can fly all about!"

"Well, that be just what I need. Now I be so heavy, it's like I'm anchored to the ground. It's just that I like the food the good Lord provides and He bless me to be a good cook and all and everyt'ing' I be makin' tastes so good…I just can't help myself."

Yeah, I know what you mean, Matti, I love eating too but I'm really trying hard to just keep my portions down and I promised myself to fast every Monday to keep disciplining myself and my will power strong."

"Well, I be very proud of you and maybe next week, I try to stop for a day or two."

"That's a good way to start, Matti. Try to fast for a whole day or even start by missing supper and slowly build up your will power. And what really works best is to pray about it. Ask the Lord if He wants you to do it. That's what got me started. For the longest time I felt prompted to fast and pray and like I said, it's the best thing I ever did in my life. The spiritual benefits are amazing, Matti. I can't tell you how much I have learned about myself, what the Lord wants me to do and I think I'm happier with myself. So, you see, it not only cleanses the body of all its toxins and stuff but it helps to heal your soul and draw you closer to God."

"Hallelujah, praise the Lord! Like I be sayin, you be an inspiration to me. Imagine goin' without food for forty days! Hallelujah. Amen and I say amen again! Now Henry, that not the main reason I be callin you. The Lord be workin mighty powerful here and I got some excitin news to share but there be a man here pullin at the receiver. He wants to speak to you so bad, he be burstin' soon if I don't let him tell you the news. It be a good t'ing', I, too, am so excited I got to go pee!"

Henry knew what the news was but thought he would just let them share it from their point of view and he didn't want to dampen their excitement in any way.

"Hey, Hank, ole' buddy, how ya', doin'? It's me, Eddy!"

"Yes, I recognize you, Eddy. I'm great and you sound great too. And I didn't notice any cough…" Henry said, trying to open the door for Eddy to let him know about the miracle in his life.

"You're not going to believe this, Hank, but I've beat the cancer in my life. A miracle has happened and that wife of yours is responsible for it happening. She must have quite the 'in' with the Big Guy for healing a messed-up guy like me."

"That's great Eddy! Tell me what happened!"

"The crew here prayed over me and asked Jenny to put in a good word for me that my cancer would be taken away. I never felt so much love and care, Hank. There was Matti, Coreena, J.J. and his family, Thomas and Neela, three other people who were friends of Thomas and the hospital Chaplain. Matti also had a daisy that belonged to Jenny. She brought it back with her when she was in Regina for Jenny's funeral. I got to tell you Mon, I couldn't believe when they told me the flower was over a year old! It looked just like it was picked for me. The moment I took that daisy with the gold center, I knew something was about to happen. Electricity flowed through me; I thought maybe God was putting me in the electric chair and zapping me for all the bad stuff I did through life."

Henry laughed. He couldn't get over how good Eddy sounded.

"Imagine, Hank, God healing me even after I didn't have much to do with Him most of my life. Most days, Mon, I never thought from one day to the next that I would be seeing the sun come up. And then out of the blue comes this miracle, Mon. Still can't believe it."

"That's amazing Eddy and I am very happy for you. How God works through His Divine Providence is truly amazing."

"What's God's Divine Providence, Mon?"

Before Henry could explain, Matti, in the background cried out, "That be how He workin' in our lives to bring us back to Him! It be takin' a long time to reach your heart, Eddy, but he arranging t'ings here and there and look at you so happy to be home. Yes sir, He be lovin' you so much Eddy! He wantin' you up there with Him, but He didn't want you smokin' the place up so He done healed you down here!"

Everyone laughed in the hospital room including Henry who heard what Matti had said.

"Hang on, Hank, Thomas wants to have a word with you."

"Yeah, that would be great."

"Hello, Henry. Matti sure keeps things lively around here."

"Have to agree one hundred percent, Thomas. How are you doing?"

"As well as can be expected for a man in his seventies. A few more aches and pains, but the good Lord still allows me to keep the garden for Him. Just wanted to say how incredible it is what Miss Jenny has done, but I'm not surprised at all. She was the loveliest flower of all in the entire estate. She was a light in everyone's life when she was here. Some days I could hardly tell who was the brighter, Miss Jenny or the sun."

"That's very kind of you to say, Thomas."

"We all miss her. When she left the estate, it was never the same again. No matter how many flowers and different kinds I tried to grow, I could never capture that same spirit. As soon as she came to visit though, she brought the light back with her. It was a special aura that dear wife of yours had, Henry. Not a spot of darkness could exist in her presence. She was the closest person to know and live a life of love that I ever knew."

Henry didn't know what to say. When he visited the Hamilton estate with Jenny, he viewed Thomas to be quiet and a man of few words unless he was asked a question or two. Henry was going to thank him again for his kind words but Thomas broke into Henry's thoughts again.

"Now, I didn't get to know Father Engelmann that well, but I felt much the same about him when he visited with you and Miss Jenny. Matti could feel the Spirit in him more than I."

"It's interesting you mention that Thomas, as it leads into something I wanted to share with all of you. You already may know, if Monsignor said anything to you about Jenny and Father Engelmann."

"He was very excited and interested to know all about Eddy's healing and Miss Jenny's involvement. He did ask us to hold off for a day or two as he wanted to tell you the news himself first."

"Yes, he mentioned that to me as well. However, he did mention something else though, that both Jenny and Father Engelmann are being considered for sainthood. Apparently, Jenny's intercession on Eddy's miraculous healing is going to be attributed to her and is the first step to Jenny's beatification!"

"My, my, that is wonderful news, Henry. But like I said, it doesn't surprise me, both are very holy people…"

"What be the news Thomas? I can see you be excited about somet'ing."

Henry chuckled as he heard Matti pester Thomas about what he had said. "Henry just mentioned what Monsignor Antonio Giuseppe said to him when he was in Regina—"

"What did the man from Rome be sayin'...tell me Thomas."

"He told Henry that Miss Jenny and Father Engelmann are being considered for sainthood. Apparently, Eddy's healing is being attributed to Miss Jenny's intercession and will be considered meeting the first requirement to beatification. Miss Jenny needs two miracles and Eddy's will count as the first one."

Henry was about to respond to Thomas when Matti let out a shout that almost deafened him.

"Hallelujah, praise the Lord!" Matti shouted as she waved her hands heavenward. "Our Miss Jenny being crowned a saint! Praise the Lord! Saint Jenny, now ain't that be the sweetest words you ever did hear!? Saint Jenny, how sweet the sound. Why she be turnin' heaven upside down with her charm and beauty. Who can resist her sparklin' blue eyes and smile that be touchin' the bottom of your heart...now ain't that so?"

"Well, we have to wait a spell, Henry. Matti's twirling around and dancing up a storm. Now there she goes running down the hall like a town crier." Thomas chuckled.

"You know Henry, a lot of people think that sainthood is out of their reach and just for very holy people who seclude themselves in some type of shelter or cave and pray all day. But as we can see in both Miss Jenny's case and Father Engelmann, they are people just like you and I who choose to give their life to God and follow Him."

"Amen to that, Thomas. Yes, both Father and Jenny were very ordinary people who chose to live extraordinary lives. Their secret was to place Jesus at the center and to receive the Holy Spirit, to live it out and look what can happen!"

Thomas was going to respond when suddenly another commotion was heard by Henry. Apparently, Matti returned and was going on and on about something else. Henry was trying to make out what it was. Suddenly Matti came on the phone and excitedly said, "Now if this ain't a sight for sore eyes not'ing' is."

"What's going on Matti?" Henry wanted to know.

"Eddy be so elated that his miracle was one which be counting for Miss Jenny's sainthood. He got out of bed and be prayin' on his knees. That man be on fire! Here Eddy, do you want to talk to Henry?"

Henry heard Eddy say, "Not now!"

Matti came back on and said, "Eddy can no longer speak to you Henry, he busy prayin' on his knees to the Lord. Why I never did see him like this in all the years he be married to Coreena. Why I would say this be a bigger miracle than the healin' of his lungs. This healin' be bringin' Eddy up the stairs to heaven for sure. For a long time, I be prayin' for him as I wasn't too sure. Why his cussing and smoking were not the best for his soul but I tell you now, Henry, this man, the way he be prayin' he just may be a candidate someday too! I can't imagine it but anyt'ing' be possible with the Lord…Saint Eddy Zeigler, it don't have the same nice ring as Saint Jenny, but I must say, it be close. Yes, hallelujah, it be mighteee close! Imagine, Saint Jenny intercedin' for us up there with the good Lord! Now ain't that somet'ing! Praise the Lord, hallelujah!

Once again, everyone chuckled.

"And how be my precious little child, Hannah? I know that little one be havin' wings soon if not already. She be one special little girl, Henry. You just wait and see. That's for sure!"

When Henry got off the phone, he was so happy and elated he fell to his knees and prayed and praised God for all these blessings. He also said a prayer to Father Engelmann and to Jenny. He could hardly imagine that they were now both candidates for sainthood and may be declared such together on the very same day!! Just think, Henry thought, praying to Saint David Engelmann and Saint Jennifer Pederson! He felt like jumping around and dancing like Matti had done earlier. Truly, unbelievable how God works in His Divine Providence!

Chapter Fifty-Six

"Good evening everyone. Thank you so much for coming out for this social get-together of our ladies' group. For the most part in our meetings the discussions focus on the role of women in a marriage and family as it relates to the teachings in the Bible. Often, we wish the men were there for their input or just to hear what was being shared that would be insightful and helpful for them to hear. Since that is not possible, I have asked Henry Pederson to speak this evening on what he perceives to be the role of the husband in the family and to address some issues for men to consider in their marriage as well. Although his remarks will be directed more to the men, it is beneficial for women to hear this too, so they know what areas to support their husband in."

Camilla, the new president overseeing the ladies' groups which Jenny had started paused and then said, "Since Henry will be suggesting things which men should consider doing as husbands and fathers; there may be the urge for us women to give the 'elbow' to our husbands...please refrain from doing so." The ladies chuckled.

"This also goes for your discussions at home. Refrain from using what Henry says as a criticism of your husband as well. This creates defensiveness and shuts out communication and also future meetings with other counsellors, should this arise in your marriage. Rather, be open to what Henry has to say and use it as a base for a non-judgemental discussion. Communication between spouses is best when both partners come together and speak openly and honestly from the heart expressing how they feel and what they would like to see in their marriages and homes to make it work better. Finger pointing or criticism is not usually successful in making positive change."

Camilla smiled, her eyes sparkling with pride and delight, "So, without further ado, here is my father-in-law, Henry Pederson."

Henry made his way up to the microphone in the church hall. There were close to two-hundred and fifty people present from all the groups which Jenny had established in various parts of the city. The ladies were also encouraged to ask their friends to come along as well. The turnout was excellent.

"Thank you, Camilla and good evening to everyone. Thank you, too, to all of you for coming and I hope my remarks are helpful and received with an open mind and heart. I left counselling over fifteen years ago to pursue my art and business career, but still have fond memories of meeting with students and parents to discuss concerns they had within their families and sometimes between the parents themselves. Over the three years that my wife, Jenny, ran the ladies' groups to discuss marriages and families in relationship to the teachings of the Bible, many of the issues which I used to deal with came up in our home discussions. Further, we had a very close friend, Father Engelmann, who had been my mentor and teacher since I was fifteen years of age often joined into the conversations which Jenny and I had.

In my talk this evening, I will be addressing some of those issues and also passing along some of the wisdom and insights that Father shared with us. He had the added insight of having been married himself before his wife, Anna, died and he entered the priesthood. I think many of you were here a few years ago when Jenny had invited him to speak on the topic of 'using the gifts which God has given us' like touch, showing affection, effective communication and so on."

Henry heard many voices softly, positively, acknowledge listening to Father's words of wisdom.

"When I first started counselling, I never brought God or Jesus into the discussion or as part of the solution to people's problems and concerns. I thought my words, wisdom and insights would be sufficient to convince people to change and solve their challenges. But, I was wrong; just like I was wrong about self help books and techniques for improvement. Yes, these are temporary fixes and offer excellent suggestions for improving our lot in life but unfortunately in most, if not all cases, in a week or so the advice fades away. We so easily slip back to our old ways of thinking and responding to life's challenges.

"That is why I am reluctant to offer a list of dos and don'ts to follow in your role as leader of your family. Like self help books, the rules, obligations or suggestions I offer may remain in your mind for a few days, but will quickly be forgotten. However, if there is one thing I can convince of you tonight is that we need Jesus in our lives. You may already know this, or even if you don't, this is something that cannot be emphasized enough and will have a better chance of being remembered.

"I say this with confidence because God is already a part of our lives. We were created by Him and despite our sinful nature, we are therefore wired to come back to Him. My goal this evening is to awaken you to that fact. We have only to look at what happens when a crisis hits our lives; suddenly we just naturally turn to God for help, regardless of the depth of our faith. Suddenly we come face to face with what is really important in our lives. There are very few atheists and non-believers in the face of death. What I want to try and do this evening is to motivate and hopefully inspire you to turn to Him now so that you are not only ready for any eventuality but you will begin to live a life that God intended for you to live.

"I believe that if we put Jesus at the center of our lives and obey His teachings and follow His example we will plainly and as a matter of course come to know what our roles as husbands and fathers are. We will not only develop a loving relationship with Him and be filled with gratitude for what He has done for us but we will come to see that our main goal as head of the family is to bring ourselves, our wives and children home to our heavenly Father. And that is why we need to build our house on a rock. One has only to look at the home they live in. If it hadn't been built on a solid foundation, it would soon crumble and fall apart. It's the same with our lives, if we don't build it on sound values and principles, it too, soon shows up in the form of sickness, challenges and unnecessary anxiety and trials.

"But I am getting ahead of myself.

"What I have learned from Father Engelmann over the years, is to use a story to instil a life lesson. We can more easily relate to a teaching this way. Jesus used parables often as they make a point and one that is remembered. Furthermore, a story is non-threatening and thus our defences are down and we are more open to see how it can affect our lives. So, by way of presenting what I think a man's role in a marriage is and a family, I would like to share a personal witness of what happened to my father in our family. By doing so, it will cover much of what I want to say to you tonight and clearly show why it's so necessary to have Jesus at the center of our lives. Hopefully, my sharing will awaken the tremendous source of life that is already within you.

"As close as the air you breathe!

"It is important to keep in mind, God is always working in each and everyone's lives, every second of every day through His Divine Providence, to bring us back to Him. It may be through a book that we read. Perhaps, my presentation tonight might touch someone's heart; maybe it's a movie you have seen, something a friend says to you, or whatever. In my dad's case it was a TV show he watched along with millions of viewers every Sunday night called, *Life is Worth Living.* It featured Bishop Sheen, who was a motivational speaker with the goal of inspiring people on problems affecting their lives. His motto was, *the family that prays together stays together.*

"At that time, our home had an underlying current of unforgiveness and insecurity. My dad had made a mistake by being unfaithful to my mother and ran off with another woman. He returned, but it was always in the back of my mind that he might do it again. Even though Dad said he was sorry and promised he would never do that again, both my mom and I never completely believed him. Our home looked fine on the outside, but it was far from fine on the inside.

"One day my dad came home from work carrying a brown paper bag and after supper we all sat in the living room when he revealed what he had. I will never forget what he said as it clearly showed God's Divine Providence at work in my father's life. Without looking at us, Dad said, 'That fellow, Bishop Sheen keeps saying that the family that prays together stays together. Well, it's a good slogan but if it isn't put into practice, it's not much good.' He then took out three rosaries from the paper bag and gave Mom and me each one and then with the remaining one in his hands, he went to the chesterfield and knelt down. He looked up at the holy picture above the couch and invited us to join him in prayer.

"My mom immediately went to his side and knelt down, but I was speechless and couldn't move. That act instantly filled me with a total trust for my dad. For Mom and me to see a proud man bow and kneel down in humility to Jesus and invite Him into our home gave me complete security in our family and my parents' marriage. At that moment, I knew, he would always be faithful to Mom and me. It was that day, when I was eighteen years of age that I learned the true meaning of what Father Engelmann tried to drill in me about building my life on a rock so I would be able to withstand the storms of life and be ever ready to meet my Maker." Henry paused and nodded,

"For me, that was the day, my dad began to build his house on a rock.

"But God's Divine Providence was at work once again the following Sunday when Father Engelmann came over for dinner as he usually did. Later, as we all sat in the living room watching dad's favourite program, Bishop Sheen talked about the Day of Pentecost when the Holy Spirit descended upon the disciples, transforming them from fearful followers of Jesus into warriors. The Bishop went on to talk that only when we are filled with the Holy Spirit can we fully experience the spiritual power and truth of the Word. After the show was over, dad surprised us all again that evening when he asked Father Engelmann to pray for him. Right then and there, Father asked Mom and I to join him as Father laid hands on my dad's head and prayed that he receive the Spirit of God in his heart. That was the first time, I saw my dad begin to weep.

"I knew God had touched him.

"From that day on, he started to get up in the morning and pray and read the Bible in the living room. He was a tough, hard man and never showed his emotions as he considered it unmanly and a sign of weakness. But gradually, he began to show his affection and love for Mom. He opened up about his concerns and problems at work and realized the great listener and counsellor my mother was. He was less stressed and more relaxed and more approachable. He never failed to give mom a kiss and hug when he left for the day or when he returned. Each time he did so, I loved it. Each time he showed affection and cried, I loved it. Each time he prayed from the heart, I loved it. Each time he was filled with compassion for someone's state in life, I loved it. I loved when he held Mom's hand and walked beside her and not two or three feet ahead of her as he used to do."

Henry paused and wiped away a tear as so many thoughts flooded his mind. Slowly, he continued, "Good memories began to erase all the negative thoughts and images of Mom hurting over what he had done and all the insecurities I had harboured for many years. I knew his change of heart and direction was authentic. He no longer swore or used God's name in vain. He grew in character. He was true to his word and totally honest.

"He walked the talk.

"Spiritual development became high on his list and he led our family in prayer in the morning, at meal times and at night which before was usually at Mom's direction. Sundays continued to be a day for church but for Dad it grew more fervent. We went earlier and stayed to pray a little longer after the Mass was over. Besides being a day of rest and family, every Sunday was special in our home. We didn't have the best china dishes or silverware but Mom always took out what we had on Sundays because that was a special day if we had company or not.

"It was a day for God and family."

Henry paused once more and took in a deep breath trying to keep his emotions in check. "You know," he continued, "As a young teenager growing into manhood, I could see that our home was only half alive to the fullness of life before Dad committed himself to Christ. It was more peaceful and stress free. We were happier and laughed more and kidded with one another, cared for one another and loved one another like never before. And what was so important for me was that I lost my fear of coming to my dad. We had so many intimate talks even though some were awkward, I will never forget the conversation we had about pre-marital sex. It was short and to the point but he made every effort to be there for me. And perhaps most important of all, I could see the benefit of having Christ at the head of our family. I no longer begrudged going to church. I looked forward to it because I was so grateful to God for healing our family and making it so happy.

"All of this, fellows, would never have happened if my dad hadn't made the decision to follow Christ and really and truly put Him at the center of his life and our home. I could have grown up not really knowing what a Christian family could be like. He could very well have lived out the rest of his life absorbed in himself and his world. He would have remained stagnant with little or no real growth towards becoming a mature man and Christian. The day that my dad humbled himself to get down on his knees and invited us to pray with him, was the day he freed my mom from an unforgiving spirit and me from a deep anger and insecurity I felt towards him. His act and choice to follow Christ was leading Mom and me home to the Father. He was dying to himself and being the servant to his mate and a leader to his family.

"The decision to accept Christ was a simple act, yet so profound and far reaching. Dad was becoming the man God wanted him to be. He was rising to new heights in the eyes of God and to those around him. He was becoming, through Christ, our hero, our teacher, our beacon of light. *He was now working for the Lord.* He was continuing the redemption that Jesus started on the cross. My dad, whether he realized it or not, and I didn't either, was teaching me how to be as a man, as a father and husband. Through his example, which was based upon the teachings and example of Jesus, my dad was living out the truth, the way and the life of Christ. He was carrying out his most important responsibility as a father to bring Mom and I safely home to the heavenly Father. He was living with eternity in mind for his own soul and that of his family.

"To me, fellows, that's leadership.

"Before we stop for a brief break, I feel compelled to share a bit more of my dad's life. Long after I left home, he continued to show leadership. Being a father doesn't stop when the children leave home. A year before he passed away, he shared something with me that touched my heart and affected my life even further. It was the daily ritual of coming to the Lord upon arising each and every day. It had become a way of life for him. Walking from the bedroom to the living room was like walking to the sea of Galilee at the dawning of a new day. There he would sit quietly and visualize Jesus standing on the hillside teaching his flock how to live. He described how the sun warmed his face as it rose into the morning sky and how he had to shield his eyes from the sun's rays reflecting brightly on the sparkling water. How the sweet scent of wildflowers filled the air, and the sound of birds singing praise along with the angels and butterflies flitting about in the blue sky.

"But most of all, it was the sight of his Lord standing high above the flock, speaking truths that went against the standards and wisdom of the world. Tears came into my dad's eyes as he described the calm clear voice of the Master penetrating the cool air, warming and touching the heart of all those present. My dad quoted Scripture after Scripture with words that were filled with hope, wisdom and insights that challenged worldly values and morals. Teachings that were so contrary to man's usual response and reaction to hatred, anger, unkindness and insult. Words filled with promise and peace and love. Words which invited Dad and others to come to Him with their burdens and receive His yoke which was light and easy.

"Dad described his morning visit with Jesus so vividly, it painted a picture in my mind's eye. It was as if I were there smelling the salt in the air and feeling the cool breeze come off the sea of Galilee right along beside him. Listening to my father was like listening to my heavenly Father. I didn't want the moment to end. When I thought how my dad was in the early years, to how he was now, was like day and night. To me, my dad had become a holy man. *He had become a saint.* This is the legacy my dad left to me and will remember until the day I die.

"I am describing one life but it could be yours.

Henry surveyed the room and smiled. "Well, let's stop here and return in fifteen minutes. I see the girls prepared a delicious snack."

Camilla walked quickly over to Henry and gave him a hug.

"That was a wonderful sharing, Dad! The close relationship you developed with your father before he passed away was so heartwarming."

"Yes, it all could have had quite a different ending,```` but God's Divine Providence thankfully was working so powerfully and fortunately, Dad responded to the calling."

"I can hardly wait to listen to the rest of your presentation!"

CHAPTER FIFTY-SEVEN

"WHAT I JUST shared with you before the break describes a man who discovered before it was too late, what his role as a father and husband were to his family. He was playing out God's design (Ephesians 5:18-33) for a family and a father's role in it. I have described my dad's life but it could very well have been yours.

"There are several points in that sharing which I want to briefly elaborate upon as they apply to our lives. Hopefully it will inspire and motivate us.

"First, we have to acknowledge the impermanence of life. One day, sooner or later, we all will die. We don't like to think about it and for most of us, we live as if we are going to live forever. But it can make us stop to think about our lives and how we are living them. For people who are diagnosed with a terminal illness, death suddenly takes priority in their lives. What is going to happen to me? Where do I go? Is there a God, a heaven and a hell? It's obvious that one of the benefits for people suddenly faced with death is that they can at least have time to prepare for it. They are now motivated to turn to God whether they are strong in the faith or not. Their job, problems, daily worries all fall away and these more spiritual questions take priority in their lives. Differences which they have had with their spouse, children, and extended family are now dealt with.

Their stubborn pride begins to fade away, replaced with reconciliation, forgiveness and love.

"Finally, we come face to face with what is really important in our lives.

"But let's bring this closer to home and more immediate and final. At any moment in time, any of us could die. This could happen to you or your wife or children.

"The question is, would you have been prepared?

"What did you, as head of the family, do to ensure, to the best of your ability, that your family was ready to meet their Creator? We don't like to think about this, but death is a constant threat and could come in the blink of an eye. Does it not make sense that we should prepare not only for ourselves but our loved ones as well? At the moment of death, we come before the Lord. All He is interested in is how we loved Him, our neighbour and how we served Him. All else that we struggle and work so hard for is of the world and has absolutely no value unless it was used to serve His kingdom.

"We can see why Father Engelmann maintained that the most important responsibility of each spouse is to have as their goal to bring their husband or wife and children safely home to the heavenly Father. To always be ready and prepared. To always live with eternity in mind. In my sharing it was clear that my dad only began to live out this obligation after he accepted Jesus. It was only then as his mind and heart were transformed by the Truth of the Word that he freed Mom and I from our unforgiving spirit and anger towards him thus opening the door for all of us to come to God. He removed the stumbling blocks; the obstacles that had imprisoned us too. His attention to the spiritual side of his life and ours prepared us to come to the Lord at any time.

"What if my father hadn't made the decision to accept Christ into his life? What would have been the fate of all of us? What kind of a legacy would my dad have left behind for Mom and me?

"Does it not make sense that we should live our lives with purpose and meaning with eternity always in mind?

"And this leads us to the second point. My dad came into his marriage with a lot of challenges just like many of us do. In some cases, there has not been much leadership in our homes as our parents had issues of their own due to the issues of their parents. The father may have been absent, or was an alcoholic, abusive, didn't show affection or spiritual leadership...the list goes on and on. Being a parent is perhaps the most important job in our lives and in most cases the one we are least trained or prepared for or give serious thought to.

"And here is the serious part. We learn by identification, especially people who are significant in our lives. By the time we are old enough to realize that our parents are not the best teachers or models, many of the teachings and behaviours and practices, for better or for worse, have become a very strong part of us. If our dad was critical or abusive to our mother, chances are in the heat of battle, we will do the same. Consciously and unconsciously what we see in our formative years becomes a part of us and how we respond to life's challenges.

"I often smile when I see my son, for example, stand the way I do or has similar gestures and habits. Sometimes his moods, the words he says and actions are similar to mine. While some of these are good and not harmful, many could be and are. We can see our behaviours are not the best, but find it difficult to change. In most cases we learn by trial and error, we wing it and stumble along. We strive to be better and live in a way which is not so self defeating but for most of us, we never stop to examine our lives or the direction in which we are heading. And even if we do see our failings, we don't know how to change or have the strength and commitment to do so.

"And here is the important point; if you agree that you were influenced by your parents who were your most powerful personalities when you were growing up, then the fact is also true that we will in turn influence our children in the same way for better or worse. We can infect our children and our marriage, family, home and our lives with good or with evil. We can make our homes healthy and spiritually sound or we can create sickness and spiritual emptiness. In the same way you were held captive to the shortcomings or strong points of your parents, so too, will be your children to your faults, values and ideals.

"In fact, many of your emotions and words, deeds, moods, values, character will be adopted by your children. They will become the recipients of your headship in the home. *And when we see where we are at and understand that it is the result of all that went before, we have a choice to either perpetuate the way we live knowing full well the effect it will have on those around us; mainly our wives and children. Or, we can choose to end the cycle and search for a new way to live not only for our own benefit but for the welfare and benefit of our loved ones.*

"Had my dad not accepted Jesus and instead continued in his old ways, I doubt very much he would have truly come to the Lord and he may very well have lost his soul. I would hate to think of the many emotional scars and negative images of dad he would have left for me or mom to deal with.

"This is pretty powerful stuff.

"It's scary when we seriously think on it. It places what may appear to some as an immense burden, to see the good or harm I can do, by the way I am living, to myself and those around me. And yet, it can also challenge us to do something about it. Even my father, in his weakest and most abandoned state, imprisoned as he was by his self-defeating thinking and actions, was able to rise up and out of his state, by accepting Jesus as his mentor, teacher and example. The living Words of Christ transformed his mind resulting in new thoughts which blossomed into joy and wholesome living!

"Doesn't it make sense that we should stop to examine our lives and the direction in which we are going?

"The way we think and live our lives can lift us and those around us to peace, harmony and happiness or lead us and our loved ones into misery and suffering; sheer hell.

"I have already alluded to the third point several times: to accept Jesus as your Lord and Saviour and commit to follow Him. Although my dad was head of the household as God designed it, he really didn't show leadership in any other area than to provide for us. It wasn't until he made the decision to accept Christ, that his role as a husband and father began to grow and be fulfilled as God intended.

"Jesus is the way, the truth and the life; no one comes to the Father but by Him.

"Like I said, we learn by identification and Jesus is the perfect role model. He is the Son of God who became man and before He died on the cross for our sins, He walked the earth for three years teaching us how to live. When He started His ministry, He called out to twelve men to follow Him and He is still calling on all men to come and follow Him today. When my dad did that, he was steadily led to a more victorious life for him and his family.

"When I accepted Christ into my life and began to come to Him daily like my Dad did to pray, meditate and read the Bible, I began to understand how my father was changed so dramatically. Recently, I made a forty day fast and prayer retreat at the prayer house on our acreage. This further helped me to draw closer to the Lord in ways I could never have imagined. I could see as one grows closer to Jesus, one's character and sinful self is exposed to the light of His Truths. You will begin to see just how far short you fall from living a fruitful, Godly life. You will see how we have lowered God's standards to our standards. How we have watered down the Gospel to suit ourselves. We see how we have become God and floundered aimlessly, guided by our selfishness. You will begin to see how your self-centeredness and ego and faulty thinking were not only a major stumbling block to your own personal growth but to that of your wife and children.

"Jesus Christ is your teacher, mentor, guide and example in becoming a mature Christian. In the marriage setting in which relationships are so close, your spouse and children will get to know and see you just as you are with all your strengths and weaknesses. It is in this setting in which you have the golden opportunity to put Jesus' teaching and example into practice and begin to really grow outside of yourself.

"I saw it in my dad, myself and countless others whom I have counselled or known. Christ takes us to the next and next and to the next higher level. It's so plain to me that when Jesus becomes a part of our daily lives, how our hearts and minds are transformed. The old falls away and a new creature is born. All of our thoughts, words, and deeds now have a spiritual side to them which are a reflection of Truth. All choices and decisions are made in light of Jesus' teachings. A peace which surpasses all understanding comes into our lives because we are no longer controlled by the world but are now led by an all-knowing God who has our best interests at heart.

"We come to trust Him in all our circumstances.

"In short, you will have the opportunity to become a hero to your family. You will learn the great secret and mystery that to die to yourself is to save yourself. Through self sacrifice and dying to ourselves, we become the child of God we were meant to be. We become the man, the husband and father we were meant to be. We rise to new heights and begin to bear fruit. It's like we were a dead seed that had to die in the ground in order to become the mighty oak that we were meant to be. It is now that we truly are able to begin to grow, to love and to lead others.

"This is when we become leaders who our families will respect and follow.

"The thought which might be entering into your mind right now may be, that this all sounds pretty idealistic. But in the real world, it's easier said than done. And some of you may be quick to point out that you have prayed and didn't see any results. I would have to agree that to try to live this way in Jesus' footsteps would be next to impossible if it were not for the rest of God's supernatural make-up and plan.

"This takes us to the fourth point. In God there are three Divine Persons: God the Father, God the Son, and God the Holy Spirit. When Jesus rose from the dead, as we celebrate every Easter and before He ascended into heaven, He told His disciples that when He goes up to heaven the Father will send the Holy Spirit to them to be their Helper, Comforter and Advocate. He may no longer be there in person to be beside them but He will now indwell in them through the power of the Holy Spirit. True to His promise, on the Day of Pentecost, the Holy Spirit not only came to the disciples but to all of us.

"Some of us have received the Holy Spirit in Baptism, Confirmation and the Jesus prayer; that is, coming to Jesus with a sincere heart of repentance for your sins and accepting Him as your Lord and Saviour. The Holy Spirit's purpose is to convict us and remind us of Jesus teachings. He is here to energize us, prompt us, motivate us, strengthen us, enlighten us, guide us, empower us to let go of the old and put on the new armour of Christ. He is the one who will help us to change and become the kind of father, husband and leader in the home which I described. We need God's Holy Spirit to live out the teachings of Jesus and to follow Him.

"It is impossible otherwise!

"The reason many of us may not have experienced the Holy Spirit in our lives is because we have free will and haven't chosen to invite Him into our lives and heart. Even though God the Father, God the Son and God the Holy Spirit through Divine Providence are always trying to bring us back to the truth and to receive their full power in our lives, we have to fully give them our lives in return. To say the Jesus' prayer that we accept Him as our Lord and Saviour and repent of our sins means little if we don't follow through with a firm commitment to truly follow Him. To pray a little today and a week or month later pray again when a crisis hits our lives, or we are really not willing to change our ways, does little good. God promises if we draw near to Him, He will draw near to us. God wants you to grow as a Christian in character and develop values and morals which make us a strong beacon of light into a world filled with darkness.

"But we must be willing to give Him our 'all'.

"Take what happened to my dad that evening when Bishop Sheen spoke of the Holy Spirit. God knows our weakness and propensity to sin. He knew my dad would never have been able to make it on his own efforts and strengths and that is why dad was quickly led to become aware of the need for the Holy Spirit in his life. Bishop Sheen may have reached millions of viewers but one thing I know for certain, my dad was destined to hear that message. He was convicted with God's Holy Spirit that night and fortunately my father stayed open to the Spirit in the days, months and years which followed.

"If my dad hadn't gotten up early every morning and made the trek down the hallway to the living room and begin to pray with a sincere heart, not too much would have happened in his life. God gave us intelligence, will power, discipline to make decisions and act. Unless we exercise these gifts and do our part, we don't grow. Consider any project where you want to learn or master something; unless you commit and work at it, not much will happen. God will not do for you what He gave you the ability to do for yourself.

"*Otherwise, how can we grow?*

"The same is true of personal and spiritual growth. If we make every sincere effort to draw near to God and grow strong in character and commitment, He will draw near to you. The good news is that we can draw near to Him on more than our human strengths. We can pray and ask the Holy Spirit for help. Each and every day, we pray to Him for the grace, strength and guidance to say "yes" to Jesus. When we give Him our 'all', we receive the Holy Spirit in full power.

"*Now we are ready to lead and truly live!*

"The final point or question is this; where are you in your role as a father, husband and leader? No matter how you look at it, it would be foolish not to consider having Jesus at the center of our lives. If you can show me another way to prepare ourselves and loved ones for eternity, to change our thinking, which creates peace and direction to our life, to be a leader to our family and create a legacy that will be remembered long after you are gone, I'd love to hear about it. If you think you can do this on your own and that your life is great just as it is, just ask the woman beside you if she thinks this is so.

"*How do we begin?*

"You don't have to search very far. The kingdom of God is within you. You are His child. Once you accept Jesus, you gain your inheritance. The door is now open to the Father, His graces and blessings.

"In much the same way you got to know your wife and grew to love her ever more over time, we get to know about Jesus. We have to commit to getting up early everyday and have a quiet time with Him in prayer and meditation. Through His word, we come to know Him. He teaches us how to live and we will see over and over, His love for us. Gradually, you will come to be filled with deep gratitude and love for Him. Imagine having someone love you so much that they give up their life for you, so that you might have life and have life to the fullest. And to top it off, Jesus did this while we were still sinners!

"Would you be willing to sacrifice your life for someone who keeps doing wrong to you? When we realize at a deep level how much Jesus must love us to do this, we simply want to return His love. Soon you will want to live with eternity ever in your mind, not so much out of fear of going to hell but out of love for Him. Father Engelmann once said, 'if we only knew how much God loved us, we would die of over joy!'

"And here is more motivation; if we look at our life at present, many if not most of us, get up every day and live out much of what we did the day before. Our thoughts and reactions to situations are basically the same. We may move ahead in our business or jobs, increase our wealth and possessions, but our personal, spiritual, family life and goals remain the same or even worsen. Considerable stress fills our lives and our marriage, in many cases, isn't what it could be.

"And what about your children? Are they growing with spiritual direction? Are they obedient, responsible, respectful and learning values and principles to live by that will prepare them for life? Or are they learning them from their friends and the world? If we are honest, all too many homes are lacking in leadership to take the time and effort required, for our marriages to blossom and our children to grow strong in faith and character.

"Like I said earlier, this can all change in an instant if a crisis hits our lives or a member of our family dies. If you maintain that you do not have time, I assure you, if a calamity hits, suddenly all that we thought was so important immediately fades into the background. And if we wait too long, we may not even have a minute or even a second to ask for forgiveness or tell our loved ones how much we care for them. If we have built our home on a rock and live with eternity in mind, however, we are always prepared for the most important moment of our lives.

"The day we meet with our Maker.

"The question we have to ask; wouldn't it be wiser if we lived more purposeful and meaningful lives before such calamities happen?

"As we can see, leadership in the home is a serious responsibility and obligation. We hold the future of our life, our wives and children's in our hands. The choices which we make, the life we lead, affects all of those around us for better or for worse. It's evident in the news, the papers and television daily that society is crumbling. We can no longer stay silent or tolerant of the ills and sins of society. Abortion, drugs, alcohol abuse, sex, pornography, rampant divorce, decline in church attendance and in many cases not at all, are all signs of a society which no longer fears God and His judgement. Obedience to His laws and teachings are being replaced by man's laws and standards. We are changing the plan and design that the Chief Architect has laid out and we are seeing the chaos that results not only in our homes but all around us.

"We are in trouble and I believe it's because the family unit, which is the building block of society, has lost its way and is failing. We have forgotten God's plan and our role as men in it.

"Men, we must step up to the plate each and every day in order to do our part in building a healthy society. In order to do that, we must restore the family unit according to God's plan. Jesus Christ must come back into the picture. We, as head of the home, must realize and understand that the growth and development of the spiritual side of our lives is more important than the air we breathe. Jesus' words and example teaches us how to live and the Holy Spirit gives us the strength and motivation to do so. This way we and our family are ever ready for eternity and we are a beacon of light in the darkness of the world.

"I say this with all my heart, not as a criticism, but as a fact of life; men who do not place Jesus at the center of their lives, men who do not attend church to develop the spiritual side of their lives and their family are doing a great disservice to themselves and their wife and children. Men who choose to drop away from their faith are missing out on the heart of human life and the strength and nourishment of the Holy Spirit and Jesus' Word and the security and direction of living that we all need to draw upon every moment of our lives as we journey through life.

"There is a Scripture which sums everything up as to what we must do: 'Seek the Kingdom of God above all else, and live righteously, and He will give you everything you need.' In other words, put Jesus at the head of your life and family, pray daily and examine the direction of your life based upon Jesus' teachings and put them into practice. Trust me guys, you will soon realize that you haven't been living at all. If you start tomorrow, I can guarantee that six months from now you will be reaping the benefits of what you have sown. If you don't and keep filling your mind with the same old stuff, not too much will be changed in our lives. Yet, if we take time to examine our lives and the direction in which we are going, in light of Christ's teachings, you will begin to see how your thinking is flawed by worldly thinking and reactions.

"As these truths come to the fore, you will pass them on to your family by being a living example to them like Jesus' living Words were to you. Very quickly you will begin to feel the peace, joy and inner confidence and strength in the light of the Word. This is how God's plan for his children works.

"The truth will set you free!

"One way or the other, you will have either chosen to grow or spin your wheels. Marriage and family just doesn't happen on its own!

"Once we give our hearts to God, we open the doors to new possibilities that we could not have imagined. He is now in control and will lead you to paths which you would never have taken otherwise. My dad is a perfect example of one who grew in ways that at one time seemed impossible. Yet, he stepped out in faith and turned his life and his family's completely around. Had he stayed on his old way of life, the opportunity to grow as a Christian person and to up-build and edify his family the way he did, would have been lost forever. In choosing to walk with Jesus, he stored treasures in heaven and on earth a legacy which will forever remain in his family's hearts.

"I can't help but to urge all of you to give this a try if you haven't already. Your wife needs you! Your children need you! God needs you! the church needs you, and the world needs you! Like Father Engelmann said to me when I first started working at his grocery store at age fifteen, 'Henry, this world so desperately needs people who have thought things through and don't go through life like a leaf tossed by the prairie wind. We need more than ever, strong people whom others will want to emulate because of the wholesome way they live.'

"Life moves rapidly on; the passage of days quickly come and go. Soon your children will be grown and gone. The leadership you give them to prepare for their future and your relationship with your wife is determined by the choices you make now. We are called to become new men in Christ. He is our mentor and teacher to help and guide us in this most important role as head of the household. He wants to take us to a new level. To become all we can be. God sent His son down to earth to show us the way, the truth and the life. God further sent us His Holy Spirit to help us follow the teachings and example of the Son. Imagine how quickly the world would be healed of all its ailments if we took God's plan to heart!

"We, as Christians, are powerful.

"We can make a difference if we choose to do so. If you and I filled our role as godly leaders in our family, I dare to say there would be an incredible revolution in the world very quickly!

"Choose to become the kind of man who understands this and sees the vision that God has so plainly lain out and follow it. Surely, once you see the overall picture, it would be very unwise not follow His plan. It takes energy to live one way or the other. Every moment, we can choose to be someone who promotes an uplifting spirit filled life or someone who inflicts tension, anxiety, fear and emptiness into a relationship and family. The blind cannot lead the blind, else both will fall in the ditch. With Christ at the center, you can be a great leader, a hero, a good husband, father and yes, even to be a saint are all within your grasp.

"Build your house on a rock, guys and you will be able to withstand all the storms of life during your earthly journey and you and your family will be ever prepared for eternity which can come at any moment.

"There is one final thing which I would like to say and it concerns the precious lady sitting beside you. Perhaps every man and woman thinks of finding the perfect mate to spend the rest of their lives with, but I am inclined to think that women dream more about the man who will come into their life. The man who will come in shining armour and sweep them off their feet! The man who is their protector, provider, friend, lover, hero...in short, the man of their dreams.

"Tell her how much you love her every day; how much you appreciate her. Never take your wife and marriage for granted. Don't get so caught up in your work and the ways of the world that you neglect the most important treasure in your life. Bring her a little gift often and some flowers. Take her out at least once a month. Show her kindness, patience, tenderness and affection often. You may be king of the house, but she is the queen and her crown needs to be polished everyday to keep it sparkling with light.

"Love her to bits, fellows."

Henry paused and turned to Camilla and asked, "How much did you say the ladies offered to pay me to say all that?"

There was a loud laughter and when everything settled down, Henry continued, "Seriously, I truly meant every word of that, and guys, you know there is truth and wisdom in those words.

"Remember what Father Engelmann said about marriage and family; one of the greatest things that parents can do for their children is to constantly show how much they love each other. It's wonderful to hear kids say, 'Oh, geez, there they go smooching again!' Even a three-year-old can understand that kind of communication between their mom and dad and the deep feeling of security it instils in them.

"It is the man who understands this and the great need to place Jesus at the center, that is the one whose wife will whisper to him on their 50th anniversary, 'Honey, you truly are the man, the husband and father who has made all of my dreams come true and more!'

"That fellows, is the result of leadership; of a man who had his priorities right on the journey of life!"

So, in closing, it all comes down to having faith in Jesus Christ and all He did for us. He reconciled us with the Father and opened the gates of heaven. It is the unwise man who ignores this immense gift of love and sacrifice. Life is short and quickly goes by. It just makes good sense to have an eternal perspective. If we don't treasure Jesus' words in the Bible and all it means and teaches we will not live a life worthy of the calling of God. If you don't choose to live according to Jesus' teachings, the full power of the Holy spirit cannot come in and neither can God's graces and blessings.

You could see this all in my dad. I told you of his conversion but it was his choice to exercise his new-found faith and live a Christian life in light of all the trials and temptations of each day. Let us learn from him and let others learn from us the true path to a fulfilled life on earth. Choose to draw close to Him and He will draw close to you and help you become all you were meant to be! Jesus calls you now as He did the apostles to be co-workers with Him. Choose to leave a legacy of faith, hope and love as a man, husband and father…in short, choose to be a warrior for God!"

Henry bowed his head and said the following prayer:

"I pray Lord that you touch the hearts of all of us here this evening with the grace of Your presence so that we know you personally in our heart. In order to lead, we must become like You. Others must see You in us. The path is not easy as true discipleship begins with the path to humility which You so powerfully exhibited during Your ministry. Within a family setting we have a wonderful opportunity to grow mature and become all we can be by dying to ourselves and allowing the Holy Spirit to take control of our lives. Otherwise we can do nothing. Let us not pass up this amazing opportunity to bring Your peace, love and healing to a world so desperately in need of the Light. We only pass this way once during our brief existence. Each precious moment should be spent seeking goals which will leave a legacy of care, concern for our family and which serve you. Amen."

CHAPTER FIFTY-EIGHT

I T WAS THE beginning of a beautiful mid-September fall day. The sun had risen only a half hour ago and both Hannah and her dad were up and ready to give thanks for the day. They decided to have an early breakfast and walk down to the prayer house to say their morning prayers and take in the glory of God's creation.

Henry had kept Hannah out on the farm with him for the entire week. He wanted to spend time with her, but also to talk about the trip to India that he and Justin were about to take in the following week.

Over the past year, Henry had brought healing back to his family. Hannah was spending more time with him and his relationship with Justin was stronger than ever. He was very pleased that his son had decided to come with him to Calcutta for three months. Henry was certain the experience would not only be great for Justin, but that their bond would further strengthen.

It was a busy year and a half as Henry began to simplify his life. He sold off his properties and turned his business completely over to his children. Although Hannah was now spending much more time with her father, Henry knew it was best for Camilla and Jeremy to raise the small child. Camilla and Jenny had discussed this prior to her death. Jenny must have had a premonition that this might happen and she and Camilla had already concluded that should something happen to her, that it was Jenny's wish that Hannah be raised by her as long as Henry was willing.

Henry understood that as well and felt blessed that such a beautiful understanding relationship and care for the child had been established. From the moment Hannah was placed in their care, Camilla and Jeremy loved and cared for Hannah as if she were their own daughter. Camilla especially loved the fact that she had a daughter now along with her three sons and also, she felt blessed to have the privilege to raise a child who had been so richly blessed by the Lord.

"The valley looks so nice, Daddy," Hannah said, as they strolled slowly down the winding road leading to the prayer house. Henry was glad that he had decided to put on a sweater and jacket. Normally the air got cooler as they descended to the valley floor, but with fall in the air, the growing coolness was even more-so.

Ginger was way ahead of them. She loved the water and Henry and Hannah fully expected to see her swimming in the stream. Sure enough, no sooner had they turned the bend in the lane exposing the full valley view and prayer house, they saw Ginger swimming like a beaver.

"Eeek! That must be so cold!"

"Yes, I often thought about that too, Hannah. I guess the fur helps to insulate dogs but still, once the hair is wet the cold must penetrate to the skin. I suppose Ginger and Coco loved swimming so much that they forgot about the cold.

"So, Hannah, we have been talking for a long time about me going to India."

"Yes, Daddy, you want to work with the poor people and help them. Why can't I come, too?"

"Well, you are not old enough, Hannah, for one thing. And for another, one can easily get sick there."

"Will you get sick and what about Justin?" Hannah wanted to know.

"Well honey, Justin and I got vaccinated to help us fight off the diseases we could get. But it's not for you just yet. Maybe, when you are a little older like Justin, you and I can go."

"I pray every day to my guardian angel to tell yours and Justin's to watch over you."

Henry couldn't get over Hannah's understanding. It always seemed as if he were talking to a much older child.

"That would be wonderful, Hannah. And I will pray to mine to tell your guardian angel to watch especially out for you too!"

When they got to the bottom of the valley and started to walk across the bridge, Ginger came running.

"Oh, Daddy we are going to get wet...eeeek!!!" Hannah cried, as she hurried behind Henry's leg. As expected, as soon as Ginger came to their side, she shook all over to dispel the water in her long hair.

Both Henry and Hannah tried to quickly step aside to avoid most of it.

"Okay, Ginger, enough... stay back." Henry tried to push her off but Ginger strived to receive affection more than listen to her master."

"Daddy, Daddy, look, I see a monarch butterfly!" Hannah pointed to the field on the other side of the stream that still had a few wild flowers that had escaped the frost.

"Are you sure, Hannah? All of the butterflies are long gone back to Mexico for the winter."

"But I saw one, Daddy. Can I go catch it?"

"Let's go to the prayer house first and say morning prayers and then you and Ginger can go look for it."

Henry was certain that it was just her imagination as it would be rare, if not a miracle, for a monarch to still be here. The distance to travel to escape the cold was just too far away. It surely would die with winter just around the corner and so many frosty mornings since August.

When they got to the prayer house, they stopped on the deck and looked at the beautiful hillside ablaze with color. Henry always loved this scene, not only the view, but the ethereal setting. Traces of mist still lingered here and there over the water. He loved how the creek meandered through and divided the valley; how it led both into and out of a naturally occurring pond. It was why he had chosen to build the prayer house on this location. The water was so calm, that the hillside reflected perfectly in the mirror like still water.

"Daddy, it's so beautiful to see all the colors God made the trees."

"Yes, honey, when fall comes, the trees and shrubs lose their summer olive green shade and turn into the bright yellow, ochre, vermillion and red colours of fall—"

"And there is purple too, Daddy...look!" Hannah said excitedly pointing across the stream to the deep purple and crimson chroma of the leafless brush and thickets. Henry was amazed that Hannah was able to not only detect that color but also, how that color harmonized in between a spectacular array of warm color.

She was developing the eye of an artist!

"Yes, Hannah, the purples and crimsons are so beautiful. I love to include them in my paintings when I paint fall scenes."

"I like to color purple in my drawings, too, Daddy."

"Yes, I noticed you use purple a lot."

As Henry stood there taking in the serenity and quiescent state of the moment, he suddenly felt Hannah's warm hand take hold of his and ever so quietly, she said, "Should we go into the chapel and thank God for our blessings and pray for everyone?"

Henry shook his head and squeezed Hannah's hand, "Yes, honey, let's go in and say our morning prayers."

As soon as they stepped inside, Hannah and Henry made the sign of the cross and waved towards the altar. Henry knew from the past, that Hannah wasn't necessarily waving to Jesus but to the two angels she sees standing on either side of the altar. Henry had questioned her on it and she described what she sees with such credibility, he had no doubt that his little girl was seeing the angels who protect the chapel. Hannah also said several times that she sees angels flying around and above the prayer house as well.

At two and half years of age, Hannah had grown not only in her perception of the world around her, but also physically. She was now over two inches taller than Jacob who was born full term and almost two months before her premature birth. It was a miracle that Hannah was born so healthy and was doing so amazingly well. The kneeler was a bit too large for her, yet, Henry still loved how her little chin was just high enough to rest on the top rail of the kneeler where Henry rested his elbows. It took his breath away to see how angelic Hannah looked there kneeling with her hands together in prayer just under her chin and her eyes fixed on Jesus.

Without any urging, Hannah began.

"Dear Jesus, bless Daddy and my mommy up in heaven. Bless Mommy Camilla and Daddy Jeremy, too. Bless Jacob, Joshua and Noah and Allison and ..."

Henry loved to listen to Hannah go on and on to include everyone she knew, even J.J., his family, Matti and all the rest of them at the estate. When she had heard of Eddy's healing, she even thanked God for that miracle, too! What Henry didn't expect to hear was when she prayed for all the poor people in India and to keep her daddy and brother safe and not to get sick!

Her love of prayer and attention span to kneel there after almost twenty minutes, Henry considered a miracle as well. He often thought about what Camilla had said one evening when he and Justin were visiting at their home. So many miracles occur so quietly, they hardly are noticeable. If only we stopped to see how the hand of God was continuously involved in our lives.

Henry had to agree, there was much truth in that observation.

After prayers, Hannah noticed all the manuscripts on top of the desk in the bedroom. A copy of the new book one, *Pewter Angels* had been printed and was ready to be released next spring, around Mother's Day.

"The silver angels look so pretty on the cover, Daddy. They look just like the one you always wear around your neck."

"That's how I got the idea for the cover and I think that is why Father Engelmann named the first book *Pewter Angels*."

Henry unbuttoned the top button of his shirt and took out the silver angel and held it by the chain. It sparkled in the light.

Hannah reached up and felt its smooth surface finish. What does that say, Daddy?" Hannah pointed to the inscription at the bottom of the angel's dress.

"It says, '*Watch over my beloved.*' That is what your mommy wanted my angel to do. And I sent her the exact same one with the same words. Isn't that amazing, Hannah? See, look closer at the cover and you will see the letters the angels are holding. The pink envelope contained the pewter angel to me and the white one was the one I sent to Jenny. Someday when you can read more, you can read about how your mommy and I met and how our guardian angels created a very close bond between us."

"I can read already, Daddy. Can I read the book? Please?"

"When I get back from India, I will tell you some parts and the rest we can read together."

As Henry laid the book down, Hannah asked about the other manuscripts, if they too were stories about him and mommy.

"Yes, there are seven books here, Hannah. I am going to make up a different picture on the cover for each one and every year from now on, they will be printed and put out into the stores so people can buy them to read."

"Will I be able to read them too, Daddy?" Hannah was excited to know.

"Yes, honey, you will be able to read them, too!"

Henry laid down the new book one, *Pewter Angels,* took hold of Hannah's hand and went back out onto the deck. Ginger was standing by the door waiting for them.

Once again, Hannah shouted, "I see the butterfly Daddy! Can I go see it closer?"

Henry looked out at the field but couldn't see the butterfly. He thought, however, it would be okay for her to run a while and he loved watching her play.

"Okay, you and Ginger see if you can find the monarch and try to have it follow you back."

Henry also wanted to sit on the deck and take in the serenity of the moment a bit longer too, before heading back up to the farm house.

He sat down and watched Hannah and Ginger scamper off. She reminded him so much of Jenny's spirit; so full of life, free, spontaneous and everything God wants us to be. It's sad that so many of us lose this joy of living in the present moment! It was amazing that Jenny, in spite of all the challenges and trials that came her way, never lost that childlike trust in life or that childlike gift of a spirit filled life.

To Henry, it was plain that little Hannah, too, would never lose it during all the trials, sorrows and challenges that she would face either. Like her mother, Hannah would express love in all its purity and joy. Henry just knew it just as he knew that *Hannah, too, was born with the heart of an angel.*

Yes, Henry thought, it is love above all else which sets us free! How unfortunate it is that this spirit of love is covered over and lost as we journey through life. So much of our lives is spent trying to return and recapture what we have lost. So much of our existence is spent searching in the wrong places and getting sidetracked with the values and ways of the world. Love is connected to everything through the cross; to all of life's challenges, trials, joys, tribulations and relationships. It is love which can give us peace and hope and is the answer to everything!

God is love. And where love is, so is God's peace, joy and healing. The night before he died as it is recorded in the Gospel of Saint John; Chapters 13-16, over and over Jesus commands us to love one another as he has loved us. Above all else, He could have said that memorable evening, it is love which Jesus commanded us to do. God is love and we are created out of love and for love.

When Jesus died on the cross for our sins, He restored our right relationship with the Father. Through Jesus and the cross, we are once again in God's family. We are once again His children and through Christ's sacrifice we are connected to each other as brothers and sisters! Yes, love connects us all to each other and to all of life!

Take any circumstance and love is partly or fully the solution or answer to the situation. Yes, God gave us free will and the entire gamut of human emotions which we can choose from to respond to life's challenges, but it is when we choose love, we return to Him and love sets us free.

"Think on it," Henry whispered, "to return kindness when unkindness is shown…isn't that giving the sacrifice of love? Isn't that bringing light to the darkness…isn't that love? The same can be said to return hurts with forgiveness, peace to replace hate and anger, to be patient when impatience is shown.

"This is love in action.

"It is plain to see that it is love which elevates us to God on high. It is love which makes us all we can be; to be gentle, bearing others faults, and shortcomings, being understanding, compassionate, consoling…yes, it is love which brings us peace and allows us to live fully in the moment of life!"

Little Hannah, like her mother, was a perfect example of this joy and freedom in the moments of life…

It wasn't long before the tranquility of the setting took hold of him. Henry's mind oscillated between thoughts of Hannah chasing an imaginary butterfly and the fond memories he had of the prayer and fast retreat and how it drew him so much closer to God. Had he not made the choice to do that retreat, he may very well be caught up in his business and the ways of the world. It is so true what Father Engelmann had professed and did all of his life; to withdraw daily and reflect on where you are going.

It is not so important in the present moment of life as to where we were but to where we are choosing to go!

If we don't take time to reflect, pray, meditate, examine one's conscience daily, how can we live a life of purpose and meaning?

Tell me, how?

As Henry gazed out upon the still pond more memories of his fast and prayer retreat came back to him in little gentle waves like the barely noticeable rippling water before him.

Something happened during those forty days.

It was not just fasting, which drew him closer to God; it was his love for the *Eucharist*. He could hardly wait for the next morning to arrive so that he could receive Jesus into his heart. His hunger for the spiritual sustenance of the Eucharist far exceeded his hunger for food. No wonder Father Engelmann loved the Mass and how the death and resurrection is enacted each time it is celebrated. No wonder, he had become so much like Jesus. Every day, his mentor died to self and resurrected with his Lord!

What an amazing, costly way God and His Son had planned to show their love for us and keep this immense sacrifice of love alive for all mankind to share in, down through the ages. So often during his fast, Henry would pretend he was celebrating the Mass. He knew every movement and word by heart, just like his mentor. He loved how, daily, he would offer his sufferings, failings, challenges, prayers and petitions to the altar and how they would miraculously mingle with Jesus' sacrifice!

Daily, he found himself through the strength and nourishment of Jesus, to be able to die to his failings and struggles and give them to Jesus and then experience the joy of resurrecting with Him at communion, full of life and feeling renewed. It is little wonder Father Engelmann loved to celebrate the Mass so he could impart this love and mystery that goes on in the Mass to his sheep!

The beauty of the Mass is not just that we celebrate the immense sacrifice of the cross which Jesus took upon himself for us but that His death led to the resurrection! His victory over death! His victory over a world that once was dead and filled with darkness, to a world which now promised hope, defeat over death and the darkness. It gave us love and life and access to heaven once more and to all the things which God promises to those who chose to follow Him!

"Yes, it is the Eucharist which is key in all this. It is how Jesus continues to nourish us and strengthen us even though he is no longer present in the flesh like he was with the apostles and disciples. Imagine, in the Eucharist, we receive Jesus into our hearts and souls."

The image of Father Engelmann celebrating that last Mass in the Poustinia flashed across Henry's mind. He would never forget Father's actions and words as he repeated the eternal words Jesus declared at the last supper:

Father took the host and said, "Who, the day before He suffered, took bread into His holy and venerable hands, and having raised His eyes to heaven, to You, O God, His Almighty Father, giving thanks to You, He blessed it, broke it, and gave it to His disciples, saying:

"'All of you take and eat of this: *For this is My body.*'"

Father elevated the Host. It was like Father was raising the sun. The image of Christ almost blinded the holy man. The risen Jesus was present in the Eucharist. Father dared to whisper, *"My Lord and my God."*

David then picked up the chalice and continued with the consecration, "In like manner, when the supper was done, taking also this godly chalice into His holy and venerable hands, again giving thanks to You, He blessed it, and gave it to His disciples, saying:

"All of you take and drink of this:

"For this is the Chalice of My Blood of the new and eternal covenant: the mystery of faith: which shall be shed for you and for many unto the forgiveness of sins.'"

Father set the chalice down and said, *"As often as you shall do these things, in memory of me shall you do them."*

The image Henry was reliving was so real he paused to savor the miracle which just took place before him. He stared with love and adoration at the bread and the wine which was now the Body and Blood of his Lord, which Father had offered up to God the Father along with his and Henry's offering.

Tears like beads of light glistened down Henry's cheeks as his love for the Eucharist and all it represented touched his heart.

Father Engelmann knew this would happen.

There was deep purpose in what his mentor and teacher did to consecrate forty hosts for him. He knew that Henry's love for the Eucharist would grow.

As Henry sat there, something deep within began to stir in his being. Something which God had foreseen from the beginning of time and was unfolding now. God's plan for Henry was to help in the Great Commission and missions, but God was calling him to more...

"Daddy! cried, Hannah.

Henry was so deep in his reverie, he didn't hear his little angel at first. He turned towards the field and saw her and Ginger running towards him.

"Daddy, Daddy, look at the butterfly!" Hannah shouted once more, her blue eyes sparkling and her happy face radiating such joy!

"Oh, honey, it's too late in the season for them to still be here. Are you sure you saw one?

Hannah's eyes and excitement, however, clearly told a different story. She was out of breath as she climbed Henry's knees and sat on his lap.

"Oh, Daddy, that was so much fun!"

Henry thought he would play along. "So, what color was the butterfly, Hannah?"

"It was orange and black, Daddy. Just like the ones at Uncle Carlos' and Auntie Maria's home in their backyard. And it was a girl butterfly, too, Daddy!"

"How could you tell, Hannah?"

"It didn't have the two dots on the back of its wings. Uncle Carlos showed me how to tell the difference."

Henry shook his head. Could it be possible that she really did see a monarch? And then, all of sudden, there it was, flitting about in front of them!

"See, there it is!" Hannah shouted, excitedly.

Hannah opened her hand and incredibly, the monarch came to rest on her palm.

"Isn't she pretty, Daddy? See, there are no black dots on her wings."

Henry was speechless as he gazed at the monarch. What on earth was this butterfly still doing here? He knew that the last generation of butterflies would have made their trek back to Mexico well over a month ago. It made a poor choice to stay behind as it is destined to die. It could have lived up to eight months longer if it had left for the Oyamel Fir Forest. And even so, how could it have survived all the early morning frosts...it should have already been dead...

"Amazing," Henry muttered. *Was there more to this?* It seemed like the monarch wanted to give itself to Hannah and Henry.

"The wings are so beautiful and gentle," Henry said, almost inaudibly as he watched the monarch open and close its wings ever so slowly.

"Just like my guardian angel. My angel flaps its wings very softly, too, when I fall asleep."

"That's beautiful, Hannah."

Henry was filled with wonder as he gazed at the beautiful creature in Hannah's tiny hand. He loved the web design on its wings and how the sun shone through when the wings were open. The wings glowed with a warm light or ... *was it love.* There seemed to be a knowing between Hannah and Henry that the monarch resting on Hannah's hand was there for a reason. It prompted Henry to say, "Carlos believes, as I do, that God uses nature to send us messages of healing and love. I wonder if mommy isn't doing that now?"

"What would she be saying, Daddy?"

Hannah's words touched Henry and unbidden tears surfaced. He thought of Jenny and her love of butterflies. "Oh, I think she would be saying how much she loves you, Hannah. Your mommy loved butterflies, too, and chased after them, just like you."

Henry reached his hand forward and gently stuck out his forefinger as his hand reached the butterfly; to pat it somehow.

Closer and closer came Henry's finger and suddenly, the butterfly flitted momentarily and then rested on his finger which now was touching Hannah's open hand.

"See Daddy, she loves you, too! She is very pretty."

"Yes, yes, she is so lovely, Hannah"

Henry wondered if the monarch was sending a message from Jenny. In a way, it was risking its life to be here for just this moment; to bring healing and perhaps... a message of love.

And as Henry and his little daughter sat together in the warm, peace filled moment, gazing at the beautiful butterfly, they both felt prompted to say the guardian angel prayer; the monarch gently flapped its wings seemingly to join in...

Angel of God, my guardian dear,
to whom His love commits me here,
ever this day be at our side...
and dear sweet Jenny and Mommy...
to light and guard, to rule and guide...
Amen.

Nine years later...

2004

Chapter Fifty-Nine

A T FIRST HENRY could not tell who the lady on the other end of the phone was until she said his name. "Hendry, how is the love of my life!?"

"Oh my, Ivania! I would never have dreamed that I would get a call from you. It's so nice to hear your voice! How are you doing?"

"Six years ago, I moved to Vancouver where our head office is located. Occasionally, I come to Regina for conferences and visit the office here. I was in the cafe yesterday and your son, Jeremy, I believe, told me about the loss of your dear Jennifer. When your son said it was over ten years ago I thought I would call if there is any chance that I could see you again."

Henry smiled. He always marveled at Ivania's boldness and outright honesty and how she came right to the point.

"A lot has happened in my life since Jenny's passing...how long are you in Regina for?"

"Until tomorrow, however, Hendry, I could easily make my stay longer..."

Henry chuckled, "That's what I always loved about you Ivania, you are not shy in expressing your mind."

"Well, I hope that is not all you loved!"

Henry chuckled again and then said, "I was actually planning on coming to Regina in about an hour. I would love to treat you to lunch if you can make it. Perhaps you have made plans... it's already ten-thirty—"

"Hendry, even if I had an appointment with the president of the company, I would cancel it to have lunch with you. Shall we meet at the cafe?"

"I was thinking of the Hotel Saskatchewan around one o'clock after the lunch rush is over."

There was a silence for a brief moment. "That sounds very promising, Hendry. I will cancel my two appointments and meet you in the dining room promptly at one o'clock."

"That's great, Ivania. There is quite a bit I'm sure we both have to share with one another."

As soon as Ivania got off the phone, she cancelled her eleven o'clock appointment, her luncheon date and her one-thirty meeting with the CEO of the Saskatchewan branch. *She felt hopeful.* She never expected to see Henry during this trip and only had business attire. She decided to go to several boutique shops and find something more seductive or at the very least…alluring.

NORMALLY, IVANIA WAS very cool and collected and in control of situations. However, she had to admit her heart was racing more than usual as she sat in the dining room waiting for the man she wished she could have won over many years ago. She recalled that dinner engagement at the Diplomat only too well when Henry shared his longing for a teenage sweetheart he hadn't seen since he was fifteen. Ivania realized though, when she finally did meet Jenny at the airport thirteen years ago, she could understand why Henry's heart had never let go of his first love. She was stunning to say the least. She was visiting her husband at the time who wasn't in good health. Ivania remembered praying at the time that Jenny's ex-husband would steal her heart back so as to open the door once again for her and Henry.

Unfortunately, it never happened and soon Henry and Jenny married. But to learn now of the remote possibility that his heart might be free again gave Ivania hope. And, for him to invite her to lunch at the hotel was very promising, indeed.

Ivania's thoughts were interrupted as the host greeted a man dressed in black with white hair and a white beard. He began to follow the host and was partially hidden behind him and so couldn't quite make out if it was Henry or not. Half-way to her table, the man stopped and was greeted by another man who was seated at a table. She briefly heard their exchange and her heart sank.

"Hi, Father Pederson, this is my business associate Jack Teeley. I'm looking forward to your talk at St. Mary's next weekend."

"Nice to see you Bill, Jack. Yes, it will be wonderful to have you attend the presentation. I hope Janis can make it."

"She wouldn't miss it for the world, Father."

As soon as the host saw Henry was finished with his chat, he continued on to Ivania's table. She looked as white as a candle when she saw the white collar around Henry's neck!

The host pulled out Henry's chair and he sat down. At least half of the patrons in the dining room had their eyes on him. They wanted to see who the man was that had a date with the ravishingly, attractive woman at the table. They were as stunned as Ivania that her date was a man of the cloth!

Ivania, nodded. "My good Lord, Hendry, Hendry Hendry... you have always been full of surprises!"

Henry reached both hands across the table and Ivania immediately responded. "Ivania, it is so good to see you. I have forgotten just how attractive you are."

"You should have remembered that before you made the decision to become a priest!"

Henry smiled and laughed nervously. He struggled to keep his eyes on Ivania's face and not her chest which clearly revealed how well-endowed Ivania was.

Ivania shook her head. "This is unbelievable, Hendry. How could this possibly happen to such a handsome eligible widower? Now I understand why you wanted to see me...yes, there is much we need to share...so, tell me what happened in your life after that day we met in the airport and Jennifer was on the way to see her ex-husband. I believe he lived in Ottawa?"

"You have a good memory, Ivania. Yes, she was off to see her husband, James who was very ill."

Henry went on to tell her that James died at Christmas time and six months later, he and Jenny got married. Henry shared a little of their life together and also about his dear friend, Father Engelmann and the tremendous influence he was in his life."

"So, what happened to Jennifer?" Ivania wanted to know.

Henry tightened his lips and said, "Well, despite her age, Jenny wanted to have a child. Her prayer was answered, but due to complications shortly after she gave birth to our little girl, she passed away."

"Oh, Hendry, that must have been devastating for you. I knew how much you loved her and I could see it even more so in your eyes that day we met in the airport. Was it difficult for you to get over her passing? I still long for my first husband, too."

"Yes, I recall he was involved in a plane accident flying up north."

"Yes, and after I knew that you and I couldn't share a life together, I married two other men but none could come close to you or my first husband. I thought when we spoke this morning on the phone that the future might be lighting up again but I see you are now married to another bride; the church!"

Henry smiled and was interrupted by the waiter. They ordered wine and a light lunch and then Henry shared what happened after Jenny's death. How he went into a depression for over a year and how he was miraculously healed. Henry explained as best he could how Father Engelmann offered up his life for him and even asked for the Stigmata so that Henry's faith in God would be restored.

"You mean the priest actually received the wounds of Christ? How can that be, Hendry?"

"It's a long story, Ivania. It has happened to others down through the years who have lived very holy lives. In any case, after he died, I made a forty-day retreat in a prayer house situated on my property and during that time of praying and fasting, I felt a deep calling to do missionary work. Six months later, when my son finished high school, we both went to India for three months to work with some friends of mine who did volunteer work with Mother Teresa. I wanted to experience firsthand, the poverty there so that I could share what I had seen with people in the west."

"So, how did you become a priest?" Ivania was anxious to know. "Didn't you say that Jennifer gave you a daughter? How does such a vocation come into play under those circumstances?"

"I was just coming to that, Ivania..."

The waiter interrupted their conversation. He placed the Mediterranean salad in front of Ivania and the soup and sandwich special of the day on the table in front of Henry.

"More wine Ma'am?

"Yes, please bring a bottle of Sauvignon blanc and an ice bucket to keep it chilled."

The waiter was momentarily put off balance by Ivania's order and didn't ask Henry if he wanted more wine under the circumstance. Surely, his lady friend would share some of the bottle she ordered.

They stopped chatting and ate their food for a bit and then Henry continued. "About six months after I came back from India, I felt very compelled to follow in the footsteps of my lifelong friend, Father Engelmann. A similar situation had happened to Father as well. After his wife passed away, he entered the priesthood later in life, too. I think what finally convinced me to do it was my friend Gary, who I mentioned earlier; he too, decided to go into the priesthood. We had much discussion about the calling of the Lord with Mother Teresa when I was over in India."

Ivania stopped eating even though she only finished a bit of her meal. She just kept shaking her head in disbelief over what Henry was sharing.

"In any case Ivania, the Archbishop at the time was set to retire within six months and I needed to make the decision before he did so. It's more difficult to be admitted into the priesthood when you are my age. When I talked to him about it, he didn't hesitate. He felt my situation was just like Father Engelmann and so I was accepted on his strong recommendation. Three years later I was ordained!"

"I must say, Hendry, the attire looks divine on you. Your white hair and beard gives you an aura of holiness but even more so, a very handsome appearance. I would hate to be the one that encourages a priest to sin but my feelings for you are still strong enough to risk my eternal fate and damnation over."

Ivania smiled as Henry chuckled nervously.

"So, what about the darling little girl? Who is raising her and how is she doing without her mother around?"

"It was all meant to be, Ivania. Jenny's daughter, Camilla was also pregnant at the same time she was. Camilla, gave birth about a month or so before Jenny and so when Jenny gave birth and had so many complications which eventually took her life, Camilla was able to take over and she raised Hannah as her own."

"Hannah. Is that her name?"

Henry nodded

"That is a beautiful name, Hendry. Who does she look like?

"She has some of my features but she is almost the spitting image of Jenny; blonde hair and sparkling blue eyes!"

"Well, if she turns out to be like Jennifer, she will have men falling all over her."

Henry chuckled and then said, "I don't think so, Ivania. She will be twelve in a couple of days and she has already committed herself to become a nun."

Ivania let out a squeal, drawing attention to their table. "My good Lord, Hendry! You are becoming a family of saints! Your friend being blessed with the wounds of Christ to restore your faith and you and your daughter coming to the Lord…what is in store for you all in the future!?"

"Truer words couldn't have been said. Both Father Engelmann and Jenny were canonized saints by the Pope three years after their deaths—"

"What!? I can understand Father Engelmann receiving sainthood but how could your wife have achieved such an honor!?"

"Well, once again that is a long story. Like Father Engelmann, Jenny did lead quite an extraordinary life. When she was miraculously healed of her terminal cancer, the archbishop began documenting her life, but it was her decision to refuse having an abortion when severe complications set in during her pregnancy that the sacrifice of her life for the child in her womb was recognized by the church as a very holy act and offering. She valued the life for the child within her womb even more than her own and…in the end that decision proved to be fatal for her."

Ivania was speechless. She just stared at Henry with wide open eyes trying to understand all this. She shook her head from side to side almost imperceptibly.

Henry shrugged his shoulders. "There is never a dull a moment when you work for Jesus, Ivania. Hannah is celebrating her twelfth birthday the day after tomorrow. If you are in town, you are welcome to come to the farm and meet her and the family."

"I would love to meet your daughter and the rest of your family but I have to get back to Vancouver."

Ivania swallowed the food she was eating and asked, "I have met both of your boys at the store but you have two daughters as well from your first marriage, how are they doing?"

"Yes, besides the two boys, Jeremy and Justin, there is Alison and Lauren. Alison married a man she met at the Bible College and Lauren became a professional dancer. She actually made it to Broadway, New York and performed for years on the production called, *Aida*."

"Yes, I remember that musical. We were going to go to that one but opted for *The Lion King*. In any case, that is quite an achievement to make it to Broadway! Is she still performing?" Ivania wanted to know.

"No, her knees gave out and she went back to college to study psychology and counselling. She is engaged to be married. And Alison has four children so she's a busy mom. Jeremy is married as you know with three boys and Justin is also engaged to be married next spring to a girl who worked for us as a server in the café. They are all doing fine. And what about you, Ivania, did you ever have any children?"

"No, fortunately. I say that as my last two marriages were not the best and would have been more complicated had children been involved. No, my darling Hendry, beside my first love, you were the only other I would have loved to have a family with, but I see now that would be impossible."

The waiter came by and filled up Henry and Ivania's glasses with more wine. As soon as he left, Ivania asked, "When you first came into the dining room, you stopped briefly at a table. I overheard the man you spoke with mentioning something about a presentation. Are you giving a talk?"

"Yes, on Friday night I am giving a presentation and slide show about missionary work in India. It's about making us aware of the needs of our brothers and sisters here and abroad. Part of the purpose is to raise funds but even more so is to motivate people to commit to Jesus and His great commission to bring all of humanity to salvation; to lead us home."

Henry smiled.

Ivania nodded. "That is a noble cause, Hendry. You are a fine man. God has chosen wisely. You are doing great things for Him."

"Thank you Ivania. Much of my talk is addressed to the men. It is my belief that many of the problems which exist around us are because men haven't been carrying out their role as husbands and father as leaders in the home. Families are the building blocks of society and when the family breaks down we can see it in the breakdown of society as well."

"That's a big responsibility you are placing on men's shoulders. What should men be doing, Hendry? Most are not like you; close to God."

Henry nodded, "That's true. God is being neglected more and more in the home. We are failing to develop the spiritual side of our lives. We have too many idols and pursuits over and above God. I was much the same, Ivania. I was a lukewarm Christian. But Father Engelmann helped me to see the light and I am trying to do the same for others.

"You're right, it is a big responsibility on men but they are the head of the house...well, in many ways it's just like you, Ivania. In the same way you are at the helm and lead your staff, so too, men have to be leaders in their home. You know if leaders falter, the company suffers. Well, that's what I think is happening in the home. Just like your staff needs a leader with a vision of how to make things work for the good and benefit of the company and the employees, so too, men need to step up with a plan and vision for their wives and children. What I am trying to convince men of is that the vision they need to follow has already been laid out for them by Jesus Christ. If they put Him at the center of their lives and model Him and implement His teachings, their lives will be transformed.

"But as you know, Ivania, you can't lead your company alone. You need CEOs and managers to help you or the company will easily falter. So too, does the husband need the strong support and input of his wife. She, too, must put Jesus at the center of her life and marriage with her husband. She, too, must give of her strength, love, encouragement, wisdom and whatever is needed there for him."

Ivania listened quietly. Her mouth was open but no words came forth. She was awestruck by the man across from her.

"It all makes sense, Ivania. In the same way you were promoted to take over because the company was failing, so too, men need to step up to the plate and become more active and responsible in leading their family home to the Lord. Just like your company is once again flourishing across Canada for the entire world to see, so too, can families, the church and thus society. flourish again. The world today, more than ever before, needs leaders who have thought things out and become beacons of light in darkness."

Ivania shook her head from side to side, "My, my, Hendry, you have become a soldier for the Lord."

Henry smiled, "You know, Ivania, there is something else which is crucial in all this. Even though men may see the vision of Jesus' teachings for them and their family; even though Jesus is the perfect mentor, model and example of the sacrifices they need to make; there is one more crucial thing necessary which is needed to make it all work."

Ivania sat up, placed her elbows on the table and rested her pretty head on top of her folded hands and asked, "And what is that, Hendry?"

"The Holy Spirit! Before Jesus ascended into heaven after His resurrection, He told His apostles He had to go but would continue to intercede for them to the Father but He would not leave them alone. He said He would send the Holy Spirit to help them, comfort them, convict them, and help them to remember all of the things He taught them. The Holy Spirit is for us, too, Ivania. We need the power of the Holy Spirit to give us the strength to follow Jesus; to help us die to ourselves and follow the teachings and example of Jesus."

Henry paused and smiled at the beautiful lady across from him who seemed to be momentarily, unusually speechless and added, "Actually, Ivania, I know how much passion you have for the vision of the company you lead. Imagine if you called upon the Holy Spirit to empower your passion even more, there is no limit to what can be achieved and the untold new heights your firm can be taken to!" Henry added with a wink, "And if you could convince your company to give to the poor, to our mission work, the Lord will reward and bless you and your company beyond measure. Jesus said, 'Give, and you will receive.' Your gift will return to you in full: pressed down, shaken down, shaken together to make room for more, running over, and poured into your lap!"

"My, my, Hendry, I can see there is no use in me trying to seduce you from your vocation and calling! In fact, if I am exposed a moment longer to such a heartfelt outpouring of service for the Lord, I might very well consider becoming a nun...!

"Heaven forbid!"

CHAPTER SIXTY

HENRY HAD SPENT the last week and half at the Poustinia working on book seven, The Heart of an Angel in the Angelic Letters Series. Just moments ago, he wrote the last paragraph, bringing the story right up to the present. He did however want to include Hannah's birthday which was just two days away, the anniversary of Jenny's death in May and perhaps a chapter or two describing the missionary work he was doing. So, there was still some writing to be done in the weeks ahead.

So many memories were revived in this last book, memories which at times he hoped didn't happen and that it was all just a story. But his dear sweet wife did pass away and miraculously through the love and offering of his dear, lifelong mentor and friend, he had survived the ordeal.

Henry sat back in the chair and brought his hands together behind his head. He gazed out the picture window and took in the restful valley scene before him. Spring came early. Tall, lush, spring grass lined the edge of the stream feeding the pond in front of the Poustinia. Old reeds had bent or fallen over and last year's weeds were just about choked out by fresh, green new growth everywhere.

The back door in the bedroom leading to the deck behind the prayer house was open and suddenly a barn swallow flew in. He'd been meaning to put an outside screen door there for years and somehow always forgot, probably because, it was at the rear and not used that often. The bird didn't stay long and soon zoomed out to add the bit of grass in its beak to the nest they were re-building above the door frame molding. The old nest had fallen off earlier that morning.

How many times did Father gaze out the bedroom window just like he was now? How many of his sermons were based upon the visions he saw from this view? There was one homily Henry vividly remembered, when Father called all the parishioners in the church to repentance like John the Baptist did. Father got his inspiration right here as he visualized John walking along the stream, making way for Jesus. And then there was that powerful sermon he gave of Jesus sitting on one of the hills teaching about the beatitudes. Henry smiled when Father said he often thought of the pond outside the prayer house as the Sea of Galilee.

Henry never dreamed that he would follow in the footsteps of his teacher. But that year following his forty-day retreat and fast when he and Justin went to India for three months was when he felt the calling. The adoration of the Eucharist at the end of each day at the Mother House of Sisters of Charity in Calcutta was so compelling that his desire to say Mass and bring Jesus; Body, Blood, Soul and Divinity, true God and true man under the appearance of bread and wine to the people, was something he had to do. His passion for the Eucharist began during his fast and prayer retreat and just continued to grow. The Eucharist was the highlight of Father Engelmann's vocation in the priesthood as well; Henry could now clearly understand why.

What a journey it has been since Father Engelmann's passing. He toured hundreds of churches across Canada and planned to begin in the United States in the New Year. He was glad he started to release the books which Father had written right after he was ordained. All of the books needed to be proofread, edited and the cover designed. He started with *Pewter Angels*, book one in the series and as he had planned, he published it under the name Pio-Seelos Books. It was released on Mother's Day, in 1999 and in each of the following years, another book in the series was released except for this last book.

As Henry had expected, *Pewter Angels* was an immediate success and with the release of each book they were all instant best sellers, too. This would be the only year he was not able to get the next book out for a Mother's Day release. Emails, letters and phone calls came in daily asking when the seventh and final book in the series would be out. Henry was already making bookings for signing events and also with churches and libraries who wanted him to speak on both his missionary work and the *Angelic Letters Series.*

Henry gazed at the six books standing on end at the back of desk. He liked the design and color of the covers. It was still hard to believe that Father authored those books and the captivating story he spun of all of their lives. Henry reached out and grabbed book three, *Angel of Thanksgiving*. He flipped through the pages and shook his head. All these books and hundreds of pages...amazing! *"Truly remarkable,"* as the Archbishop would say.

What an inspired story!

Henry knew after he had read them during his forty day retreat they would be 'best sellers.' Father's conversational style of writing touched hearts instantly. Over and over, readers said that they couldn't put the books down once they started the story. To date, thousands of dollars had been raised for the missions and Henry saw no end.

Since the last book contained Jenny's death and the birth of Hannah, Henry had planned to talk to his daughter about that and his subsequent depression. He had said things about Hannah's birth being the cause of Jenny's death and that he had wished she had never been born. These were thoughts said out of intense sorrow over the loss of a loved one during a time when his world was falling apart. Henry wanted to make sure Hannah understood that before releasing the book. This was also another reason why he held off releasing this book until Hannah was old enough to understand. He realized now that it really wasn't necessary as Hannah's comprehension and empathy were far beyond her age.

Henry got up and made his way to the bedroom door. As

soon as he walked into the chapel, he pictured Jenny at the kneeler; her hands were together in prayer and her head bowed. She was such a beautiful picture of reverence to the Lord. The scene dripped with intimacy; she was so close to Jesus. How many times over the past few years had he vowed to paint that picture. Henry could feel the oneness; her spirit entwined with that of her Lord. He had seen that intimacy all of his life with Father Engelmann and Jesus, yet it was more obvious with Jenny; so pure, so beautiful, so deep and yet, so free!

Just beyond the kneeler, Henry immediately saw the image of Father lying on the floor bearing the wounds of Jesus. He would never be able to erase that scene off the screen of his mind. What a moment in time that was when he walked into the Poustinia and saw that Father had received the Stigmata. And to learn that Father had offered up his life for him to save his soul was what Henry would be eternally grateful to Father for.

Henry gazed at the altar and tried to replace the image he was still holding with one that saw Father Engelmann still alive and celebrating Mass. His mentor's presence was felt so strongly when he had said Mass earlier that morning. The Mass was offered up in memory of Jenny and all his love for her. So many memories, so many wonderful memories of the three of them here in this little chapel praising Jesus. If only Father and his dear Jenny were here now, they would sit by the patio windows or go out onto the deck and chat about life, the challenges they faced and how to bring the love of Christ to others.

The day when he and Mr. Engelmann walked through the store for the last time and then went out back and sat on the old grey crates came back to Henry. He chased one memory after the other of all the good times they had over the years. In a way this was similar. This was a close to the story, even though it would go on forever through him and his family and all those readers whose lives the characters in the story touched. *In a way*, Henry thought, *we will all be sitting out back on the old grey crates listening to the teachings of Jesus so entwined in the captivating love story.*

It's remarkable how the Lord through His messenger, Zachariah, inspired Father to write it. Henry shook his head. Father must have felt so inadequate to write a book and yet, he stepped out in faith and wrote one best seller after the other. Henry could only imagine the countless number of people who are called to step out in faith and fulfill the plan which God has for them. There is tremendous reward for those who do. It gave Father such purpose in his declining years.

Henry gazed at the cross above the altar and crossed himself. He turned and walked out into the sunlight closing the door behind him. A beaver spotted Henry and slapped its tail on the water. Instantly, the reflection of the hills and valley on the pond before him were obliterated in the ripples. Slowly, the water came to rest, mimicking once again the fresh green foliage of early spring on the banks in the mirror like surface.

A shout from the upper deck at the farm house startled him as it echoed in the valley. Hannah was waving. "When are you coming up for lunch, Dad? I made some sandwiches."

Henry looked up to the house on the hillside and waved back to his daughter. "I was just getting ready to come up. Be there in ten minutes."

"Did you see any monarchs, yet?"

"No, it's still too early, Hannah."

"They will be coming soon to visit Mom at the cemetery. I'm sure some will fly here, too!"

Henry chuckled to himself. Hannah was probably right. Everything seemed to be blooming early and it was incredible that the monarchs arrive one to two months earlier than normal.

The meadow was ablaze with color; Henry marveled how the wildflowers seemed to blossom early that year. It seemed as if the monarchs and flowers, like him, couldn't wait to see Jenny running through the meadow and wanted to be with her too...like him. Carlos thought the same thing as he witnessed year after year how early in the spring the flowers grow and the monarchs return to Jenny's back yard garden in the city.

Jenny knew the secret of nature and its power to heal and bring peace. Both Jenny and Father knew the need to withdraw and dwell in God's creation; breathe in the fresh air and allow the peace and calm to permeate and heal the soul. Somehow, nature brings us back into the moment and cares vanish; the beauty, the soothing rhythm of the babbling stream, the sound of birds who are always rejoicing and singing in praise.

A serene silence enveloped Henry as he stood there taking in the beauty surrounding the prayer house. He knew he was about to hear God's messengers whispering to him. As he marveled how the rays of the sun shimmered on the gentle ripples across the pond, it came to him that just as the grass and flowers need sunshine and water to grow and flourish giving beauty to the world, so too, do we need the light of Jesus in our hearts to make our faith grow. If we were only to water our hearts daily with His Word, others will see the beauty in us just like the breathtaking beauty of God's creation before him.

He felt the presence of Father Engelmann inspiring him further as the shimmering water sparkled like diamonds under the rising sun. Words seemed to bubble out of Henry to proclaim to the whole world,

"Yes, yes, oh my Lord! Let us see that each and every word You speak are like diamonds, too, jewels that we place in our heart each day. These are the treasures we must seek. The light and truth we gain from Your word will make us sparkle, too, and has far more worth and lasting value than all the gold and silver of the world."

Henry was so grateful for the passion and love for the Lord which flooded through him that tears of erupting joy blurred the glorious, sunlit valley before him. He could feel the gentle touch of his mentor's hand on his shoulder and the warm, morning breeze moving across the pond toward him, carrying the sweet voice of his dearly beloved friend.

Lovingly, soothingly Henry heard Father Engelmann whisper Ecclesiastes. 2:26…

"For to the man who pleases Him, God gives wisdom, and knowledge and joy!"

CHAPTER SIXTY-ONE

"HAPPY BIRTHDAY, TO our dear, sweet Hannah! Happy birthday to you! Yeahhhhh! Whoopee!" everyone yelled and clapped and cheered.

Henry bent down and rubbed his cheek next to Hannah's as Jeremy snapped another picture of the two of them beaming from ear to ear. Hannah had just blown out all twelve candles on the chocolate cake that Matti had baked.

"Happy Birthday, sweetheart," said Henry as he gave Hannah a peck on her cheek. Henry stood up and watched the others wish Hannah best wishes as well.

What a wonderful practice they had started on Hannah's second year birthday. More than anything, Jenny wanted family and did everything to encourage it. The fruit of her efforts were showing since her passing. For all important occasions, the family got together. J.J. easily brought the entire estate to Regina for the celebrations in the company's private jet.

Gary, who also became a priest, was there along with John. John had become part of the Pederson family since the death of his mother. Although he didn't make it to all of Hannah's celebrations, he came whenever he could. Peter and his wife Angelika had grown very close to the Pederson family over the years. Usually, Peter's children came for the celebration, but both were busy with other events in their families.

The most unexpected guests were Eddy and his wife Coreena. Eddy was supposed to have died years ago but since his miraculous healing from lung cancer, Eddy has been fit as a fiddle! Sadly, Thomas had passed away three years ago. He suddenly had a heart attack while working in the garden on the estate. He died doing the work God wanted him to do; to make the world beautiful. And that's what Thomas did. J.J.'s estate was written up in several magazines as one of the most beautiful gardens in all of Canada.

Neela, Thomas' wife, kept coming to the family events and always brought a bit of her husband's spirit with her by her gracious charm and eloquence. She usually stayed with Carlos and Maria and came with them to the party. Henry's children were all there; Jeremy and his family, Alison, Lauren, Justin and his fiancé, Susan and finally the Carters. Jack reluctantly retired from medicine five years ago, giving in to Vera's insistence and with the help of a cane, both Jack and Vera were in fine shape for their age.

All in all, it was a fine gathering of family and friends. Jenny would be beaming and happy as a lark if she were present! However, they all knew that she was there in spirit.

"Be takin' some ice cream with your cake, Henry?" shouted Matti, snapping him out of his reverie.

"For sure, Matti. I can't have chocolate cake without ice cream."

"Even though it's several years since your ordination, I keep confusing you with Father Engelmann," observed J.J.. "You thinning out a bit on top and your hair and beard is just as white as his was."

"Yes, yes," said Henry, chuckling, sounding just like his mentor, too. "It is said, that when two people have a lifelong friendship and love one another with deep respect and affection, that they begin to emulate each other and even look like one another!"

Matti just heard what Henry had said as she brought his cake and ice cream to him. "That be true, J.J.. When I see Henry from the back, I swear I be seein' the holy man, especially with that aura of light which be surroundin' him. Just don't you be letting it go to your head, know what I'm sayin'?"

Henry chuckled, "No worries there, Matti. Father Engelmann's shoes are hard to fill, and that's for sure!"

"It's sure good of you to find the time in your busy schedule to make it here each year for Hannah's birthday."

"I wouldn't miss it, Henry," replied J.J.. "Family is something I missed growing up and since Dad's passing, I promised to keep up what he had started on the estate during his last couple of years... it has been a wonderful blessing. As we all know though, it was really Mom's presence on the estate which actually started all of us growing together as one big family. I wouldn't give it up for the world."

Just then, Peter came over and joined the conversation, "Justin mentioned that you went back to India again this past year."

"Yes, I did. They needed a priest to say daily Mass while many of the staff went on vacation. It's good for me to see what goes on there just to remind me of the extreme poverty and the many problems which exist in India. The caste system itself creates such human misery. So many people are considered the lowest of humanity and untouchable. And then there is the sanitation, so many living on the streets, so many children abandoned, the sickness and lack of food for so many from day to day. It's quite a struggle for literally millions of people."

"It must be very disheartening for the sisters and volunteers. It would be understandable for them to throw up their hands and say that it is impossible to overcome all these challenges," said J.J.

Henry nodded, "I felt that the first time Justin and I went there but Mother Teresa encouraged everyone to just take one soul at a time and extend love. She was quite the lady. A saint in our midst."

"And how did Hannah like the experience?" J.J. wanted to know.

"Yeah, I struggled with the decision to take Hannah but I'm sure glad I did. She is quite mature for her age and is very

attracted to the poor and doing God's work. I thought I would
have to shield her from some of the misery but she handled
it better than I. Sometimes I forget that she is still a young
girl and not a young lady. She is already talking about joining
Mother Teresa's order when she finishes high school."

"J.J., you be wantin' some more cake?"

"Yeah, excuse me fellows." As J.J. turned to leave, he said,
"The corporation will be making a contribution to your
Missionary Foundation later next month, Henry."

"That's great, J.J., much appreciated," said Henry.

"When you're in Calgary, please include my parish on your
tour. We already help out several charities but we will do whatever we can for you."

"Thanks, Peter. It would be wonderful to visit your parish.
How is church attendance by the youth?" Henry wanted
to know.

"It was declining but we do notice a comeback since we really
started praying to the Holy Spirit to revive our parish. It all
happened one day as I was searching for the Lord to help me
that I read Acts 19: 1-2. It was when Paul visited Ephesus and
observed that some of the Christian disciples were lacking
something in their faith. It was what Paul asked them that
really jolted me about something that I had neglected in our
parish. 'Did you receive the Holy Spirit when you believed?'
They answered much like many parishioners in our church do.
They knew of the Holy Spirit but didn't see Him as important
or necessary in their lives.

"It was like a light bulb went on in my head. Although I
had spoken of the Holy Spirit in many of my sermons, somehow, it didn't register with the congregation. I immediately
spoke to the people about it, asking that we come before the
Lord in repentance and that we receive the Holy Spirit in our
heart. The result was like the Pentecost came to our church.
Since then, attendance has increased and many youths are
accompanying their parents once again. I believe it has to do
with the deepening of faith by the parents and living out their
spiritual side more during the week."

"That's a wonderful sharing, Peter. I do believe you are correct that many parishes are lacking the indwelling of the Holy Spirit in their church. The Holy Spirit is such a powerful advocate in helping us and yet, the least prayed to and invited into our lives. I think you are onto something Peter; seeing how the Spirit moves and convicts us, is faith building and contagious. When I tour the country, I also emphasize the importance of the Holy Spirit. Like you said, if parents live out their faith at home, strengthened by the Holy Spirit, it's bound to have a good effect on the children. In my presentation, I actually put a lot of focus on the men as leaders in the home to put Christ at the center of their lives and follow Him; and to do so, they need to be empowered by the Holy Spirit."

"Yes, Henry, we have developed a marriage cou—"

The two men were interrupted by Henry's daughter-in-law who was also Peter's daughter! "Hey, Dads," said Camilla, "You two will have to talk shop later. Hannah is about to open her presents."

"Yes, of course," said Henry. He put his arm around Peter's shoulder and the two men made their way into the overcrowded family room.

"I can't get over how Hannah is looking more like Auntie Jen. Every year when we come back, her features and gestures are so spontaneous, bubbly and her blue, sparkling eyes, exactly the same! And just look how tall she has grown—at least two or three inches since last year." observed Chloe as she stood next to Henry.

"Yeah, her personality is very much like Jenny's. She has the heart of a little angel, that's for sure, like Matti would say."

"So, how—" Chloe's comment was interrupted by an excited Hannah.

"Oh, what a beautiful white jumper, Matti. I just love the daisy flowers all over!" exclaimed Hannah, as she opened Matilda's gift.

"Oh, you be lookin' just like your momma, honey. You will have to try it on later make sure it be fittin' okay. You growin' so fast it soon no longer fittin' that beautiful body of yours!"

Henry recalled Jenny having a spring dress similar to that and so did Camilla. There were too many look-alikes around! It was the last gift which Hannah didn't open in front of everyone. It was a letter from Jenny. Before she passed away, Jenny had written over eighteen letters. The first sixteen were for Hannah's birthdays and the last two had to do with special occasions off in the future. Jenny had secretly given Camilla the letters soon after Jenny had learned of the complications developing in her pregnancy. Jenny had hoped that they would never have to be delivered but just in case, she wanted to keep in touch with her daughter and share what she would have, had she lived.

Reluctantly, Camilla agreed to accept the letters. She was glad she did, as they were so precious to Hannah. Jenny would have written more, had she not died so unexpectedly after she was discharged from the hospital. Henry recalled each of the letters that Hannah had received so far. Jenny did a wonderful job of leaving such heartfelt messages to her little girl appropriate for her age.

Jenny would always begin by wishing her daughter a birthday wish followed with some mother daughter thoughts. As Hannah grew older, Jenny would share a bit about herself and what she liked to do at that age. Since Jenny didn't anticipate Hannah maturing so quickly, some of Jenny's thoughts didn't seem to fit where Hannah was in life's journey. In any case, the letters were always read out loud to all those present. When Hannah celebrated her fourth birthday, she read the letter to all those present for the last time. Beginning on her fifth birthday, Hannah told everyone that she wanted to open the letter in private when she got to her room.

Although Henry and all the guests would have loved to know what Jenny had to share with her daughter, everyone understood the personal intimacy of the letter from Jenny to Hannah. Hannah wanted to savor the letter and the gift of the heart which her mother had expressed to her.

The other gift that elicited a special interest from Hannah was the Monarch Butterfly Kit that she received from Chloe and Robbie. While everyone was chatting outside on the deck, enjoying the beautiful early spring day, Hannah stayed inside and began to set up the kit. Just as Hannah had opened the two-foot-high net enclosure that the butterflies would be born in, Chloe came inside and sat next to her.

"I just love this gift, Chloe! I can't wait to get it set up. I was thinking the other day that it would be another month or so before the butterflies come back to the prairies and now, I can see them even sooner and watch how they change from a caterpillar to such a beautiful butterfly!"

"Yes, it's truly a miracle. When I was your age that's what I always called it. Your Mom and mine loved it when I used to say that it was a miracle."

"When I visit Carlos and Maria with dad in the summer time, Carlos always shows me how the monarchs lay eggs on the back of the leaves of the milkweed plant. I will never forget when I was six years old, I began to watch how the larvae soon begin to eat their way out of the egg and don't stop until they become a huge caterpillar."

Chloe picked up the clear glass container that came with the kit. "Look, Hannah, I see about five larvae in there resting on a lot of food. In about two weeks they will be like what you saw with Carlos; huge caterpillars!"

"What will they hang from, Chloe?" Hannah wanted to know.

"It must be from the underside of the lid somehow." Chloe picked up the instructions and after a bit said, "Yes, look here, Hannah. See how the caterpillars stick their back end to the lid and hang from there until they hide inside a chrysalis, a sort of cocoon they grow around themselves."

"And inside the chrysalis, the caterpillar changes into a butterfly! That's called metamorphosis, isn't it?" asked Hannah.

Chloe looked at Hannah in surprise. "That's right, Hannah! That's the miracle! Isn't that something!?"

Hannah nodded, "God has made so many amazing things for us."

Chloe had come to admire Hannah's faith in God and related comments.

"Daddy told me that your mom and mine were best friends."

"Yes, Jenny and Tammy were like two peas in a pod, Hannah. They loved each other like two sisters."

Hannah looked up at Chloe, her big blue eyes sparkling with wonder, "How old were you when God called your mom?" Hannah asked.

"I was eight years old, four years younger than you are today."

Just the thought of that fateful, memorable day being beside her mother when she was shot, brought tears instantly to Chloe's eyes.

Hannah sensed Chloe's sadness and reached out and touched her hand. "That must have been so sad. You still miss your mom, don't you, Chloe?"

Chloe nodded. With her free hand, she brushed away a tear rolling down her cheek. Chloe was touched by Hannah's empathy.

"I wish my mom was still alive, too. Everyone tells me how nice she was. They say she looked a lot like Camilla and that I look like her, too!"

"Yes, do you ever! I was telling your dad that earlier when you were opening up your gifts. The resemblance is amazing."

"Camilla shares a lot about Mom with me. For the longest time when I was growing up I thought Camilla was my mom rather than my older sister. Camilla always explained to me that she was my second mother in absence of my real mom, but still she is so loving towards me, I considered her as my real mom."

Chloe patted Hannah's hand. "Yes, Camilla has done a wonderful job in raising you just like your mom helped me so much, too. After Tammy died, Auntie Jen sort of became my mom. We didn't live together like you and Camilla but we were always on the phone. Auntie Jenny helped me get over my mom's passing and explained to me so beautifully that Mom's spirit is alive in heaven just like angels are."

Hannah looked at Chloe and asked, "How did my mom explain that to you, Chloe?"

As soon as those words left her lips, Chloe anticipated that question from Hannah who was so perceptive and mature, well beyond her age.

"Well, I remember that day before Mom was buried, I was walking with your mother in the garden when she lived at the estate with J.J. in Ottawa. It was fall and all of the butterflies had left on their trek to Mexico except for one. Like I said, I was only eight at the time and had difficulty understanding how Mom's spirit was alive in heaven. The butterfly flitting about that day gave your mom the idea to compare Tammy's passing to that of a caterpillar dying in a cocoon."

"In a chrysalis. Is that what you mean, Chloe?"

Chloe nodded and went on, "We may feel sad and think that the caterpillar has died but as you know Hannah, it is only going through an amazing transformation as we do too when we die. Instead of looking down at the dead caterpillar in the chrysalis, look up and see the new life it has become! See the beautiful butterfly fluttering about so radiantly happy overhead.

"So, Hannah, in the same way that the caterpillar had a beautiful butterfly inside that miraculously comes alive and is so happy and free to flit about in the sky, the spirit which was inside of your mommy has undergone a new life from earthly wings to spiritual ones. The moment she died, the spirit that was in her body while she was alive, left her body and emerged as a beautiful, free spirit like an angel. She is now free in heaven. We can't see her spirit but we know she is here and will be for the rest of our lives to help, guide and protect us.

"That is what happened to your mother, too. At times you will sense her presence so strongly that you will become over-whelmed with joy. We will all have another angel at our side! I can just imagine how your mom and mine are so happy together in heaven."

Hannah had tears in her eyes. "That is so beautiful, Chloe...I remember reading about that scene in the *Angelic Letters Series* but I loved hearing about it from you. I tried to visualize myself there with you and Mom. That was such a special time."

Chloe hadn't thought about how her sharing with Jenny at that time would elicit thoughts and feelings from Hannah such that she wished it was her there with her mother.

"It is eerie reading about our parents in those books, Hannah. It was incredible how Father Engelmann in his near-death experience was allowed to see into the lives of people in the past and then assigned to write about your parents and to include all of us in this epic story!"

"It is so amazing, Chloe. I would have loved to meet Father Engelmann. I don't know how many times I read the first five books and I'm reading the sixth book over again for the third time. With each reading, I am learning more about life, God and the importance of putting Jesus at the center of your life."

Chloe gazed at Hannah, lovingly and compassionately. She knew in book six was when Jenny had conceived Hannah and was faced with the decision to abort her when eclampsia had set in. Chloe also recalled reading that Henry wanted to save Jenny's life over Hannah's. In a way, a similar situation was developing with Hannah that happened in her life too. Her dad, Robbie, didn't want her initially either and had pressured Tammy into considering an abortion. But her mother never went through with it. Robbie eventually realized the huge mistake that would have been and had expressed his sorrow many times for even having thought such an alternative. Chloe was wondering if Hannah had similar feelings about what her father was going through, when Jenny's life was threatened by the critical medical situation she faced.

"I read book six, *The House Where Angels Dwell,* too, Hannah. That must have been such a difficult time for your mom and dad when Jenny started to have complications in her pregnancy."

Hannah, nodded. "Yes, that was so frightening when mom went into a coma and daddy was struggling with the decision to terminate the pregnancy or not. I recall in the last chapter of the book, Dad called you to ask your opinion and advice."

Chloe nodded to the perceptive and sensitive young girl in front of her. How must she be feeling to read about this and the terrible situation her father was in; so torn between saving the life of his dear wife and seeing the abortion of their baby as the best option.

"Yes, I recall talking to your dad about that, Hannah. It was such a difficult time for him, but in the end, he had made the decision to carry out the wishes of what your mother would have wanted to do; to deliver you!"

Hannah had tears in her eyes. Chloe anticipated what the young girl must be thinking. Although Jenny had long passed away and Hannah also knew the deep love that her father has for her, yet in book seven which soon will be released, would deal with the death of Jenny. That in itself could be so traumatic for Hannah, but to also deal with her father's ensuing depression and the entire gamut of emotions he would go through, could be completely overwhelming for Hannah, no matter how mature she is. Judging from the detail described by Father Engelmann of their lives from previous books, what would be revealed in book seven about Henry's feelings over the loss of his wife after giving birth to Hannah, might be too painful and hurtful for the young girl to deal with.

Chloe was concerned that Hannah may feel that she was rejected by her father and that she was the cause of her mother's death.

"When is Henry going to release book seven, Hannah?" Chloe wanted to know.

Hannah brushed away a tear rolling down her cheek and said, "I know he's still working on it. For the most part, it's finished. He just wants to bring it up to date and all to some conclusion. I think he plans to release it either this fall or next spring, around Mother's Day like he has with all of the previous books."

Hannah hesitated for a moment and then opened the door for Chloe to discuss what was weighing on her heart.

"I have a confession to make. I hope dad won't be upset with me. When he was away touring some of the churches in Alberta, I came across the manuscript at the prayer house for book seven which dad was working on.

"Did you read it, Hannah?" Chloe was anxious to know.

Hannah nodded, "Yes, I read it Chloe, in fact, I read it three times…"

Hannah began weeping and couldn't go on. Chloe moved closer to her and put her arm around Hannah, tears surfacing in her eyes as well. Chloe waited for Hannah to speak. She wanted to know where Hannah was at.

"It was so sad Chloe, and daddy went through such a tough time in dealing with it all. Over the years, dad has talked to me about Mom's death and his feelings at the time to prepare me for this, but still, to read about it and dad's struggles touched my heart so deeply, Chloe."

Chloe could only imagine what Hannah had read and what her father felt and said. After collecting her thoughts, Chloe spoke softly, "Your father loves you so much, Hannah. That was such a difficult time he went through and in the moment, all of us go through so many irrational thoughts and emotions… do you recall in book two, *Another Angel of Love,* when my mom was pregnant with me? Remember how Robbie, wanted Tammy to have an abortion and all the struggles he went through along with my mom?"

Hannah nodded, "I remember, Chloe, but it is as you just said, at the time, we all go through such struggles with what is the right thing to do. This is where we are at, at that point in our lives. And like you said earlier, Robbie eventually came around to see what a huge mistake it would have been to abort you and how much he loves you."

Chloe was taken aback by Hannah's response. The young girl had almost taken the words out of her mouth as to what she was going to say to comfort her!

"Yes, that is so true, Hannah. I was just thinking the same thing about what you must be going through. I don't know what you read in the story but I'm sure you realize the deep love your mother had for you and the sanctity of life. Your dad, too, although he was struggling so much with the loss of Jenny, overshadowed at the time, how dearly he loved you and the gift which Jenny left behind for him. Oh, Hannah, you are so deeply loved and cherished not only by your dad but all of us."

"I know," was all Hannah could say before the two girls hugged one another. They both knew above all else, God created them and all of humanity. Life was a gift and must be honored at all costs. Their mothers knew that and that was why they were here, embracing one another, to acknowledge their deep gratitude to them.

Although the noon day sun was streaming in through the living room windows warming Chloe and Hannah's spirits, the special aura surrounding the two girls was enhanced by not only their guardian angels but the presence of their mothers' spirits as well.

CHAPTER SIXTY-TWO

AROUND MID-AFTERNOON, THEY all walked down to the Poustinia to celebrate Mass. It looked like a small pilgrimage was being made to a holy shrine. And it was! Many miracles had occurred there including Father Engelmann's receiving of the Stigmata.

The tiny chapel was too small to hold everyone, so they left both patio doors wide open and many stood outside on the deck. It was difficult for all those gathered there to get used to Henry officiating, rather than Father Engelmann.

Following the Mass, they had a barbeque and a sing along which was led by Alison and Carlos playing their guitars together. While Alison played fireside songs such as; This Land is Your Land, Home, Home on The Range, She'll Be Coming Around the Mountain, and You are My Sunshine, Carlos played many songs with a Mexican flavor: Vaya Con Dios, Seven Spanish Angels and more. Every one enjoyed Lauren's impromptu dancing when Carlos sang and played Vaya Con Dios. In between some of the singing, Justin performed magic tricks that he had taken up as a hobby years ago.

It was a wonderful mix of entertainment but it slowly came to an end. They all wished it could go on forever. J.J. and his crew were the first to make a move to leave along with Chloe and Robbie who were flying out later that day. Matti always found it the most difficult to say goodbye.

"Oh, Henry, or should I be callin' you, Father Pederson?"

"Henry is just fine, Matti."

"Well, I be missin' you and your wonderful family already. You be one fine man. I just know Jenny be proud of you workin' for the Lord. I can just hear her up there singing praise and shoutin' hallelujahs! That for sure!"

Matti no longer had to bend over to give Hannah a hug and kiss. "My, my, you growin' child. Next time I see you, you be taller than me."

Matti smiled and continued, "You be a special girl, honey child. I just know you be just like your mommy...another earthly angel."

One after another they said their good bye and by nine o'clock, everyone had gone except for Justin, his fiancé Susan, Alison and Hannah. Lauren went into Regina with Grandpa and Grandma Carter as she had to catch a midnight flight back to Toronto. Hannah wanted to spend the night at the farm and was already in her bedroom.

"Well, Dad I am going to take a shower and then come down for a visit."

"Sounds good, Alison. Sorry that man of yours couldn't make it."

"He was looking forward to coming but just couldn't get away from work."

"I am going to watch a bit of TV with Justin and Susan. I'll see you later then."

HENRY, ALISON, JUSTIN and Susan chatted for about an hour and then they all decided to call it a day. As Henry was going to his bedroom, he noticed the light to Hannah's room was still on. Henry knocked on the door and walked in. She was reading Jenny's letter. Henry knew she had probably read it for the tenth time. Hannah had tears in her eyes.

Henry sat on the edge of the bed and said, "What a great party that was. It's so nice to see everyone like that and get caught up on the news."

"I love it when everyone comes, Dad. I wished they lived closer so we could see each other more often."

Henry nodded, "Family is so important. We need each other, to be there for one another and to feel we are loved and belong."

"It's so sad when people do not have a home and children are left on the streets like we saw in Calcutta. It must be so scary being all alone on the streets like that."

"Yes, that is why we need each other and to help one another. Like the girl you write to in an orphanage in Calcutta; what is her name?"

"Alisha. She is eight years old and hasn't' got either parent. So many times, she wishes that she had parents like I do."

"There are many abandoned children, honey. Not only in India but all over the world, including here in Canada. Even though many children have a mom and dad, they are not looked after properly. That is why we have to care and help one another and pray for each other."

"I was thinking about going into the Carmelite order like Saint Therese, the little flower. They devote their lives to praying for the world but I think Jesus wants me to be out helping the poor."

Henry nodded. He wasn't surprised any more by conversations like this with Hannah. For several years, she had been talking about entering a convent and doing God's work. She was struggling with the choice to live more in seclusion, as a nun, like some of the orders do. Or, to be called a 'sister' and lead a more active apostolate, like Mother Teresa's Sisters of Charity.

"Both are important, Hannah. The world needs prayers and lots of it. But it also needs people to go out and serve more directly. In a way, Hannah, you are doing both. You are praying much of the time and you also want to help; you give all your allowance to the poor, last month you chose to have jeans that are less expensive than the ones at the specialty store. And besides Alisha, you are writing to nine other girls in different parts of the world—"

"I loved helping you and the other volunteers at Mother House in India when we were there last year," blurted Hannah, excitedly. "I wish I could enter the order after I finish high school."

"You are still too young, Hannah. Since you skipped two grades, you will only be fifteen when you finish grade twelve and it would be good for you to spend a couple of years at university."

"But, Dad, I know what I want to do and St. Therese entered the Carmelite convent at age 15 and she too, like Mom, loved flowers…"

Henry nodded, "We will have to keep praying and waiting on God's guidance in the matter, Hannah. You are still young and things are different now. God will direct your path and let you know in due time."

Hannah's face showed a hint of dejection as Henry tried to change the subject.

"I see you have the butterfly kit all set up on the dining room table."

"Chloe helped me. I will have to set the jar with the larvae near the sunlight tomorrow. We have to watch it doesn't get too hot as condensation might form on the inside of the jar. It needs to stay dry."

Henry smiled and nodded again.

"I just finished reading the first five books in the *Angelic Letters Series* for the fifth time and have started to read book 6, *The House Where Angels Dwell* for the third time. It's such a wonderful love story and I love how the guardian angels are involved. It's so cool how I already know so much of what happens in the story from what you and Camilla have shared with the family over the years."

"Yes, I had that same feeling when I first started to read the story from Father Engelmann's writing. It's so true to life and what actually happened."

"And I love the way Father worked in so many life lessons and his sermons are so powerful. Oh, how I wish I could have met him."

"Well, you do get a good portrait of his life and character and love for the Lord from the story. When I edited each book, I added a lot of things about Father which he was too humble to put into the story."

"I was wondering why Father's name wasn't on the books? He wrote the first six, right?"

"Yes, he did, however, in a note to me, he requested that I edit the books and put my name on them. I did so reluctantly but actually, Hannah, neither Father nor I wrote the story. It was a gift from God. Father and I were only instruments used to pen the words. Zachariah, Father's guardian angel delivered the message that this was one of the missions God wanted of Father.

"The Holy Trinity and the messengers of God were the true authors of the books. Father Engelmann and I were simply the instruments through which the series was written. Truly, it was all divinely inspired. Father and I may have held the pen but the words, insights, wisdom and twists and turns which flowed from it onto the pages were guided.

"The series, all of it, was a gift to Father Engelmann and I to share with the world! In any case, the story itself reveals how it all came about."

"Wow, that is all so amazing. When are you going to release the seventh book, Dad?"

"I had planned to finish it up by this fall, but I have so many speaking engagements coming up, it probably won't get done until February or March of next year. I am hoping to release it in the spring around Mother's Day. It will also be in remembrance of Jenny's passing."

"That will be Tuesday, May 2, 2006, just twenty days after my thirteenth birthday! I looked it up last week."

"I can't believe that when the time comes, thirteen years will have passed since Jenny went to heaven."

"You can always remember by how old I am."

Henry gazed at his lovely daughter and smiled trying to hide the fact that it's not the best way for a daughter to remember her mother. He was also concerned about the content of book seven. Although Henry had talked to Hannah about the circumstances surrounding her mother's death and his subsequent depression, still, so much emotion and detail was revealed in the book. He didn't want Hannah to feel that in any way he blamed her for Jenny's passing or that he didn't love her deeply.

Hannah must have been reading her father's mind.

"I have a confession to make, Dad. When I was down at the prayer house one day while you were away, I discovered the manuscript for book seven and I couldn't help myself, I just had to read it. Please don't be upset with me and I don't want you to worry about anything. I know how much you love me. I know how much you love Mom and all the pain and turmoil you went through…"

Tears had already surfaced in Henry's eyes. He was so concerned about that and was trying to think of the best way to discuss this with his daughter. In fact, he purposely delayed finishing the book for another year to go by so Hannah would be older and more mature. But, she was more than ready; mentally, emotionally and spiritually. Just the way she just responded was to let him know that she understood and felt totally loved.

Hannah reached out and took her father's hand, "Oh, Daddy, I love you. I, too, wish so often that Mom was alive but she is in heaven and so close to both of us. For some reason, God took her…if he hadn't, you wouldn't be a priest nor doing the things you are doing. And…and, when you shared all you went through when you did the fast and prayer retreat and how close you drew to God… maybe that was a way for you to finally find Jesus in your life like Father Engelmann did. Maybe, that's why God allowed Mom to develop complications when she was carrying me. If Mom hadn't had me, perhaps she would have had an accident and been taken home some other way. You write so strongly about God's Divine Providence and Father Engelmann is constantly telling us to live with eternity in mind because life is so short and any of us can be called to go home to Jesus at any time…if all this didn't happen Daddy, maybe you never would have found what you were searching for all of your life; to truly have Jesus at the center of your life."

Henry couldn't believe how insightful and understanding and consoling Hannah was. It was as if Saint Jennifer and Saint

David Engelmann were speaking through his dear daughter telling him over and over what his wife and dear mentor have been telling him for years and years; God causes all things to work together for good to those who love God, to those who are called according to His purpose.

"Oh, Hannah, I am not upset that you read the manuscript but rather more concerned about the content and the circumstances surrounding your mother's death. It was such a difficult time for me and I said things about Jenny and the baby which may be hurtful to you or that you were the cause of it all."

"Oh, Dad, I understand how much you loved Mom and wanted her by your side but it was God's will for things to end up this way. I know how much you love me and do not feel that you resent my birth or that I was the cause of Mom's passing. This was Mom's lifelong wish to bear a child for you and through that pregnancy her belief in life, her love for you and I was lived out. I feel so honored to have had a mother who loved me so dearly that she would sacrifice her life for me.

"And, and…Chloe and I were talking about this, this afternoon. She mentioned that her dad had struggled with similar feeling when Tammy carried her. But he realized too, how much he loves Chloe. Death is the beginning of true eternal life. Just like Mom gave life to me, so too, death gives life and new birth in heaven's kingdom. She is alive in her new state and praying for us. Life on earth is so short Dad, soon we will all be together in heaven."

Tears surfaced in Henry's eyes and it took only one more blink for the tears to spillover and roll down his cheeks. Henry could barely believe the healing and insightful words coming out of his young daughter. What incredible understanding. Rather than him consoling her, it was the other way around! "Oh, honey, I was so worried about you reading about your mother's death and all the things that happened and I didn't want you in any way to feel that your birth was the cause of it all. It makes my heart soar at your understanding, Hannah!"

Henry reached over and hugged Hannah. "Jenny said you are the gift she wanted to give to me all of her life. I am so blessed to have such a wonderful daughter."

Hannah nodded, "You were blessed to have Father Engelmann as your lifelong friend, too, Dad. He was such a holy man. Imagine being able to go down to the prayer house like you did and celebrate Mass with him and sit on the deck and talk. Do you miss him, Dad?"

"I think of your Mom and Father every day, Hannah."

A silence fell over the room. Henry looked down at the letter Hannah was holding and asked, "So, what does Mom have to say this year?" Henry would love to know.

Hannah picked up the letter and said, "She mentions you a lot…she loves you very much, Dad. There is so much in her letters to me that are also revealed in the story. Since she didn't exactly know what was in the books Father wrote, she didn't realize that she would be repeating much of her life to me in her letters. But still, I treasure them and it's all so amazing how this is playing out in my life. I am so honored and blessed to have such a wonderful mother and to think, she is a saint! I want to be just like her! And you, Daddy, are a priest! I couldn't be closer to Jesus!"

She looked down at the letter and began to read to Henry:

"Dear Hannah,

Happy twelfth birthday! I will be at your party in spirit. So many of us here in heaven are filled with joy and laughter as we celebrate with you and the fun you are having!

I can just see how pretty you are in the white jumper that Matti or Camilla bought for you. I gave them a list… that's how I know!

When I was twelve, I still remember what I wished for when I blew out the candles. I wished we could live in Vancouver forever. My dad, who is also your grandfather, by the way, got transferred many times with his job. This was our fourth move and I loved British Columbia; the beautiful scenery and ocean. I wished we would stay in Vancouver forever. However, three years later, he was transferred again to Regina, Saskatchewan. At first, I didn't want to go but that all changed very quickly because on the second day we moved there, I met the man of my dreams, who of course, is now your father! More about that later in another letter!

If you are like I was when I was twelve, there are so many thoughts and feelings about life to deal with along with all the changes going on inside. There are some things you may feel more comfortable talking with Camilla about, but your dad is one you can trust all your life with, too. Even though I am not there with you, I am in spirit. You can come to me and share you're your joys, heartaches, crazy thoughts and wild ones, dreams and aspirations. I am ever so near to you.

Remember too, that you are a child of God. He is your heavenly father and is always available to you. Trust Him with all your heart and He will guide your life, perfectly. Things may not always turn out the way you want, but trust that it is the will of God and He will turn all things into good. Count your bless- ings every day and give thanks and praise to God for everything.

I know by now you have made a lot of new friends, but especially cherish the ones you feel most comfort- able with and trust. I had one true friend you may have heard about from family. Her name was Tammy. She and I were like to two peas in a pod. It is such a blessing if we have such a close friend in life who we can bear our hearts with beside family if at all possible.

I just know you have grown close to Jesus and have placed Him at the center of your life. You are a *special child, Hannah. Explore life to the full so you know the talents and abilities God has blessed you with. He has a plan for your life and wants you to work with Him and for Him. All of us are meant to be co-creators with Him.*

I wish I were there to hold and hug you and look into your sparkling eyes. They were blue when I held you so many years ago. I have a feeling though, that they still are.

Give a hug to Daddy for me, too!

Hannah, I love you always and into eternity!

Mom

CHAPTER SIXTY-THREE

A LTHOUGH TWELVE YEARS had passed, Jenny's death was still very fresh in Henry's mind. He would never be able to erase those last few minutes of that day in the hospital from his memory; how he held Jenny's hand as she slipped into heaven.

The very life Jenny had given birth to was next to his side. Henry could feel his dear sweet wife through Hannah's hand as they strolled through the cemetery. As soon as Henry entered the Memorial Gardens, he parked the car. It was about a block and half away from Jenny's grave site but it was such a beautiful spring day, he wanted to just unwind and enjoy his time with Hannah. They also liked to stop at the gravesites of other family members on the way to say 'hello' and a prayer.

Grandma and Grandpa Pederson were the first they came to and about one hundred yards further along was where Henry's own family was buried; Julean and Benjamin. An unmarked grave was designated for him when the time came. Henry wished he could have gotten a plot for Jenny near to where Julean was, but there were none available.

Henry placed the bouquet he was carrying at the base of Julean's tombstone and whispered a prayer to his dear first wife. Hannah squeezed his hand knowing the loss that her father was feeling. Henry was always astonished at his young daughter's empathy for what others were feeling. Often, he could hear her soft whispers praying to God asking that He comfort them.

Just as they were leaving Benjamin's site, a friendly voice greeted them. "Padre Pederson and Miss Hannah, it is so good to see you!"

Henry and Hannah turned to see Carlos and Maria walking towards them.

"Hi Carlos, Maria, I thought we might run into you."

"Yes, Señorita Jenny's site is flowering as beautiful as ever and just as I anticipated, some of the monarchs are there a month ahead of schedule. It is as if they know each year to the day when Jenny passed away."

"It is true," reiterated Maria, "Many of them must have perished trying to get here. It is too early to travel that great distance just to give their love to our precious Jenny."

When the friendly gardener and his wife were in front of Henry and Hannah, they warmly hugged one another.

"You look so much like your mother, Hannah. Señorita Jenny would have loved to see how her little angel is growing into such a beautiful girl."

"Thank you, Uncle Carlos. Please put a daisy in the Angel of Thanksgiving's basket for dad and me."

"I already did, Hannah," said Maria. "I also put a daisy at the foot of statue of the Blessed Mother, too. Jenny and Mary had such a close relationship."

"How are the ladies' groups doing, Maria?" asked Henry.

"We had a meeting this morning that was very powerful. Sometimes the sharing is so deep; we can all feel the presence of the Holy Spirit."

"I am pleased that you are continuing on with them."

"Oh, yes, and after all those years, some of the ladies still talk of that wonderful speech you gave to them and their husbands. Some said, their spouse took your words to heart and the home has grown in leaps!"

"That is good to hear, Maria. Praise the Lord that the Holy Spirit worked through me that evening."

"Yes, a very fine talk, Padre. Perhaps you and your family can come this Sunday for dinner? Your son and his family are at the grave site and we have asked them to come too.

Maria can prepare a wonderful Mexican dish for you and all the family."

"I would love that!" Hannah piped in.

Henry nodded and smiled, "Yes, that would be very nice, Carlos."

"We will see you again on Sunday. Adios and vaya con dios my friends."

"And may God go with you, too, my dear friends," Henry replied.

They had not walked more than ten steps further when Hannah said, "I see where Mom is sleeping from here, Dad."

"Yes, I see it, too. It looks beautiful."

Henry looked across the sea of tombstones but Jenny's was readily recognizable with the radiant wildflowers covering the mound over her grave site. When Jenny was buried, all the flowers which covered the coffin went down with her that day. The following spring everyone was surprised, especially the caretakers of the cemetery how the wildflowers shot up through the dirt and covered the entire mound. Henry suspected that might happen and he smiled thinking on the fruit which Jenny's angelic heart continued to bear.

As they approached the site, Camilla and the boys were already waving towards them. Henry couldn't get over how Noah was growing into such a fine young man. He was finishing grade twelve that year and off to university in the fall. There was no sight of Joshua as he was in the College of Engineering in Saskatoon. Jacob, who was Hannah's age, suddenly came into view. He was hidden behind Jenny's tombstone.

"Hi, Jeremy, Camilla," said Henry as he gave them both a hug. Hannah laid down the bouquet of white daisies with the yellow center she was holding amongst the other wildflowers and then quickly stood and gave everyone there a hug as well.

"It's truly amazing how the flowers keep coming up each year," remarked Camilla.

Henry shook his head. "It is a miracle—"

"And look at all the monarch butterflies flitting all about! That, too, is a miracle!" shouted Hannah.

"And look, there are countless more monarchs coming our way." echoed Jacob.

"Carlos was going to ask the cemetery groundskeeper if he could plant a milkweed plant at the grave site to attract butterflies but when we spoke earlier when they were here, he thought it may not be necessary. The monarchs seem to be just naturally drawn by Jenny's love for them."

"I agree, Jeremy. And with all the flowers here, there is probably enough food to feed them all."

"You should have been here an hour ago, Grandpa," said Noah. "Uncle Justin came and brought his blue kite and was flying it as he ran around the tombstones."

"It was such a sight, Dad!" said Camilla.

Henry smiled. He knew why his son did that. He still missed Jenny so much. "The kite has special meaning to him."

"I remember reading about that day when Justin and Mom were flying the kite behind the house up on the hill. That was the day Mom's love for him reached Justin's heart. I loved that scene in the book, Dad."

Unbidden tears surfaced in Henry's eyes. He couldn't speak for a moment and just nodded. He wished they had come earlier; he would have loved to see Justin trying out the kite.

Jeremy and his family stayed for another fifteen minutes while they all stood around Jenny's grave and said the rosary. When they left, Henry and Hannah said some more prayers and spoke with Jenny for over an hour. They both felt her presence and the warmth of her love. Tears surfaced in Henry's eyes as he gazed at Hannah, so much like Jenny in so many ways. Her hair shone like gold in the sun and her clear blue eyes sparkled just like her mother's.

Thank you for the gift of our daughter, sweetheart, Henry silently prayed. *She gives light to my days and joy to my heart, just like you did. Thank you for this beautiful gift. You knew I would need her when you were gone. She is so precious and you were blessed to give her back to God. He has a special plan for her life and she truly has your angelic heart. I love you, darling.*

After visiting all of their loved ones, they began to meander back to the SUV. Henry stopped abruptly as he came into a familiar area of long ago. There before him was the large tombstone with the inscription:

JACOB STEVENS
ETERNALLY I ASK
FOR FORGIVENESS

"What's wrong, Daddy?"

"Oh, I am just thinking about that tombstone, honey. It means a lot to me how God used it in so many ways to bring healing to my family."

"Yes, I remember reading about that in book two, Dad. It was such a beautiful scene between you and your father after Anna's interment."

Henry simply nodded. His daughter had learned so much about his life through the story. At times it was a little unsettling. Almost as if she could see into his past life and how he felt about things that happened to him.

He recalled that day as if it were yesterday and smiled at the thought of how God uses every opportunity to work through His Divine Providence; how He used an inscription on a tombstone to touch his dad's heart and seek forgiveness for what he had done.

His mom was touched by the inscription too, and thanked Mr. Stevens for prompting her to seek reconciliation for her lack of forgiveness to Bill for his unfaithfulness.

Hannah read the inscription out loud, breaking into Henry's thoughts. She then asked, "What did this man do to ask for forgiveness forever, Dad?"

Henry stared at the inscription and said, "Well, that's the thing, Hannah. At one time, I used to think it was for something bad which he did, but now, I think he might have had a different meaning in mind; maybe something for all of us to think on."

"And what is that?" Hannah wanted to know.

"Well, I think Jacob was simply saying he was sorry for all the times he was disobedient to Jesus; when he turned his back on Him and did what he wanted and not what Jesus wanted him to do. He was like all of us, honey. We all make mistakes and do things we shouldn't do. Time and again we ask Jesus for forgiveness for being so foolish and the hurt we cause Him.

"It seems to me, Mr. Jacobs realized as he journeyed through life the great sacrifice which Jesus did for him by dying on the cross so he could go to heaven. Perhaps, Hannah, as we realize this in our heart, we, too, like Steven, will eternally ask for forgiveness."

Hannah reflected on what her father had said and then offered her thoughts on the matter.

"But, Daddy," Hannah began, "We don't have to keep asking Jesus for forgiveness forever. If we say we are sorry with all of our heart, He will forgive us. We don't have to be sad and feel guilty all the time like Mr. Stevens. God is our Father in heaven and we are His children and He loves us just like you do, Dad.

"It almost seems like Mr. Jacobs was trapped by his sins or whatever great act he committed. Maybe he didn't understand how merciful, loving, and forgiving Jesus is. Maybe he didn't realize that Jesus died for our sins, He paid the price for all of them and if we come to Him with a sincere heart, it is forgiven and forgotten."

Hannah paused for a moment. Henry was going to respond but Hannah went on. "I don't think God wants us to focus on ourselves, or our sins as it means we don't take Him by His word that our sins are forgiven. We should feel free of fear and guilt and living with eternity in mind for ourselves, our family and neighbor.

"And, and, … didn't you say in your books over and over that God is present in the present, the now of life. The now is when we are present to God and others. It all makes so much sense, Daddy. That is when our service to God's will is with us. We are at one with Him, we are at peace, our minds are clear and alert to love and heal and bring the light. I wonder if Mr.

Jacobs thought about that or did he dwell on his sins. Did he fail to claim his victory in life and enjoy the gift!?"

Henry could see the fire in his daughter's eyes. They flashed and sparkled with excitement and conviction. And once again, before Henry could respond she went on.

"Mr. Stevens and all of us should claim that victory. It's free! Let us be filled with joy, praise and gratitude. The more we reflect great joy because we are filled with the Holy Spirit and the indwelling presence of Jesus, the more we will draw others to Jesus, Dad. Not dwelling on our sins eternally..." Hannah's words trailed off.

Henry stopped and turned towards Hannah, amazed at her comprehension and astounded by her answer. He had to admit that he, too many times, was trapped in his guilt, shame and sins. He didn't take Jesus at His word that he was forgiven and should move forward with joy, and thanksgiving.

Hannah was beyond her years and yet, Henry thought at 12 years of age, Jesus, was about His Father's work, too. He was already teaching the church elders in the temple. In a similar way, Hannah was filled with the Holy Spirit. Her heart overflowed with Jesus and His love. She radiated Jesus. Why would she not be blessed with wisdom and grace!? She, too, was about her Father's work. She had the added advantage of not only being born blessed as a child who belonged to God but by reading the story over and over and all the wisdom she gleaned from Father Engelmann, her mother and from Henry's failings in life and final redemption. It all filled her mind with God and Jesus and all He did. It drew her to the Bible and Jesus' teachings. Hand in hand, with the story and the Bible, she grew close to the Lord and filled with wisdom. And further, she knew she was a child of God and she, more that most children, lived with this purpose and meaning in mind. She was destined to do God's work in a mighty way.

"The answer you gave was filled with much truth and wisdom, Hannah, but there is something we can learn from this. Yes, maybe, Mr. Stevens had it wrong. Maybe he didn't understand how merciful, loving, and forgiving Jesus is. Yet,

God is the God of possibilities, He knows how to use any circumstance and bring good out of it.

"Take Jacob Stevens for example, God took Jacob where he was at in life. In spite of Jacob being trapped in his search for forgiveness, as we are surmising, look how God used the statement he had chiseled out on the tombstone for good. Look at how many people have come by here over the years and seen this tombstone like my dad or my mom or even me. We didn't see what you just saw Hannah but rather we were reminded by God for the need to seek forgiveness.

"In my dad's case, he said he didn't want to go through life trapped by what he did and sought forgiveness. In Mom's case, she knew that it was this tombstone which motivated dad to change and seek forgiveness and to forgive himself. In my case, it motivated me to forgive John for being the cause of Julien's death. So, while it may have held Jacob back from true fulfillment and joy in the goodness of what Jesus had done for him, God turned it all into good and who knows, Jacob may have received true joy from God for asking for forgiveness eternally.

"You see, Hannah, there are always different ways of looking at things based upon a person's life experiences. In any case, God sees possibilities for growth and ways to draw people back to Him in every situation."

"That's beautiful, Father. I understand. See, it all goes back to the cross. Through such a horrific act as the crucifixion would come such good in so many different ways surrounding forgiveness. You have given me something more to ponder in my heart."

Henry smiled at his daughter and wished Jenny was here and could have heard those words and see the fine young girl, Hannah was growing up to be. Then again, he had the feeling that his dear sweet wife was near.

He looked up but only saw the fresh green leaves of spring fluttering in the breeze. High on one of the elm trees, he heard the sound of a meadow lark. He couldn't see it but there was no mistaking the melody it sung. Henry smiled, just one more sign that Jenny was close by.

New life was abounding everywhere despite the fact that they were surrounded by death. Tall stones of shaped granite standing like sentinels marked those who have died. But their spirits were alive and life goes on bringing us closer with each passing year to our eternal home, too.

Hannah must have read his mind. Softly she asked, "How many people here do you think lived a happy life, Daddy?"

"That's a good question, honey. It all depends on how they chose to live. I can say that those who took the time to know Jesus, were the ones who were more at peace. They were people who trusted Jesus with their worries and cares and thus were freer to live in the present moments of life. They were the ones I believe that came closer to being all they could be in this life—"

"And they were the ones whose hearts were filled like mommy's; with praise and gratitude."

Henry turned to his daughter, "Yes, Hannah, when we realize the goodness of God and all he has given us, we do live a life of continual thanksgiving for all our blessings!"

"Just like mom did!"

Silently, they gazed across the sea of tombstones. Yes, the people here were all now at peace from their life in this world but where were they now in eternity?

That was the question.

Henry took a deep breath of fresh air and detected a hint of lilac fragrance in the air. He looked around but there weren't any lilac bushes and it was too early for them to be in bloom. He looked up again and back at Hannah. He shook his head and thought he might play a game with Hannah and get his mind off the supernatural.

"So, Hannah, what else might Jacob Stevens have written on his tombstone instead of what he did?"

Hannah thought for a minute and said, "How about, Eternally, I am grateful to Jesus."

"Hmm, that's a good one, Hannah. How about, Eternally, I will Praise God."

Hannah nodded, thought a bit more and said, "Eternally, I will love Jesus."

"Now that gets to the heart of the matter, Hannah, I think it pretty well sums it up. If we love God with all our heart and soul and mind and everyone else like ourselves, we will be eternally happy forever and ever in God's kingdom."

Hannah gazed up at her father; her blue eyes sparkling in the afternoon sun and said the final word in the matter...

"Amen, Daddy!"

No sooner had the words left his daughter's lips when suddenly a rain shower came out of nowhere. They were at least a half block from the truck. "Quick, Daddy, quickly, hold my hand."

The words startled Henry. Hannah had never said them before. Without hesitation, Henry reached out but it wasn't Hannah's hand he felt at that moment. Henry would never forget the feel of Jenny's soft, warm hand in his. He looked up at the lone, rain filled cloud sailing tranquilly in the vast expanse of the prairie blue sky. Just the way it wisped in the heavens, it looked like an angel with extended wings.

A knowing smile played on Henry's lips as he whispered soft as a feather...

"I knew you were here, Jenny..., I love you!"

And the thought immediately came back to him, "I love you all the more."

Chapter Sixty-Four

I T WAS LATE October and the temperature was just above freezing. Snow had fallen earlier in the week but quickly melted. There was always that transition period on the prairies when one had to adjust to a new season emerging. The older one gets, the more difficult it was to make that adjustment; especially from fall to winter. Henry would have preferred to be home by the fireside and yet his passion to advance the kingdom of God far overpowered his own comforts and the challenges of nature.

Every night last week, Henry was doing presentations that he had booked earlier that past spring and summer. It was three years since he had done all the churches in Regina and he was invited to do them all again. Parishioners were not only anxious to hear how Henry's missionary work was doing but they also wanted to listen to what he had to say about the *Angelic Letters Series* which he and Father Engelmann had written.

Henry had tried to have the last book seven in the series, *The Heart of an Angel*, all completed and released that fall but the many commitments he had during the year made it impossible to get it out. He knew many people would be disappointed if he didn't release it next spring. He was not hopeful that might happen either as the New Year seemed even busier.

Henry, along with Hannah, pulled up to the parking lot behind the church and next to the hall where he would be speaking that evening. They were early. Their breath hung in the cool air as they walked briskly to the hall. They had to set up the slide projector and get the other audio equipment ready for Father Pederson's presentation. Volunteers were watching for their arrival and ran out to help them as soon as they had parked their car.

While Henry set up the screen and projector, Hannah and church volunteers got books from the SUV and began setting up a display on several tables at the back of the hall. When the presentation and talk was over, Henry would go back there to help with the sales of the series and to sign the latest sixth book, *The House Where Angels Dwell*. At seven-thirty, they were all ready for Henry's talk and presentation which was set to start at eight o'clock.

As was Henry's usual practice at these events, he sat in the front row and waited until the time for him to begin. He still couldn't believe that after all those years he had dreamed of doing missionary work, he was finally doing it! He realized that his time with Father Engelmann was his novitiate to speak for the Lord. He was in a lifelong training program. It started in grade eight as a novice and it had taken almost a life time to finally be ready to fully enter into the service of God. Although he had anticipated doing some type of work to help the missions, what he never anticipated was that he would be doing so as a priest and author.

He marveled at God's Divine Providence as he looked back and how finally he was able to free himself from the clutches of the world. He had given most of what he had away to his children and charities he supported. All he wanted was to retreat to the prayer house occasionally to continue his writing and painting whenever it could work into his busy schedule. Service to God and others was now first and foremost in his life.

Henry checked his watch; it was fifteen minutes to eight. He started to feel twinges of nervousness, but his feelings never escalated to the point of becoming debilitating as he was always surrounded by the comfort and assurance of his unseen loved ones. Whenever he approached the podium, he always felt the soft touch of his guardian angel on the back of his shoulder and the warmth of Jenny's and Julean's hand in each of his. What calmed Henry completely though was when he gazed out to the audience; there in the front row in the seat which he had occupied was his mentor. Henry knew when he received Father's signal, the hearts of all those present were touched by the Holy Spirit and would now be receptive to the Word and his message. At that point, Henry always felt he was now empowered by the Holy Spirit and ready to begin.

By eight o'clock, the hall was filled to capacity and Catherine, the hostess for that evening, approached the microphone to introduce Henry. This was the second time Henry spoke to members of that congregation but still there were new parishioners and this time Henry's talk was not so much about his missionary work, but on the series of books which he published under the name of Pio-Seelos Books.

Catherine described Henry's eclectic career; how he journeyed from being a teacher, counselor, professional artist, gallery curator, entrepreneur and author, to becoming a priest and aligning himself with missionary work. Catherine went on to inform those present that Henry would come to speak about all the books in the series to date and the final book seven which would hopefully be released next spring on Mother's Day following a brief slide presentation and talk.

As Catherine left the stage, the lights in the hall slowly dimmed and after a minute or two a calm, peaceful atmosphere was created. Out of the silence emerged the sound of a voice that could only be described as angelic. The purity of the sound was so sweet and melodic it took ones' breath away. Instantly, one was transported into another world by the words and calling of her song. As Margaret Tearhorst began to sing "Whatsoever you do," the images projected on the screen came to life and touched the hearts of all those present...

The slides required no explanation; it was easy for people of the western world to see poverty in all its forms: families living on the streets, their homes defined by strings and cardboard and pieces of rags and plastic. Men laying in the gutters, children drinking water from a polluted river or lake, children wearing rags and sharing but a handful of food at supper time.

People, young and old, just skin and bones, staring wide-eyed, revealing the emptiness, hunger and desolation.

Margaret's words mingling with each image calling for compassion and aid...

> "What so ever you do to the least of my brothers, that you
>   do unto me.
> When I was hungry you gave me to eat,
> When I was thirsty you gave me to drink,
> Now enter into the home of my Father...
>
> What so ever you do to the least of my brothers..."

And then, the slides took on an encouraging, heartening course; pictures of hope showing what was done through the care, kindness and compassion of people supporting the mission. Happy children, clean and dressed in uniforms sitting in classrooms or playing in a fenced lot; children eating lunch in a cafeteria. Children were witnessing the love of Jesus lived out in action through the love of His people reaching out to their brothers and sisters. Now, the crosses hanging on the wall was meaningful. Now, the cross hanging in hospitals, dormitories, churches had significance. Now, the people were praising and thankful for the water wells and the volunteers who came to teach them how to look after themselves and their people. The basics of life being met by people who cared and reflected the love of Jesus. Now, the great commission was being lived out in action and good works.

People in the audience could not only see the great needs of their brothers and sisters but could put an image as to how the money which they gave was used. Father Pederson didn't just want people to write out a cheque but to feel the responsibility they had towards people who had so much less in so many ways. Father wanted charity to become a way of life. Helping others out of love and compassion; to witness to others by their giving; teaching charity in the home so their children grow up with their brothers and sisters in mind. This is not just some isolated act that we do once or twice a year but year-round. *Jesus is the vine and we are the branches.*

If there was anyone amongst the crowd of people there who was affected most deeply by Henry's words, it was his daughter, Hannah, sitting in the front row. She was so proud of her dad and what he was doing. She too wanted to do the same.

When her father had finished book six and they discussed its contents, Hannah learned of the covenant her mother had made with God concerning her. The story helped her to understand the deep calling she felt to go into a vocation. It all began in her mother's womb and God's heart. She loved the Scripture, Jeremiah 1:5; "Before you were in your mother's womb I consecrated you." Hannah understood the real significance of this passage was becoming clearer in her understanding of her calling. She was given back to God and the desire to do His will was so powerful and strong in her being. She loved to be present with her dad when he said Mass in the Poustinia and she would spend hours in prayer there as well.

This past year, Hannah had read about so many different orders; the Carmelite Nuns, Sisters of the Precious Blood, the Poor Clares, the Dominican Sister of Peace and many others. Even at her young age, she was already thinking about whether she was called to be a 'nun' and lead a cloistered or semi-cloistered life of quiet and prayer or be a 'sister' who lives, ministers and prays within the world like the sisters who belong to Mother Teresa's order. Both were vital to the salvation of the world. Both required vows of poverty, obedience and chastity. She was still young and had several years to decide, but for now, her heart tugged in the direction of joining her father and helping him to bring the peace, love and justice of Jesus to the world.

Hannah sat up as her thoughts entered once more into the present moment. It was at times confusing for her to separate Henry as being her dad and also that he was a priest. Father Pederson was coming to the end of his talk about helping missions and now relating it all to the *Angelic Letters Series*. Hannah loved the love story about her mother and dad. She loved Father Engelmann and wished she had known the holy man. She loved to read of his wisdom and teachings and could see so clearly how his mentorship had rubbed off on her father. But more than anything, she loved the essence of the story to become like Jesus and bring His light into the world.

This was the part she especially liked about her father's presentation. He was coming to the end of his talk which she always found so inspiring. She sat up in her chair and listened and dreamed what kind of a story she would write in her life and what she was going to do. She listened to her father now...

"We often feel that we are helpless and insignificant in changing the world for the better. This is not so, as witnessed in my sharing with you the ripple effect of what happened when Father Engelmann stepped out in faith and began to write this story. It's important to remember that we are all God's children created out of love for love. Through Jesus, we are all connected, all brothers and sisters, all one with the Father. Everything we do affects the entire family of God. Think of it this way: a cup of water spilled into the sea may seem like nothing and yet the entire ocean just expanded by that one cup of water.

"In the same way, it may seem what we do is insignificant, but the tiniest act of love we do affects the entire world because we are all connected! A friendly greeting, a smile, an act of kindness not only affects others but can be used by God to transform lives. He sees all, knows all, even the number of hairs on our heads. He knows instantly when the world He created just got better because of an act of love.

"If there is a message I would like to leave with you is that we are co-creators with God. His creative spirit, through His Divine Providence, is at work in our world every second of every minute of every day. This story is only one small example of it. As Father Engelmann and I stepped out in faith, God was right there to guide, lead, inspire us and expand it all tenfold, hundredfold and more! Without Him there would be no *Angelic Letters Series*. Both Father Engelmann and I are the first to admit this entire story is a gift from Him. And yet, without Father or me saying yes, and using our free will and beginning, there would not be a story either.

"We are co-creators with Him. We have all been gifted with the great responsibility of serving as good stewards of all of God's gifts to us. The parable of Jesus giving the three men different talents, telling them that they should faithfully use them, in Matthew 5:14-30, confirms this. He has called us from all eternity to be His hands, His arms, His eyes, His legs and His ears and His heart. When we fully understand our purpose on earth and place Jesus at the center and receive His light, strength and grace to do the will of the Father, then we will be able to bring the Lord's healing love into every situation and advance His entire kingdom. That is how we carry out the three great commandments of Jesus; to love our God, to love our neighbor as ourselves and to carry out His great commission.

"This, my brothers and sisters in Christ, is the message at the heart of the *Angelic Letters Series.*

"In closing, I would just like to say that we are not all called to be authors of books. But whether we realize it or not, all of us do in a sense write our own life story. Daily, we wake up to a new day in which we write another chapter of our lives by the way we *choose* to live. The person who disciplines himself or herself to pray and meditate upon awakening is the one more likely to write a bestseller of their life when they close the cover to their story on earth.

"Starting the day in this way is the one thing Father Engelmann stresses over and over in the series. If we want to know what God's plan is for our lives and be able to do His will to achieve His divine purposes, it is imperative to retreat each day to quiet the incessant chatter and endless noise that continuously bombards our minds. The distractions today are endless. Our thoughts so much of the time are like the rapids of a raging river. We need to find a place of calm in our home or in nature beside a calm, placid pond which reflects the peace and love of God.

"Imagine you are by the prayer house where angels dwell. Imagine you are sitting with Father Engelmann on the deck by the pond in the presence of God the Father. Imagine the peace, serenity and soothing sound of the babbling stream and meadow-lark. Imagine the beauty of the green hills, trees, shrubs and wild-flowers reflecting in the sparkling water under the rising sun. Slowly your mind, hearts and very being is brought into the present moment.

"*Your spirit is quiet and at rest and receptive to the Lord...*

"In between the silence you will hear the flutter of wings as God whispers words of wisdom and what He wants of us. Only then can you begin to see the wonderfully, creative way to write a chapter that draws more and more people to Him through our lives. This is the kind of book we want to write! And at the end of the day as we write the last chapter and we close the book of our lives, may we feel that our writing reflected God's will and Divine Providence. It may not be a New York best seller but surely a best seller in heaven, only because, Jesus was always the main character in our story."

Father Pederson paused for but a moment and reached out his hands to the audience and fervently said, "Come, quickly hold my hand, together...we will bring the light and peace and love of Jesus to the world!"

Henry stepped down from the raised platform and holding out his hands, made his way to the people. They in turn stood and took each other's hands and raised them upwards to the heavens and together they sang along with Margaret, *I will Choose Christ**:

I will choose Christ, I will choose love, I choose to serve.
I give my heart, I give my life, I give my all to You.
To You. I give my all to You.

How many times must He call my name
and show to me that He is God?
And as a servant He calls to me,
"You must serve too."...

---

*   By Tom Booth

Early Spring

Two years later

GOOD FRIDAY

APRIL 6, 2007

CHAPTER SIXTY-FIVE

ALL THE SNOW was gone. Spring was early. Winter had its cold spell at the beginning of March and a week later, the temperature rose above freezing and it stayed there. The weather was so mild that by the end of the week, most of the snow had melted except for those patches that hid in the shadows.

Hannah loved to watch the spring runoff in the valley. The stream which meandered through the valley rose over three feet that week above the banks, running wild all-over the valley floor. It looked like spring was there to stay at the beginning of April, but two days ago, a sudden storm ran across the mid-southern part of the province, reminding prairie folks what they had learned time again; one never knows for certain on the prairies what the weather will be like at times, from hour to hour.

During the last two days spring was back in full force. A chinook came in from Alberta and once again, most of the snow was gone. Little rivulets ran all over the road leading down to the prayer house. It reminded Hannah of Grandma Vera Carter's face. So many wrinkles had etched into her face over time and the image of seeing her lay in the coffin over a month ago, still remained in the young girl's memory. Hannah chuckled to herself how the mind can conjure up and mix together totally disconnected images.

By the time she got to the Poustinia, Hannah's shoes were so muddy, she had grown over three inches. She tried to kick off the big clumps before she stepped onto the deck, but the mud was so packed and sticky, Hannah's effort to remove the gumbo was in vain. Frustrated, she sat on the edge of the deck and removed her shoes. It felt good; they weighed a ton!

Father Pederson was supposed to come home for lunch and pick up Hannah and together they would return to the city for the three o'clock service at St. Mary's Church. However, an emergency came up. He had to rush to the General Hospital to give someone the last rites and visit with the family. All the other Pederson family members were busy and so, Hannah decided to walk down to the prayer house and make the Stations of the Cross and have some quiet time with the Lord. In effect, Hannah believed that her prayers would unite with all the other churches and prayers offered up to God in memory of the crucifixion and death of His dearly beloved Son, our Lord and Savior.

Hannah was still savoring the service her dad and Father Knuka held at the church last night. It was such a humble act for both priests to re-enact what Jesus did the night before he died by washing the feet of twelve parishioners. For her dad and Father Knuka to do that was one thing but to picture the Lord Himself doing that seemed unthinkable and yet, that is what Jesus, the Almighty King of the universe did. "Oh, my dear Lord, please help me to serve and be humble like that," Hannah whispered.

The sweet odor of sanctity filling the air in the prayer house complimented the young girl's thoughts. Hannah knew that it was the smell of humility. The fragrance of Father Engelmann's spirit, whose heart was filled with mercy, compassion and love, lingered in the atmosphere. Hannah considered it an honor and privilege to be surrounded by so many dear people who picked up their cross and followed Jesus so completely. Her mom, dad, Father Engelmann, Camilla, Jeremy and so many other family members had been such powerful influences in her life. What Hannah didn't yet realize was how her life, too, was instilling faith not only to her family, but to everyone she encountered.

Hannah's heart went out to Jesus as she knelt before the large cross hanging above the altar. The sculptor who had chiseled out the form and image of Christ, accurately portrayed the fate of that sorrowful Friday so many years ago when Jesus gave up His life for us. The wooden spikes, trails of blood from the wounds on His hands, feet and side where the spear penetrated Jesus' chest and heart, were clearly shown. It was all so beautifully sculpted out in wood and yet, no matter how skilled, there wouldn't be anyone alive who could ever capture the pain, agony and torture the Lord had endured for all of mankind.

The suffering of Jesus was evident throughout Hannah's entire being. Glistening tears were soon revealed in Hannah's eyes as she relived all the grief and sorrow of that momentous day. How Jesus, like a lamb, was led to the slaughter; quietly, purposefully and offering no resistance. He accepted His mission; to die for our sins and make right our relationship with the Father.

The white Sunday Missal she held in her hands belonged to Julean, her dad's first wife. Henry had given the book along with a rosary to her before they got married. It was all recorded on the inside cover of the Saint Joseph Sunday Missal:

This missal belongs to:
Julean Carter
I hope this missal and rosary
increase your love for Jesus and
devotion to Mary.
August 19, 1962
With all my love,
Hank

Hannah tried to picture the other woman in Henry's life but her distraction was brief. She quickly went back to meditate upon the scenes of the different Stations of the Cross which were depicted near the back of the missal.

Imagine, the King of the universe, all things in heaven and earth created through Him, agreeing to become man and undergoing what He did for us. How could Jesus allow Himself to stand before Pilot and be judged when the only thing He was guilty of was loving the earthly judge, the man standing in front Him, and all of us, too much!

His crime was 'love!'

Hannah couldn't begin to imagine the scourging at the pillars; the kicks and blows to the head and body. Being spat on and mocked. Cords, tied around his hands, lifted him up on the column to expose his body for the whipping that followed. Whips made of leather with metal balls at the tips were alternated with whips that held sharp metal hooks at the ends.

Hannah winced as she saw in the screen of her mind her dearly beloved Lord's flesh pulled off and flung through air with each excruciating lash. If only she could have been there to tend to His wounds and plead for them to stop. It was unbelievable that the scourging didn't kill Jesus at the pillar. How did He survive it all? He was so drained of blood and weakened by the bruises, suffering the repeated lashes and crown of thorns. How in that condition could He carry the cross up the hill to Calvary? Surely His spirit could have given up at any time. He had already suffered too much!

It must have been the 'cross' that sustained Him. The cross which would become the eternal symbol of His love for us.

Yes, there was more to suffer. More pain to endure; the metal spikes tearing through His hands and feet and ripping through His flesh as the cross was raised and the weight of his body pulled down. There, against the backdrop of the heavens, hung our Lord, fully exposed, so the memory of it all would be burned into our hearts and minds, how dearly, totally and completely He loved us. There is no greater love than to lay down one's life for a friend.

There is nothing more to give!

"Oh, Lord," Hannah cried out. "So often, we take this all for granted. So often, we don't give this day and all You suffered a second thought! You have shown us the extent of your mercy, grace and forgiveness and yet, how often we fail to do the same. At the slightest remark against us, how quickly we hold resentment and forgiveness back. How quickly we forget the cross, failing to extend the mercy and forgiveness you have shown us to others."

It was as if Hannah were at the foot of the cross next to Mary. The horror and indescribable torment of it all swept through the young girl's vivid imagination so clearly, she fell to floor and began weeping.

Deep sobs of sorrow pulsed through her body as she gasped for air. She smelled the odor of blood. She recalled Father Engelmann lying there where she was now. Henry had shown her where he had found his dear mentor and friend that memorable day. Hannah couldn't imagine how Father was blessed with the Stigmata and received all five wounds. She wanted to ask God for that rare gift too but was too afraid. All she could do was cry out to Jesus to have mercy on her and the whole world. Over and over, she pleaded for mercy, repenting how sorry she was.

Hannah tried to understand the love that Jesus had which would make Him undergo such an immense sacrifice. To be so humble and submit to all He endured. When Henry spoke to the congregation last evening at the service, he reminded everyone that even though Jesus was true God, truly Divine, He was also truly man; body and soul. Jesus showed His humanity the night before He died when He prayed in the Garden of Gethsemane to God that this cup be taken away from Him. He revealed that all He would undergo and suffer would be felt the same as any human being on this earth.

Hannah couldn't fathom making such a sacrifice for sinners; people who are so cruel and unappreciative and turn their back to you at every turn. And it was not just the suffering and pain but there was that moment before He died in which He was all alone; hanging there, carrying her sins and those of all mankind.

Completely separated from the Father. The words of Jesus asking His Father why He had abandoned Him, *haunted her.*

How could this be? What kind of love is this?

Her father would never do that to her and yet, God allows pain and suffering to achieve His purposes. Look at the good God brought out through the crucifixion of His Son. Jesus fully trusted the Father and was obedient to Him and as a result, the gates of heaven were opened and we were once again part of the Father's family. Jesus came to serve and save mankind. He came to wash everyone's feet and He wants us to do the same.

Hannah felt the nearness of Father Engelmann. His love was rooted in Jesus' love on the cross. He embodied the prayer he said every day in honor of the sacred wounds:[*]

My crucified Jesus!
I adore the Wounds in Thy Sacred Head
With sorrow deep and true
May every thought of mine today
Be an act of love for You.

I adore the Wounds of Thy Sacred Hands
With sorrow deep and true
May every work of my hands today
Be an act of Love for You

I adore the Wounds in Thy Sacred Feet
With sorrow deep and true
May every step I take today
Be an act of Love for You.

I adore the Wounds in Thy Sacred Heart
With sorrow deep and true
May every beat of my heart today
Be an act of Love for You.

Amen

---

[*] Written by Fr. Bob Weiss, C.P.

Father Engelmann was one who lived out, obeyed and followed Jesus' example so that he might bring his beloved Lord to others. Look at the pain and suffering he endured when the wounds of Christ were inflicted upon him. Father Engelmann had offered his life for her father. Imagine the love Father Engelmann had for Jesus to bring Him and His immense sacrifice to the doorstep for Henry to see and accept the love Jesus had for him.

"Oh, Lord help me to reflect Your love to others, too. Love which comes from You is forgiving, healing and compassionate. How could Your love not be anything but merciful and filled with grace? Please, Jesus, help me to die to myself so I can be filled with Your love from the cross."

Hannah rose and sat behind the kneeler and continued to gaze at the cross. Such a powerful symbol that embodied so much...so very much. What a perfect way, yet so costly, for God and His Son to show Their endless love for us. In dying, the blood and water that poured out from Your side and wounds flowed out as a font of mercy and compassion for us. What an incredible, powerful, love filled moment that was; the moment we were allowed to come home again! Hannah could feel Christ's endless mercy that opened that day and will continue to eternity.

Tears rolled down Hannah's cheeks as she thought how often we ignore and take for granted the unfathomable love which Jesus wraps around all mankind.

Hannah began to pray out loud again. Her words softly echoed off the walls of the holy chapel. "Oh, heavenly Father, never allow me to take lightly what the Lord has done. Let me always remember that it is through us that Jesus reveals Himself to others! Look at Mom and Father Engelmann and my dad. Seeing Jesus in them instills faith and belief in others. This is our task; to love as You have shown us how to love. It is so wonderful to read about Mom and how she had the heart of an angel; how the fruits of the Holy Spirit flowed from her heart. Peace, love, forbearance, patience kindness, forgiveness and gentleness were irresistible gifts she passed onto all those whom she encountered.

"How could others not help but see Jesus?

"And Father Engelmann who lived by the Scripture: 'I have been crucified with Christ; it is no longer I who live, but Christ who lives in me; and the life I now live in the flesh, I live by faith in the Son of God who loved me and gave Himself for me.' How fortunate daddy was, to have such a teacher, friend and mentor. Mom and Father Engelmann knew, as Dad does too, the great responsibility we have, to live for Jesus. How fortunate I am to have a saint for my mom and such an inspiring father. Oh Lord, bless me that I, too, have inherited their hearts! I dedicate my life, my every thought, word and deed to Jesus so that it reflects Him continuously to all I meet."

The Holy Spirit had made His home in Hannah's heart as soon as she was born. She was baptized in the Spirit. She had grown up with the Spirit so strong in her life that it was not unnatural for her to speak in tongues. For the longest time, Camilla thought that the babbling was just baby talk and then rambling on that children sometimes do. Gradually, though, her step-mom realized that Hannah was speaking in tongues. It just naturally flowed from her lips. It was not unlike the times Camilla had heard Father Engelman pray over people.

Hannah knew at the core of her being, as she stared at the cross, that Jesus had shed His blood for her and it was her life mission to return that love. She belonged to Him and prayed constantly that He reveal His plan for her life. She loved Saint Therese and identified with her. She was just a year older when she entered the Carmelite Order. Hannah loved the way Therese loved flowers like her mom did. She also loved the way Therese promised to send roses to people who prayed for her intercession.

Yet, as much as she loved the cloistered order and the great need to pray for mankind and ask mercy for our sins, she loved working for others too. One of the highlights of her brief life so far was when she went to India with her father for three weeks. Oh, how her heart went out to the poor, sick and dying. She had no revulsion in holding their hands or praying for so many in the moments of their passing.

Hannah heeded her father's advice to wait upon the Lord to show her His plan for her life. She was blessed to have such great models! Her heart's desire was to follow in the footsteps of her Mom and Father Engelmann. They both lived lives which flowed with such sweet calm and inward peace, because they had Jesus at the core of their being. Her heroes clearly showed that it is not what they did for Jesus but what He did for them. Without Jesus we can do nothing but with Him we can do everything. The graces and blessings abound! Our lives come alive! We can even become saints!

It was getting late. The light in the prayer house was growing dim. Hannah got up and looked outside. The shadows were rapidly spreading across the valley floor as the sun was sinking in the western sky. She thought she better head back up to the house before it got too dark.

She prayed for her guardian angel to protect her.

As she was about to say the guardian angel prayer, the first prayer that miraculously came to her so early in life and said countless times, her thoughts returned to the cross. Today, after witnessing the effect of sin on our Lord, Hannah seemed prompted to add another sentence to her heartfelt prayer as it flowed from her lips in a soft whisper:

Angel of God, my guardian dear,
through whom God's love
commits me here.
Ever this day, be at my side,
to light, to guard, to rule and guide.
From sinful stain, oh keep us free.
And, in death's hour, our helper be!

CHAPTER SIXTY-SIX

TODAY, WAS MAY 2, 2007, exactly 14 years since Jenny's passing. Henry and Hannah had planned to visit the grave site that afternoon like they did every year. They not only wanted to celebrate the Mass at the prayer house in honor of Jenny's memory, but also for her intercession, along with Padre Pio and Father Seelos, to spread the final book in the Angelic Letters Series across the world.

Book seven, *The Heart of an Angel* was printed the first week of April and was going to be released on Mother's Day in stores across Canada in just eleven days! Acting on behalf of Saint Padre Pio and Father Francis Xavier Seelos, as publisher, Henry was very pleased with how the book turned out; the cover was attractive and filled with symbolism, the contents and message was inspired to touch the hearts of readers and this would finally bring the epic story, after months of many delays, to its conclusion.

When Henry came down for breakfast, he noticed a light on in the kitchen and a note on the counter:

Hi Dad,

*I went down to the prayer house. I'll wait for you
to say Mass.*

*Love you,
Hannah*

Henry couldn't get over how much Hannah loved to pray, read the Bible and be with the Lord. He was so eager to celebrate Mass, that he decided to skip breakfast, too, and head straight down.

The air was fresh, the wind calm and the sky was clear blue, just like St. Jennifer's eyes. It was the beginning of a glorious day! He took a deep breath of morning air and began his trek to the prayer house. Even though Ginger had died over four years ago, he still missed not having her at his side. He decided not to get another dog as he was so seldom at home with being on the road, travelling from parish to parish, doing his missionary presentations. Justin moved into the city after he got married and so much of the time, the house was empty, except for those times when Camilla and Jeremy and their children came out to enjoy the valley and visit the Poustinia.

It was a hectic several weeks; the rush to get all the details involved in getting a book ready for publication was demanding enough but Hannah's birthday, just under three weeks ago, kept things hopping as well. As usual, everyone came to celebrate Hannah's fourteenth birthday and some of the family stayed longer than usual. It was a sad time in part as both Jack and Vera passed away during the winter within weeks of one another. Jack was the first to go and while it was attributed to natural causes, Vera's passing was clearly due to a broken heart and not just old age.

Another tragedy had also occurred during the past year; Eddy and Coreena both drowned when the boat Eddy was working on for over twelve years capsized during a storm on its maiden voyage. Unfortunately, the incident occurred a mile or so away from the Island of Jamaica and their bodies were not recovered. All four were deeply missed at this year's re-union and party. That was one of the reasons why some family and guests stayed longer, just to reminisce and help heal the memories of their dear friends passing.

All in all, it was a wonderful party for Hannah. She had grown so much; tall and very beautiful, just like her mother. She looked older than fourteen and to talk to her was like talking to a fully mature lady who was very perceptive, insightful, intelligent and as close to the Lord as her skin. If it hadn't been for her strong social skills, development and mature appearance, the school would not have accelerated her a third time. At fourteen, Hannah was finishing grade eleven and at the top of her class.

At the party, it made Henry think of the similarity between Jeremy and Hannah. Jeremy, too, had accelerated quickly through school. He grew tall and matured quickly. Henry had always believed it was part of God's Divine Providence so Jeremy would end up meeting Camilla and amazingly, how it was a major factor in bringing Henry and Jenny back together again.

But the similarity stopped there. Jeremy never grew so close to the Lord as Hannah had. Even though, Alison was very close to the Lord and so, too, was his mother, Mary, that fervor and closeness to Jesus wasn't the same. In fact, besides Father Engelmann, Jenny and his friends, Gary and John, Henry had never known anyone so close to Jesus' heart. It was as if they beat as one. Especially one so young; there was something very special about Hannah and her relationship with God. The meaning of her name seemed very appropriate too, 'to show favor'. It was not only Henry who thought that his daughter was favored by the Lord, but others did too.

Perhaps it was because Jenny had given Hannah back to God like the Biblical Hannah did in the story of 1 Samuel. Hannah bore a son, Samuel, and gave him back to God as she had promised and her faith in God had consequences beyond anything she could have imagined. It was Samuel, who would anoint King David, who would propose the building of the temple in Jerusalem and establish the house into which Jesus, the Savior of the world would be born!

Henry knew Hannah was favored too, and wondered, what possible plan God had for her. It wouldn't be as earth-shaking or as historical an event as it was with Hannah's son, Samuel, yet still, he felt, she would affect countless lives in some way, as he had dreamt near the end of his forty day fast. He recalled how overwhelmed he was when he woke from that third dream. He could not remember the vision he saw, other than Hannah was in the midst of countless people.

Henry, however, would not have to wait long to know the plan that God has for his daughter. Before Hannah and Henry would leave the prayer house that day, Henry would begin to see the path God has chosen for Hannah and… how he fit into it! She may be his and Jenny's daughter but she belongs to the Lord and is destined to do mighty works!

As Henry came to the bend in the road leading down to the prayer house, he had to stop and take in the glorious view. He never tired of seeing the prayer house at the edge of the pond, surrounded by the green hills of the valley. Each time he came down, he also tried to re-capture that morning when Father Engelmann celebrated his last Mass. The light that surrounded the Poustinia, the stillness in the air and the electrifying light imparting the Stigmata to Father was the most powerful vision he had ever seen nor would ever see again. He could still see Zachariah, lifting the spirit of the holy man he was assigned to protect, heavenward.

Unconsciously, Henry reached out to both sides as if to take someone's hand. Although their presence wasn't visible, Henry's two wives were on either side of him. The fragrant odor of lilac was on his right side this time; *Jenny was there.*

When Henry got to the prayer house, he quietly stepped in through the kitchen door. As he suspected, Hannah was kneeling at the foot of the altar. She was so deep in prayer, she didn't hear him come in. Jenny's rosary dangled from her finger-tips; the glass beads sparkled in the light. Hannah was ecstatic when she had received the rosary from Henry for her birthday. Hannah claimed that she felt the warmth and touch of her mother through the beads. *Henry did, too.*

He tiptoed into the room and quietly knelt down at one of the kneelers, then crossed himself. Unbidden tears surfaced in Henry's eyes at the beautiful sight of his daughter expressing such a deep love and devotion for the Lord and His mother, Mary. An aura of light surrounded the angelic image before him.

The chapel glowed.

Henry knew what Hannah's prayers would be about. She had been struggling with the decision for some time, to either be a nun and live a more cloistered life like St. Therese, the little flower who had joined the Carmelites. Or, should she become a sister and lead a more active apostolate. She would be praying for guidance not only to the heavenly Father but to her mother, Saint Jennifer as well.

Hannah suddenly turned; she felt her father's presence. "Oh, Hi Dad." She got up and came to him and kissed him on the cheek. "I can hardly wait for you to say Mass and receive Holy Communion. I am so excited to visit Mom at the cemetery, too. I wonder if the flowers are blooming yet? It's a bit early and the weather has been cool, still, I have the feeling her grave will be covered with beauty and monarch butterflies flitting all about in the air. It's always such a glorious sight!"

Henry nodded, "Yes, I am sure all that you are anticipating will prove to be true based upon what has happened in previous years. I'll put on my Mass vestments and then we will get started."

Henry returned within ten minutes from the bedroom and began Mass. Justin and the other members of the family said they would attend Mass at St. Mary's Church and so it was just the two of them there.

When it came to the offertory, Henry offered the new book up to God praying that its contents would honor Him and bring glory to His name; that its message would touch the hearts of all who read the book and lead them to Jesus, helping them to become a light to the world. Henry turned towards Hannah and asked her to place her petitions, prayers and aspirations on the paten as well. He noticed that Hannah was crying. He stopped saying the Mass and asked what the matter was.

Hannah brushed away a tear rolling down her cheek and was about to speak but her weeping escalated. Through her sobs she said, "Oh Daddy, when you came in, I was praying the rosary to Mary and I was thinking about all the things she pondered in her heart about her Son. And as you were bringing Jesus towards the cross in the Mass, being nailed and hung, the pain He must have experienced is so unimaginable... but, think of the pain his mother felt too! There she was, at the foot of the cross, watching her beloved Son, so in agony, hanging there. My heart goes out to Jesus but also to Mary. I can't fathom the deep, deep sorrow and unthinkable pain."

Henry approached his hurting daughter and put his arm around her.

"The crucifixion pains me too, Hannah. Jesus was all alone, feeling abandoned by the Father, carrying the sins of all mankind...I can't imagine the pain either and yet, Jesus saw what you saw too; His mother in the midst of such grief and He tells His disciple, John, that she was now his mother and that John was now her son. Imagine, at that moment, in His pain and suffering, Jesus was still concerned about his beloved mother. Imagine now though, Hannah, if Jesus' death was final and there wasn't a resurrection—"

"Oh, Daddy!" Hannah cried, "that would be the end of it all. There would be no victory over sin or death. No hope... it would be just like any other horrific death!"

"Yes, Hannah, but He did resurrect and that is what carries us past this appalling scene. Jesus did rise and opened the gates of heaven for all of us. He restored our relationship with the Father. God knew all this would happen and that's why He didn't take the cup away that His Son had to drink. Can you imagine the joy in Mary's heart when she learned that her Son had defeated death! See Mary in your heart and mind now, Hannah. Focus on that and be filled with the joy that God wants you now to feel as we celebrate the rest of the Mass. See the risen Christ in the Eucharist and you will see Jesus as Mary saw Him on the third day. Imagine her joy! This is the joy God wants you to feel as well!"

Henry brushed Hannah's shoulder soothingly, turned and went back to the altar. When he came to Communion, he stared at the Eucharist for the longest time just like his mentor did. In many ways, Henry was to Father Engelmann as Hannah was now, to her father. Not only was Henry carrying out the tradition of celebrating Mass at the prayer house but also being a mentor to Hannah.

As Henry was removing his vestments after Mass, Hannah came into the bedroom and picked up a copy of the new book seven and remarked, "I just love the cover of the new book and the title is perfect; *The Heart of an Angel!* Seeing Mom running through the meadow takes my breath away. She is so pretty and free. It captures her spirit perfectly, Dad."

"I like it too, Hannah. Did you figure out all the symbolism on the cover?"

"Well, like I said, the image captures Mom's spirit of freedom, gaiety, love of life and nature: look at the monarch butterflies, the wildflowers, the valley, stream and… oh yes, the angel in the sky holding a heart expresses that Mom, too, has the heart of an angel and…the dove could represent the Holy Spirit."

"Very perceptive, Hannah. Yes, the dove is usually the symbol for the Holy Spirit but you will note there are three doves."

"So, the other two represent God the Father and Jesus."

"Yes, I thought I would represent them all in the form of doves. They are one God, even though, they are three distinct persons. It reminds us of the Trinity and how God is active in our lives and yet each person of the Trinity plays a different role. So, when we see the Holy Spirit, we are also seeing spiritually, God the Father and God the Son."

Henry paused for a moment to let Hannah absorb what he said and then went on, "And…, what about the color, Hannah? Any thoughts on that?"

"I love the bright red color and it's very eye catching. Is that what you mean?"

"Well, it does draw one to the book but I chose red for the last book to represent the Precious Blood of Jesus. Note that the cover is not only red, but so is the roof of the prayer house, the red door that enters into the chapel, where the sacrifice of Jesus is celebrated in the Mass and of course red represents the heart, not only of Jesus but also of Jenny's angelic heart. She had the heart of an angel!"

"Yes, and so did Father Engelmann!" Hannah concurred.

"That's right and that is denoted by the sub-title; *We are all called to be earthly angels*, aren't we?"

Hannah thought for a moment. "Yes, Dad. We are called to follow in the footsteps of Jesus and look what happened to Mom and Father Engelmann, they were declared saints! I think earthly angels are also saints."

Henry nodded, "I agree. For some reason, most people seem to accept being called an earthly angel rather than a saint. There's the perception out there that sainthood is for people who pray from morning to night and live in caves or secluded monasteries, but as you can see, ordinary people can lead holy lives. They are a *light* to the world. Not only did they enjoy more peace, but also they enjoyed their lives and were very content."

"To be a saint; that would be a beautiful goal in families, Dad. Imagine parents teaching their children to be a light. To be saints! To be true followers of Jesus and bring His peace, love and mercy to others. I want to be just like Mom. I want to live a free life placing all my trust in God."

Hannah paused and asked, "Why don't more people see that as such a worthy goal, Dad?"

Henry paused as well and shrugged his shoulders. "Well, besides what I just said, parents have to be models and leaders in this regard. For the most part, I think it's the way we are brought up. Once again, there are so many perceptions out there that it is weak to pray to God or it's too personal or we do not want people to think we are holier than them or some kind of Jesus freak. You have to have strong faith and know how you want to live your life; for God or yourself or others. I can see such a difference in your attitude and belief in God and how mine was at your age. I rarely thought of God. My mom was a faith filled person but dad wasn't at the start. I really learned about Jesus and Christian values from Mr. Engelmann when I worked for him before Anna died and he became a priest. If he hadn't been my life-long friend and mentor, I doubt very much that I would be a strong follower of Jesus Christ today, let alone a priest!"

"That is so true, Dad. I realize that more and more all the time. Jesus reveals Himself through those who place Him at the center of their lives and do His will. That would be one my goals, Daddy, to motivate young people to accept this challenge. Imagine, young people seeing their goal in life, to become like Jesus; to live saintly lives!"

"What a refreshing thought, Hannah. That's the key. To even think about the possibility; that it is not something remote or impossible, but a worthy goal, is to take a step in that direction."

Henry paused. He so enjoyed having these amazing discussions with Hannah. It reminded him of when he was her age and working for Mr. Engelmann and the talks they had out back of the grocery store.

"How did we get on this topic? Oh, yes, we were talking about the cover."

"Oh, Dad, the cover is all so beautiful and well planned out. Oh! I just noticed something else... Is that you standing on the deck beside the patio doors?'"

Henry smiled, "I wondered if you would notice. Yes, that's me. I couldn't resist putting myself in there watching Jenny as she ran through the meadow. If you could see a close up, you would see a happy smile on my face and joyful tears in my eyes. It gave my heart such immense joy to see her amongst the flowers chasing butterflies. When I saw her do that Hannah, it made nature even more beautiful for me... she completed nature for me..." Henry's words trailed off.

"Oh, Dad, that is so beautiful. I can see the deep love you had for Mom and...you still miss her so much..."

Henry simply nodded and quickly changed the subject. "So you can see, Hannah, there is a lot that goes into the design of a cover, besides of course, all the work and thought that goes into writing the book itself!" Henry added with a twinkle in his eyes.

"Yes, it's amazing, if one day, I, too, will write a book or two, I know who to come to for help with the cover!"

Henry smiled, "You may very well be the author of another series, Hannah."

"Oh, Daddy, I wish the series would continue and never end. I love the characters so much. The amazing thing is, they are all my family in real life! And what is further so incredible, is that through the story, I have come to know and love my mom and Father Engelmann who I never knew in real life. Yet, through this story, it almost seems as if they are still alive somehow! In a way, Dad, the characters have become family to so many readers, too. I'm sure they feel the same as we do. They would like to see the story continue on."

"Yes, Hannah. I am sad to see the series end but it's time to bring it to a close and hopefully as I just said, you may spawn another series and take it all to another level!"

Hannah smiled. "I don't think I will ever be able to write such a beautiful love story."

"Well Hannah, your love for the Lord and His endless love for us is really the greatest love story ever told and it continues to unfold. I think Hannah, the best story may just be around the corner."

"I would love to do that, Dad. I am learning so much from the books and your mentoring. So, perhaps later when I'm ready, I may continue to write about us and the new life experiences God creates in my journey that He wants me to share with others. Like you said, God works amazingly in our lives through His Divine Providence."

"I have a feeling, you just may do all that, Hannah. You certainly have a head start on us, learning about all the life lessons you have absorbed through the series."

Henry gazed intently at his daughter. He still had some concerns about the content of book seven but was very happy that Hannah was mature enough to handle it. Over the past year, they had many discussions and it always seemed as if Hannah was helping him deal with his past depression and Jenny's passing than Henry trying to convey to his daughter, how much he loved her and that her birth was in no way the cause for her mother's death.

As he took the book from Hannah, he asked, "So, you're okay with the contents of book seven and what others might say?"

Hannah nodded, "I am fine with it all, Dad. Let us stop coming back to that and enjoy the release of the book. Congratulations, Daddy; that is quite an accomplishment and the book will touch the hearts of so many people. I just know it."

And then Hannah thought of something else to ask her father along the same line, "Are you going to write another book, Dad?"

"As a matter of fact, Hannah, there is a book I wanted to write when I was a counselor in my thirties, but it was also the time I started to become an artist and so writing that book fell to the way-side and I never did write it. It was just as well. As I look back, I really wasn't ready to write that book. I have learned so much about life from Father Engelmann and his writing and from my writing of the last book, too. I do feel ready to finally get at it."

"Do you have a title, yet? What is it about, Daddy?"

"Yes, I even had a title at that time. It's going to be called, *"To Be or Not To Be...that is the question!"*

"The title sounds great, Dad. I sort of have an idea what it will be about."

"Yes, the title is suggestive about life and how we live it."

Henry reflected a moment, then gave a brief synopsis. "It's a continuation of the speech I was motivated to write when I gave my valedictory speech to the grade twelve students when I was eighteen. I had learned so much about life and how to live it from Mr. Engelmann that I was highly motivated to share what I had learned. It mainly revolved around making choices and decisions based upon Christian values and the need to read to the Bible every day. The book would be a continuation of that and more."

"I remember that speech in book two, *Another Angel of Love*. It was powerful! I loved the demonstration you gave at the end how our character is based upon the choices we make. You used a large sheet of paper painted white on one side and black on the other. That was so effective. I bet that image was burned into the minds and hearts of so many of your class-mates.

"And… yes, that's right, you did give the title of your book back then! I remember now how you related it to one of the lines in Shakespeare's play; *Hamlet*. Yes, you said the title back then, Dad. Do you remember?"

Henry shrugged his shoulders. He recalled giving the speech but not sure if he eluded to the title at that time. But Hannah remembered and said, *'To Be Or Not To Be, that is the question!'* You added something like; every day when we get up, we have a choice to serve others or ourselves, to build relationships or to tear them down, to be happy or sad, kind or unkind, grateful or complaining, forgiving or unforgiving , to be truthful or untruthful and on and on…yes, Daddy, to be a person of integrity or not to be, is a question we must ask ourselves daily without fail!"

"My gosh, Hannah, your memory is amazing!"

"It's just that I have read the books so many times they are burned into my heart. In fact, each time I read them over, I learn more or I read something I didn't see the other times or missed the meaning of. There is so much wisdom and truth in the books and they not only motivate one to read the Bible, but the books go hand in hand with the Bible. Every time I come to a Scripture in the books, I look it up in the Holy Book."

"That's wonderful, Hannah. It is my prayer and I know it was Father Engelmann's too, that the books would encourage readers to get up each day and read the Word of God and learn of Jesus's teachings."

"That's exactly what the books do!"

Henry stared lovingly at his daughter. She had become such a joy in his life.

Henry had to say what was in his heart. "You know, Hannah, like your mother, you have such a beautiful way of looking at life and at others. That is why you are so happy with yourself. You are a child of God and you are so proud and joyful to be in His family. So many miss that truth, Hannah. When we view life with our minds filled with anger or resentment and look for the bad in others, it is simply a reflection of ourselves... because that is what is in our mind. We see what we are filled with in our heart... we choose every moment to really live in the present, or half live, and all too often, live not at all."

Hannah smiled at her father and said, "Thank you Daddy for seeing me in that light...you are right, to be or not to be is the question we must ask each and every moment of our lives."

A silence fell between them as they both made their way out to the living room and stood in front of the patio windows and gazed out at the beauty of nature before them. They were so in tune with the soothing and healing power of God's creation, they just naturally allowed their spirits to drink in the scenery before them.

Softly, Henry broke the stillness. "See the beauty of God's creation, Hannah. This is but a drop in the ocean of all the immense glory and loveliness of what is out there across the world. Yet, regardless where we are, the magnificence of it all is that nature always fulfills what is was created for: to give beauty, solace and peace to the world just by being! Nature is always there desiring to give all it has and never changes. Jenny saw the power of nature.

"To simple be!

"We never tire of sunsets, waterfalls, flowers, beautiful trees, because they just are. They exist to give glory to the one Who created them. There is no strife between them, One flower does not try to outshine the other or the tree next to it; they just are. The sooner we realize we are children of God and that through Jesus we can all become one, too. We can all blossom just like the flowers in the valley before us."

"Yes, Daddy, the world could be so much happier, joyful and more loving if only we were in harmony with the beauty of God's creation!"

Henry nodded and after a brief silence, Hannah added, "Why can't we just be the way God created us too? Human beings are God's greatest creation and yet, it's sad that so much of our beauty and happiness is covered over with worry, hurt, harboring resentment and not forgiving others. It steals our precious moments away to be fully alive in Jesus and being there for one another."

"That is very true, Hannah. There is so much goodness, loveliness, talent and beauty which is locked inside of us because of the way we think, how we respond to life's trials and challenges, our fears and lack of faith."

"But we can choose to be live fully alive if we have Jesus in our hearts."

Henry nodded again and said, "Yes, there is great power and potential in all of us. It's just a breath away if we begin to decide to take time to reflect on our lives and —"

"To place Jesus at the center of their lives!" Hannah blurted in. "He can unlock the door to so much more of life, Daddy! The Holy Spirit will help us become all we can be. Jesus came to help us to live with joy and abundance. He is the way the truth and life!"

Henry was about to respond but Hannah excitedly added, "Oh Daddy, let us uncover and remove the obstacles and walls we build up so no one would miss out on the gift and joy of life any longer. Let us help people to be happy and fully alive! Mom was such a good example of one who had so many challenges and yet, through her love of nature and having Jesus at the center of her life, she was able to rise above all those things which could have pulled her down. I love the way she gave thanks daily for her blessings and how she offered flowers in such joyful gratitude for life and for all the challenges and trials which came her way. Through her love of life, she was able to blossom like the flowers she loved. She existed just for Jesus in the present moments of life.

"Oh, Daddy, we can all blossom like that too! We can work in harmony and peace just like nature does. We can lead saintly lives! It is as you say, Daddy, *To Be or Not To Be, that is the question!*"

Henry shook his head, talking with Hannah was like chatting with Father Engelmann. "Oh Hannah... my dear, sweet, Hannah, the Holy Spirit has truly given you many gifts and an extra dose of wisdom. Your heart oozes with compassion and understanding. Your desire to help others is palpable and I am so proud to have you as my daughter. I know Jenny is too, but I wish for just a moment I could see the utter joy in her sparkling eyes that she has for you."

The proud father turned to his daughter and said, "It seems to me that another similar cycle of life is playing itself out. In the same way Father Engelmann was a mentor to me when I was fifteen, so too, I am a mentor to you. When Anna died, he became a priest and now, with Jenny's death, I too, have become a priest. There was one big difference however; I will never be able to impart to you, what Father Engelmann has taught to me through our journey in life. Hannah, you have learned much and grown to be very wise in the Lord, many days I don't know who the teacher is and who is the student."

Henry wrapped his arm around his young daughter and said, "Come, let us go out to the deck and sit a while and warm our spirits and faces under the sun."

Hannah felt so blessed, her heart nearly burst as they made their way outside. She loved these times talking to her dad on the deck just as much as he did with Mr. Engelmann when they went out back of the grocery store and sat on the old grey crates.

They both stopped on the deck and breathed in deeply the morning fresh air and allowed the peace and calm to permeate and heal their soul.

"See Daddy, how nature brings us back into the moment and cares vanish; the beauty, the soothing rhythm of the babbling stream, the sound of the birds who are always rejoicing and singing in praise.

Henry chuckled over how similar Hannah's love of nature was like that of her mother. He also enjoyed, too, how similar Hannah's thoughts were of how their relationship was developing as his had with Mr. Engelmann. He turned to Hannah and asked,

"So, tell me, Hannah, has the Lord made His plans for you any clearer?"

CHAPTER SIXTY-SEVEN

B EFORE THEY SAT down on the deck chairs, Hannah broke
loose from Henry's hold on her shoulder and looked at
him excitedly, "Yes, Daddy, God is revealing His plans for me
and I can hardly wait to share it with you. God sent me two
dreams the other night; the first was that I was a nurse caring
for the sick and dying at the Mother House in India! There
was so much to do and so many people to care for. The Lord
was telling me that I needed help...lots of help. The needs
were so great!

"In the second dream, I was older and my outfit had changed
from a nurse's dress to a white coat. I had become a doctor!
This time, though, the scene was in a hospital setting. It was
brand new! At first, I didn't know where I was at, but then, I
realized I was still in India as all the patients were Indians. In
one scene, I was prescribing medicine to people who were sick
and in another I was doing surgery! The dream was expressing
my wish and deep prayer to help cure leprosy and to make all
those people with cleft lip and palate deformity to smile and
be pretty and handsome and happy!"

Unbidden tears were already in Henry's eyes as he listened
to his excited daughter.

"See, the Lord is directing your path, Hannah. It looks like you are being called to a more active apostolate and maybe not into the religious life at all. So, what else is the Lord telling you?"

"Well, He definitely wants me out there working with the poor and the sick. Because I am only 14 and will finishing off grade 12 in another year, I think I will go into the College of Nursing for two years, work in the field for another two years and then go back to study medicine. I feel such a strong desire to cure and heal so many diseases."

"You're filled with compassion, Hannah, but that will require a lot of study of different fields of medicine."

"But that's it, Daddy, I am young and a whole life-time a head of me. I can study general medicine, internal medicine, plastic surgery, heart surgery and whatever else I need to study to help people!

But there is more, Daddy!"

Henry beamed from ear to ear. Hannah reminded him of how excited Mr. Engelmann got when he came up with a new idea for the store. Henry knew now, how his mentor felt.

"Come, let us sit down, Hannah. This is all too much for me and it sounds like you have a lot to share."

Reluctantly, Hannah sat down, turned her chair to face her dad directly, her eyes flashed and sparkled. She was so much like her mother and Henry loved it!

"So, Hannah, tell me what else the Lord has directed you to?" Henry asked again.

"It's like you said, if we wait on God, He will direct our paths."

Hannah was silent for a long time as if deciding where to start... "There is so much to share, Dad. There are so many needs and so much to do. I think we were meant to work together! In fact, in the second dream I was telling you about where I was a doctor in the hospital, everyone was so hopeful and happy and excited. The staff were whispering and talking about this priest who was coming there that morning. Apparently, he was the one whose Foundation was responsible for the building of that hospital. And then someone shouted, 'He is here!' I turned and looked down the hall and there was the hospital administrator walking next to a priest. It was you, Daddy!"

Hannah gazed into Henry's eyes, "Isn't that a sign that we are meant to work together? The work you are doing raising money to build hospitals, schools, digging wells for clean water is desperately needed. This is the active part of what we do to meet the immediate needs of countless people. This will bring them to Christ! They will see our love and care for them is motivated by Jesus!" And before Henry could respond, Hannah blurted out,

"But there is more!"

"Oh, Hannah what more could there be?"

"I keep having this vision to reach other young people and fill their heart with the love of Jesus like my heart is. The work is so great, it will require an army of helpers to meet all the needs which exist in the world. I see this vision of countless students offering their learning, talents and abilities for others. Teachers, doctors, nurses, engineers and whatever is needed will come forth, Daddy."

The words Hannah just spoke gave him some understanding of the third dream he had near the end of his forty day fast. The first two dreams had to do with his missionary work in India and the need for adoration at the end of the day. But the third dream had to do with Hannah. *A light was beginning to go on.* At least part of that dream and vision he saw that night was coming alive. The thousands of people he saw in the dream were young people inspired by Hannah. Yes, Hannah was playing a significant role in it all!

Neither Jenny nor he, either alone or together, could do what Hannah in her youth could do; *energize the youth of today with a cause.* She was already a leader; a leader filled with love and power of the Holy Spirit. He knew his daughter was on fire with the Lord. She had a vision and was already receiving direction from God how to fulfil it. Henry could feel the adrenaline flowing through his veins just listening to her. Silently, Henry prayed that young people would catch a glimpse of what Hannah saw. The earlier and sooner youth see the truth of placing Jesus at the center of their lives, the better; before idleness, passivity, fear and self-defeating habits and thoughts were ingrained and the ways for the world firmly established.

Hannah was going to share something else, but Henry began to respond to what she said. "Oh, Hannah, this is great news! We need more Hannahs in the world to set more hearts on fire; a vision that stokes passion until it bursts into courage and love; passion which ignites the soul to revolutionize the world!! Hannah, I see such a fire growing in you...soon it will be like a wildfire spreading here and there. Soon the flames will leap across the seas into other countries!!

"Share your vision with others like you did in high school and when you go to university you can try again through the student council as well."

"Yes, Daddy, I plan to do that and I will also write to the Carmelite Orders, the Sisters of the Precious Blood and all the cloistered nuns to pray for all of us but especially the young people so that God infuses them with the vision to make a difference during their journey in life...to change and restore the world!"

Hannah paused for a moment and beamed. "Daddy, there is something more I need to share with you!"

Hannah was at the edge of her chair bubbling over with something she couldn't hold back a minute longer. "Daddy, there is one big plan God wants me to tell you. It's the answer to all of what you just were saying; how to reach young people with this vision.

"Well, here is what God wants me to tell you!

"In the same way that I learned so much about life, how to live it and brought me to read the Bible was through reading *The Angelic Letters Series*. Daddy, we have to get every high school student to read these books! It could be as recommended extra-curricular reading or part of their ethics class. In fact, Mr. Chorney, my ethics teacher who has read the series is already doing that. Friends of mine who have also read the book told me they found the story so gripping, they couldn't turn the pages fast enough."

Henry turned white as a candle. It was an 'aha' moment. The rest of the third dream he had at the end of his fast unraveled instantly before him. It suddenly burst into light! The idea had been skirting all around him and now, God, through his daughter, made him see how he fit into this incredible mission as well. It was as if the sun suddenly got brighter.

"Of, course, Hannah, that's it! What an amazing insight! What better way for young people to learn more about Christian values and how to live them out than through a captivating story, a story they cannot put down and will touch their hearts…an inspiring love story that has incorporated so many biblical teachings at that!"

"Yes, Daddy, they will learn just as much as I did and even more! They, too, will get as excited as I am to work for the Lord!"

"Hannah, that's a brilliant idea! The youth of today need to sink their heart into something life changing. Something bigger than themselves like we were just talking about. Something that will stir the hearts of mankind."

"There is such power and determination in young people, Daddy. I've seen students band together when they see a worthy cause. I can just see, poverty, sickness, disease, war and all the ills of society eradicated. It may sound idealistic, but I can see it all coming! And it's like Father Engelmann kept saying throughout the books and so did you, Daddy, 'This world so desperately needs people who have thought things through and don't go through life like a leaf tossed by the prairie wind. We need more than ever, strong people whom others will want to emulate because of the wholesome way they live!'"

"Yes, Hannah, I remember that as if it were yesterday. I was fifteen at the time. He and I were talking about Gary and so many things. Father would be so excited to hear your idea to promote this very thing. Yes, through this story, inspired by the Holy Spirit, is the perfect way to help young people think about their life and the direction they want to go!"

If Henry thought he was on a roll earlier, he would now see his match. Hannah excitedly blurted out, "Imagine if more and more youth were made aware of their purpose in life, dedicating themselves to different careers and wanting to travel around the world to give of their time and knowledge to help those less fortunate. Their hearts will be touched like mine was when they see so many who have nothing and live under such horrible conditions like the countless people we saw in Calcutta. This is what God wants! Jesus clearly said, feed the hungry, heal the sick, treat everyone as your brother and sister. And did Jesus not say, 'When you do this to the least of My brothers, you do this for Me?

"Oh, Daddy, we want young people who see the world and its values for what it is and make change that will make a difference. Young people who see that it does not profit them to gain the whole world and its riches and lose their soul...youth who live in the present and see every opportunity to do all they can for their fellow man. Young people who realize that it is through Jesus they can become all that they can be! Youth who see the fallacy of storing up treasures on earth and rather, seek the great reward to lay up treasures in heaven. Youth who chose to enter by the narrow gate. Youth who know the Holy Spirit and are on fire for the Lord. Youth who answer the call to be true disciples of Jesus and want to be known for their love of others. Youth who are filled with the truth and wisdom and compassion and are dedicated to eradicating sickness, hunger, war, racism and all the ills, inequality, abuses and injustices of the world!"

Henry shook his head and began to laugh. Hannah's comments reminded Henry of what Father Engelmann would say, 'Ach, mein lieber Gott, Danke, danke! Miene geliebte Tochter sieht das Licht! She sees the Light!' He noticed such a difference in Hannah than when he was young. She is so confident, posed and possessed a quiet, yet powerful boldness. She believed in God and wasn't afraid to express her faith and beliefs. And she did it so eloquently and powerfully. She knew her purpose in life.

There would be no stopping her.

"Oh, Hannah, your words are inspiring! You know so much. At your tender age, you know what has taken me a life-time to learn. You are bold and confident and I note you seek the approval of God and not others or be swayed by their opinion."

"Now that I am so aware of it from reading about it in the books, I see it, even in myself at times. I've learned to put Jesus at the center and not be too concerned about what others think. I am living out my life for Him and seek only His and the Father's approval. I know if I do that, I will just naturally meet everyone's needs like I am supposed to. I can do no wrong to others or myself. Living for God means loving our neighbor as myself. Living for God brings us peace, joy and fulfills His commandments."

Henry listened in awe. His daughter had learned so much about life. He noticed Hannah was hesitating to say something else but then she added, "The rumor has spread that Mom is a saint. Perhaps someone's parents heard about it and told their daughter or son and word got out. Sometimes, I get teased about that and am called St. Hannah. I try to project an image that I don't consider myself holier or better than anyone. I participate in most sports and activities that interest me and have time for to let others know that I am normal and just like them. Still, some students object to my values and reject me. So be it. I can handle that as I know the truth."

Hannah gazed at her father. She didn't want him to worry about her, so she added, "For the most part, Dad, everything is fine. Most of my friends talk about boys, sex, clothes or their appearance...I must admit that I am an odd ball in the crowd much of the time. I'm not interested in partying or drinking and really not interested in boys either and at times feel out of place...but like I said, I know who I am, a child of God and I want to be obedient to Him. I am not afraid to follow Jesus no matter what. I am here to serve and make a difference, Daddy. I want to be a saint, just like Mom."

Henry nodded, "The Lord has blessed you in another way which takes years and years of struggle, trials, pain and suffering for the truths of life to take hold. Hannah, you not only have this wisdom and insight into life in your mind but the Holy Spirit has sent it to your heart and that's where passion is, where commitment is, where dedication is, where tireless effort is. It is so visible in your enthusiasm; it's contagious, Hannah!" Henry shook his head as he gazed into his daughter's crystal blue eyes. The depth and clarity he always saw in Jenny's and Father Engelmann's eyes was the same in Hannah. She reflected her love for Jesus so beautifully. It was plain that every thought, word and deed was filtered through Jesus' Word; her mind constantly seemed to ask, 'What would Jesus do? What would He have me do or say or sacrifice or whatever, to do His will? Henry couldn't help himself, he just had to blurt out, "Oh, Hannah, you are so filled with the Holy Spirit!"

Henry clapped Hannah's shoulder and said, "Hannah, we have work to do. We need to convince principals and superintendents and pastors of churches that students in their high schools should read these books. There is so much out there that is not good or wholesome for youth and gets them on the wrong track. The story, through the lives of the characters, encounters so many of life's challenges along with insights on how to deal with them. In so many cases, young people turn to their friends who often don't know any more how to handle certain situations than they do. It's like the blind leading the blind. So often, young people are reticent to go to their mom or dad and talk about sensitive issues like sex. At the very least, the books would enlighten their minds and give them guidance based upon sound values and teachings."

"And it's so easy to read! That's the beauty of the series, Daddy. It's written in a style which is easy to understand and I've learned so much of the Christian faith; it's given me something to anchor my life on and shown me how to live with purpose and meaning. So many of my friends just flounder about aimlessly and never seem to think about the choices they make based upon sound values. Many do not realize how day to day decisions can develop their character and the quality of life they live.

"Oh, Daddy, it's the perfect way for young people to see the big picture and how important it is to have Jesus at the center of their lives. Having the series as part of their reading would be an awesome way to reach students and help them through so many difficult times! The contents of the books have helped me immensely!"

Henry paused and then began to laugh. "This is all so amazing, Hannah. It was always a dream of mine when I was both a teacher and counselor in my thirties that we should have a course for students about living: how to anchor one's life on solid values, the role of a father and mother in the home, how to deal with their children and relate to one another and so on. I often thought schools were lacking in that regard. And now, almost forty years later, it may be realized just like the writing of the book, *To Be or Not to Be, that is the question,* soon will be, too. I am astonished how God's Divine Providence works. All I can say is thank you, Lord!"

"Well, Dad, it looks like we have to work together." Hannah winked at her dad and said, "See, you will raise money from the adults and seniors to advance the missionary work and the young people will do the work; take on the challenge of renewing the face of the earth! Isn't that usually the way it works?"

Henry chuckled as he shook his head, "No, sweetie, the adults usually raise the money and do at least most of the work, too, but in this case, I think if young people catch on fire like you and see the vision you are seeing, they will pursue and follow this incredible goal."

"And if the Holy Spirit is behind it, success is a certainty!" Hannah exclaimed to settle the matter.

Henry just beamed. The slight wrinkles which time had begun to etch around his eyes, gathered joyfully at the corners. It was wonderful to see a young person so in love with the Lord and how naturally, she reflected this love to others.

Henry stood and turned towards the pond and the valley beyond and took in a deep breath of warm air. The peace of the valley filled his heart and the holy fragrance of his beloved teacher that lingered in the air, touched his spirit. He turned to his student with a twinkle in his eyes and wearing a benevolent smile like his mentor before him usually did, Henry softly said, "It makes me want to continue writing just to let readers know the way the Lord is moving in your life, Hannah. In a way, I am sad to bring the story to a close but soon your story will take life and your sheep will follow your lead and continue the story until the day Jesus returns. Until that day, Hannah, we have work to do. Each day, the Lord, through His Spirit, will give us our orders. The Lord has given us the vision; the plan to follow and now, He will guide us each step of the way. It is as you say, Hannah, that we are a father-daughter team!

"Well, Hannah, are you ready to revolutionize the world for Jesus?"

Hannah stood up, her sparkling blue eyes radiating the task that lay before them. "Yes, Father. I am scared, nervous, excited and ready..., all at once..."

Henry smiled as he nodded, "The path will not be easy. You will be challenging the establishment; the values and norms of society, just like Jesus did when He walked the earth. You will meet resistance, persecution and criticism just like Jesus did, too. But in the end, Hannah, your cause and belief will prevail. You are building your life on a rock that will be able to withstand the storms of life. I can see it in your eyes and heart, Hannah, how fully connected you are to Jesus and through Him to God and empowered by the Holy Spirit. Remain obedient to Jesus as He was to the Father and like Jesus, your belief will be contagious, your faith will be inspiring, and your vision noble as it all gives glory to God!

"Your words are so uplifting, thank you, Daddy!"

"I often recall what Father Engelmann did when he felt weary and lacked the courage to go on. He followed the words of the Scripture in the 23rd Psalm. It begins by advising us to come and rest by the still waters and restore our souls. That is why he so often came here to the prayer house in the valley. Father knew the great need to quiet the soul, recoup, reenergize and refresh the spirit.

"In the next two sentences the Scripture assures us to have courage as we walk through the world and not be afraid as the Lord is at our side and His staff and rod will comfort us.

"And, yes, we will meet obstacles along the way but what does the Scripture say?"

Hannah chimed in, "He will prepare a meal for us in the presence of our enemies, He will anoint our heads with oil, our cups will run over!"

They both smiled at one another and almost in unison they uttered the closing words of the Psalm; "Surely goodness and mercy shall follow me all the days of my life: and I will dwell in the house of the Lord forever!"

The radiance of their faces seemed to glow brighter than the sun rising into the glorious sky, as they stood together on the deck and chuckled over the goodness of the Lord.

"See, Hannah, always trust in the Lord with all your heart and don't lean on your own understanding. He will direct our paths and light our way and keep us from harm. So, let's take the first step towards the dream that God has put in your heart."

Hannah smiled and with a wink, she added, "I know what you are waiting for me to say, just like you always say in your closing remarks when you give a presentation; 'Quickly, hold my hand and together we can bring Jesus to the world.' When you say that, I always know that Mom is right here taking our hand, too, along with Father Engelmann. It will always make me know that what I am doing has the blessing of my family and gives honor and glory to God!"

They thrust out their hands to each other and their other hands into the air for their spiritual companions and stepped off the deck. Henry followed Hannah's gaze into the cloudless blue sky and caught a glimpse of countless angels flitting about the prayer house ever so jubilantly. He felt Hannah squeeze his left hand and the electrifying warmth of his dear sweet Jenny in his right hand; his two angels!

A few steps further along the path, Hannah let go of Henry's hand and began to chase a monarch butterfly into the meadow of fresh, spring, wildflowers. She stopped momentarily to pick a white daisy with a golden center. Wisps of her blonde, wheat colored hair fluttered in the prairie breeze and her radiant, luminous skin shimmered in the light. Hannah breathed in the intoxicating fragrance of the glowing flower held lightly in her delicate fingers and just like her mother before her, began running through the field as cheerful and bright as the dazzling daisy she waved happily in the warm sky.

Such a spirit filled girl, thought her father...thank you, my love, for this beautiful gift!

Henry tightened his hand around Jenny's and softly whispered, "She will lead so many on the path to inner peace and a joyous life. Oh, Jenny, you have given Hannah your heart. Our dear sweet daughter overflows with loveliness, grace and truth...

"She has the heart of an angel!"

An unstoppable exuberance filled Henry's heart as he raised his hands towards the heavens and sang rejoicingly throughout the valley, "Here we are Lord. It is Hannah and I Lord, we have heard You calling in the night. We will go Lord, wherever You lead us. We will hold Your people in our heart!"

Hannah turned to her father, her blue eyes sparkled as she excitedly cried out to him, "Yes, Daddy, come, together we will bring the light of Jesus to the world!"

The End

Coming Soon

TO BE OR NOT TO BE...
that is the question!

HENRY K. RIPPLINGER
Best Selling Author of Pewter Angels

Following is the introduction…

INTRODUCTION

TO BE OR NOT TO BE ... *that is the question*, is a book about life and how best to live based upon the way we were created. Yes, it involves God, Jesus and the Holy Spirit because we are all part of the total plan of creation and this is why we are here. We are wired to come back to Him and live for Him. If we don't, that is when we run into trouble. A simple analogy is with the vehicle we drive. If we put in water or any liquid other than gasoline problems soon develop. In a similar fashion, if we don't have Jesus in our lives and accept His ways and teachings, we too, soon run into trouble.

In my earlier years when I was a counselor, I thought my insights and words of advice would be enough to help others in their search for peace and overcoming their challenges. I soon discovered however, that as we worked on their spiritual development, they made real and permanent progress in their lives.

To Be Or Not To Be, is based upon the belief of accepting Jesus into our life and the inheritance which comes along with it. It is Jesus who sets us right with God the Father and we become part of His family. We accept our inheritance as a child of God and are loved beyond measure. Knowing this, I believe, results in a greater acceptance and love for ourselves which in turn encompasses others. We can only give what we have. We can only love others to the extent we have a wholesome love of ourselves. To fully 'BE' in this context means to know the wonderful, loveable person we are in Jesus. This has nothing to do with pride or lack of humility. Remember what Jesus said, "We are to love others as we love ourselves."

When we know we are loved and are a perfect child of God at a deep level, we automatically reflect God's love. We treat ourselves and others with respect and kindness. We look after our bodies, the temples which house the Holy Spirit; we are true to ourselves and able to accept others unconditionally. Fear, control of others, worry, being judgmental and unforgiving (some of the conditions that often plague our lives), can gradually be eliminated. With the indwelling presence of Jesus in our hearts and the strength of the Holy Spirit, our old selves fall away and a new creature is born. Rather than live mediocre lives, we begin to experience a deep sense of joy and fulfillment.

For many of us reading this, it may appear as too religious but I would ask for you to bear with me. It all begins with the decision to place Jesus at the center of your life. Beginning each day with a quiet time with Him to pray and meditate, not only fills us with inner peace, but helps us to develop the right mind set for dealing with all of life's challenges throughout the day. We are more aware of what is going on in our present moments and how God's Divine Providence is working through us to meet the needs of ourselves and others. But perhaps most important is that we are living our lives with purpose and eternity in mind.

It is not so much as what we do or who we are, but rather what we become in life which is everything. So many live under the false illusions that our worth comes from our wealth, what we own, what others think of us and the talents and abilities which we possess. All this and the many other worldly values in the end contain shallow and worthless promises.

Our identity and worth come from being a child of God.

In fact, the purpose of this book will be to show that in all circumstances, trials and challenges, as well as our joy and well-being, are all connected to who we are in Jesus.

But I am getting ahead of myself. I just want to let you know that the foundation upon which this book is based on is the acceptance of Jesus into my life. Many have tried on their own with some success, but were they happy and did they have inner peace? Were they prepared for eternity? When a crisis or death knocks at our door which can come at any moment in time, most of us, if not all, turn to God. There are very few atheists at death's door.

We need to understand why we are here and discover our purpose. We need to live in harmony in the way we were created. Techniques, how to do's and don'ts, don't work for long. Insights which we thought were so great are soon forgotten and old habits and self-defeating ways of thinking quickly work back into our lives.

Faith in God is the key to life. Without belief in Him, our deepest yearnings will never be satisfied. We will never become all we were meant to 'Be." It's like the sunlight that is required for plants, trees and flowers to grow.

We need the "light" too.

Many of the choices we make are based upon our weaknesses and self-centeredness which all too often are not the best for ourselves or others. God knew this would happen in giving us the freedom to choose our destiny, but He didn't leave us alone to drift like a leaf in the wind. He knew we would need guidance on how to live successfully and save ourselves from the temptations and pitfalls of life. So, *"To Be Or Not To Be"* comes down to a choice. We can accept Jesus; His immense sacrifice out of love for us and His teachings or reject it.

In the pages to follow, I would like to make a case for this. To be a happy person, at peace with ourselves and others, will happen when we live in harmony with the way we were created and designed to live in an imperfect world in which we all have free will. It's all about making the one big choice; to be a *light*. It is then on that basis that we continue to base all of our other choices from moment to moment as to how we live our lives. Yes…

To Be Or Not To Be…that is the question.

HENRY RIPPLINGER IS the best-selling author of *Pewter Angels, Another Angel of Love, Angel of Thanksgiving, The Angelic Occurrence and Angel Promises Fulfilled,* and *The House Where Angels Dwell,* the first six books in the seven book series "The Angelic Letters." The overwhelming response by readers to Henry's novels gives testimony to Henry's gifts as an author to write books that touch human hearts and offer direction to their lives.

Henry's empathetic abilities, combined with his lifelong experience and eclectic career as an educator, guidance counselor, professional artist and businessman, prepared him to craft this inspirational, spirit-filled love story and indirectly realize his aspirations of writing a self-development book.

Henry is also one of Canada's foremost prairie artists. His work is on display at private and corporate collections across Canada, most notably in Saskatchewan, his home province, and can be seen in the critically acclaimed book, *If You're Not from the Prairie.*

As both author and artist, Henry communicates from the heart, painting pictures with words that are so vivid and real that readers can feel and visualize every aspect of their own lives intertwined with the lives of his beloved characters.

Henry resides with his wife in the panoramic valley setting of Lumsden, Saskatchewan, Canada.

Please e-mail Henry at: henry@henryripplinger.com or visit the web-site: www.henryripplinger.com for more information on Henry's work and art. He would love to hear from you!

PEWTER ANGELS
BOOK ONE OF THE ANGELIC LETTERS SERIES

Pewter Angels, book one in the seven book *Angelic Letters Series* is an award winning national bestseller. The epic story follows the lives of Jenny Sarsky and Henry Pederson along with their guardian angels. Their uplifting yet tumultuous journey through life's struggles and victories inspires the miracle of deep, enduring love.

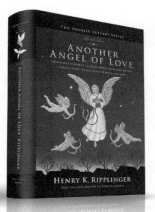

ANOTHER ANGEL OF LOVE
BOOK TWO OF THE ANGELIC LETTERS SERIES

Another Angel of Love, book two of the series, continues the saga of Henry and Jenny and their families. The powerful life lessons revealed through the author's beloved characters, especially Mr. Engelmann's mentoring goes beyond fiction and is life changing. The novel glows with moments of tenderness…deeply inspirational …is captivating the hearts of people everywhere!

ANGEL OF THANKSGIVING
BOOK THREE OF THE ANGELIC LETTERS SERIES

Angel of Thanksgiving, takes the reader further into this incredible journey of faith, hope and love. Make a huge space in your heart before you begin to read book three in the Angelic Letters Series as it will quickly fill with love's beauty and wonder between Henry and Jenny.

THE ANGELIC OCCURRENCE
BOOK FOUR OF THE ANGELIC LETTERS SERIES

The Angelic Occurrence, book four, delves into the ever-widening circle of influence Henry's and Jenny's guardian angels bestow upon them. The twists and turns in this thrilling and heart-stopping adventure will keep you gripping the book tighter and tighter. The Biblical themes will touch your soul… the essence of your being where faith is born.

ANGEL PROMISES FULFILLED
BOOK FIVE OF THE ANGELIC LETTERS SERIES

Angel Promises Fulfilled, book five brings surprises and satisfaction beyond the reader's most wishful imaginings The characters, the words, the spiritual content will consume your thoughts and heart completely! Only angels could bring about such a hard to put down tender-hearted saga of life, miracles and enduring love.

THE HOUSE WHERE ANGELS DWELL
BOOK SIX OF THE ANGELIC LETTERS SERIES

Come, sit on the deck beside the prayer house along with Henry and Jenny who talk to Father Engelmann about life challenges that really matter. Often, there is a silence between the sounds of nature in which you will hear the flutter of wings as God whispers to His angels to speak to your heart. Whatever your state in life, once you read this book, you will never be the same again.

THE HEART OF AN ANGEL
BOOK SEVEN OF THE ANGELIC
LETTERS SERIES

You will not want to miss the exciting conclusion of the Angelic Letters Series.

Hailed by reader's as the most inspiring story they have ever read.

The Angelic Letters Series is an experience which you will not forget.

If You're Not from the Prairie, written by David Bouchard and illustrated by Henry Ripplinger, is a poetic and visual journey depicting the prairies and the people who have made this diverse land their own…a treasure for the mind and soul.

All books available for purchase from web site:
www.henryripplinger.com Order your personalized copy today!

The Angelic Letters Series

Now in:

Audio-books

Book One - Pewter Angels
Book Two - Another Angel of Love
Book Three - Angel of Thanksgiving
Book Four - The Angelic Occurrence
Book Five - Angel Promises Fulfilled
Book Six - The House Where Angels Dwell

Available for purchase at audible.com

Ebooks

All six books in the series are in ebook format and available for purchase from Amazon, Kobo and iTunes.

Join Facebook

Join Henry's Facebook for words of wisdom from Father Engelmann, book signing tours and schedules, blog posts, future books and more.

Visit the web site: www.henryripplinger.com

Ripplinger Fine Art Gallery

2175 Smith St.
Regina, Saskatchewan S4P 2P3
Tel: 306 791 7888

Ripplinger Fine Art Gallery is an award winning heritage style complex which includes:

HENRY'S CAFÉ, A CLOTHING BOUTIQUE AND SEVERAL GIFT SHOPPES

Ripplinger Fine Art Gallery, Henry's Café and Boutiques is one of Saskatchewan's main tourist attraction visited by people from all over Canada, USA and abroad!

The ambiance, warm friendly atmosphere and heritage style create a memorable experience you will never forget!

Come, visit us soon!

Ripplinger Fine Art Gallery presents
FRAMEABLE ART CARDS

Card size: 6 x 9 inches
Retail Price: $8.95

All art cards are also available as a Limited Edition Print.

Examples of Framed Art Cards

Title: Autumn Road
Image size: 5 X 7½ inches
Overall framed size: 11 ½ X 14 inches
Retail price: $50.00 plus shipping and handling.

Title: Prairie Harvest AND If You're Not From The Prairie
Overall framed size: 13 ½ X 25 inches
Retail price: $145.00 plus shipping and handling.

Note: the cards can be framed vertically and
in sets of three art cards per frame.

Title: Hockey on the Creek
Image size: 5 X 7 inches Overall framed size: 11 ½ X 13 ¾ inches
Retail price: $50.00 plus shipping and handling.

For a complete selection of all art cards in full colour and for more
details and shipping information visit the web site:
www.henryripplinger.com